LADY RUTHLESS

NOTORIOUS LADIES OF LONDON BOOK 1

SCARLETT SCOTT

Happily Ever After Books

Lady Ruthless

Notorious Ladies of London Book 1

For my Sassy Readers

CHAPTER 1

LONDON, 1885

How dare the Duke of W. and my wife betray me? My confrontation with His Grace had done nothing to allay my furious need for vengeance. Nor could it stop the darkness in my soul. The solution I arrived upon was a final one, dear reader. It was death.
~*from* **Confessions of a Sinful Earl**

*L*ady Calliope Manning, sister to the Duke of Westmorland, social darling, and one cunning, vicious harridan, was about to learn that when a man had nothing left to lose, he was bloody well dangerous.

She was also about to learn that her efforts in chasing off all his future marital prospects had been for naught.

And that telling the world the Earl of Sinclair had killed the previous Duke of Westmorland and his former countess both came with ramifications. Dire ones.

Sin waited in the shadows as Lady Calliope left her publisher's office and moved toward her waiting carriage. She was so accustomed to running wild all over Town and doing whatever she pleased, she did not even bother to cast a glance around her. If she had, mayhap she would have seen him watching.

Mayhap she would have known how much trouble she would soon find herself mired in. Or, at least, she may have had an inkling. But because the self-absorbed chit had never had to worry a day in her life about how she would afford her silk Worth gowns fresh from Paris or her lavish balls or live with a roof over her damned head that was not leaking, she never looked.

She never saw him coming.

Nor did she appear to take note that her driver had been replaced with a man he trusted. A man who had been paid with what little funds Sin had remaining at his disposal to drive them to the country. Her driver would have come to by now, suffering from the very devil of a headache in a nearby alleyway thanks to Brinton's left hook.

Sin strode forward, timing his every action with utmost care. One false step, one precipitous move, and all his plans—and indeed, his only chance at saving himself—would be dashed. She was nearly within the carriage now, her back to him, foot on the step. Sin caught her waist in his hands, his grip firm, and shoved her inside.

She made a startled cry as she heaved forward in a mess of skirts and petticoats, sprawling over the Moroccan leather squabs. Sin joined her in the carriage and slammed the door, then knocked on the roof. He sat on the bench opposite her as the conveyance swung into motion.

Just in time for her to scramble around, terror on her pretty, treacherous face. The fear was chased quite neatly by recognition. Her lips parted on a gasp.

"Lord Sinclair? What the devil do you think you are doing in my carriage?" she demanded.

"I am abducting you," he told her with a sangfroid that was owed partly to the whisky he had swallowed to fortify him just prior to this mission of desperation. And partly to his desire to make the alarm return to her features.

She scoffed. "You cannot abduct me, my lord."

So much for her alarm. But there was plenty of time to draw blood. The journey ahead was long.

Sin held up his hands, gesturing to the interior of the carriage. "Observe, Lady Calliope."

She raised a dark, elegant brow. "All I see before me is an interloper in my carriage. What are you doing here, Lord Sinclair? Do you not have an innocent to debauch? Some opium to eat? Another murder to plot?"

He was going to enjoy destroying this despicable creature.

Sin gave her his most feral smile. "You have been paying attention to my reputation, my lady. I am all aflutter."

"I hardly pay you any attention at all." She frowned at him, her dark eyes flashing with defiant fire. "You are beneath my notice."

Lying witch.

"Indeed, Lady Calliope?" He reached into his coat and calmly extracted the blade he had secreted there for just this purpose. For *her*. He tested the point at the tip with his thumb, watching her.

Her gaze had fallen to the blade. Beneath her hat, which had been knocked askew when he had shoved her into the carriage, her skin paled.

"Why do you have a weapon?" she asked.

"Perhaps I am plotting *your* murder," he suggested, slowly running his thumb down the length of the blade. "Since I have already killed your brother."

She stiffened. "If you think to do me harm, my lord—"

"Has no one informed you it is poor form to threaten the fellow with the knife?" he interrupted. "*Tut, tut*, Lady Calliope."

3

"I daresay no one has ever wielded a knife in my presence," she snapped. "What is this about, Lord Sinclair? I have other calls to make today, and you are wasting my time with your nonsense."

How she deluded herself.

"There will be no other calls." He stroked his thumb back down the blade, this time with too much force.

He knew a quick sting in the fleshy pad, followed by the wetness of his blood. What irony. The first blood he had drawn was his own.

"You cut yourself," she gasped. "You are bleeding everywhere."

So he had, and so he was.

"It is a minor scratch," he said, unconcerned. "It will stop. This knife is very sharp, Lady Calliope. I would hate to have to use it upon your tender flesh, to cut you."

"You are attempting to frighten me," she countered, her eyes narrowing. "I do not know what you want or why, but surely you must realize this is madness and it needs to end at once." She rapped at the ceiling then. "Lewis! Stop this carriage."

He laughed, the sound bitter. "Do you truly think I would be stupid enough to abduct you with your own driver?"

Confusion stole over her expressive face.

It was a pity he hated her so much, because Lady Calliope Manning was one of the most stunning women he had ever beheld. Stunning and deceitful and reckless. He would crush her before this war she had begun was over between them.

"What have you done with Lewis?" she asked, fear making her voice tremble.

All her bravado leached away.

Good. Perhaps she was beginning to realize the gravity of her situation.

"Mayhap I killed him, like the others," he growled. "Like

my wife. Your brother. That is what you think, is it not, my lady? That is what you wrote for all the world to read and believe, pretending to be me."

She went paler still. "I do not know what you are speaking of."

"The false memoirs you have been writing and publishing in regular, despicable little serials," he elaborated, bringing his cut thumb to his mouth and sucking the blood clean. Copper flooded his tongue. "*Confessions of a Sinful Earl*, I believe you titled the deceitful tripe. Not terribly clever of you, but then, your sole intention was to make certain everyone had no question in their minds that your vicious fictions were about me, is that not right?"

"I read the memoirs along with the rest of London, but I am not the author, my lord," she denied.

He had known she would not confess her sins easily. He was prepared to refute her claims. He had been waiting. Watching. Preparing. Lord knew he had nothing else to do since all the doors in London had been closed to him.

"And yet, I just caught you paying your weekly call to the offices of J.M. White and Sons, the same publisher of *Confessions*," he countered.

"J.M. White and Sons publishes pamphlets for the Lady's Suffrage Society." Her response was quick. "That is the reason I pay calls there regularly."

He smiled. "An excellent excuse for your trips, is it not? But how do you explain the manuscripts in your bedchamber at Westmorland House, Lady Calliope?"

Her eyes widened. And an expression stole over her face then, one he imagined mirrored that of a wild beast staring down its hunter. "How would you know what is in my chamber?"

His smile deepened, along with his triumph. "Because I was there. I saw it myself."

But his triumph was short-lived. Because in the next breath, the virago launched herself at him.

* * *

Callie knew the Earl of Sinclair was desperate.

She knew he was dangerous.

She believed he had murdered her beloved brother and his own countess, who had been engaged in an *affaire* and had mysteriously died on the same day in suspicious circumstances.

And she also knew she had unwittingly led the wolf straight to her door. Now, he was out for blood. But she was damned if she was going to allow him to spirit her away somewhere to do Lord knew what with her. Kill her? Because she was the author of *Confessions of a Sinful Earl*?

It seemed unlikely he would commit murder again, with so many suspicions raised about him.

Still, she was not taking any chances. Callie launched herself at him, hands balled into fists, pummeling his chest. But he was stronger than she was. He caught her wrists in an iron grip. Belatedly, she remembered the blade. His cut. Wetness smeared over her skin, over her madly flitting pulse.

His blood.

"That was foolish, Lady Calliope," he snarled.

He was right, she realized. She was astride his lap, and his relentless hold on her brought their faces near. He was a handsome devil. She could not deny it; there was a reason why the Earl of Sinclair was better known as Sin.

Because he was the personification of it.

"Unhand me," she demanded with a bravado she did not feel.

He had all the control.

"I think I like you here, my lady." His lip curled. "How does it feel to be at my mercy? I daresay you do not like it."

His breath was hot. She felt it on her lips. It was also scented with spirits.

"Are you drunk, Lord Sinclair?" she asked instead of answering his question.

His appetite for pleasure was renowned. Excess in all forms. Little wonder the former Lady Sinclair had sought solace in Alfred. Her brother had been kind and good. Everything this beautiful, cruel waste of flesh was not.

"Far too sober," he said, his brown gaze so dark it was almost obsidian. "Am I going to have to tie you up? I had not wanted to, but admittedly, there is something so very pleasing about the thought of your wrists and ankles bound. About making you as helpless as you sought to make me."

She tugged at her wrists, struggling to free herself without any effect. He was immobile. "I do not know what lunacy you are spouting. I did not write those memoirs."

"Your denials are as useless as your attempts at escape." His voice was low, his expression an impenetrable mask. "I was inside your chamber. I saw the drafts on your writing desk."

How had he gotten into her chamber? Was he bluffing? How did he know she had a writing desk? Or that it was where she kept her drafts of *Confessions of a Sinful Earl*?

The questions were endless. Too many for her brain to work through.

Most immediate was the pressing need for escape. She knew where men were most vulnerable. She moved quickly, attempting to strike him in the groin with her knee.

But he anticipated her movements, and steered her away. Her knee connected with his inner thigh instead.

"Release me, you lunatic!" she cried out, thrashing against him wildly.

Her fear was very real now, a bitter, metallic taste in her mouth. Her heart pounded. When he had first invaded her carriage, she had been startled, but when he had blithely announced his intention to abduct her, and when the carriage had not slowed when she had demanded Lewis bring them to a halt, and when Lord Sinclair had removed that wicked, gleaming blade, her calm had fled.

With a suddenness that stole her breath, the earl moved them both, whipping her around so she was on the bench and he straddled her lap. He pinned her there with the strength of his big body.

"I think we both know which of us is the lunatic in this carriage, madam, and it damned well is not me," he growled as he reached into his coat and extracted a cord.

Dear God. What did he intend to do?

She shrank back into the squabs and renewed her efforts to escape him. But it was fruitless. She was out of breath, outmatched by Sinclair in strength. She could not fight him off her. He looped the cord around her wrists and knotted it with a haste that suggested the action was familiar to him.

Her wrists were bound.

"You cannot abduct me," she told him, hating herself for the tremble in her voice.

He bared his teeth, looking like nothing so much as a lion she had once seen in a menagerie. "I already did."

Fear ricocheted through her. Sinclair was serious. He was carting her off somewhere and for some nefarious purpose she could only guess at. Strike that—for a nefarious purpose she had no wish to guess at.

"You are mad," she gasped, still struggling beneath his weight, desperate to free herself.

A feat which was becoming less and less likely by the moment.

"I am perfectly lucid," he sneered. "Which is far more than I can say for you, Lady Calliope. Your actions have certainly been those of a madwoman. What did you hope to accomplish by blackening my name and filling pages with vicious lies about me? Did it entertain you? Were you bored in your castle, *princess?*"

He spat the last as if it were an epithet.

The vitriol emanating from him was as potent as it was lethal. The Earl of Sinclair despised her.

"I do not know what you are speaking of, my lord," she maintained, breathless from her attempts at escape. Her heart was pounding faster than the hooves of the horses beyond the carriage. "If you allow me to return home, I will never speak a word of this to anyone. I promise. It is not too late to put a stop to these plans of yours, whatever they may be."

He laughed, the sound dark and relentless, sending a chill down her spine. "You can cease your false protestations of innocence at any time. I know beyond a doubt you are the author of the memoirs. Did you believe I would sit idly by whilst my life became fodder for scurrilous gossip and all the doors in London closed to me? Did you truly imagine I would not do everything in my power to prove I am not a murderer?"

His voice trembled with fury, cutting as the lash of a whip.

"You cannot possibly have proof I am the author of those serials," she snapped.

She had been careful. So very careful. Only Mr. White knew she was the author of *Confessions*. He had promised her his utmost discretion, and she trusted him. Not even her beloved and overprotective brother, Benny, the Duke of Westmorland, knew the truth.

"The younger Mr. White sang like a bird when introduced to my fists," Sinclair told her calmly, jerking her bound wrists to an ivory handle on the interior of the carriage and securing them to it with another series of knots.

He was not wearing gloves. She stared at his knuckles as he worked. His fingers were long, his hands large. She did not doubt he could inflict a great deal of damage with them.

The senior Mr. White had promised her he had not shared her identity with anyone. Was it possible he had told his son? Mr. Reginald White was a thin, frail-looking gentleman. She had only met him once, but she was quite certain the massive brute abducting her would decimate him with one blow.

"Nothing to say, princess?" he taunted.

"Get off me," she gritted.

She was unaccustomed to having a man in her lap, and he was deuced heavy. Not to mention terrifying.

He raised a dark brow, that gaze of his sweeping over her, filling her with a curious combination of cold and heat all at once. "Are you going to behave yourself now?"

Never.

"Of course," she lied through clenched teeth.

He finally removed his weight from her body, returning to the other bench with a sigh. "You will not escape those knots, and your legs are too short to reach me. I suppose I may as well settle in for our journey."

Journey?

The word made something inside her freeze. Somehow, she had imagined they would be remaining within London.

But the prospect of a journey... *Dear God*, it filled her with dread. Where could he be taking her? And for what purpose?

"Surely you do not believe you will get away with a third murder, my lord?" she asked boldly.

"Oh, I have no intention of killing you, Lady Calliope," he said, bending down to retrieve his discarded blade from the floor.

His tone was calm. As if he had not just taken her hostage, threatened her with a knife, and bound her wrists.

He truly was a madman, just as she had feared.

"What are you intending to do with me, then?" she prodded him through lips that had gone suddenly dry.

He cocked his head, raking her with that fathomless, dark gaze as he ran his bloodied thumb back over the gleaming blade. "I am going to marry you."

CHAPTER 2

You ought to have seen the look upon her face, dear reader, as I closed my hands around her elegant, treacherous throat. When she begged me for mercy, perhaps I ought to have listened. But for her, I had no pity. She had betrayed me. She was a candle that was mine to extinguish. My fingers tightened. I cannot deny I enjoyed the sound of her struggling for breath, the power I had over her...
~from **Confessions of a Sinful Earl**

One of the excellent things about abducting Lady Calliope Manning and bringing her to Helston Hall was that it had long since been closed up, with no curious or well-intentioned servants about to question him. Or to stop him.

But also, there were *no* servants.

Which meant he would have to play footman, cook, lady's maid, etcetera, to the woman who was currently glaring at him with murderous intent. That fact rather hit him now, with nothing but an old oil lamp to light the way, and no one but the two of them, since his man was tending to the horses and carriage and would bed down for the night in the stables.

To be bitterly honest, the stables were probably more rain-tight than the main house. The previous Earl of Sinclair had been deuced fond of horseflesh and gaming, in exactly that order.

"*Wumf fifflemal wamam,*" Lady Calliope spat at Sin around the gag he had been forced to put in place halfway through their journey when she refused to shut up.

The hour was late, and the cold, stone great hall of Helston Hall suffered a leaky roof. When he had stopped to gather provisions in the village, it had begun to rain, and the deluge had not stopped. Which meant all about them, the echoing of rain pattering to the stone floor echoed, mingling with his prisoner's muffled threats.

"Welcome to one of my ancestral hovels," he announced grimly, offering her a mocking bow. "Forgive the lack of servants and proper roof. Familiar coffers are depleted at the moment, as I am sure you are already more than aware."

Her eyes narrowed. "*Gah er el.*"

He was reasonably certain the troublesome baggage had just told him to go to hell. She need not fear. He was already there. And it was time for her to join him, since she had delivered the final deathblow to his reputation.

Just to further irk her, he feigned confusion. "I cannot understand you, I am afraid."

Her hands were still bound. Her hat was gone, her gown was rumpled, and she was furious. Somehow, in her imperfection, with her Gallic beauty and flashing eyes, she was more beautiful than when she'd had not a hair out of place earlier in the day.

His cock stirred.

Bloody hell.

"*Ayeisoff,*" Lady Calliope said, lifting her bound hands and attempting to tug at the cloth he had tied in place during one of her stinging diatribes.

She had been ranting about how he was fit for the lunatic asylum and he had murdered her brother and his own wife both. And Sin had finally had enough of that. The remainder of their travel had been so much more pleasant after she had ceased squawking.

Marriage to this woman was going to be wretched. But Sin had already suffered one hellacious marriage, and that one had not even come with enough coin to settle his inherited debts. Fortunately, Lady Calliope Manning hailed from a family of obscene wealth. And he intended to obtain enough of it to rescue himself from ruin. All at her expense.

He would not feel a modicum of guilt about that. Because she had brought this on herself with her vicious lies. The she-devil owed him.

"Come," he told her, taking her elbow and guiding her to the rickety stairs. "You must be tired after our travels. I will take you to our chamber and you can tend to yourself as you must before dinner."

Her eyes went wide and she yanked her elbow from his grasp, making a strangled noise.

Blast. He supposed he would have to untie the gag if he was to communicate with her. Unfortunately.

He extracted his blade and used it to slice through the silk handkerchief he had used as his makeshift gag. "There you are, my lady. What was it you wanted to say to me?"

"*Our* chamber?" she demanded. "You truly are a madman if you believe I will lower myself to share a chamber with you."

"You think you are in a position to make demands of me?" He laughed. The sound held no levity. His laughter never did these days. Had not in years, perhaps.

Her lips thinned into a harsh line. "I am a lady. You are a lord. Surely that ought to account for something? Have you forgotten who we are in your merciless plans?"

"Amusing of you to remind me. Had you not thought of something similar before penning your spurious accounts of my supposed memoirs, all so you could ruin me?" he countered. "Tell me, Lady Calliope, where did you come upon some of the information included in those memoirs? The orgies, in particular. Could it be you have experienced them yourself? How shocking for a young, innocent, unwed lady to write such filth. It you were to be revealed as the author to all London, I cannot help but to imagine the scandal."

Indeed, such a revelation would prove her ruination. The doors of polite society would be forever closed to her, regardless of her brother the duke's immense wealth. They could overlook her eccentricities, but a fallen woman, and a fallen woman who was hell-bent upon ruining an earl with false memoirs…

She paled. "I told you, I did not write those memoirs."

"And I told you, I saw them on your writing desk at Westmorland House after I paid a visit to your brother. For a man who led the Special League, he is quite inept at making certain his visitors leave when they say they do." He caught her elbow again, not above forcing her to the chamber. "And before that, I managed to get the truth out of the younger White. You made it far too easy to find you, Lady Calliope. But I am glad for that, because you are precisely what I need."

"I will not marry you," she insisted.

Carrying the lamp, he led her up the steps, taking care to avoid the loose board on the fifth stair. He had made a trip here as part of his plans, just to make certain Helston Hall was yet livable. The answer had been yes.

Barely.

"Your argument is pointless," he told her. "The dye has been cast. Do watch that step. It is rather rotten, I fancy. Tread with care."

"Where the devil have you brought me?" she demanded.

"This leaking monstrosity is more fit to be a ruins than a home."

"Not for long," he said calmly, hauling her to the top of the stairs. "With the proper coin, it can be repaired and restored to its former glory."

"Is that what this is about?" She yanked at her elbow again, making herself a dead weight as he attempted to pull her down the hall toward the state apartments. "You have abducted me so you can convince my brother to pay you ransom and settle your debts? Are you truly that desperate?"

"Yes, I am that desperate," he snapped, pulling her with all his might. "But I am not that stupid. "I do not want a ransom. I want a lifetime of reassurance. Only marriage will buy me that."

"I repeat, I will not marry you." She attempted to wrest herself from his grasp once more, but it was futile.

He was far stronger than she was, and he simply dragged her into the chamber. "Yes, you will."

Unfortunately for his captive, this chamber was the sole habitable one of the lot. Which meant they would be sharing both the room and the bed.

"I do not know what you are about, Lord Sinclair," she huffed with more of that signature bravado of hers, "but abduction is against Her Majesty's law. Nor can you force me to marry you."

"Who said anything about force, princess?" He lit another lamp, all while keeping a firm hold on his wife-to-be, lest she attempt to clobber him with a random household object.

The chamber smelled of must, but evidence of its former glory abounded in the plasterwork on the ceiling and its sheer size. A shame, truly. This ramshackle old beast was once a prized jewel in the Sinclair earldom's coronet.

She laughed, the sound shrill. "If you think I shall willingly marry you, my lord, you are even madder than I thought."

Oh, he was definitely madder than she thought.

"If you wish to use the chamber pot, you will find it behind the screen just over there," he told her coolly, gesturing to the shadowed corner of the room. "I will await you, and then we will dine before retiring for the evening. The journey has left me tired."

Her gaze narrowed on him. "And where will you be awaiting me, Lord Sinclair? Surely not within this chamber."

"Wrong again, princess." He flashed her a grin. "I will be right here. Naturally, I do not trust you not to get yourself into trouble, should I offer you even a moment alone. Therefore, I shall wait."

* * *

Callie gaped at the Earl of Sinclair, trying to control the fear threatening to clog her throat. She was terrified of him, it was true. How strange it was to at last be face-to-face with the man she had turned into a veritable devil in her mind. Before her brother, Alfred's, death, she had scarcely ever crossed paths with the earl, her social circle being quite a bit removed from Sinclair's dubious connections. In the wake of Alfred's death, she had fled to Paris and her aunt Fanchette, and the man responsible for Alfred's sudden demise had been a world away.

She had forgotten how handsome he was. She wished he was a great, ugly gargoyle of a man. That she could take one look at him and see the evil somehow reflected upon his visage, burning from his eyes.

Instead, he was not hideous. Nor had he been particularly

violent or vicious thus far. But he was certainly a lunatic. He watched her now with an implacable calm, as if he had not just ordered her to use a chamber pot *within his hearing*. And as if he had not suggested she would willingly become his bride.

"I require privacy," she told him, pleased that her voice did not betray even a tremble.

In the battle she waged with this despicable foe, she knew she would need to maintain as much ground as she possibly could.

"And you shall have it," he agreed. "Behind the screen."

She was in desperate need of relief. They had traveled hours from London—she knew not how long. But he had not stopped for her comfort, and as a result, she was about to burst. Still, she had her pride.

Callie shook her head. "I cannot possibly do it."

"You will have to accustom yourself to all manner of intimacies with me after we are wed, princess." He quirked a brow at her, unrelenting. "This will be the least of them."

His words chilled her to her core. "Considering you murdered your former countess and my brother both, I will never marry you, my lord. Nor will I use the chamber pot within your earshot. Get out."

He chuckled, and even that sound was sinister. "You seem to be confused about which one of us holds all the power. Allow me to educate you: your hands are bound. You are at my mercy. You have no choice."

The insistent pain in her bladder reminded her he was close to being right. But she was not going to give in just yet. Her mind spun.

"I cannot use the chamber pot with my hands bound," she tried next.

If he forced her to humiliate herself, at the very least, she could perhaps have her hands free so she could attempt to escape him. Her eyes went around the chamber in search of something with which she could bludgeon him and settled upon a strangely shaped figurine on a nearby table.

"Of course you can," he countered, frowning.

"I cannot." She held up her bound hands and made a show of attempting to grasp her voluminous skirts. "Unless you wish to aid me, I must have my hands freed. You may continue to preside over me as my gaoler as you wish. But at least grant me the decency of tending to myself."

His wide jaw tensed beneath the shadow of dark whiskers covering it. "Only until you have finished, and then your wrists will be bound again. And if you attempt anything foolish, it will not go well for you, princess. I have no qualms about hurting you. Do you understand me?"

Her heart pounded. "Perfectly." She held out her bound wrists to him.

He pulled that same, wicked-looking blade from within his jacket and sawed through the bindings with ease. "Nothing foolish, Lady Calliope."

Blood rushed back to her fingers as he freed her, making Callie cry out as tingling pain seared through her. She had not realized how tight her bindings had been until their removal. She rubbed her wrists and flexed her fingers, wincing.

His hands were on hers then, and an unwanted heat skipped up past her elbows at the touch. He rubbed her fingers in his, cursing bitterly. "Was it too tight?"

"Why would you care?" she asked, jerking herself from his grasp.

What a strange man he was, acting as if he were concerned. She did not trust him. If he was concerned, it was for his own plans and not for her wellbeing. That much, she knew without doubt.

She turned away from him and went behind the screen,

where more shadows and a chamber pot awaited her. Grimacing, she made the necessary motions to relieve herself, terribly conscious of Sinclair's presence on the other side of the screen. Also terribly aware that she would somehow have to get her hands on the figurine and deliver a blow to the earl's head with it.

Though she hesitated to harm anyone, her ability to escape him grew fainter by the moment. He had taken her somewhere well beyond the boundaries of London, and she had no hope finding her way back unless she did something drastic.

She took her time, rising and settling her undergarments and gown back into place.

"Are you finished?" came his voice, low and impatient.

"Almost," she hedged, swiftly crafting her plan.

If she hesitated, lingering behind the screen, it was entirely likely he would come for her, and then she could distract him by throwing the screen onto him, giving her enough time to get her hands on that figurine.

"What is taking you so bloody long?" he demanded, his booted footfalls striding nearer.

Nearer.

She held her breath. At the last moment, she shoved the screen, upending it onto him. His muffled curses were not far behind her as she raced for the figurine. Her fingers closed upon it, and she turned, raising it high, striking him over the head with it.

The figurine smashed into hundreds of ceramic shards, raining all over the floor.

He growled.

But he did not topple over. Nor did he pass out. Instead, he lunged for her.

And that was when she knew she was in desperate trouble.

CHAPTER 3

After they were both dead, dear reader, I wish I could tell you I experienced a measure of guilt. However, I knew not even a modicum. I gloried in my crime. The Duke of W. and the Countess of Sin deserved their fates.
~*from* **Confessions of a Sinful Earl**

The witch had broken a porcelain figure over his head. Sin supposed he ought not to be surprised. Leave it to Lady Calliope Manning to find one of the few pieces remaining within Helston Hall which had yet to be sold off or bartered because it was too bloody ugly, and to clobber him with it.

But she would pay for her folly.

He was not in the mood to find amusement in her attempts to beat in his brains, as it happened. His reaction, he had to admit, was rather something of an overreaction. There was no need to tackle her and pin her to the thread-bare carpet beneath him. No reason save his own fury.

And the desire to have her beneath him.

He would not lie about that. As much as he loathed her,

Lady Calliope was a dark-haired, dark-eyed beauty with a feminine form to tempt a saint. The need to overpower her, to show her just how helpless she was, had become a physical ache that swelled beyond the mere tides of lust.

Sin caught her hands, pinning them over her head. His thighs bracketed hers, and he leaned down, so their noses nearly touched. She was breathing heavily, thrusting her full bosom into his chest.

"That was a mistake," he told her as he allowed his gaze to flit over her face.

Her eyes were wide, luminous pools of darkness. Her lips parted. "Let me go, you brute."

Why the hell was she so damned beautiful? So alluring? So traitorous?

He ground his jaw, forcing back a wave of desire that crashed over him when she writhed beneath him. He was not supposed to want her, damn it. "I am the brute? Need I remind you which one of us has just attacked the other?"

"You abducted me!" she shouted, struggling to free herself. "You killed my brother!"

She was panting beneath him, fighting him with all her might. He had to admit, she possessed surprising strength for such an elegant duke's daughter. He also had to admit, he liked the way she fought him. His cock was hard.

What the hell was wrong with him? She had ruined him and had just accused him of murdering her brother, a crime which he had most certainly not committed. How could he be randy at a time like this?

"I abducted you," he snapped at her. "I will own that. But I can assure you, I did not kill your brother. The sainted Duke of Westmorland achieved his demise all on his own."

"A fall down the steps in the middle of the night after you had attacked and threatened him within earshot of the servants," she scoffed, breathless. "And on the same night as

22

your wife's sudden death. So many curious deaths, all revolving around one despicable man."

"Unfortunately for you, I am the same despicable man you are going to marry." His lip curled. "How will it feel to spend the rest of your life bound inextricably to the man you wanted to destroy, princess?"

He was taunting her, it was true. In truth, it had been a long day. A long journey. He had been filled with rage and desperation for far too much time. And now, it was all mixing with the heady potency of lust. A dangerous combination indeed.

She moved beneath him with increasing, futile violence. "I will never marry you."

She had no notion that her thrashing only rubbed her breasts against his chest and ground her curves into his straining prick. She had no idea her breathlessness and open berry-red lips called to him. Even her anger excited him. Her hatred made him want her. He had not been prepared for the depths of his own depravity.

But there was a reason he was known as Sin.

Part of him reveled in the depraved.

And this physical battle between them? It was the stuff depravity was made of.

"Oh, marry me, you will," he promised her.

And then he gave in to temptation, to wickedness. He pressed his mouth over hers. He would not call it a kiss, because it was not that; it was less and yet so much more. It was a claiming. It was also possession. He would never raise his hand to a woman, regardless of what she had done to him, but he wanted to dominate Lady Calliope Manning. He wanted her weak. On her knees.

He would settle for her mouth. He kissed her viciously, with bruising force. And it startled him, how much he liked it. How suddenly ravenous he was for her, this woman he loathed, this capricious chit who had brought about his ruin with her wild imagination and poison pen.

There was something between them. Something more than hatred. More than lust. He kissed her, and he forgot why they were here, what she had done, how he had taken her from London, her subsequent attack with the worthless piece of pottery. For a moment, he forgot all the reasons. Forgot everything but the woman beneath him. She smelled sweet and exotic at once, like lavender and tuberose. He inhaled her scent, her breaths, her fear.

Her lips moved against his. She was breaking, giving in. Kissing him back. He lost himself. Lost reason. Had to taste her. He slid his tongue into her mouth. She made a mewling sound, her tongue moving against his.

And then, the spawn of Satan bit him. His tongue, specifically. Hard enough for him to rear his head back, severing the connection. With enough force to draw blood. For the second time that day, the copper flavor of his own blood was in his mouth.

"Vicious princess," he ground out, staring down at her.

"I will never marry you," she returned, all fire.

He smiled. He was enjoying this far more than he had anticipated. Enough of these games, however. He had no intention of consummating their union until she was officially his countess. And before that could happen, he would have to lay out the plain facts for her.

But first, he was hungry. Not just for her beneath him, but for his dinner.

"I will enjoy proving you wrong," he told her, and then he moved quickly, rising to his feet and hauling her along with him. "Do not try anything so foolish again, Lady Calliope. I would hate to have to cut your pretty flesh, but I will if you make me. It is only fair, since you have drawn first blood."

He did not want to bind her wrists again. When he had

cut her bindings and she had made a sound of undeniable pain, guilt had eaten at him. He was good with knots, but he was not accustomed to binding another for longer than what bed sport required. And despite the fact that he despised this woman and what she had done to him, he had no wish to cause her physical pain.

He withdrew his blade as a reminder, and then he tugged her along with him. "Come. It is time for us to have dinner and to talk."

* * *

Callie did not want to have dinner with the beastly Earl of Sinclair.

Nor did she have any inclination to speak with him.

And yet, she found herself seated opposite him at a scarred old table in the kitchens of the ruins where he had taken her. She had watched in amazement as he had filled plates with cold chicken, hunks of bread, and cheese. Simple fare, and yet, somehow, she had not expected a heartless murderer to care enough to make certain her stomach was not empty.

And as she watched him fussing over the meager meal he had somehow acquired in the brief pause in their travels earlier in the day, when he had left her in the carriage, her lips stung. They stung with the reminder of those awful kisses. Who could have anticipated his hated lips would have felt so very right upon hers?

She had never before been kissed in anger. Nor by someone she despised. She had not expected to *enjoy* it. Indeed, her wits told her she should have abhorred everything about what had transpired between them—his weight upon hers, his big body crushing her, his hot breath fanning over her mouth, and then his wicked assault of her lips.

And yet…she had liked it, much to her shame.

She had liked the kiss of the man who had killed her beloved brother.

What was the matter with her?

She stared down at the plate Sinclair had laid before her, determined she would not eat a bite of it as penance for her sins. Even as her stomach rumbled with the reminder that it had been a long time since she had taken tea and biscuits with her friend, Lady Jo, back in London. It had only been hours ago, and yet seemingly a lifetime had passed.

"Afraid the heartless murderer of wives and brothers has poisoned your supper?" asked Sinclair, his tone dark, angry, and bitter.

"Have you?" she asked.

His lips flattened. "No."

Did she detect disapproval in his voice? Hurt?

She fiddled with her fork but made no effort to pick it up. "Are there no servants in this ruins to which you have forced me?"

"None, princess. You will have to see to yourself, or you will have to rely upon me." His smile was insincere.

Yet still beautiful.

He was a dreadfully handsome man, and his sobriquet had never made more sense than it did to her now, in this low light, as she was the beneficiary of all his attention. After his lips had devoured hers.

Sin.

How fitting.

She ground her molars and returned her stare to her plate. Her stomach growled once more, imploring her to eat at least a bite. Her pride would not allow it.

Her captor had no such reservations. He was gustily

consuming his chicken and cheese. Strangely, his voraciousness did not disgust her. Rather, it intrigued her. She found herself stealing glances in his direction, only to find his eyes were always upon her.

Almost black, those eyes.

Fathomless.

"You are not hungry?" he asked suddenly.

She cleared her throat at his question. "No."

His lips twitched. "You will only spite yourself, Lady Calliope. If you do not eat your dinner, you will go to sleep with a hungry belly."

She doubted very much she would be able to sleep this night. First, she would be far too busy attempting to orchestrate her escape. Second, how could she sleep, knowing she was this man's captive? She laid down her fork.

He made a low sound of disapproval. "Eat, princess."

His directive naturally made her balk. "I am not hungry."

"That is a lie. I heard your stomach rumbling from here," he said.

Blast him. He likely had. She was starving.

She pasted a false smile to her lips. "I am sure you heard nothing of the sort. I have no wish to eat the food of my captor. Therefore, I am not hungry."

"This is the food of your future husband." He lifted a bite of chicken to his well-sculpted lips. "I am not your captor, Lady Calliope."

She tried not to watch him chewing, tried not to allow her gaze to linger upon his lips. Upon those lips that had so recently been moving over hers. And she most definitely banished any lingering tingling sensations caused by the memory.

"You *are* my captor," she reminded him as much as herself. "You took me from London, against my will. If I am free to go, why did you bind my wrists and threaten me with a blade? Why do we not return to London now?"

"I prefer to think of myself as your host. The man to whom you will bind yourself in holy matrimony." He took a generous sip of wine.

She watched the bob of his Adam's apple, nettled at his lack of concern. Irritated by his blatant masculinity, too. "I prefer to think of you as a madman."

"You may as well eat," he told her. "There will be nothing until breakfast."

"I will not eat your food." She compressed her lips and pinned him with a glare.

Her stomach growled again.

He gave an indolent shrug. "Suit yourself, princess."

And then he continued to eat.

Each clang of his cutlery upon the simple plate irked her. How could he be so unaffected? So cool? Part of her was frightened, part confused, part terrified. And another part? Intrigued.

"You truly suspect I poisoned your food?" he asked suddenly, reaching across the table and spearing a hunk of chicken on the tines of his fork before bringing it to his own plate. "Witness: I will prove to you it is perfectly safe to eat."

She watched him tuck into the thieved chicken with the same enthusiasm he had shown the rest of his meal. "Why do you care if I eat or not?"

His jaw tensed. "I do not give a damn about you, Lady Ruthless. You are a means to an end. But if you starve yourself before I can make you my wife, you will be of little use to me."

Lady Ruthless.

She did not like that sobriquet any more than she liked *princess.*

28

She tilted her chin up in defiance. "Perhaps I shall starve myself, then. It seems the most palatable solution."

If only her stomach agreed. She was desperately hungry. So hungry, she was beginning to feel ill. She ought to have eaten something more significant when she had the chance. Ordinarily, she did. But she had been so preoccupied with stealing away to the publisher with her friend Jo's newest pamphlet for the Lady's Suffrage Society and her own latest installment of *Confessions of a Sinful Earl*.

It was the wickedest part of the serial to date. And even she could admit to herself that by now, the character she had created—the Earl of Sinfulness—had taken on a life of his own. Nothing in what she had written had a basis in truth. It had been written with all the rancor in her heart. The words were meant to hurt the man before her. To cut him deeply. To ruin him.

He raised another bite of chicken to his lips, catching it between his teeth. Even the way he consumed his dinner was sinful. She had never seen a gentleman dine in such a blatantly carnal fashion. He was aiming to shock her, she suspected.

Her cheeks warmed in spite of herself as she watched his mouth move. As she stared at his tongue gliding over his upper lip. She told herself to look away, but somehow that seemed like surrender. She was determined to win this battle between them.

"Starving is a better option than marrying an earl?" he asked, before biting into a hunk of bread.

Her heart was beating fast again. Faster than the wings of a hummingbird, it seemed. "When the earl in question is you, yes."

"You may change your mind, darling." The smile he flashed her was darkly amused.

"Never," she vowed bitterly. "And do not presume to call me your darling."

"Never is a long time." He raised a brow, then took another calm sip of his wine. "At least have a drink, princess. You must be thirsty."

She was, blast him.

Callie swallowed. "I would prefer tea."

"Alas, I have none." He settled his wine back upon the weathered table. "I am afraid it is wine or nothing."

The dearth of food, drink, and servants suggested he did not intend to keep her here long. Or if he did, he would need supplies.

"Nothing," she clipped.

She would not accept his food or his wine. He could go to perdition where he belonged. She must remain firm and strong, for Alfred's sake. Her beloved brother had been a saint among men, rivaled by only her brother Benedict, who had become duke after Alfred's death. She owed it to her brother's memory to continue this mission of vengeance. Alfred was gone. Surely she could summon enough strength to abstain from cold chicken and wine.

"As milady wishes."

His mocking tone was not lost on her. Nor was the sting in his regard. He looked at her as if *she* were the detestable one, between the two of them. She had done nothing wrong. At least, nothing that was not deserved. If she had caused him misery and agony, it could hardly compare to the suffering he had dealt her when he had taken Alfred away forever.

She pushed the plate away from her, sending it across the rough surface of the kitchen table. And then she slid her wine toward him as well. "There you are, *milord*. I will not be consuming any of your tainted food or drink."

His nostrils flared. "It is not tainted. I am not a murderer, in spite of your feverish fantasies to the contrary. Nor am I an opium eater. I have never touched the stuff."

Her wrists were no longer bound. She was feeling bold. Callie stood, her chair legs scraping on the rough stone floor. "I do not have fantasies, feverish or otherwise. I have facts. My brother is gone. You are responsible. And your poor wife too, though I scarcely knew her."

The former Lady Sinclair had been beautiful. Callie well understood why Alfred had fallen in love with her. She had been golden-haired, a perfect English rose. Callie had only ever met her once, in passing. She had come alone to a ball Alfred hosted.

How different life had been then.

Alfred had been alive. Simon had already been gone.

Her heart gave a pang at the remembrance of her betrothed. So much loss. Such a short amount of time. She occupied herself well now, keeping her mind from thoughts of the lost. If she lingered too much upon her painful past… Well, she had done that in Paris, had she not? And she had almost lost herself in the process.

"Sit down," Sinclair ordered her.

Still calm, so calm. As if he were paying her a call in his brother's home during her at-home hours. As if he were a suitor. As if he were not the architect of the demise of her family as she had known it. Three siblings—Alfred, Benedict, and Callie. The alphabet, they had once been known. And now, one of them was missing.

"No," she denied. "I will not sit. I refuse. I will not eat, I will not drink, and I will not be a part of your mad scheme a moment longer."

With that, she spun on her heel and began stalking from the dank, shadowed kitchens. It was a large room. From the looks of it, this familial rubble where he had secreted her had once been a vast, proud estate. Now, it looked better served

31

to host spiders and rodents than guests of the human persuasion. Either way, she cared not. She was leaving.

Fleeing him.

But he was on his feet and chasing after her. Footfalls echoed on the stone, hard and forceful. She gathered her skirts in her hands, lifting them—cursing herself for abstaining from her traditional divided skirts earlier—and breaking into a run.

The Earl of Sinclair was faster. Stronger. Hands caught her waist in a punishing grip, staying her flight. He yanked her backward, into his tall, lean frame.

His face was near. Against her back, she felt the pounding of his heart. His breath was hot on her ear. "You did not truly think you would escape me that easily, did you, princess?"

Her eyes fluttered closed on a wave of misery. She attempted to elbow him in the ribs, but he anticipated her movement, catching her arm in a swift grip. His body radiated heat into hers.

"What are you seeking to prove?" she demanded wearily.

"If I said my innocence, would it make a difference?" His lips were so near, they grazed the shell of her ear when he spoke.

She could not quell the shiver that went down her spine. "You cannot possibly prove that when you are guilty."

"As I thought." His tone was grim, his grip still tight upon her, the heaviness of her skirts crushed between them not enough to separate her from *him*. "You have already decided you are right and I am wrong. That I am evil and you are the innocent who has been wronged. Have you not, Lady Calliope?"

Her eyes opened at last, and all she saw ahead of her was the dankness of the unused kitchens. Vast fireplaces, an outmoded stove, all of it lifeless. The air smelled damp, and it was apparent there had been no inhabitants within for some time. The busyness of the kitchens at Westmorland House had always been a secret source of pleasure for her. From the time she had been a girl, she had adored sneaking into the kitchens, which had always smelled of baking bread.

The disparity between that happy place and this dark, dank kitchen, her captor at her back, made her shiver again. At least, she told herself that was the reason, and not the way he felt, molded to her. So strong. So dangerous and feral.

"Why the sudden quiet, my lady?" he demanded. He anchored her to him with one steely arm, entrapping her, and then, his hand was on her throat. His fingers encircling. Bare skin on bare skin.

She held herself still, as a new fear swept over her. Callie swallowed. "If you are going to kill me, have done with it. There is no need to play with me the way a cat paws at its prey."

CHAPTER 4

*What sin can possibly quell the ceaseless urges of a villain like
myself, dear reader, after murder? It was the question which drove
my days, the obsession that consumed me. I developed a thirst for
innocence...*

~*from* **Confessions of a Sinful Earl**

She had tenacity, Lady Calliope Manning. Sin would
grant her that much. But she was also stubborn and
foolish. And now, with his fingers wrapped around her sleek,
pale throat, she gave away her fear. Her pulse beat a rapid
staccato beneath his touch.

"Are you afraid, princess?"

He posed the question directly into her ear, and he had to
admit, perverse bastard that he was, frightening her brought
him pleasure. More pleasure than he would have imagined.
Or perhaps it was not her fear but the feeling of her body
pressed once more against his that had his cock at half-mast.
Difficult to believe a woman he hated with all the fury of his
black soul could also make his prick hard.

But when had he ever been a normal man?

Never.

His past sins were proof of that. The many women he had bedded. The wildness of his youth.

"Strangle me if you wish," she said, her voice bold and brazen as you please.

Stubborn to the last. Had he expected any less? Ever since he had uncovered the true author of the memoirs which had ground his already dark reputation so far into the mud, it could never be retrieved, Sin had been studying her. Watching from afar. Planning. He knew she had her brother, the Duke of Westmorland, wrapped around her pinky finger. He knew she had all London on its knees for her.

Not many unwed ladies could return from Paris in a swirl of rumors and yet move freely amongst the *crème de la crème* of society. The famed painter Moreau was rumored to have been one of her lovers. A distasteful thought. When they married, she would have to wait until she provided Sin with an heir and spare before cuckolding him the way his last wife had done. But then, Celeste had proven herself a vengeful bitch with relative ease.

Suiting that he was about to bind himself to another woman who appeared to be cut from the same cloth.

"If I strangle you, darling, I cannot make you my wife," he murmured, giving her throat a gentle squeeze.

Just one flex of his fingers. Nothing more. Nothing that would cause her pain. Contrary to what she believed of him, he had never harmed another, whether beast or man. He did not even enjoy the hunt.

She trembled beneath his touch. He felt her inhalations. Fast and shallow. She was afraid.

Good. Let her know some fear. Some desperation.

"I have told you, I will never marry you, and you cannot force me to do so," she bit out.

"Fortunately for both of us, I will not require force." He released her throat and stroked it.

She was soft and warm and feminine. He liked the way her skin felt beneath his questing fingertips. And despite his rage toward her, part of him had to acknowledge that bedding her would not be a chore.

What the devil was wrong with him? He ought not to be enjoying this in the way he was. Nor ought he to be enjoying *her*, his enemy.

How long had it been since he had last shagged a woman senseless? Too long. He had been attempting to win the prim Miss Mary Vandenberg and her American father's fortune. He had been on his best behavior. But it would seem playing the saint was not good enough for Mr. Vandenberg when rumors of the murders his potential future son-in-law had committed were being bandied about London drawing rooms. Miss Vandenberg had cried off with all haste.

"I am already betrothed," she bluffed then.

It was a futile ploy on her behalf. He knew everything there was to know about her.

"Lord Simon Montbatten," he said calmly. "Difficult indeed to marry a dead man, is it not?"

Lord Simon had been of frail constitution. Two years ago, he had gone to Italy to aid his ailing lungs and take the waters. And he had never returned. From all accounts, Lady Calliope had been devastated by his death. Theirs had been a love match. Lord Simon had been the heir to Viscount Suttworth, an old title that hailed to the times of the Conqueror, much like the Dukes of Westmorland. The perfect dynastic union.

Lady Calliope stiffened, inhaling sharply. "How dare you?"

He stroked her pulse, reluctant to stop touching her. "How dare I speak truth?"

She resumed her struggles. "How dare you speak of him so callously? He was a wonderful man, a true gentleman. Your better in every way."

"I have no doubt he was, but he will not save you, princess." He dared to nip her ear, just to show her which of them held all the power in this odd dynamic. "Dead men cannot play Sir Galahad. No one can save you now."

She fought him harder. "I do not need anyone to save me. This is madness, my lord. I did nothing to provoke this."

What a liar she was.

"Nothing indeed?" He spun her about so she faced him at last, careful to keep his hold upon her tight enough that she could not escape or strike him.

Her dark eyes met his. She was pale. Her lips were the red of summer roses in bloom. Parted. He thought about how soft they had been beneath his. And then he banished the notion.

"I did not write *Confessions of a Sinful Earl*," she said.

But her eyes drifted to a point over his shoulder as she issued the denial.

He shook his head. "This is all fruitless, Lady Calliope. I know you wrote those bloody serials. Your publisher admitted it. I saw your mad scribblings on your writing desk in your chamber. You may as well acknowledge the truth."

Her eyes returned to his, blazing with fury. Wild. "I wrote them. Every word. There. Is that what you want from me, Lord Sinclair? It matters not in the end who wrote those memoirs. The truth is, you murdered my brother, and then you murdered your wife."

Now they were getting somewhere.

"That is the truth as you see it, is it not?" He searched her gaze. "You think it was perfectly acceptable to ruin me because I am guilty. You believe I hurt you, and so you sought to hurt me in return. But you went beyond hurt. You ruined me, utterly."

Her jaw tightened. "You ruined yourself. If you were not such an insufferable ogre, your wife would never have gone to my brother for comfort."

"My wife was a manipulative whore," he bit out, fury vibrating through him.

Celeste had torn him apart. He had fancied himself in love with her, once. She had been the woman who had tamed London's most notorious rake. A flaxen-haired siren come to tempt mere mortals into perdition. He had fallen for her. Fallen for her schemes. Believed she loved him. But when he had inherited the earldom, she had changed.

In the end, all she had done was lie to him, spend the little of his funds that remained upon her vast, ever-mounting gambling debts. And cuckold him. She had seduced him into marriage and turned into a monster, taking everything from him.

By the time he had realized the depths of his foolishness, it had been too late. They had been inextricably bound. After their daughter had been stillborn, she had only grown bolder. Collecting the hearts of men had been one of Celeste's prized entertainments. The former Duke of Westmorland had merely made himself one more of her victims.

"My brother said she was a goddess among women," Lady Calliope snarled, her lip curling.

"Your brother was duped by her the same way so many other poor sods were, myself included," he ground out.

"I do not believe you." Her eyes were wide, desperation making her voice quake.

She was afraid.

Very afraid.

The knowledge ought to please Sin, and yet, it did not.

"You do not have to believe me," he told her. "It is the truth even if you refuse to acknowledge it."

"You want me to think you so innocent in all this," she spat. "But yet, you have abducted me. You have threatened me with a knife. You have bound my wrists. Put your hands on my throat. Your story speaks for itself."

"And what of you, princess?" he asked, unwilling to allow her to continue playing the innocent. "Do you imagine I would have even noticed you, had you not meddled in my life? I was betrothed. Do you think I would have pursued a selfish, vainglorious chit such as yourself to this extent if you had not ruined me with your outlandish, false tales?"

"Prove to me they are outlandish and false!" Her voice rang through the empty kitchens, echoing off the stone walls.

Suddenly, thunder roared overhead, seemingly out of nowhere. One violent crack. The flash of lightning followed not long thereafter, brightening the room with a flash of light for an instant.

"Prove to me you did not write *Confessions of a Sinful Earl*," he countered.

After all, she had not truly admitted she was the author of those infernal memoirs. Those vicious, insidious serials of utter tripe. The entirety of it was so salacious, so ludicrous… and yet, it barely skimmed the surface of his true sins. Imaginary sins had been heaped upon him—murder, opium eating, all manner of horrible tales. But the truth of it was, his sins were of a different variety than those which *Confessions* depicted. The memoirs were clearly the product of an overeager imagination of a woman who had not witnessed the darkness in life that he had.

There was a reason he was called Sin. But it had nothing to do with murder and everything to do with pleasure.

"I wrote it," she admitted at last, her tone defiant as ever. "You are correct, my lord. I wrote every word. And I can assure you that the latest serial I delivered today is even more depraved than the previous editions. If you were ruined before, you will be decimated now."

How smug she sounded.

His nostrils flared.

He tightened his grip on her. "You are playing with fire, Lady Calliope."

But she remained as unrepentant as ever. "Then let it burn me, Lord Sinclair."

He had a feeling she was going to regret those words and her defiance both.

"Oh, it will, princess," he warned her grimly. "It will."

* * *

"This is where we will spend the night. Make yourself comfortable as you must and then settle in," the Earl of Sinclair informed Callie as he finished tying the knot on her wrist, leaving her bound to the headboard of an imposing old bed.

Her restraint was long enough to give her freedom of movement, but short enough to prohibit escape. As she stood on the threadbare carpet before the bed, however, her bindings were the least of her worry.

We, he had said.

The Earl of Sinclair still expected Callie to share a bed with him.

An answering frisson of dread mingled with something else rolled down her spine. It was the *something else* that troubled her every bit as much as the idea of spending the night in a bed with him.

Alone.

"I will not sleep here with you," she vowed.

"Yes," he told her calmly, "you will. This is the only bed. I am tired after our journeys. And I need to keep an eye on you."

"This is the height of impropriety." She could not seem to wrest her gaze from that big, imposing bed. "You cannot expect me to…"

She could not bring herself to say the words aloud. Could not bear to think them. Surely he was not so depraved that he was going to attempt to force himself upon her.

"Do you think I will ravish you, princess?" he asked, sounding darkly amused.

His query sent a strange sensation blossoming through her. Her heart raced. Unbidden, the memory of his lips on hers returned, bringing with it an unexpected flare of heat.

"Is that your intention?" she returned, forcing her gaze to his.

His mouth quirked into a dangerous smile. "No. A cossetted duke's sister who spreads filthy lies about me is the last woman I would ever want to bed."

His words stung. He was a conundrum, this man. If he loathed her, why did he want to marry her? What were his plans? How long would he keep her in suspense?

"Good," she managed. "But forgive me if I find that hardly reassuring. I will not share a bed with you, regardless of your intentions."

"Yes, you will." Calmly, his stare never wavering from hers, he removed his coat.

Alarm skittered through her. Along with that unwanted *something else* once more. His shoulders were broad, his arms thick. He was so very tall and well-formed. He tore at his neck cloth, then removed that wicked-looking blade once more, laying it upon the bed as he began undoing the buttons on his waistcoat.

Another roar of thunder cracked through the night. The late-spring storm was raging in full force. Lightning followed not long after, filling the room with false brightness before plunging it back into shadows. Lord Sinclair was pulling the buttons on his shirt from their moorings now, toeing off his boots.

He raised a challenging brow, eying her in a fashion that was far too familiar. "Like what you see, Lady Calliope?"

Her cheeks went hot. "Of course not. I am merely horrified you would dare to disrobe before me in such shocking fashion. You are repugnant to me."

And he was, she reminded herself. His beautiful exterior could not abate the evil festering within him. She had heard all the vile stories of his past. All London had. He had not been meant to be the earl. According to common fame, his mother had been the concubine of a German grand duke before suddenly marrying his father. Rumor suggested he was the product of that illicit *affaire*. The death of an obscure cousin had left him next in line to the earldom. But it was not the murk of his ancestry which caused the most wagging of tongues. Rather, it was the manner in which he had chosen to live his life.

Orgies.

Depraved parties.

He ruled over a club of decadent lords who devoted themselves to pleasure. Voluptuaries, wicked sinners. How easy it had been to believe his wife had fled from their marriage into the arms of another man, given the shocking stories Callie had heard. Her wild days in Paris may as well have been spent in a nunnery by comparison.

"It is just as well that you find me repugnant," he said, his deep voice cutting through the night as another crack of thunder rapped in the distance. "I would hate to think you would ravish me."

Her lips compressed. How dare he make light of her in the midst of this wretched situation?

She was not certain which was worse—the severity of the muddle in which she now found herself, or the knowledge that no one would even miss her. Perhaps the servants would? Her lady's maid?

She thought of her brother Benny, and his new wife Isabella. They were on their honeymoon, happily in love, off to the countryside. Aunt Fanchette was supposed to have arrived from Paris to act the duenna, but she had failed to appear, in true Aunt Fanchette style. Callie had not minded, as it meant she had run of Westmorland House whilst her brother was gone.

Now, her freedom had proven her downfall.

The sound of Sinclair shedding his shirt filled the chamber. She remained where she was, on the opposite side of the bed, wondering how she could escape. The knot on her wrist felt as final as a noose.

"Nothing to say, princess?" he taunted.

She inhaled slowly, attempting to gain control over her anger. "I will sleep on the floor if you will not at least pretend to be a gentleman."

"You will share the bed with me, and that is final." His voice was closer. Without his boots to warn her of his approach, his footfalls had been damningly silent.

She jerked toward him, startled to find him right behind her, within reach. Without a shirt, his entire chest and abdomen were on display. She promised herself she would not look, but focus upon his eyes instead. "The floor shall be more than sufficient. Indeed, it is preferable to compromising myself in such fashion."

"Your protests are rich, coming from a lady who was painted in the nude by Moreau," he said, a sharp edge to his voice.

Callie had heard that rumor herself more times than she cared to count. Philippe had been a true gentleman. And the truth was, he was in love with the incredibly talented watercolorist, Monsieur Claude Bisset. He had eyes for no one else. But that was not her secret to tell. Philippe and Claude's love had oft caused her a stab of envy. It was what she should have had with Simon, but she was happy for her friends, that they had each other, even if her other half was forever lost to her.

"I was wearing a *robe de chambre*," she corrected the earl coolly, tearing herself from her thoughts.

"As much as you have familiarized yourself with all the rumors concerning me, I have also had ample time to learn about you, my lady." His stare was upon her, undeniable. Impenetrable.

She could not look away. "Oh? And what do you think you know about me, Lord Sinclair?"

"Turn," he told her.

She swallowed. "No."

"You cannot sleep in all your layers," he pointed out.

She could not deny the truth of that. Sleeping in a corset was deuced impossible. To say nothing of her cumbersome gown, petticoats, and chemise. Stockings, impractical shoes...she was weary and tired after their hours-long journey from London. If she were honest with herself, she would admit that all she wanted to do was slip into fresh bedclothes wearing nothing more than her chemise.

But not with the man before her.

Never with him.

"I would die before I lie down in a bed with you," she told him.

His hands seized her waist. She flinched at the touch. Not violent, but possessive. As if he had every right to command her with such familiarity. He spun her around with ease.

Of course he did. He out-muscled her. And she was bound to the bed. There was only so far she could travel.

His fingers were on the buttons at her nape, plucking them one by one. She moved away from him, but he caught her, hauling her against him once more. Never had she felt so inconsequential. So incapable.

"What are you doing?" she demanded, struggling against him, though it was futile.

"Playing lady's maid." There was a hint of amusement in his baritone.

She did not like it.

"How dare you?" She fought against him with greater furor, attempting to kick his shins and tear herself from his grasp.

All to no avail.

Her bodice was gaping.

And he laughed, the devil.

"Take care, princess. If you incite me too much, I may be tempted to hasten our wedding night," he warned grimly.

She stilled, believing him. Thunder clapped with ferocious intent. Lightning flashed almost instantly afterward. Rain lashed the windowpanes.

"Do what you must," she told him.

She would suffer what she had to suffer. Lord knew there was only one man she would ever love, and he was forever lost to her. To find vengeance for her beloved brother, she was willing to endure anything.

Her gown and all her undergarments save her chemise were gone in mere minutes. Swept away as if they had never been. The sole issue had been in the sleeve of her gown. Because he had already tied her to the bed, he had not been able to remove it, and had instead used his wicked blade to slice it from her arm.

"I will have nothing to wear tomorrow," she said, when at last he had finished and released her.

She was breathless.

From fighting him, of course.

And she was also irritated by her own susceptibility.

"Perhaps I shall keep you in your chemise and nothing else."

He was still near. Too near.

She spun about to face him, heart pounding. "What do you intend?"

He gave her a faint smile. Thunder cracked again. Wind railed against the exterior of the old pile of rubble. "Sleep."

And then, much to her surprise, he left her, standing there in nothing but her chemise, drawers, and her stockings. He skirted the bed, returning to the opposite side, and shucked his trousers. Standing there in nothing more than his smalls, he met her gaze.

"Good night, Lady Calliope. Our business shall resume in the morning."

He slid into the bed and drew the counterpane over his beautifully masculine form. She had done her best not to look, but there was no denying the sheer strength of the man, the corded muscle, the sinew. He was as flawless as any sculpture she had ever seen. A god come to life.

An evil god. A wicked god.

A demon, more like.

"Are you intending to stand there all evening?" he asked, settling himself comfortably, the bedclothes round his ear. He even sighed, then yawned.

She wondered what he had done with the knife.

Wondered how she could escape him now.

"The blade is beyond your reach," he said, as if he had read her thoughts.

She stiffened. There was a chill in the room. Her nipples

46

were hard. Gooseflesh pebbled on her arms. The heaviness low in her belly, pooled between her thighs, was tension, she was sure. Anxiety. Hatred. Despair.

Mercifully, the bonds tying her to the bed were slack enough she could lower herself to the worn carpets. They were woolen and scratchy and dusty, but they would have to suffice.

She would not even ask for a pillow. Her pride would allow for no concessions from this man who had taken her as his prisoner. This man who had murdered her brother, she reminded herself.

"Suit yourself, princess," he said, curt. "Sleep well with the mice and the spiders."

He extinguished the lamp, bathing the chamber in darkness.

The booming of thunder punctuated his edict with a chilling finality. A reminder of how small she was in the world, of how little control she possessed over her own future and wellbeing.

Slumber proved elusive for quite some time.

CHAPTER 5

I forced my mouth upon hers, dear reader. Her trembling fear did
not slow my desire to ravish her. It only made me want her more...
    ~from **Confessions of a Sinful Earl**.

ucking hell.
        Sin could not sleep.

He told himself it was the storm and not the fact that his
beautiful captive had chosen to bed down on the rug with
nary a pillow or blanket for comfort that kept him up. But he
lied to himself.

There was an odd sensation prodding at him, all sharp
angles from within: guilt.

Not that he ought to feel even a modicum of it. Lady Calliope
had brought this on herself. She had started this war, not him.

The storm was rumbling on now, moving farther away.
He was weary to the bone. He ought to be happily slumbering. He turned onto his side, peering into the darkness, in
her direction. She was sleeping on the floor. The hard, dusty,
cold floor. Though it was nearly summer, nights in Helston

Hall were damp and draughty. They had been even before it had fallen into such an appalling state of disrepair.

On a growl, he threw back the bedclothes and rose. He stalked around the bed and found her on the floor, curled in a ball rather reminiscent of a cat. Sin scooped her into his arms with ease.

"What are you doing?" her voice was sleepy, and it lacked the vehemence of her previous protestations.

Had she fallen asleep after all? She was warm and soft in his arms. All woman. *Damn*, but the lack of her feminine trappings meant his arms were filled with lush, sweet-scented curves. He fought back a swift rush of desire.

"I am seeing you settled for the night," he snapped, irritated with himself for the hoarseness in his voice. "You are too stubborn for your own good."

"Mmm." With a throaty sigh, she nuzzled his throat.

Bloody hell, the woman was definitely half-asleep. And he was half-erect.

He swallowed and lowered her to the bed, settling the bedclothes over her. Cursing himself, he skirted the bed once more. She made a sleepy sound that should not have made his cock twitch.

You hate her, he reminded himself.

She is a deceitful witch.

But as he made his way back to his side of the bed, his inner protestations did not do one whit of good. Gritting his teeth, he slid beneath the bedclothes, attempting to get comfortable. Her even breathing filled the silence of the chamber. She was asleep.

Of course, she was.

How was it that she had been the one to bed down on the unforgiving floor and yet he, in the comfort of the bed, had been unable to find peace? How was it that *he* was still, even now, being assailed by the twin sensations of guilt and desire?

Perhaps she possessed no conscience.

That would certainly explain it. How else could she write such blatant falsehoods about him?

The air was filled with the soft, faint sounds of Lady Calliope's snores. *Good God*, could the woman sleep through anything? Her wrist was bound to the headboard. She had been on the floor with no blanket, no pillow. He had lifted her from the floor and settled her on the bed, and still, she had scarcely stirred.

Again, a twinge of guilt returned. He had spirited her away from London and brought her to this dilapidated hovel. She was frightened of him, that much he could plainly discern. And he had every intention of persuading her of the necessity of their marriage, whatever that took. He was not going to allow her to leave until he had secured her agreement.

Still, alone with his thoughts and the distant rumble of thunder, his mind swirled with unwanted questions. What if she believed what she had written? His reputation was black, and he knew it. He was at fault for that. Guilty of most of the sins ascribed to him.

But not the worst.

He had never committed murder. Celeste had died by her own hand. And he could hardly say what had befallen the last Duke of Westmorland. He had heard it was a fall, a broken neck, and Lady Calliope herself had claimed he had fallen down the stairs. Regardless of the means by which Westmorland had met his end, Sin had been nowhere near the man when it had happened.

Instead, he had spent the night in the arms of his former mistress. When he had returned to his own townhome that afternoon, it had been to discover his wife had already taken her life. Admittedly, he had lost control after that. His *affaire* with Tilly had ended abruptly, and he had been adrift. He supposed he could see how his subsequent flight from London, to the Continent, could have made him appear guilty.

Instead of mourning Celeste, he had celebrated his freedom from her. A fortnight of overindulgence in drink and quim. He had fucked his way through Paris. And then he had fucked his way through Italy, too.

But those memories were hazy. Nothing more than ghosts.

He could prove his innocence to Lady Calliope if he gave a damn.

Which, of course, he did not. Let her think what she wished. Let her believe the worst of him. Let her think him a monster. Some parts of him *were* monstrous. Most parts, in fact. He had earned his reputation the hard way.

He would not allow his conscience or his attraction to her to get the better of him. His plans would not be compromised. Far too much depended upon his ability to secure her fortune. Thanks to Lady Calliope Manning, she was his last chance to save himself.

Most importantly, she was his last chance to save the only person who mattered to him.

His mother.

On an irritated growl, Sin turned, rolling to his belly. His cock was rigid as stone, burrowing into the mattress. It was going to be one hell of a long night.

* * *

Callie woke to a numb hand and a furnace at her back.

A hard, citrus-and-musk scented furnace.

And an arm banded around her waist.

And a mouth upon her bare shoulder, soft, smooth lips kissing her there.

Truly, it would not have been an unfortunate manner in which to wake, except for her hand.

Early morning light streamed into the chamber, brightening all the shadows from the night before, reminding her she was in a strange place. With a strange man. She could not be farther from her cozy bedchamber at Westmorland House, where she kept fresh roses on her writing desk and had chosen every stick of furniture and picture on the wall.

Remembrance hit her.

The Earl of Sinclair had forced his way into her carriage, and he had brought her to some crumbling ancestral ruins hours away from London. He had discovered she was the author of *Confessions of a Sinful Earl*. Worst of all, he had informed her of his intentions to force her to marry him.

She was tied to the bed.

And she was *in* the bed.

How was she in the bed? She had fallen asleep on the floor, just to spite her captor. At first, it had been deuced uncomfortable, but then she had been so exhausted by travel and the accompanying fear of being unexpectedly absconded with by her mortal enemy...

It was *his* arm around her waist. And *he* was the source of the heat. To say nothing of the delightful masculine scent filling her senses. Or the mouth.

He kissed her skin once again, reminding her she was clad in nothing more than her undergarments. Her chemise had shifted in her sleep, sliding down to bare her shoulder.

"*Cherie, vous séduisez,*" he muttered.

A shiver trilled down her spine, sending an unwanted surge of desire to the apex of her thighs. She pressed her legs together to stay the ache. Forced herself to recall she did not like this man.

In fact, she loathed him.

He was responsible for Alfred's death.

For her numb hand. For her presence in this bed. For so much pain and sorrow.

His hand slid from her waist, gliding over her chemise until he cupped her breast in his palm. Her traitorous nipple stiffened instantly. His thumb traced over the peak, sending a spark of unwanted flame shooting through her. A natural reaction, she reassured herself. It would have happened had any man's hand been upon her.

"Je veux faire l'amour," he whispered, his voice a low rasp.

She was certain he was asleep. Whispering to her in French. More proof of his depravity. He could fall asleep with a woman he professed to loathe and then attempt to seduce her. *Good God*, he had not bedded her, had he? Surely she would have remembered such a thing.

How had she come to be in this bed?

So many questions, so few answers. Only one man knew, and he was sleeping, holding her tight. He would never be able to anticipate what was coming to him.

Good. It would serve him right, the rotter.

Using her unbound arm, she sent her elbow into his solid midsection with as much force as she could muster. The breath fleeing his lungs was as hot as he was, coasting over her bare skin in a sudden rush.

He coughed into her back, sputtering awake. "What the devil?"

His arm tightened on her waist, dragging her backward, so that she was pressed against his frame. There was an unmistakable ridge prodding her lower back. Even as he cursed her and reacted to her abrupt attempt to sever their connection, he held her closer still.

She was not as innocent as some unwed ladies in her acquaintance were. She knew what portion of his anatomy was so rudely making itself known against her back. And she also knew why.

He desired her. His body was reacting to hers, the same way that hers had been affected by his proximity and warm strength radiating against her back. The same way her nipple had tightened when he had cupped her breast.

Instinct. Nothing more. Had not Aunt Fanchette said all men suffered similar maladies in the morning?

It mattered not. All that did matter was that Callie herself was not attracted to the odious Earl of Sinclair.

"Release me, you scoundrel," she gritted, struggling to free herself of his grasp.

"Sheathe your claws, woman," he ground out. "I told you last night, I have no intention of ravishing you."

"You were kissing my shoulder and being crude in French," she accused, wriggling to free herself.

Unfortunately, the action only served to wedge her backside more firmly against his manhood, which seemed to have grown even larger. *Good heavens.* Her cheeks went hot, and that alarming sensation between her thighs would not stop blossoming.

"I assure you, I am crude in every language." He laughed then, the oaf, and the sound lacked the bitterness of the night before. "I can hardly be held responsible for imagining myself somewhere far more pleasant in my sleep, with a bedmate of my choosing."

His implication nettled, she had to admit, in spite of herself. But then she remembered the mystery surrounding the manner in which she had wound up in the bed.

"I fell asleep on the floor," she reminded him coolly. "How did I end up here?"

"Perhaps you wanted to be closer to me," he suggested, his tone wry.

He was responsible for her presence in the bed, she was sure. "Never!"

She moved some more, but the devil was still disturbingly near. And firm. So very firm. She attempted to scoot from him, and he groaned.

"Devil take it, woman. Cease moving about."

"Let me go, you vile wretch," she returned, increasing her struggles.

"Stop wriggling," he gritted in her ear. His hand had settled upon her hip. His manhood was still nestled against her bottom, firm and insistent and hot.

So hot.

So wrong.

She stilled, swallowing past a knot in her throat. The knowledge that he was affected by her proximity was unsettling. Displeasing, she told herself. Vexing. Horrifying.

Intriguing.

No! She struck the unwelcome notion from her mind. His desire for her was not what she wanted. He was an evil monster. His protestations of innocence aside, he was most definitely guilty of forcing his way into her carriage and spiriting her away. And he was also guilty of binding her. Of insisting upon a marriage between them…

"Mayhap I should ravish you after all, princess," he suggested, tracing a lazy pattern on her hip.

His lips grazed her flesh as he spoke.

Her heart was pounding fast. With fury, of course. Not with…anything else. She was not attracted to this odious villain. Decidedly not.

"Stop this madness," she ground out, shifting again, to no avail. "I will not marry you, and nor am I attracted to you in the slightest."

"Then I suggest you cease bloody moving, because it is damned difficult for a man to think straight with your bottom rubbing all over his cockstand," he growled.

If her cheeks had been hot before, they were positively scalding now. *Dear heavens*, had he just said what she thought he had said? The man was an unrepentant rogue. Scandalous and horrible and evil.

"Lord Sinclair," she chastised past her own shock. "How dare you speak to me with such vulgarity?"

"Do you truly fancy me a murderer?" he asked then, taking her by surprise with his query.

She blinked. "Yes."

But within her, deep within her, confusion reigned. She was not entirely certain, now that she had met him at long last. Oh, he was a villain. That much was clear. But her brother, Benny's, words returned to her now, suddenly.

Our brother's death was an accident.

Benny was wrong, because he had been too lost in his work for the Special League to investigate the truth. She could hardly blame him. He was weighed down with so much responsibility—Fenian bombers running rampant all over London, attempting to blow up the London Bridge and the Tower and even Parliament itself.

But after her mind had cleared from the terrible grief infecting her in Paris, she had seen the answer with such shocking clarity, it had stolen her breath. Alfred had been in love with Lady Sinclair. Lord Sinclair was a devious scoundrel. Of the three, only one of them remained. Logic suggested the culpability of one man and one man alone.

Alfred had fallen down the stairs at his home in St. Johns Wood. But only *after* Lord Sinclair had paid him a call there, argued with him, and threatened him over his illicit relationship with Lady Sinclair. She must not forget that the man holding her captive was the last who had seen her beloved brother alive, aside from the servants. Or that his wife had died that same night. Two problems, gone from the earl's life.

Forever.

"I have never killed anyone or anything," the earl told her solemnly, his lips far too near to her ear. "Not even a damned pheasant. I hate to dispel you of your notions that I am a murderous monster, princess, but I am not."

She thought about the evil-looking blade he kept upon his person. And his abduction of her.

"Do you truly believe I will accept anything you say as truth?" she demanded.

"Suit yourself." He released her at last, rolling away. She tried to ignore the sense of loss, as unwanted as his presence had been. "But I have never harmed another soul. I did not kill my faithless wife. I did not kill your foolish brother."

She turned toward him, stymied by the binding on her left wrist, which held her captive as surely as he did. "My brother was not foolish. He was one of the most intelligent, good-hearted men alive."

Indeed, she had never known anyone better, aside from Benny and Simon.

Her mouth went dry as the Earl of Sinclair slipped from the bedclothes, revealing his bare back to her. He was all muscle and sinew. Broad shoulders, lean waist. And the way his smalls clung to his firm bottom was… Positively sinful. That was what it was. She could not entirely banish the effect he had upon her.

He turned toward her, catching her staring, and raised a brow. "My former wife was a coldhearted shrew who ate good-hearted men for breakfast. I am sure your bloody brother never stood a chance against her."

He spoke with such rancor that it took her aback. "You hated her."

The three simple words hung in the air between them.

His brown gaze was upon her. Searing her. "I loved her once. Stupidly and without reason, other than that she was beautiful and told me everything I wanted to hear. The hatred, however, was earned. She worked hard for that. She deceived me, cuckolded me, and stole from me more times than I can count."

Sinclair's admission shocked her. But then, his earlier words returned to her. *My wife was a manipulative whore.* For a moment Callie could not think of a single response. Her impression of Lady Sinclair, aside from the recollection of her loveliness, was vastly different. She had been a stunning woman, almost ethereal. The perfect foil to a man of the earl's dark, sullen masculine beauty.

"She was quite gracious when I met her," Callie managed to say.

"I have no doubt she was." His tone, like his expression, was grim. "The heartless bitch would have been better served had she trod the boards as an actress."

"My lord," she gasped, shocked. "It is unwise to speak ill of the dead."

"Or what?" The grin he sent in her direction was cold. "Hmm? They shall haunt us? Too late for that, princess. That woman ruined me a long time ago. There is nothing she can do to me from the grave that holds a candle to what she did to me when she walked this earth."

So much unabated vitriol. And for his own wife.

He retrieved his knife then and stalked toward her side of the bed, still indecent in nothing more than his smalls.

Callie stiffened at his approach but refused to flinch away from him.

"You have nothing to fear from me, Lady Calliope," he told her curtly, taking her wrist and slicing through the cord which had bound her wrist. "I will not hurt you."

"I am to believe the man who has taken me captive?" she bit out, rubbing her newly released wrist.

The freedom felt exhilarating.

He shrugged. "Believe what you like. You already do."

His chest was fascinating. She tried not to look at him, truly she did. But aside from the artwork and sculptures she had seen in Paris, she had never before had such a thorough view of a man's naked torso. The Earl of Sinclair's was splendid. There was no other word for it.

She blinked, forcing her gaze away from those sculpted slabs of muscle. "You were the last person to see Alfred alive, my lord, aside from the servants, who overheard you threatening him. It seems an impossible coincidence for both the wife you loathed and the man she loved to die on the same night, does it not?"

"Not impossible if it happened," he corrected calmly. "I am sorry for the loss of your brother, my lady, but I am not responsible for it."

His sympathy took her by surprise, but she refused to trust him or his words. "Of course you would deny it. I hardly expect you to admit to having committed murder."

"And so you thought to falsify my confession through your vicious little book?" he guessed.

Correctly.

Blast him.

"I was attempting to right a wrong," she defended herself. "If I cannot have justice for Alfred's death, then destroying the remnants of your reputation will have to suffice."

There. Some raw honesty for him.

His countenance was unreadable, but his jaw was rigid. "What a vivid imagination you have for a gently reared lady."

She lifted her chin, eying him with all the defiance teeming inside her. "Pray do not act as if I shocked you. I am certain my work pales in comparison to the sins you have committed."

He gave an indolent shrug, his stare hard upon her. "Perhaps. Or perhaps I am not as evil as you imagine me."

Ha! She most certainly did not believe that. There was a reason he was known as Sin, after all. She was sure the rumors she had heard about him were true. All of them.

"Only an evil scoundrel would abduct an innocent woman from London and take her prisoner," she countered.

"Ah, but I hardly think you are an innocent, Lady Calliope." He stroked his thumb over the sharp edge of his blade as he watched her.

"You will cut yourself again," she warned him before thinking better of the words.

He raised a dark brow. "Concern for me, princess? Take care, or else I shall think you have taken a fancy to me. Then again, I did take note of the manner in which you have been admiring my physique."

Her cheeks went hot anew. Of course he had noticed her silly ogling of him.

"I was not admiring you," she denied crisply. "You repulse me."

His gaze dipped to her mouth. "Your nipple said otherwise earlier, darling."

He had been *awake*. The utter knave!

Even her ears went hot. "How dare you?"

He had the audacity to flash her an unrepentant grin. "A man may as well grow familiar with the woman who will be his wife. I had to be certain you are not frigid. I will require an heir, after all."

With that, he sauntered back to the other side of the bed, still holding his blade as if he were a common footpad wielding a weapon rather than a peer of the realm. Gritting her teeth, she rose from the bed, clutching the counterpane to her breast for modesty's sake.

"I have already told you, I have no intention of marrying you," she told him. "You cannot force me."

"Force will not be necessary, princess." He was still grinning, the fiend. "Your protestation grows tiresome."

"As does being your prisoner," she returned, her voice sharp.

"Need I remind you that you brought this on yourself?" he inquired mildly as he donned his trousers.

She pinned him with a glare. "I did nothing to deserve being abducted by a depraved villain."

His smile faded. He shrugged on his shirt. "You fired the first volley in this war of ours, my dear. If you had not done your damnedest to make certain you ground my reputation into the mud, I never would have even noticed you. Right now, I would be happily between Miss Mary Vandenberg's thighs."

He was such a boorish devil.

"You are coarse and horrid." And she was burning, her cheeks aflame at his wickedness.

"They call me Sin for a reason, princess." He gave her a grim smile, working on the buttons of his shirt and hiding his chest from her view.

The moment was strangely intimate. Wildly inappropriate. It was, she imagined, what husbands and wives did, rising together, dressing in each other's presences. Only, in her mind, a husband and wife ought to love each other, the way she and Simon had.

She forced herself to look away from the Earl of Sinclair, to search instead for her own garments. And that was when she recalled that her gown had been savaged by his blade.

How could he expect her to go about wearing yesterday's gown, with a sawed-off sleeve?

"Do you need my assistance in helping you to dress?" he queried, disrupting the tense silence that had fallen between them.

His abrupt change of subject took her by surprise, as did his offer. "Of course I do not require your help."

"As you wish." He stalked to the door. "I will wait for you to dress. Do not try anything foolish, princess."

She watched him go, determined to find a means of escape.

CHAPTER 6

You may find yourself wondering, dear reader, whether I ever
thought about the lives I had so ruthlessly ended. The answer may
well shock you, for I did not.
~from **Confessions of a Sinful Earl**

Sin's first indication that something was amiss came
in the form of Lady Calliope Manning's grumbled
curses.

The woman had a filthy mouth.

But of course, he already knew that, having read the
drivel she had attempted to pin on him. The bit about the
orgy had been most riveting, but now was not the time to
reminisce.

The second indication arrived in the form of her squeal
and the sound of rending fabric.

Bloody fucking hell.

What was the maddening creature doing now? He did not
bother to knock. He threw open the door and was instantly
greeted by the sight of the she-devil's rump framed by the

window casement. Her gown was torn, having been hooked on the hinges, and she looked as if she were about to jump.

He was not about to have her death upon his conscience. If the fool jumped, she would break her damned neck.

"What the hell are you doing?" he demanded, crossing the chamber to where she dangled herself from the window.

"Getting away from you by the only means possible," she retorted, but her voice was tense.

He did not miss the fear.

She was terrified.

And well she ought to be. There was nothing to break her fall below save a pair of decrepit Grecian urns.

He caught her around the waist and hauled her back into the chamber. "Plummeting to your imminent demise is more like. Have you no wits in that pretty head of yours? There is no way to descend to the ground below save jumping, and jumping from this height will only have one outcome."

She was trembling in his arms as he pulled her away from the window. The skirt of her gown tore more as he shifted her, ripping a strip off it entirely. But he had hacked off one of her sleeves the day before, so the dress was already fit for the dustbin. The proof of her terror left him oddly shaken. And furious.

"Plummeting to my demise seemed a better fate than remaining trapped here with a madman," she bit out, her hands clawing at his as the fight returned to her. "Release me, you oaf. You have ripped my gown."

"You ripped it yourself with your ill-fated attempt at playing a bird," he observed, spinning her about so they were face-to-face.

Her eyes were wide, framed by lashes that were impossibly long. "Return me to London, and I will not tell a soul what you have done."

Did she truly believe she was the one who possessed the bargaining power between them?

His grip on her waist tightened. "I will return you to London after you have agreed to become my wife."

"Then I suppose we shall both remain here for all eternity!" Her gaze flashed with defiant fire.

Even after almost falling to her death, she remained stubborn as ever. He supposed he ought not to be surprised. The woman had been fighting him at every turn. Clearly, his plan was going to require some additional effort. Spiriting her from London had not had the intended effect of forcing her hand.

Instead, she had been all the more determined to flee him.

Her bosom was heaving with her breaths. She was glorious in her ire, in her bravery. He could not deny it. Lady Calliope Manning was a ravishing creature. Infuriating. Wrongheaded. Vicious, too. But there was something about her that fanned the fires of desire within him into raging, blistering flames.

"Eternity is a long time to wait," he told her with a calmness he little felt. "Too long for me to wait to secure a wife."

"Find a different wife," she spat, fighting him with renewed vigor.

"I would have," he gritted from between clenched teeth. "You chased them all away with your lurid tales and heartless lies."

That much was true, lest she had forgotten. She was the reason for this war.

But like earlier when they had been abed, her fight stirred the beast within him. Her spirited rebellion made his cock hard. Preposterous, especially since he detested her and what she had done. Nevertheless, it was true.

Her nostrils flared. "I would never have written those serials if you had not murdered my brother."

"A stalemate once more, my future beloved," he said. "As I have already informed you—ad nauseam—I did not harm your brother. Has it ever occurred to you that he alone was at fault for his demise? Perhaps he was soused or otherwise behaving in reckless fashion when he fell."

"Alfred was not reckless," she insisted.

"Says the woman who was attempting to leap from a window," he observed. "Have you never wondered, in all your fantasies about me, why I would have wanted to kill your brother? He had already been cuckolding me for months, and he was hardly the first to do so."

"The servants said you argued with him," she returned. "They heard raised voices. You left in a rage, they said."

Perhaps he had; in truth, he could not recall. The time after he had realized the depths of Celeste's betrayals remained something of a blur of drinking himself to oblivion and attempting to discover the extent of her debts.

Devastating, as it had turned out. She had sold off every jewel he had ever bought her. Even the Sinclair emeralds and rubies were gone.

"I did not like him, Lady Calliope, but I did not kill him." And then, because she was still squirming and attempting to get away, he did the reasonable thing.

He bent and scooped her over his shoulder.

"Put me down, you brute!" she screeched, pummeling his back with her dainty fists.

He swatted her bottom. "No. We are going to have breakfast, and you are going to listen to me. And no more attempts at jumping out the blasted window."

* * *

Callie glared at the Earl of Sinclair from across the battered kitchen table.

"Eat," he told her, gesturing to the plate he had placed before her.

Somehow, he had procured fruit and cheese and some delicious-smelling bread. Perhaps his accomplice, the man who had replaced Lewis as her driver? Whatever their origin, fresh strawberries had never looked more tempting than they did now, mocking her on a chipped piece of crockery.

She crossed her arms even as her stomach growled. "No."

He had even managed to make her what looked and smelled to be a passable cup of tea. Her lips were parched and her throat was dry, particularly after her near-demise earlier. As it turned out, attempting to leap from a second-floor window was not as excellent an escape option as she had supposed when she had been standing safely on the floor. Halfway out the window, she had not only gotten her dress hung up on the hinges of the casement, but she had also been assailed by a troubling burst of dizziness.

It had not been one of her finer moments.

Or one of her better ideas.

And it had ended in the Earl of Sinclair pulling her to safety and then hoisting her over his shoulder as if she were a sack of flour.

Also not one of her finer moments.

"You will eat, damn you," he growled. "I even made you some bloody tea."

Had he recalled her request the night before? It hardly seemed likely he would have gone out of his way to please her. After all, he made no effort to disguise his disdain for her.

"You cannot force sustenance down my throat," she told him brazenly.

In truth, he was wearing her down. Part of her dizziness

had been down to the unexpected height of the fall from the window to the ground below. Nary even a tree in which to shimmy onto a branch. But the other part of her faintness was being caused by the lack of food and drink she had stubbornly enforced since the evening before.

"Do not tempt me, oh darling future wife." Grinning at her, he held a strawberry to his own lips and took a bite.

What was it about the sight of his sensual lips moving? Those white, even teeth flashing? There was nothing carnal about eating a strawberry, and the man before her was her sworn enemy. She ought not to be affected by the mere act of him breaking his fast. She ought not to think about those lips claiming hers.

About those kisses…

Those hated, awful kisses…

She frowned. "I am not your future wife."

"You love your brother, do you not?" he asked mildly, before taking another bite of the strawberry.

Callie clenched her jaw. "Of course I loved Alfred. That is why I wrote those memoirs. That is why I have been seeking vindication for his death."

His protestations that he had not been responsible for Alfred's death meant nothing to her. The timing was too suspect. Lord Sinclair's rage and hatred for his dead wife was still palpable, a year later. She would not believe a word that slid from his lying tongue.

"Your *other* brother, my beloved betrothed. The current Duke of Westmorland." The earl took a sip of his own tea. "Mmm. I do prepare a fine cup if I say so myself. The tea is a bit old, but you would never be able to tell by taste."

Vile man.

She wrinkled her nose, casting a glance around the cavernous, stone walls of the kitchen. Last night, much of it had been bathed in shadows and darkness. By daylight, all its details were plainly visible. Including the fact that it had been abandoned for some time.

"Where did you find it?" She would not be one whit surprised if there had been rodent offal mixed in with the tea leaves if he had found it within the sparse depths of this centuries' old kitchen. "And I love Benny as much as I loved Alfred. They are my brothers, my blood. The three of us were inseparable."

"Fret not, Countess of Sinclair-to-be." He sipped at his tea again, cool and calm as could be. "The tea is safe to drink. No poison or rat droppings, if that is what you suspect."

She cast a longing glance in the direction of her own tea before she could quash the urge. So thirsty. She was so very thirsty, and the tea certainly smelled sweet and inviting. She could practically feel it gliding over her tongue.

But there remained one insurmountable problem: *he* had prepared it.

"I would sooner leap from the window upstairs than become your next countess," she returned with what she hoped was equal composure.

"Ah, but you had your chance, did you not?" He cast her an amused smile. "Instead, I saved you. You are welcome, by the way. I did not hear you thank me for sparing you the certain fate of the bird who cannot fly."

He was so smug.

So horrid.

She wanted to lunge at him, strike him. Run from him. She wanted to escape him and never again blight her life with his presence.

"You were the reason I was attempting to leap from the window, so I shan't thank you," she bit out.

Her stomach growled again. Quite noisily this time.

His smile deepened, and he picked up another strawberry, holding it to his lips. "These are fresh. So succulent and sweet. You ought to try them, my darling bride. I just heard your stomach revealing you for the liar you are."

Her nostrils flared. "If there is a liar amongst us, rest assured it is you, my lord, and not I. And nor will I be your bride. You shall have to find another woman to force into the loathsome position."

"Westmorland recently married, is that not so?"

His calm query set her on edge.

Why was he so preoccupied with Benny? Her beloved brother had nothing to do with her quest for vengeance against the Earl of Sinclair.

"Yes, he did," she allowed, searching his gaze for answers and finding none.

He was unreadable as ever, the blighter. Slowly, as if he had all the time in the world, he sipped from his tea. "His choice of duchess was somewhat *unexpected*, was it not?"

She stiffened. Her new sister-in-law, Isabella, had been the proprietress of a ladies' typewriting school when she had first met Benny. Though Isabella's mother was of noble birth, her father had been a merchant, and Isabella had initially been in Benny's employ.

"There is nothing unacceptable about his duchess, if that is what you are implying," she defended.

She loved Isabella like a sister. Isabella was good for Benny—Callie had seen it almost from the start. And she had done more than her share of matchmaking, attempting to throw the two of them together to facilitate that connection.

"I imagine Westmorland has quite a bit of scandal on his hands at the moment," Sinclair continued. "A common wife…"

"Isabella is not common!" she protested.

"Special League matters," he continued as if she had not spoken. "He has stepped down as the leader, has he not? There were rumors, I believe, that he would be removed after the bombings in the House of Commons and the Tower of London. Some said he was too preoccupied with chasing after his new duchess."

She gritted her teeth. She had heard those rumors as well, of course. They were being bandied about. "Benny is a hero. He is responsible for bringing a dozen Fenians to justice and for keeping London safe. *The Times* has been nothing but effusive in its praise of him, as is well-deserved. He took his duties seriously, and anyone can see that the war against the Fenians is being won thanks in part to his tireless work."

"What would happen, I wonder, if word of his sister's attempts to ruin the Earl of Sinclair were to become public knowledge at such a sensitive time?" the earl asked, stroking his jaw with his long, elegant fingers, his tone contemplative.

Something inside her froze. With fear. Understanding.

Finality.

In her lap, her hands clenched her ruined skirts. "What are you suggesting, my lord? Speak plainly, if you please. I grow weary of this game."

"The Younger Mr. White is willing to attest to the true identity of the author of *Confessions of a Sinful Earl*," he said, his gaze skewering hers. "You, darling betrothed. I have a letter from him, written and signed in his own hand, waiting to be posted to *The Times*. One word from me, and Young Mr. White will reveal all to every scandal sheet and journal in England."

His calm pronouncement hit her with the force of a fist to the gut, robbing the air from her lungs.

No.

No.

No.

One word—denial—it was all she could think, a litany, a waterfall. Rushing through her mind, obliterating everything else. She had been so careful. Careful to keep her identity a secret. Careful to always use the Lady's Suffrage Society as the reason to visit her publisher's office.

"You appear shocked, princess." The bitterness had returned to the earl's voice, and so, too, the sharp edge. "Imagine, if you will, the impact such troubling information would have upon Westmorland's reputation, which already hangs in the balance. His innocent sister—one who caused tongues to wag with her daring behavior abroad—writing tales of orgies and opium eating. Writing the sort of filth a proper lady never ought to be acquainted with. No one shall be surprised, and with the younger Mr. White ready and willing to swear to the truth of his statement, we both know who will be believed, do we not? I do wonder at your carnal knowledge myself, beloved betrothed, but perhaps it will prove a boon. At least in the procuring of my heir and spare. You certainly seemed amenable earlier this morning."

The bastard.

He had entrapped her. He had outmaneuvered her. If this had been a game of chess, it was checkmate. She knew better than anyone that her place in society was precarious at best. Her reputation was already somewhat tarnished from her days in Paris with Aunt Fanchette.

But if it became common fame that she had written *Confessions of a Sinful Earl*, her reputation would not be salvageable. In truth, she did not care for herself. Callie's heart belonged to Simon, and he was forever lost to her. She had no intention to marry. However, it was not herself she was concerned for.

Benny and Isabella…their marriage was so new, so hard-fought, so well-deserved. Isabella and Benny had nearly been killed by a Fenian in her typewriting school. It had only been Benny's bravery and timely intervention which had saved her. And now, they were married, on their honeymoon, savoring each other and their love.

If Benny returned to Callie's ruination, he would be devastated.

And he had just found his happiness.

The woman who was meant to be his wife, just as Simon had been meant to be Callie's husband. If she could not have the life she had dreamt of, she would be damned before she would allow anyone to take that from Benny. She loved her brother. Fiercely and devotedly.

Worse, this black mark against her, if it were to be made known, could do far more than cause Benny and Isabella upset and worry. It could harm them as well. Sinclair was correct, damn him. There had been a great deal of rumors surrounding Benny and Isabella. With Isabella's life in danger, Benny had diverted Scotland Yard agents to her protection. If scrutiny were to be placed upon him because of her...

"I see your devious mind at work, my future countess."

The earl's voice cut through her wildly spinning thoughts.

She met his gaze. "What manner of despicable villain would seek to hurt a man who is courageous and good, a man who has devoted himself to keeping us all safe from danger? A man who has nothing to do with any of this?"

He inclined his head. "A man who has nothing left to lose, princess. A man you ruined." He took a lingering bite of his strawberry. "Me."

* * *

Sin watched as understanding dawned on Lady Calliope's expressive face. For a fleeting moment, her countenance took on that same haunted quality of a wild creature facing down her hunter. He knew a moment of guilt at what he was doing, but then he ruthlessly squelched the inkling.

She deserved this.

She *had* destroyed his reputation—not that it had required much effort on her part—with *Confessions of a Sinful Earl*. And she had not stopped after that. Rather, she had enjoyed her vengeance. She had continued.

Only now, too late, did she realize that in so doing, she had made herself vulnerable to him. Oh, so very vulnerable. Yes, she had brought this on with her madcap scheme to decimate his chances at making a match. Before she had disseminated her tripe, he had been about to secure the hand and vast dowry of Miss Vandenberg.

Never mind that Miss Vandenberg paled in comparison to the delectable, dark beauty of Lady Calliope. He did not need to desire his wife. Lord knew, by the end of his marriage with Celeste, he had been so repulsed by her, he had not been able to touch her.

"This is blackmail," Lady Calliope accused then.

Quite accurately, as it happened.

"You are damned right it is." Smiling, he nibbled at another strawberry.

She was looking rather pale at the moment, his future countess. Likely because she was still refusing his offer of food and drink. He could outlast her in a battle of stubbornness, however. Perhaps she was also feeling bilious at the notion of being forced to marry a man she erroneously believed had caused her brother's death.

Again, a stab of something akin to guilt prickled at his conscience.

Again, he sent it to the devil.

"If I agree to this…this horrid plan of yours, how do I have any proof you will not still reveal I am the author of *Confessions* just to spite me?" she asked next.

He swallowed his bite of strawberry, his grin deepening. "Why would I want to harm my own wife?"

Her pallor grew even more heightened. "Why indeed?"

Ah yes, she believed him a wife murderer as well as a brother murderer. How could he have forgotten? The creature certainly had a wild imagination. But then, he knew from his own experience that having someone to blame always felt better than the realization that one was completely and utterly at the mercy of the universe.

"You have my word as a gentleman that I will take your secret to my grave," he reassured her, keeping his tone light. "I have had enough scandal to last a lifetime. It will be an even exchange—you marry me, and in return, I will never reveal the truth, and nor shall the younger Mr. White. When we return to London, I will pay a call to your publisher on your behalf, explaining to him that he is no longer permitted to publish the next installment of the serial, and further, that no more shall be forthcoming. I will instruct him to deliver the manuscript to me, for safekeeping. You are amenable?"

"Amenable as I must be," she allowed. "However, I will not share your bed."

Still imagining she possessed the power to bargain, the foolish chit.

He chuckled. "Yes, you will. I cannot very well get an heir on you if I do not bed you, my lady."

"You cannot possibly expect me to suffer your attentions." Her lip curled, as if the notion of his touch disgusted her.

And mayhap, in a sense, it did. But her body had been most responsive to his earlier. Her mind may be convinced he was a heartless devil, but her body could easily be persuaded otherwise. He knew the feeling—after all, he loathed Lady Calliope Manning. Yet kissing her and touching her and waking with his prick nestled against her feminine curves had given him a cockstand just the same.

"Only until my heir is secured," he told her. "After I have my heir and spare, I will never return to your bed."

Her lips compressed. "Do you swear it?"

He raised a brow. "Madam, I have no wish to share a bed with a conniving jade. If it were not for your dowry, I would ruin you in the blink of an eye. I need your funds, and I need an heir. You can give me both, and then you can go to the devil for all I care."

Her stomach growled once more, reminding him she had yet to eat.

On a sigh, he rose and dragged his chair nearer to hers.

She stiffened, eyes going wide. "What are you doing, my lord?"

"Plotting your murder," he told her wryly.

Her expression said she believed him.

"Bloody hell," he swore, snatching a strawberry from her plate and holding it to her lush lips. "I am feeding you before you perish from starvation, you wrongheaded virago. Take a bite."

She rolled her lips inward and shook her head.

He shoved the strawberry into her mouth with less finesse than he would have liked. But he nevertheless achieved the desired goal—there was food in her mouth.

"Chew," he told her as if she were a child.

Her countenance was mulish as ever, but she chewed slowly, then swallowed.

"Good." He held the half-eaten fruit to her lips once more. "Another bite."

This time, instead of attempting to seal her lips, she opened her mouth. He slid the strawberry inside and the bloody harridan bit him. Pain shot up his arm as those pretty teeth of hers clamped on the fleshy pad of his thumb before releasing him.

He ground his molars to stave off an exclamation of pain.

He would not allow her even a moment of triumph. "That was not very nice, my dear. Or particularly wise."

"I was obeying your orders." She blinked at him, her expression one of contrived innocence.

He brought his throbbing thumb to his own lips and sucked, easing the sting. "Fair warning, princess. Next time you bite me, I will bite you back."

He would start by nibbling on her creamy throat. Then catching her lower lip between his teeth. Then, he would work his way lower. Bite those pretty nipples he had felt through her chemise…

Damnation.

Desire pounded through him, reminding him it had been far too long since he had last bedded a woman. That was the only reason he was attracted to the woman he had spent the last few weeks despising and plotting against.

"Forgive me," she said, her voice radiating with insincerity.

Never, he vowed inwardly. Forgiveness was for fools. Lady Calliope Manning would be his enemy forever. He had learned that particular lesson thanks to his former countess, and it was one that would serve him well in the next loveless union he faced. If there was one source of solace he could find in this hellacious mess, it was that this time, he was too wise to fancy himself in love with his wife.

It would be a marriage of convenience in the truest sense.

No danger to his heart. No betrayal. No pain. No lies.

"Eat your breakfast, beloved betrothed," he told her. "The sooner we can get back to London and you are my wife, the better."

After all, he did not just have himself to fret over.

CHAPTER 7

*My rapacious hunger for conquests became a dangerous obsession,
dear reader. The more I reveled in the depths of my depravity, the
more I sought it, like a true satyr. Imagine, if you will, a chamber
filled with dozens of men and women, all of them nude, writhing in
their shared, forbidden passions...*
~*from* **Confessions of a Sinful Earl**

*C*allie was bedraggled, tired, and wretched. Not
necessarily in that order.

Her captor, however, was dozing comfortably on the
Moroccan leather squabs opposite her, his long legs
stretched out across the interior of the carriage, his booted
ankles crossed. The deep, even sound of his breathing
suggested he was slumbering without a hint of conscience,
now that he had gotten what he wanted and they were en
route back to London.

In repose, he looked somehow less menacing. Less like an
angry god. More like a mere mortal. Still more handsome
than sin.

She was going to marry this man.

Callie could hardly credit the knowledge. The last day seemed more like a horrible nightmare from which she would wake safe in the comfort of her bed at Westmorland House than reality. The man she had spent the last year believing responsible for Alfred's death, the man she had ruined, the man with the blackest reputation in London, was forcing her to become his bride.

How she hated him.

She thought suddenly of his blade. Now that she had agreed to Sinclair's demands, she was no longer bound like a prisoner. Mayhap it was not too late to escape him after all. She had no wish to truly hurt him with the knife—indeed, she did not think she could stomach it. But if she could somehow get her hands upon it…

Slowly, she made her way across the carriage, until she had settled herself beside him on the bench seat. He continued sleeping as the carriage went over a rut in the road, jostling them both. She held her breath, praying he would not wake, and then she slid her hand inside his coat, to the hidden pocket where she had seen him secret it earlier.

His heat seared her fingertips. Gently, she searched his lean form, seeking the blade. All she felt was hard, male chest. Another bump in the road made the carriage sway, knocking her into him. She froze, studying his face for any sign he had awoke.

His expression remained serene. His dark lashes were long, fanned on his cheeks. Almost too long for a gentleman. His cheekbones were proud slashes. His nose was a sharp blade bisecting the handsome symmetry of his face. His jaw was proud and wide, his lips full.

But she was not meant to be admiring him. She was meant to be divesting him of his weapon. She moved at last, searching once more for the blade.

His lips twitched. Before she could remove her hand, he

snagged her wrist in an iron grip. His eyes opened, his gaze almost obsidian, shockingly alert. There was not a trace of slumber in them.

"Are you attempting to seduce me, princess, or were you hoping to kill me in my sleep?" His rich baritone was undeniably amused.

"Neither," she said on a gasp as he yanked her into his lap. "Lord Sinclair, please..."

"Such pretty protestations," he said, his gaze flitting to her lips. "I like it when you beg me."

Resistance rose within her. She struggled to remove herself from his lap, but her actions only served to mire her more firmly against him and twist her skirts around her. How neatly he had trapped her once more. She wondered if he had even been sleeping at all.

Her pride would not allow his comment to go unanswered. "I would never beg you for anything."

Another of his rare smiles curved that wicked mouth. "I would not be so certain of that if I were you, sweet."

She had not found his blade, and now instead of outwitting him at his own game, she had failed abysmally yet again. "I am more certain than I have been of anything else."

She would beg him for nothing.

Ever.

Not even for mercy.

"More certain than you are that I am a murderer?" His smile had disappeared now, but his stare was still upon her lips.

She licked them, wishing she could not still feel the imprint of his mouth on hers. "Do you have proof of your innocence?"

His stare flicked back to hers at last. "If I told you I do?"

Her heart pounded faster. "If you do, then I demand to see it."

"Such a brazen creature," he said, his thumb tracing over her wrist in slow, lazy circles.

Belatedly, she realized he was no longer holding her wrist in a manacle-like grasp. Instead, he was caressing her. And she was not unaffected by that touch, regardless of how desperately she wished she was not.

What was the matter with her?

She yanked herself free of him, reminding herself she must think of Alfred. "What is your proof?"

"My mistress," he replied easily. "I was with her the night your brother and my wife died."

His mistress.

Of course he had a mistress. She ought not to be surprised by his admission. He had legions of them. That was what all the rumors suggested, was it not? That was the reason he was known as Sin—his love of debauchery and the pleasures of the flesh.

But somehow, the notion of the Earl of Sinclair having a mistress made her feel strangely perturbed.

"Why did you not say anything in your defense, if that were true?" she asked him.

"My mistress was a married lady, and she had no wish to be drawn into my scandals lest there be repercussions with her husband," he told her calmly. "I respect her enough not to involve her purely for my own gain."

She searched his expression for any indication he was lying. But he met her gaze as boldly as ever, his regard unrelenting. Several things occurred to her simultaneously: firstly, that she had never even considered he may have been elsewhere that awful night, that someone else could vouch for him. She had never supposed he was innocent. She had always believed him hopelessly, irrevocably guilty.

Furthermore, he had said his mistress was a married lady. Did that mean his mistress was no longer married? Or that she was no longer his mistress? Also, why should she care?

She told herself she should not. That he was sinful and amoral. That she loathed him.

"What is the matter, princess?" he taunted. "Does the realization that I could not have committed murder disappoint you?"

"I would have to trust your word," she countered, trying to scramble from his lap.

He caught her waist, holding her still. "You would also have to admit that your campaign of vengeance was all for naught. That you ruined an innocent man for no reason at all."

She did not want to think about that. "Release me."

"Make me," he challenged.

How could she? He was stronger than she was. She had been fighting him for the past day and losing at every turn. Even now, she was still losing. And she would continue to lose. She was going to have to marry him, this man she loathed.

What if her reason for loathing him was all wrong?

What if *she* had been all wrong?

"You know I cannot make you," she admitted at last, defeat tasting bitter on her tongue. "You have won, my lord. I have agreed to marry you for my brother's sake. What more do you want from me?"

His smile returned. "Your surrender, princess."

"You cannot have that."

He lifted her effortlessly to the opposite squab. "We shall see about that, Lady Calliope. We shall see."

* * *

Sin was not about to take any chances that his future wife would attempt to break her promise to marry him, which was why he had accompanied her into the vast mausoleum that was Westmorland House, despite all her protestations to the contrary. The house was every bit as imposing as he recalled, a rambling Mayfair palace and a testament to the vast Manning family wealth.

The butler had been obviously relieved to see Lady Calliope returning safely.

Her aunt had been most distressed with her failure to return the day before, the servant had announced, casting a disapproving glare in Sin's direction. For Sin's part, he was not certain he cared for the tender manner in which the domestic had fretted over his future wife.

"Callie darling!" exclaimed the aunt now, sweeping into the lesser salon where the butler had shepherded Sin and Lady Calliope.

Westmorland was, conveniently, on his honeymoon with his new wife. Which meant that the woman with the French accent, dressed in a billowing silk dressing gown, had been tasked with acting the part of duenna.

A task which she had failed at.

The aunt smelled of violet perfume and powder. Her dark hair cascaded down her back, unbound. It was rather familiar and odd. In all his life, the only women who had ever greeted him clad in their dressing gowns had been those he had taken to bed.

"*Tante* Fanchette!" Lady Calliope threw herself into the elder woman's arms, quite as if she were being rescued from the gaping maws of a fire-breathing dragon. "You have arrived after all!"

"*Ma chère*," crooned the aunt, casting a suspicious glance toward Sin. "Where have you been? According to the servants, your coachman returned with a splitting headache, claiming he had no recollection of what had happened. I am so sorry I did not arrive as planned. When I made it to Westmorland House and you were nowhere to be found, I was about to contact Scotland Yard. What have you been doing? And *who* is this gentleman?"

Sin took that as his invitation.

He stepped forward, offering his best attempt at a bow. "The Earl of Sinclair, *madame*. It is a pleasure to make your acquaintance."

It occurred to him that he did not know much about this aunt. He knew the former Duchess of Westmorland had been of French ancestry, but that was about the sum of the information he possessed about the family. That and their hideous wealth.

Oh, and the fact that the last duke had been fucking his faithless wife.

One dare not forget that salient bit of information.

"It is *mademoiselle*, Lord Sinclair. I am not married." The aunt frowned at him. "Your name is familiar, but I am afraid I do not recall why."

He smiled grimly. "I am sure I know the reason, but it hardly matters."

The aunt withdrew from the embrace with Lady Calliope, taking a step back and examining her. "What is the meaning of this, my beloved niece in such tatters?"

In truth, Lady Calliope did look as if she had just returned from war. Her hair was plaited into a messy braid she had fashioned herself. One of her sleeves was missing. Her elegant gown was wrinkled and torn.

She looked thoroughly compromised.

He cleared his throat and jumped in before Lady Calliope could explain away her disheveled appearance. "I witnessed Lady Calliope's carriage being overtaken by footpads yesterday. They delivered a vicious blow to her driver's head. I gave chase, but in the crush of the street traffic, I was unable to reach her. Rather than seek the authorities and sound the alarm, I deemed it best to chase after her myself. By the time I was able to overtake her carriage, the brigands had reached the countryside."

His betrothed's eyes widened at his subterfuge. The excuse was rather silly, he had to admit, but he had not bargained upon an interfering aunt when he had formulated his plan.

Her aunt gasped. "Footpads! *Mon dieu*, I cannot believe it. How fortunate that you were there, my lord, to come to her rescue."

"I managed to scare the villains off, but a violent storm was rolling in," he continued, warming to his cause. "I was left with no choice but to remain with Lady Calliope on one of my estates, overnight, rather than travel in the storm with no coachman. Knowing that I have compromised her, I have offered Lady Calliope my hand in marriage, and she has graciously accepted."

"My lord, I am eternally grateful to you for rescuing my beloved niece! But I cannot help but to think a marriage is precipitate," her aunt said. "After all, Westmorland is on his honeymoon. No one even knows Callie was alone with you."

"Unfortunately, I was unable to act the gentleman," Sin added, hoping the maiden aunt would understand what he was intending to convey without too much detail.

The aunt frowned. "Do you mean to say…"

"Yes," Lady Calliope interrupted, glaring at him. "It was all rather…hasty and sudden. The *drama* of the moment over-came us both."

He grinned back at her, enjoying her irritation, the orchestration of her ruin. "My love for Lady Calliope blos-somed overnight. I have long admired her from afar, but since the fates have so conspired to throw us together, I find myself unable to live without her. I was so pleased when she confessed she feels the same way about me. I realize this is all highly irregular, of course. My lapse in propriety was egregious, and I will be pleased to rectify the matter with as much haste as possible."

"You are in love?" the aunt asked, her gaze flitting between Sin and Lady Calliope.

"It is a new love," his betrothed said with a pained smile.

"Desperately in love," he added.

"Well, our family is known for our eccentricities. I cannot say I am pleased with you for violating propriety in such a shocking fashion, but I do understand the temptations of being alone, overnight, especially given the horrors the two of you had been through. I am so thankful to you for saving her." The aunt paused to beam at him. "All is forgiven, my dear boy, as long as you promise to take very good care of our beloved Callie."

Bloody hell. This was going better than he had imagined.

Of course, if Westmorland were here, he would likely have resorted to fisticuffs. Sin and Westmorland were acquaintances, but not friends. However, he knew the man well enough to know he would not be impressed with Sin having absconded with Callie overnight, only to return with her wearing a tattered gown. Nor would he have swallowed Sin's flimsy tale so readily.

How obliging of him, getting married and leaving on his honeymoon.

This eccentric French aunt was no match for Sin.

"I promise to take excellent care of Lady Calliope," he told the aunt. "It will be my greatest honor to make her my countess."

And to use her dowry to save myself from ruin.

Wisely, he refrained from adding that bit. She owed him,

86

after all, Lady Calliope. She was the reason for his desperation. She was the one who had forced his hand.

The aunt pressed a hand to her heart, looking overjoyed. "Oh *ma chère*! Your brother will be overjoyed when he hears you are marrying after all."

"Yes, I imagine Benny will be pleased." Lady Calliope's voice was wan, her smile unconvincing.

"When does Westmorland return from his honeymoon?" Sin prodded now. Because he was running out of time. He needed to get married within the next few days, not within the next few weeks.

Nor could he afford to wait for Westmorland to drag his heels or otherwise attempt to wrest his sister from Sin's grasp. He fully expected Lady Calliope to do everything in her power to extricate herself from her promises. The less time she had to achieve her goal, the better.

"Not for over a month's time," Lady Calliope answered.

"How much time have we to prepare the wedding?" the aunt asked, clapping her hands.

"One week," Sin said.

"A few months," Lady Calliope said simultaneously.

Her gaze was alarmed when it flew back to his. "One week?" she squeaked.

He grinned. "Since I have compromised you, my darling, I am afraid we must get married as soon as possible."

"Oh yes, you must," agreed the aunt quite helpfully. "This is all my fault, for arriving late. But do not worry, darling girl. *Tante* Fanchette is here now!"

And thank fuck for that, Sin thought to himself.

The first part of his plan had been accomplished. Next, he was going to pay a call to the offices of one J.M. White and Sons. He had a manuscript to collect.

Confessions of a Sinful Earl was at an end, and so, too, were his problems.

He hoped.

* * *

Callie hated lying to her beloved aunt.

But short of confessing everything, including her role in writing *Confessions of a Sinful Earl* to Aunt Fanchette, she did not know what she could do. To make matters worse, in true fashion, her aunt had decided that Callie was madly in love with the Earl of Sinclair and that spending the night alone with him had been *très romantique*.

Callie did not have the heart to correct her assumptions. Fortunately, her aunt was of a far more liberal persuasion than her brother. If Benny were here, he would beat the Earl of Sinclair to a pulp and then he would lock Callie in her chamber for the next month. Then again, the earl was frightfully strong and well-muscled. Perhaps Benny would not defeat him with such ease.

Better that Benny was not here.

Better that he was instead enjoying his honeymoon with Isabella.

When he returned, it would be too late for him to embroil himself in her problems, and that was precisely how she wanted it to be. It was precisely how it *must* be. For she had gotten herself into this disastrous predicament, and she was the one who must pay the forfeit.

With her life.

How horrifying a prospect.

"You will need a dress," Aunt Fanchette was saying. "I daresay it is too late to commission one. A Worth gown would have been most agreeable. I do know a *modiste* here in

London who hails from Paris. Perhaps she will have something that can do, in a trice."

Callie blinked. Her mind was still awhirl from everything that had happened. Her entire life had changed forever in the span of one day. Although the Earl of Sinclair had taken his leave at last, the tension had yet to drain from her. Because what loomed before her—marriage to him—seemed akin to a prison sentence. Even if his protestations of innocence were true and she had been wrong about him, she did not even know him. He was a stranger to her. And after she had lost Simon, she had sworn to herself she would never become another man's wife…

"Lace and satin would be just the thing, do you not think?" her aunt asked.

"I do not care what manner of dress I wear, *Tante*," she said grimly.

That much was the truth. Her nuptials to the earl would not be a happy occasion.

"We must send word to Westmorland at once," Aunt Fanchette continued. "Undoubtedly, he and the duchess will want to be in attendance, even if it means interrupting their honeymoon."

"No!" Callie bit out with more force than necessary.

Her aunt flinched and gave her a curious, searching look. "But of course, we must send word to your brother. I know you have long since reached your majority, but Westmorland will want to be present."

Callie could not bear for that. If Benny returned before her marriage, he would interrogate her until she revealed the truth. And she was doing everything in her power to keep the truth—and scandal—from tainting him.

"I…" She faltered, struggling to find a plausible excuse for keeping her beloved brother from her own nuptials. "I am ashamed, *Tante* Fanchette. Benny will be very upset with me for being so reckless with Lord Sinclair and spending the night alone with him. I do not dare wait."

"Oh my darling," said her aunt with such sympathy and tender caring that Callie felt a corresponding rush of guilt all over again. "Pray do not believe you are the only lady who has found herself in such a position. And look at what happened—Lord Sinclair is a hero, rescuing you from those brigands! I am certain Benedict would be understanding."

"I am not," Callie countered, and that, too, was grounded in veracity. "But more importantly, I could never forgive myself if I were to interrupt his honeymoon because of my own lapse in judgment. It took him weeks to recover after he was shot, *Tante* Fanchette. He deserves this time of unfettered happiness with his bride."

Callie could not hide the earnest feeling from her expression or voice. She meant that, even if marrying the Earl of Sinclair was essentially a prison sentence for her. She had already lost her chance at happiness when Simon had died. The least she could do was make certain Benny and Isabella were unaffected from her actions.

Her aunt nodded. "Very well, darling *nièce*. Are you certain this is what you want?"

No, she wanted to cry out again.

Anything but this.

Her smile felt tight and insincere. "Yes, of course. Now do tell me what you have in mind for a dress, if you please."

"Something burgundy, perhaps," Aunt Fanchette continued. "Or scarlet. Crimson? Cerise? Hardly ivory, I should think. Warm shades complement your lovely dark hair. You must wear my diamonds, I insist!"

Although Aunt Fanchette had never married, she was an incurable romantic.

"Whatever you decide shall be fine," Callie said.

Though mourning black would be the most fitting for the

occasion. How to explain such a choice to dear, fawning Aunt Fanchette?

"We will need flowers as well," Aunt Fanchette said. "Lilies of the valley, do you think? No, roses. Red roses, and your lady's maid will entwine some in your hair the way she did in Paris when you met Moreau and he decided he must paint you…"

Callie gave herself over to her aunt's excited plotting even as desperation unfurled deep within her.

One cursed week.

How could she save herself?

CHAPTER 8

She could have saved herself, dear reader, had she never become my wife. Her only sin was in marrying a man who could not silence his inner demons or overcome the evil in his soul.

~from **Confessions of a Sinful Earl**

"*W*hat do you mean you are getting married to the Earl of Sinclair?"

Callie winced at the shrill disbelief emanating from the voice of her dear friend, Lady Jo Danvers. "Pray do not be so loud, lest *Tante* Fanchette burst in here with more notions about dresses and flowers for the unhappy event. I mean precisely what I said. The villain has forced me into accepting his suit."

She and Jo had bonded instantly over their mutual work for the Lady's Suffrage Society. They were like-minded in many ways, though opposite personalities in others. Where Callie was bold and devil-may-care with her reputation, Jo was quiet and circumspect. A wallflower to Callie's butterfly. And yet, they were the best of friends.

Only Jo knew Callie was responsible for writing *Confes-*

sions of a Sinful Earl and the reason behind it. Well, Jo and their publisher. And now, the Earl of Sinclair.

"Do not fret over your aunt," Jo said, lowering her voice. "I do believe my sister has her cornered for an intense meteorological discussion. When I made my way here, she was going on about rainbands and spectroscopes in the picture gallery."

Although their gathering today had a larger purpose—a meeting of the Lady's Suffrage Society—Callie had managed to pull Jo aside for a private chat in the grand library at Westmorland House since Jo and her sister had both arrived early. Their premature arrival had been down to Jo's sister, Lady Alexandra, whose science-loving mind refused to even contemplate such a disgraceful notion as tardiness.

"Thank heavens for Lady Alexandra," Callie said. "I find myself in a dreadful muddle, Jo. I am to marry him in one week's time."

"How can he force you into such a thing?" Jo demanded, sounding outraged on her behalf. "Callie, you believe he murdered your brother. He is known as Sin. His reputation is more scandalous than my brother's once was, and that is rather saying something. Julian was a wretched scoundrel before he married Clara."

Jo's brother, the Earl of Ravenscroft, had been a notorious rogue prior to his love match. But she was correct. The Earl of Sinclair's reputation was decidedly worse than Ravenscroft's had once been. No small feat, that.

Thanks, in part, to Callie's efforts.

She sighed heavily. "He discovered I am the author of the memoirs."

"What?" Jo frowned. "That is impossible. You went to such great lengths with the publisher to make certain you retained your anonymity."

Yes, she had. But it had all proven to be for naught.

"Mr. White's son divulged my identity to Sinclair," Callie admitted, stalking to the opposite end of the grand library where a wall of books was interrupted by a massive fireplace.

She was in such dudgeon, she had been pacing the Axminster. It was a miracle she had not already worn a hole in it.

Jo followed her, her shocked gasp echoing in the cavernous chamber. "How dare he?"

She spun about to face her friend. "Apparently, Sinclair threatened to persuade him with his fists or otherwise frightened him."

"He is a dangerous man," Jo said grimly. "You cannot bind yourself to such a scoundrel. I refuse to allow you to do it, Callie."

"I am afraid I have little choice." Quickly, she relayed her tale of what had happened to her from the moment Sinclair had spirited her from London to their abrupt return. "So you see? If he reveals I am the author of *Confessions*, I am afraid my scandal will taint Benny and Isabella. I love them both too much to be the cause of any suffering. To say nothing of the Lady's Suffrage Society. I had not even thought of that. Oh, Jo. Everything we have been working toward shall be irreparably damaged unless I do as he has demanded and marry him."

Jo placed a staying hand on her forearm when Callie would have once more stalked to the opposite end of the library. "Have you not thought of contacting your brother? Surely Westmorland would want to return from his honeymoon to help you. He would not stand for this bullying from the earl."

Callie shook her head. "I cannot bear to reel him into this, Jo. He will be stubborn, I know he will. After everything he and Isabella have endured, they deserve their happiness more than anyone. He nearly died saving her. No, I cannot do that to either of them. I have created this monstrous mess, and I alone can remove myself from it."

"What does your aunt make of all this?" Jo asked next.

"Aunt Fanchette believes it is all wildly romantic." She heaved another sigh. "I cannot afford for her to think anything is amiss, for fear she will contact Benny herself. I am afraid I have no choice but to marry the brigand, unless I can come up with a means of my own rescue."

"Perhaps my brother could be of assistance," Jo suggested. "Julian can be quite formidable when he chooses to be."

"I will not have my problems become someone else's, Jo," she denied. "I must face my own reckoning."

"But what of Sinclair's wife? Your brother?" Jo asked, her countenance troubled. "If he is a murderer as you suspect, he could plot your death next."

Of course she had thought about that.

She had lain awake in her bed last night, scarcely sleeping at all, watching the shadows in the corners of her chamber and worrying over what was to become of her. Worrying over whether or not she had been wrong in going after the Earl of Sinclair. Whether or not he was guilty. Whether or not marrying him was safe.

"He claims innocence," she told her friend. "He suggested he was with his mistress, but that he chose not to involve her."

"If that is true, then you must speak with the mistress," Jo urged. "You cannot marry Sinclair if he is plotting to murder you. I refuse to allow it, Callie. Say whatever you like to the contrary. Friends do not allow friends to marry murderers. You need answers, and you cannot take Sinclair at his word. We both know he is not a man of honor."

No, he decidedly was not.

But then, unbidden, she thought about the manner in which he had worried over her eating. She thought about the way he had pulled her to safety from the window. The manner in which he had carried her to the bed in her sleep and tucked the bedclothes around her so she did not spend the night on the floor.

Of course, he had also abducted her, threatened her with a blade, and forced her to agree to marry him. None of those actions were the hallmarks of a gentleman. They did, however, suggest his desperation. A desperation which she had driven him to…

What a hopeless, horrid muddle.

"If I knew the identity of the mistress in question, I would ask her myself," Callie said then. "But he did not volunteer it."

"You must force him to tell you," Jo said, her eyes flashing. "Tell him you need proof or you cannot marry him. Tell him you need more time than one week. And please, please consider contacting Westmorland. This situation is untenable. I cannot bear for anything ill to befall you."

Callie caught her friend in an impulsive embrace. "Thank you for worrying over me. I promise you that I shall be fine, whatever happens. This is my battle to fight, and I will do everything in my power to win."

Jo hugged her back. "You had better win, Calliope Manning. You cannot allow that scoundrel to best you."

* * *

Sin stared in bemused silence at the woman who was to become his wife.

Surely he had misheard her.

Surely he had consumed so much whisky that he was imagining her presence in his threadbare study at half past ten in the evening. No sensible woman would dare to make demands of him. Or to arrive wearing a veil as if she were here for an assignation and to suggest to his elderly and long-suffering butler—one of the last remaining staff members he possessed—that she was expected.

It was a miracle Langdon had even heard her at the door, truly. To say nothing of hearing her clearly and shepherding her through the house without incident. Yet, somehow, he had.

"I beg your pardon, Lady Calliope," Sin said slowly now, "but did you just tell me you will not marry me unless you are granted an audience with my mistress?"

She nodded primly, as if this were an ordinary social call. "Yes."

The foolish wench had taken a great risk in coming here this evening. He wondered if she had even been accompanied by a servant. If she had stolen away without her eccentric aunt's knowledge. If she had taken a hired cab.

He pinned her with his most condemning glare and took a sip of his whisky. Oh, the bloody irony of it. He was fretting over propriety. For most of his life, all disapproving glances had been cast in his direction rather than the other way around.

"I do not have a mistress," he said at last.

Also ironic. His appetite for the pleasures of the flesh had been considerably dimmed in the last year. He had scarcely even visited his club, the Black Souls. Perhaps it was one more way in which Celeste had ruined him forever.

Lady Calliope's dark brows snapped together into a disbelieving frown. "Of course you do. You likely have more than one of them."

She thought she knew so much about him, the virago.

And she knew nothing.

Had not even the slightest inkling. The manuscript he had collected from her publisher more than proved that. He had made it one quarter of the way through reading her wild imaginings and had been too enraged to read one sentence more.

"Ah, yes," he said grimly, making a steeple of his fingers and watching her over it. "According to you, I have deflowered countless debutantes during the times when I am not hosting wild bacchanalian orgies and drinking the blood of virgins."

Her lips pinched. "I never wrote that you drink the blood of virgins."

"I beg your pardon. Perhaps it was that I eat their hearts," he suggested, inexplicably moved by the urge to nettle her.

"Nor that."

"I am, however, an evil fiend who murders brothers and faithless wives, am I not?" Sin could not resist prodding.

Her chin went up in a show of the stubborn nature that had almost sent her tumbling from the window two days prior. "You claim you are not, but I find myself loath to accept your word. After all, you have proven you are decidedly not a gentleman and that you possess no honor."

"Honor is a luxury for the men with enough coin to afford it," he snapped.

"Yet you have enough coin for whisky and ladies of ill repute," she countered.

His patience for her was fast waning. "What was the purpose of your call at this time of night, Lady Calliope?"

"Because I needed to speak with you. Alone." Her lashes fluttered as she lowered her gaze to the hands she had kept folded in her lap.

"I thought you said you needed to speak with my mistress," he taunted.

That dark gaze of hers was back upon him in an instant, flashing fire once more. "I thought you did not have a mistress."

She was brazen and bold. And beautiful. Foolish and reckless and heartless, as well. But then, Sin's last wife had been beautiful and heartless and conniving and faithless. He may as well marry what he was accustomed to.

"I do not," he agreed.

Her eyes narrowed. "This discussion is going nowhere."

"Which is precisely where you should have gone, princess," he countered. "Nowhere. How did you find yourself here at this time of the evening? Did you steal away from Auntie Feather-wit?"

"Her name is Aunt Fanchette," Lady Calliope gritted.

"Did you come here unaccompanied?" he demanded, ignoring her correction.

Only a woman with the brains of a chicken would be pleased by the sight of her niece returning from a night alone with a man to whom she was not wed, her dress in tatters. Only a fool would have believed his story of footpads and his own heroics.

But aside from that, he disliked the notion of Lady Calliope flitting about London alone at this time of the evening. Anything could have happened to her.

The sole reason for his concern was his need of her dowry, naturally. He was not truly concerned, he reassured himself. He despised her for what she had done.

His betrothed pursed her lips. "Why should you care how I arrived here?"

He raised a brow. "If something ill befalls you, how can I marry you?"

Lifting his whisky to her in a mock salute, he drained the remnants of his glass.

"You are despicable." Her voice was cold.

He had certainly been called worse.

Sin shrugged. "I am honest."

"I brought my own carriage here," she said. "A footman accompanied me."

He wondered if it was a handsome and brawny one. That had been one of Celeste's old tricks, fucking the servants. Once, it had been a groom. On another occasion, two of the footmen at once. She had always made certain he would catch her.

That had been half of the fun for Celeste.

He clenched his jaw. "Do not go sneaking about in the night again."

Her spine stiffened. "You have no right to issue orders to me."

"Yet." He gave her a grim smile. Matrimony held no allure for him, aside from necessity.

Raw, bare, ugly necessity.

"Ever," she bit out.

Holding her gaze, he poured himself another whisky, this one fuller than the last. "Go home, Lady Calliope."

"Not until you give me an answer."

Fucking hell, why did she have to be so determined? He took a lengthy sip of his whisky, relishing the burn. "I already gave you the only answer you are going to get from me. Go home. Return to your Aunt Featherbrain and plan our nuptials like a good little betrothed."

Her lip curled, her reaction to his dismissal exactly as he had supposed it would be. Feral. "No."

He strummed his fingers on the surface of his desk. It had not been dusted since what seemed like the reign of Richard III. Give or take a century. "You have not the right to deny me. How many times must I explain this to you, Lady Calliope? I have all the power in this farce of ours. You persecuted me for no good reason, and you were not careful enough about hiding your tracks. You trusted the wrong people. I hold all the trump cards."

"You cannot expect me to marry you in this fashion," she protested.

Devil take it, one day into their arrangement, and she was already attempting to weasel her way out. He should not be surprised, he knew. But he was irritated, just the same. He had gotten what he wanted from her: her concession. He did not bloody well want to have to win it again.

"I can, and I do." Doing his damnedest to keep his stare from lingering upon the pink fullness of her mouth, he took another draught of spirits. "I have been quite clear. You marry me in return for my silence. That is all."

"I require proof that you did not murder my brother," she said.

Her words seemed to echo in the silence of the chamber.

Rage surged within him in the seconds afterward.

Again with this nonsense.

"You require proof," he repeated with a calm he did not feel.

"Yes, that is what I just told you." Her gaze did not waver this time, searing his. "You want me to marry you and to provide you with an heir. I cannot give myself to a man I believe responsible for the death of my brother Alfred."

No, no, no. This was not what he wanted to hear. Mayhap if she was desperate enough to avoid marrying him, she would shoulder the burden of her actions and face all the scandal that would rain down upon her. She could not vacillate on him. He did not have the ability to wait much longer.

A muscle began to twitch in his jaw. "Yesterday morning, you said you could."

"Yesterday morning, I was at your mercy," she dared to counter.

That was bloody well *it*.

Sin rose and prowled around his desk, not stopping until he was between Lady Calliope, still seated opposite him, and the burled walnut. He braced his hands on the arms of her chair and leaned forward, until they were nearly nose to nose.

"This evening, you are still at my mercy," he warned her. "Right here, right now, you are very much at my mercy, princess. I could do anything I wanted to you here. I could scoop you up in my arms, haul you over my shoulder, and carry you off to my chamber. I could lay claim to you tonight, planting my seed in your womb. There is no one here to save you."

She swallowed. "The butler—"

"Is hard of hearing," he interrupted. "And nearly blind as well."

The only reason Langdon was still in Sin's employ was that the previous earl had not looked after the stalwart and loyal retainer in his will, and Sin had been left without the coin to offer him a comfortable life in the country to spend with his beloved Skye terrier, Eloise, as he deserved. It was an egregious transgression Sin hoped to rectify upon his marriage to Lady Calliope.

"Is that why he bumped into one of the marble busts laid out on the floor?" Lady Calliope asked, her brow furrowed.

Her query gave him pause. "There were marble busts on the floor?"

Whilst most objects of value had been sold off, a few collections remained. The marble busts of former Earls of Sinclair and the previous earl's collection of Chinoiserie among them. But there was only one reason why the busts would have been on the floor, and he had a feeling it meant his mother's nursemaid had been tippling her laudanum once again.

Fuck.

"Yes," Lady Calliope said. "I presumed your staff was in the midst of rearranging them, though why they should do so at this time of night is rather perplexing, as was the fact that none of your chambermaids were in sight. Your butler stubbed his toe quite soundly, I fear."

He closed his eyes for a moment, which was as long as it took him to remind himself that he needed to force the woman before him to recall she had no choice. Because he had no choice. And because *she* had made it that way for the both of them.

"As I was saying," he began.

"I am firm on this, Lord Sinclair," she broke in. "I cannot marry you unless I first speak to your mistress."

Tilly was not his mistress any longer. But he was not about to allow her to be interrogated by his future wife. To do so would be an insult to both women.

"You cannot speak to a mistress I do not have," he countered. "And even if she were my mistress, I still would not allow you to conduct a tête-à-tête with her. Not only would that be the height of impropriety, but it would be terribly disrespectful to the both of you."

"Then I cannot marry you."

He gripped the arms of her chair with so much force, his knuckles ached. "Yes, you can. And yes, you will. You have already promised to do so. I have compromised you quite thoroughly, as your aunt knows. You require my silence. I require your dowry. That is the end of this particular tragedy, my dear. Acquaint yourself with your fate."

"Not without speaking to her," Lady Calliope insisted, as if she had a choice in the matter.

One thing was for certain. This woman was going to be the death of him. She was going to drive him mad with her nonsense before he could save everyone he cared about.

"Look at me," he ordered her. "I am deadly serious when I tell you that if you cause me any more trouble, I will forget all about marrying you and simply shout from the proverbial rooftops what you have done."

He was bluffing, of course. Sin had no way of knowing if Miss Vandenberg would reconsider their betrothal if he were to be acquitted of the charges which had been laid at his door by Lady Calliope's scribblings. Even if she would, Miss Vandenberg had demanded a lavish wedding that would not be accomplished with haste or ease. He could not even last the next month on what little he had remaining.

"Very well," Lady Calliope said. "If you will not arrange for a meeting, I shall be left with no recourse other than to find her myself and to pay her a call."

"You have no notion whom to pay the call upon," he countered.

"I have a list," she said calmly. "I shall begin with Lady Fonthurst and then I shall move on to Viscountess Lisle. After her, I shall go to the Marchioness of Durham. Then, the Duchess of Pembroke. There is also an actress, I believe, Mrs. Westlake. To say nothing of Lady Jane Carlton—"

"Enough," he bit out.

Where the devil had she gotten so much information about him? When he had read *Confessions of a Sinful Earl*, some of the accounts had been painfully accurate. But others had been wild flights of fancy. Yet, hearing so many familiar names roll off Lady Calliope's tongue with such ease was nothing short of alarming.

She was far more of an opponent to him than he had imagined.

Yes, he had underestimated the cunning vixen.

"Is it true that you are also well acquainted with the bawd who owns the Garden of Flora and Fauna?" she asked next, utterly astonishing him by rattling off the name of an exclusive house of ill repute.

A very wicked, very exclusive, very secretive house of ill repute.

Or, at least, so he had thought.

"Where have you come by all this information, my lady?" he asked.

By God, he would suffer anything before he chained himself to another Celeste. Strangely, however, something inside him told him the petite, dark-haired woman before him could not be further from Celeste than the moon from the sun.

"Will you have me pay calls to all of them?" Her composure was impeccable. She showed nary a hint of fear. "Or will you tell me which of the many ladies in your *acquaintance* I must meet?"

Sin did not know what came over him then. One moment, he was at a complete impasse with Lady Calliope, and the next, he was slamming his mouth down on hers. He told himself it was to shut her up. To stop her sharp tongue from its endless wagging. To remind her which of them was in control.

But the saddest bit of it was, the moment her lips moved beneath his, he was stunningly, surreally aware of where all the control lay.

In her power.

In her bewitching lips.

He was not kissing her to command her.

Rather, he was kissing her because he *wanted* to kiss her.

This would not do.

He reared back, ending the kiss before it could deepen. Glaring into her dark eyes, he growled, "I will come for you tomorrow afternoon at three o'clock. Do not be late."

Her tongue glided over her lips, and it was all he could do to suppress a groan at the sight and not chase it with his. "Tomorrow. That shall do, my lord."

He nodded, then moved away from her, needing distance between them. "And Lady Calliope? Do not again put yourself at risk by gallivanting all over London in the midst of the night."

She nodded, and he took the jerky motion as her acquiescence as she rose from her chair, her cheeks blossoming with twin patches of scarlet. "Good evening, Lord Sinclair."

He watched her flee his study then, cursing himself for a fool.

CHAPTER 9

I write these memoirs, dear reader, as a warning to you. Our world
is rife with villains. Most of their crimes are never exposed.
~from **Confessions of a Sinful Earl**

Callie had told Aunt Fanchette she was going for a drive with Lord Sinclair.

That much had not been a lie.

She had neglected to mention, however, that the earl was taking her to meet with his mistress. Strike that—his *former* mistress. Or so he claimed.

"I will have your word that after today, you will not give me further trouble," Lord Sinclair said as he deftly guided his barouche down Rotten Row.

The conveyance was not new. Its benches were in need of repair, and the whole affair seemed as if it had belonged to a previous decade. His horseflesh was adequate, but could hardly compare to the equine snobbery of their fellow lords and ladies parading through the fashionable part of Hyde Park. The state of his barouche, along with the state of his townhome—sparsely decorated, pictures missing from the faded wallpaper, threadbare carpet, and a minimal staff—suggested how impoverished he truly was.

"If I find this day satisfactory," she said, blotting out a stab of guilt at the last thought.

After all, it was hardly her fault that the Earl of Sinclair had depleted all his funds. He had done so before she had begun publishing *Confessions of a Sinful Earl*, surely.

Had he not?

"You will find it satisfactory, or I will find it satisfactory to tell the world what a vicious, scheming harridan you are," he returned.

She stifled her umbrage, telling herself she did not care what this man thought of her. "We shall see, my lord."

He made a noncommittal sound low in his throat, part growl, part grunt.

He said nothing for a few clops of the horses' hooves, forcing her to study his profile. His jaw was tense, his lips tight. The memory of his swift kiss the night before returned, along with a most unwanted tingling in her own lips. She wondered if hating him would be easier if he were less handsome. Was she so shallow, so incapable of controlling her baser reaction to him, that she was allowing him to alter her perception?

Because something had shifted between them in the past few days. The glimpses of him which proved he was not entirely evil had perhaps aided in that. Still, how was it possible that she was so drawn to a man she had so recently viewed as her nemesis?

She pursed her lips and turned her attention back to the throng of fashionable carriages around them. "I fail to see how being in the midst of so many people will afford us an opportunity to speak with your mistress alone."

He cast a look in her direction, his dark gaze searing. "Who said anything about speaking with my mistress?"

"You did," she shot back.

"No," he said slowly, giving her a long, thorough perusal that made something melt inside her stomach and slide between her thighs. "I did not."

The bounder. "Of course you did."

How she would like to launch herself back at him in the same manner as she had when he had absconded with her in her own carriage. Yet, she did not dare, for they were surrounded by hundreds of sets of curious eyes.

Leisurely, he returned his gaze to the track ahead of them, eyes upon the horses once more. "I said nothing of the sort, Lady Calliope. What I said was to be prepared for me to call upon you at three o'clock. As expected, you were half an hour tardy."

Her lateness had been intentional. The notion of making him wait had held infinite appeal. The frustrated rage emanating from him had been worth every minute she had paced the carpet in her chamber, consulting the ormolu mantel clock with each pass.

"A lady needs time to prepare herself," she said.

"You are wearing trousers, madam," he bit out. "I hardly think such a fashion choice required much preparation."

"Divided skirts," Callie corrected him once more. "These are all the rage in Paris."

"Pity we are not in Paris." His voice was dry.

If he disapproved of her divided skirts, he could take his opinion—as unwanted as his kisses and his forced marriage —elsewhere.

Mayhap not his kisses.

She plucked at the drapery of her silk divided skirts. They raised eyebrows, it was true. But for ease of movement, divided skirts were ideal. "London would be better served to ease its fusty ways."

Such as this promenade of the wealthy and the well-known.

The purpose was to see and be seen. Which was why concern prodded her anew, along with his denial that he had agreed to her demands the previous evening.

"London changes for no one," he said grimly. "Not even a duke's daughter descended from one of the wealthiest families in England."

He was right about that, in some ways. Since her return from Paris, she had been bold enough to push boundaries which had once seemed forbidden. But there was eccentricity, and there was going too far. She did not doubt he was delivering her a subtle reminder that if her identity as the author of *Confessions of a Sinful Earl* were to be revealed, she, too, would become a pariah. Already, her presence in his barouche was drawing whispers and curious stares from every direction.

"I shall endeavor to weather the tide," she snapped at him. "I grow weary of this incessant parade. Too many people are watching us. When are you taking me to your mistress?"

"Former mistress," he corrected quietly. "And I told you, I never agreed to do so."

She thought over his words from the previous evening.

I will come for you tomorrow afternoon at three o'clock. Do not be late.

That last demand had been her reason for dawdling. But...damn him. He had not agreed at all, had he? She had been so deuced flustered from the sudden press of his mouth to hers—that brief, chaste, *hated*, wondrous kiss—that she had simply taken his words as accord.

"What is the matter, beloved future countess?" he drawled, sounding amused. "Nothing to say?"

He was toying with her. Enjoying this.

She glared at him. "Are you taunting me because I made you wait half an hour for me?"

"*Moi?*" He cast a smug glance in her direction, grinning. "Never."

She had suffered quite enough of his games and his presence both. "No more of this nonsense. I demand you give me the audience I requested, or I will not marry you."

"Do not shout, princess." He turned away from her once more. "Everyone is watching the most notorious man in London and society's darling, traveling together in the same barouche. How shall we convince them of our love match if you do not gaze upon me as if I have just descended from the heavens?"

"More like dredged up from the fiery depths," she grumbled.

"I beg your pardon?" His lips compressed.

"You heard me." Her vexation increased by leaps and bounds with each passing moment.

"Tsk, princess." He clucked his tongue in admonishing fashion. "Being a brat will not get you what you want."

"I am not a brat." She scowled at him.

"Only a brat would invent such ruthless, damaging lies about a man the way you did," he countered coldly. "Did you think your chicanery would not bring about the utter ruination of my reputation? Did you not think labeling me a murderer who would seek to profit off his own sick acts would be the end of me in this unforgiving society of ours?"

Of course she had thought she would ruin him. That had been her intention.

What if you were wrong about him?

That same, uninvited voice returned. Her conscience, she supposed.

What if he can prove his innocence?

She sent the voice to the devil. Because she needed answers first.

"Spare me your endless games, my lord." She pinned a false smile to her lips when she noted everyone around them continued to watch.

Of course they were watching. All London thought he had killed his wife and her brother. Thanks to her.

At least they were finally reaching the end of the promenade. She wondered if he had any intentions of taking her to meet his former mistress after all.

"And spare me your theatrics," he returned. "As I have warned you before, you are not in control any longer. You may have begun writing this farce, but I am the one who will end it, and we will do so in my way, as I see fit. Now smile for all your admirers, and then laugh as if I have just delivered the cleverest sally you have ever heard."

The truth hit her then. He had orchestrated this drive through the park, on Rotten Row, at the fashionable hour, specifically so they would be seen together. He was further entrapping her.

Because he did not trust her to hold to her word.

Fair enough. She had no reason to trust him either.

If she had to play by his rules to get the reassurance she needed, then she would. Callie beamed at him. Then she laughed. Loudly, while holding a hand to her heart. He cast a suspicious glance in her direction, and then something else crossed his face. An emotion she could not define.

He clenched his jaw and inclined his head. "Better. We will pay our visit on our return trip to Westmorland House. I will have your promise, however, that you never write a word about her."

She detected a roughness in his voice, a note of caring she had never before heard.

Her curiosity was instantly piqued. "Why are you so protective of her?"

"I owe you no explanations, Lady Calliope," he snapped. "You will be my wife, not my jailer. Your promise or I will take you directly home instead."

"Fine," she bit out, for he was leaving her with little choice in the matter. But her quarrel was not with the woman who had once shared his bed. Rather, it was with him. "You have my promise."

He nodded.

The rest of the drive was marked with silence.

* * *

Sin and Lady Calliope seated themselves in the private salon where Tilly always greeted visitors. No stranger to Haddon House or the Duchess of Longleigh's private apartments, Sin had left his barouche in the mews and entered through the rear with his reluctant betrothed, no formal announcement—Tilly expected him. Although he had not visited her in months, it all was so familiar to him that he was beset by an eerie sense that no time had passed since he had last been a welcomed guest in Tilly's life. In her bed.

But that had been a lifetime ago, and so much had changed.

Tilly was gracious as ever, ethereally beautiful with her golden tresses styled in a thick knot at her crown with ringlets falling down her back. She was dressed in green silk, which complemented her vibrant, emerald eyes. But there was a difference in her now—a maternal beauty that could not be denied, along with the full roundness of her belly.

"Lady Calliope," Tilly greeted, smiling in that slight, elfin way of hers. "Lord Sinclair. You will forgive me if I do not rise? My feet are quite swollen at the moment, in my ungainly state."

Sin chanced a glance in Lady Calliope's direction. Her eyes were wide, her pallor pronounced. She swallowed. "Of course you are forgiven, Your Grace. A lady in such a delicate condition takes precedence over social niceties."

He knew what his betrothed was thinking. He could practically see the wheels inside her mind churning. She thought Tilly's babe was his.

"Thank you for your understanding, my dear." Tilly's gaze flicked between Sin and Lady Calliope, a question in her eyes.

His note to her had been brief and circumspect, lest Longleigh intercept it. The duke was a desperately jealous man. Tilly had suffered enough in her marriage; Sin had no wish to be the cause of further pain.

"Lady Calliope has agreed to become my betrothed," he explained, treading carefully. "However, she is in need of some reassurance from you."

Tilly stiffened. "Reassurance? I am not certain how I may provide such comfort."

Regret sliced through him at involving her. He and Tilly were old, trusted friends. Their bond had begun well before their relationship had become physical. Before her marriage to Longleigh as well. He knew, better than most, how private she was, and how she guarded her secrets. Her life with Longleigh depended upon it.

"Forgive me," he entreated softly, hating this. Hating the depths to which he had been forced to sink. "I would not come to you were it not imperative."

He was well aware how out of the ordinary this call was. How beyond the depths of propriety. *Affaires* were conducted in privacy, behind closed doors. The notion of introducing his future wife to his former mistress was beyond the pale, even by Sin's standards. But Lady Calliope had left him with no choice. He only hoped Tilly could forgive him.

"Your secret is safe with me, Your Grace," Lady Calliope added, avoiding Sin's gaze. "You have my word that whatever you are willing to share with me will not go beyond these walls."

Tilly's lips parted, as if she were weighing her next words with care. "What became of Miss Vandenberg?"

He was surprised Tilly had been aware of his efforts to woo the heiress and their short-lived betrothal. He and Tilly had parted ways amicably, but he had been in a dark place after Celeste's death, and the decision had been Tilly's. Sin could see now how right she had been—they made better friends than lovers. Sadly, however, friends who had once been lovers could never truly return to being friends once more. Still, Tilly was the only woman Sin trusted aside from his mother.

"Miss Vandenberg's father took exception to the serials being published," he said, choosing to keep Lady Calliope's authorship to himself. "Perhaps you have read them."

"I would never read such vicious tripe about you, Sin," Tilly said earnestly. "You ought to know that."

Gratitude swept over him. He had not utterly ruined her opinion of him.

"Thank you, Tilly." He inclined his head.

Lady Calliope's gaze settled upon him, searching. A frown furrowed her brow.

"You need not thank me for knowing you are a good man and for honoring our friendship," Tilly told him, before turning to Lady Calliope. "Pray tell me you have not read that horrid drivel, my lady, and believed it?"

Ha! The vixen had authored the horrid drivel in question.

The irony was not lost upon Sin. Lady Calliope looked as if she had swallowed a fishbone.

"I was rather hoping you could help me to disbelieve it," Lady Calliope said. "Lord Sinclair assures me that when my brother and the former Lady Sinclair died, he was with an acquaintance of his. An acquaintance who cannot be named but who would be willing to vouch for his presence with her."

Tilly's full lips tightened in obvious displeasure. "Sin was with me, all night long."

Relief joined the gratitude. He had not been certain Tilly would be willing to make such an admission to anyone. He knew how tenuous her marriage with Longleigh was.

"Thank you," he told her. "I have no wish to cause trouble with you and Longleigh."

"Longleigh is happy for the moment, as he has gotten what he always wanted." Her hand rested on her swollen belly, which not even the clever drapery of her French gown could hide.

Sin swallowed against a rush of bile. He hoped to God Longleigh had not forced himself upon Tilly. "If there is anything I can do for you, please, do not hesitate to contact me."

She gave him a sad smile. "You and I both know there is nothing you can do for me at all. But I made my choice, and I alone can live with it." She looked to Lady Calliope then. "Sin was with me when the former Lady Sinclair chose to poison herself and end her life. She chose her fate, and after the horrors to which that wretched woman subjected him, it was the least she could do to give him his freedom at last."

The vitriol in Tilly's ordinarily calm, tender voice took him by surprise. He had known she had no love for Celeste, but he had not realized the depth of her emotion. Still, it was not public knowledge that his wife had ended her life by her own hand.

Lady Calliope's shocked gasp echoed through the small salon. "She drank poison?"

"She was an unwell woman, Lady Calliope," Tilly said. "I do hope you will be a better wife to Sin. Lord knows he deserves it. He has been through more than most men can even fathom."

"As have you, Tilly," he could not resist pointing out.

Though their contact had been sparse, he cared for her as much as he ever had. He knew how much she had longed to be a mother, and when she had written him with the news, he had been happy for her. He had also hoped she had not made too great a sacrifice to achieve what she wanted.

"I shall do my utmost, Your Grace," Lady Calliope said, stealing his attention away from Tilly. "Thank you for your confidence. I promise you nothing but my greatest discretion."

Sin had to squelch a bitter laugh at her pronouncement. In his experience, the bloody woman had no discretion. But he dared not admit it before Tilly. She had enough worries ahead.

"We should take our leave now," he said then. "Thank you for seeing us. And please remember what I said. If you should need anything at all—"

"Thank you, Sin," Tilly interrupted. "I do appreciate the offer. It was wonderful seeing you again. You look well. Lady Calliope, it was a pleasure making your acquaintance."

His betrothed rose from her seat and dipped into an elegant curtsy, her countenance unreadable. "The pleasure was mine, Your Grace."

Sin and Lady Calliope took their leave from Tilly in grim silence.

It was not until they had returned to the barouche and

were once more on their way to Westmorland House that she finally spoke. "Is the child yours?"

His grip tensed on the reins. "No."

There was no point in prevarication to make her squirm; he would only add further injury to Tilly's reputation, and he had no wish for that.

"Are you in love with her?" she asked next.

He was not in love with Tilly. He never had been. But he did care for her, and deeply.

"Of course not," he bit out. "Love is a chimera."

"Hmm," was all she said in response.

He cast her a glance. "Are you still holding a candle for your dead betrothed?"

She looked away, breaking the connection of their gazes. "That is none of your concern, my lord."

"Just as the Duchess of Longleigh is none of yours," he countered. "You have had your call with her and you have heard what she said. I will hold you to your promise to never utter an ill word about her."

"Contrary to what you think of me, Lord Sinclair, it is not my pleasure in life to go on spreading lies about others."

Her voice was quiet, with a sharp, accusatory edge.

As if *he* had been the one who had wronged *her*.

"You promise you will not speak of this again?" he demanded, needing her concession. Tilly had appeared the most contented he had ever seen her today, and he would not have that ruined for all the world.

"Of course not," Lady Calliope said. "I have no quarrel with the duchess. She seems like a kind woman."

"She is infallible," Sin agreed. "We have known each other since our youths. She has never wavered."

"Is it true, what she said, that the previous Lady Sinclair died by her own hand?" she prodded.

Her question took him back to that long-ago day.

Although he had been desperate to gain his freedom from Celeste, nothing could have prepared him for the discovery that she had killed herself. Too much laudanum. She had left him a letter, and it had been convoluted and twisted as her mind had been. Even in death, she had been beautiful.

Deceptively innocent.

"It is," he bit out, trying to shake himself from the painful ghosts of his past.

"There was no mysterious illness, then?" Lady Calliope prodded.

"Her mind itself was ill," he admitted tersely. He did not like to speak of Celeste. Not to anyone. But he supposed this acknowledgment was necessary if he meant to follow through with making Lady Calliope his bride.

And everything depended upon making her his wife.

Everything depended upon *her*, the woman at his side.

The one who wanted vengeance against him.

Silence reigned between them once more, until the vast, imposing façade of Westmorland House loomed within sight.

"Why did you not tell me?" she asked.

"Would you have believed me?" Sin countered, already knowing the answer.

"No."

He glanced at her once more, taking in her beauty. "And do you believe me now?"

"I am not certain." Her dulcet voice betrayed her confusion.

At least she was being honest.

He believed her answer. But it was not the answer he needed.

"You have five more days to persuade yourself to see common sense and reason, princess," he hissed, frustration

119

rising, along with the same old rage. "Because like it or not, you are going to become the next Lady Sinclair."

She said nothing, merely turned her gaze to the street ahead.

Damn her.

CHAPTER 10

The Duke of W. deserved to die, dear reader. I knew it the moment
I pushed him on those stairs. I watched him fall. I felt nothing.
~from **Confessions of a Sinful Earl**

"*Y*ou met Lord Sinclair's mistress?" Jo asked, *sotto voce*, as she and Callie made their way through the Westmorland House orangery the next afternoon, under the guise of Callie showing off their newest pineapples.

Aunt Fanchette was blessedly easy to avoid, especially since she was drinking champagne and plotting Callie's hasty wedding with inebriated glee.

"His former mistress," Callie corrected grimly as they reached a row of strawberry plants bursting with ripe, red fruits, which needed to be collected soon.

She did not know why she bothered to make the distinction. Perhaps because she had seen how beautiful the duchess was. Perhaps because she had taken note of the glances the earl and the duchess had exchanged. They cared for each other, and that much was certain, in spite of his vehement declaration that love was naught but a chimera. Callie could not help but to wonder, with a bitterness that did her no credit, whether or not every woman in the Earl of Sinclair's life had been a golden-haired goddess. She had never been more aware of her dark hair and eyes.

"Former mistress, then," Jo corrected, waving a hand as if it were neither here nor there.

Perhaps it was. Certainly, it ought not to matter to Callie. Even if the Earl of Sinclair had not killed his wife or Alfred, she still had no reason to feel anything for him other than resentment and hatred. He had abducted her, and he was forcing her into a marriage that was unacceptable and unwanted.

"I met her, yes," Callie agreed, biting her lip as she moved toward the lemon trees. Fat, yellow fruits hung in abundance.

The late-spring day was warm, the sun piercing the thick London fog overhead to beat through the leaden panes of the glass-domed roof. Everything in the orangery was green and lush, so very alive. Blossoming, the air perfumed with the sweet scents of blooms and exotic fruits. Filled with promise. Of all the rooms in Westmorland House, the orangery would always be one of her favorites.

She would miss it here, she realized with a sudden, stricken pang. In less than a week's time, Westmorland House would no longer be her home. Instead, she would find herself inhabiting the threadbare townhome of the Earl of Sinclair.

"And what happened when you met her, Callie?" Jo asked, dragging her from her desolate ruminations.

"She supported what Sinclair claimed," Callie conceded grudgingly.

If she were honest with herself, she would admit that her call upon the Duchess of Longleigh had left her more conflicted and confused than she had been prior to their brief interlude. She had wanted, so desperately, to be right about Sinclair. Because if she was wrong about him, then she had been so blinded by her grief over Alfred's death that she had ruined an innocent man. But the duchess, who had been gracious and welcoming despite the unprecedented awkwardness of the situation, had seemed ingenuous.

"Do you believe her?" Jo asked, eyes wide, concern evident in her expression.

There was sympathy, also.

They both knew Callie was facing a lifetime of misery in a loveless marriage.

She closed her eyes for a moment, shaking her head to banish the image of the duchess, so serene and beautiful, a veritable Madonna, in her green gown with her growing belly on display. The earl had denied the child was his. But depending upon the timing of the dissolution of their arrangement, there was every possibility he was the father. The knowledge lent another layer of sorrow to her predicament.

Her eyes fluttered open again to the stark brightness of the sun and her friend's worried visage. "I think I do believe her, Jo. She seemed honest. She certainly has no reason to lie, particularly if their association is truly at an end, as he claims."

Jo raised a brow. "Who is she?"

Callie shook her head. For although she trusted Jo implicitly, she had promised secrecy to the Duchess of Longleigh. Or Tilly, as the earl had called her. The reminder of the intimate manner in which he had addressed his mistress—*former* mistress—still nettled. However, she intended to hold true to her promise.

"I am not at liberty to divulge her name," Callie explained. "I promised her I would not tell a soul. All I can say is she was not any of the names on the list we compiled. He was discreet with her."

Speaking that observation aloud sent another unsettling emotion through her. She refused to believe it was jealousy. It was nothing of the kind. Most assuredly not. All she could say for certain was that Sinclair was very protective of the Duchess of Longleigh.

There was that stab of something decidedly unwanted once more.

She tamped it down. Forced it to go away. Ignored it.

"I understand," Jo said easily. "Think nothing of it. What I care most about is that you are not about to tie yourself to a murderer."

Not long ago, she had been absolutely certain. Convinced of the suspicious timing of the deaths. Of Sinclair's motive— the man who had been cuckolding him, the wife who had. One by one.

And yet, she was increasingly conflicted.

Increasingly unsure.

She wet her suddenly dry lips. "God help me, Jo, I do not know. Part of me wants to go on believing what I always have. The facts have not changed. Alfred died in the midst of the night in a fall down the stairs. The earl was one of the last people to see him alive, and they argued. Lady Sinclair died suddenly afterward. It makes sense that he was responsible for both deaths, and yet…"

She allowed her words to trail off.

"And yet," Jo prompted softly.

"And yet, the d—his former mistress, told me that Lady Sinclair intentionally drank poison, that she was unwell," Callie said, correcting herself before she revealed more than she intended. "Her death was not sudden in the sense I had supposed, nor inexplicable. If she died by her own hand, the earl could not have been responsible."

Because of her brother, Benny's, close ties to Scotland Yard, she had been able to discuss her suspicions with a detective. However, as far as she knew, the case had never been pursued. She had been told repeatedly that the fall had been an accident. She had assumed it had been because Sinclair was a peer of the realm. However, now, she was no longer so sure.

What if he had never been investigated because his wife had truly ended her life at her own hand? What if the previous Lady Sinclair had indeed been mad? And what if Alfred's death had really been an accident? He could have been walking in his sleep. Or perhaps inebriated, though it was rare that he imbibed…

"But even if Lady Sinclair took her own life, the earl still could have pushed your brother down the stairs that night," Jo pointed out, frowning.

"He could have, yes." Callie paused for a moment while she gathered her thoughts. "His former mistress vouched for his presence there with her for the entire night, however. She does not strike me as the sort of woman who would lie about such a thing. Indeed, lying to me would serve her no purpose now."

That was what bothered Callie the most. The duchess had no reason to protect Sinclair. Indeed, it hardly seemed that admitting what she had to Callie yesterday had been worth the risk for her. The other woman's reluctance had been almost palpable. It was that hesitation, more than anything else, which suggested she told the truth.

"Do you believe he is innocent, Callie?"

Jo's question was the very same one which had been churning endlessly in her own mind since the day before.

"I do not want to," she admitted. "Because if he is, it means I ruined him for no reason. It means I was wrong, and that I must beg his forgiveness. That I must somehow make amends for what I have done."

"Marrying him would certainly make amends," Jo observed grimly. "Do not forget the man abducted you, spirited you away from London, and refused to return you to your home until you agreed to become his wife. To say nothing of his reputation. There is a reason why he is known as Sin."

Jo shuddered.

A frisson went down Callie's spine. Again, she thought of his kiss. His touch.

She swallowed hard. "What would you do, Jo, if you were me? No matter what I choose, I am doomed. I cannot bear for this to become Benny's problem. He and Isabella have been through so much. And it is possible that I owe Lord Sinclair."

"You have to do whatever you feel is right, deep in your heart." Jo sighed. "Oh, Callie. I do wish you were not in such a dreadful position. I beg of you, contact your brother. Ask for his help."

Callie was not going to make her problem Benny's problem. She loved him far too much for that.

"I have already promised myself to the earl," she said, resolute. "I must be a woman of my word."

And hope for the best.

Young intruded upon their tête-à-tête suddenly then, his expression pained as he appeared at the threshold of the orangery, visible at the end of the row of persimmon and lemon trees. "I beg your pardon for the intrusion, Lady Calliope. However, the Earl of Sinclair has arrived. I did tell him you were not at home, but he refuses to leave."

He was here.

The air fled her lungs.

"Shall I speak to him for you?" Jo whispered. "I would be more than happy to box his ears. Or punch him in the nose."

Her friend's staunch support won a reluctant smile from Callie. "No, dearest. But I do thank you for always championing me. I am afraid this particular monster is one I must slay on my own." To the butler, she added in a louder voice, "See him to the private library, if you please, Young, and ask him to await me there."

* * *

Sin was not a patient man.

Which was why being told his betrothed was not at home left him infuriated. When the supercilious butler finally returned, wearing a pained expression of dislike, and escorted him to a small library to await Lady Calliope, he had gritted his teeth with so much force his jaw ached. Now, having paced the length of the chamber at least two dozen times, his strides eating up the luxurious carpets, he was more than annoyed.

He was irritated.

Infuriated.

Angrier than a hive of bees which had just been prodded with an unforgiving stick.

He reached into his waistcoat and extracted his pocket watch to consult the time yet again. She had kept him waiting for half a bloody hour already. How much longer would she force him to stand here like a vassal awaiting his queen?

Devil take Lady Calliope Manning. She was an asp dressed in silken skirts. And occasionally silken *divided* skirts, as she had informed him.

"Trousers," he muttered to himself, nettled that his own mind even seemed to be kowtowing to the vexing creature.

The reason for his call was simple. He was not convinced he had allayed Lady Calliope's fears with their visit to Tilly the previous day. And whilst he hardly desired to play the role of dutiful swain and see her once more, it was necessary.

But the cursed woman had yet to materialize.

Biting off a curse, he stalked toward the closed library door, incensed and determined to find her hiding place and haul her from it. *By God*, she would cease playing games with him. Yesterday, she had made him cool his heels for half an hour. Today, she was up to more of the same nonsense.

No more, he vowed.

The library door opened when he was within three strides of reaching it. Lady Calliope hovered on the threshold, ridiculously fetching in a day gown of plum and mauve with pale-pink roses trimming the bodice and a flounce of blonde lace on her skirts. She looked like a bloody queen, regal and perfect, her dark hair piled high on her crown and curling tendrils framing her face.

As with every time he laid eyes upon her, Sin felt as if a fist landed firmly in his gut. And then his prick instantly twitched to life. More reasons to resent her.

Damn her beautiful hide. Why did he have to want her the way he did?

He forced himself to bow, recalling that he must maintain civility. At least until she was his in name and deed. "Lady Calliope."

She, however, refused to curtsy. Instead, she swept into the library, all elegant poise. She looked upon him as if he were beneath her. As if he were a puddle that had ruined the hem of her gown.

He would ruin far more than her gown before they were through.

"Lord Sinclair." She moved past him in a swish of skirts and the decadent, sweet scent of lavender and tuberose.

She had left the door ajar. As an ode to propriety? Hardly, he thought. Aunt Featherhead would not even care if he were to throw Lady Calliope over his shoulder and take her home. More likely because Lady Calliope did not trust him.

Fair enough. He hardly trusted her, either.

Sin stalked toward the offending portal and snapped it shut before turning on his heel to face the woman who would become his countess in a few days' time. "You are not pleased to see me, darling beloved? I cannot fathom why not."

"I was not expecting you, my lord," she gritted.

He moved toward her, drawn by more than an urge to unsettle her. Drawn to her for *her*, damn it all. She was the opposite of every woman he had known before her, and somehow, it heightened his desire.

"Do you need to expect me?" he asked. "I am, after all, your betrothed, am I not? A few short days from now, you will take my name and become mine."

He would be lying if he said the prospect did not bring his cock to a raging state of awareness. He was the hardest he had been since he had awoke pressed against her at Helston Hall.

Her defiance was on full display now, her shoulders back, chin up. "I will never be yours, my lord. I will always be my own person, even in the event of our marriage."

In the event, she had said, as if their nuptials were not a foregone conclusion.

As if they were a possibility instead of an absolute.

"Are you suggesting we will not wed?" he asked carefully, noting the manner in which she withdrew from him.

For each step he took forward, she took one in retreat. The trouble with her strategy was that in another few feet, she would reach a wall. For a moment, he thought about capturing her there. Pressing his body to hers, pinning her to the dark damask and taking her mouth, then lifting her skirts…

No.

He had not come here to seduce her. He had come here to make certain, once and for all, that she would become his bride. He had met with Westmorland's solicitor earlier that morning. Lady Calliope had reached her majority, as he had already made certain. She could marry without her brother's approval. Her dowry was unimpeachable.

And soon, it would be his salvation.

First, he had to make certain she would not attempt to thwart him.

"I am not suggesting we will not wed," she denied, sounding breathless, her eyes wide.

He had been so caught up in his turbulent thoughts he had failed to realize they had indeed reached the end of the room. There was nowhere else for her to flee. Her back hit the wall.

Perfect.

He stalked nearer. "Then what were you suggesting, princess?"

She licked her lips. "I was suggesting that I am my own person. Now. Always. You will not own me."

He knew he should have mercy for her, but he had none. He moved closer still. Until his body was aligned with hers. Until her petticoats and skirts surged into his legs. Until he was so near to her that her warm breath fanned over his lips in the prelude to a kiss.

A kiss he wanted to take. A kiss he *had* to take.

Right bloody now.

He dipped his head and claimed her lips for his own. Her mouth was soft and supple, giving and hot, so hot. Hotter than the fire in his blood, raging with the need to possess her. She did not resist. Instead, she sighed into his mouth, and her hands settled on his shoulders. Not pushing him away. Her fingers dug into him, spurring him on.

Everything about her was fierce. Each time they kissed, it was feral. Elemental. They were two wild creatures, madly clashing. He thought of the first time he had taken her lips, of how she had bitten his tongue until she had drawn blood. Oddly, the memory only heightened his driving need.

His cock pressed against the fall of his trousers with painful insistence, and his ballocks ached. His body cried out with the need to raise that gown and plunge inside her. But he would not do it. Not yet.

For now, he would mollify his ravenous lust with her mouth.

He sucked on her lower lip, taking his time, consuming her. She tasted sweet, like chocolate. When he caught that fullness between his teeth and nipped, she made a small mewl. Sin took her face in his hands, holding her still for his onslaught. Her skin was smoother than silk. Her pulse beat a wild pattern.

She wanted him as much as he wanted her. He was certain of it. What a pair they were—two enemies who despised each other. Together, they were combustible. Who would have thought? Perhaps their marriage bed would not be a cold place after all.

Still taking his time, Sin kissed the corners of her lips, then the perfectly formed upper bow. Her mouth was gorgeous. Made for sinning. Made for kisses. It was the color of crushed berries and just as succulent. He wondered how it would feel, wrapped around his aching cockstand.

Groaning, Sin deepened the kiss. His tongue swept inside her mouth slowly. He explored her, running his tongue against hers, the velvet recesses beyond. She tasted even sweeter, even more delicious. And her lips were moving against his. Her tongue slid into his mouth, too. One quick foray. A silken glide.

Fuck.

He had not anticipated the surge of overwhelming desire that little flick of her tongue sent through him. He had never expected to want her this much. Her response made an answering pulse of need throb to life. His fingers sank into the sleek upsweep of her dark hair, finding pins and plucking.

The need to dismantle her careful *toilette* hit him, full-force.

He wanted to mark her. To claim her in every way. He wanted her to see her reflection later, in the glass, and remember he was the one who had kissed her senseless, let down her hair. To remember she would be his.

And soon.

Not soon enough.

Pins were dropping, and her hair was falling around her shoulders in thick, luxurious curls. He bit her lip gently and then forced himself to break the kiss. Instead, he kissed her chin, her jaw. He found her wildly flitting pulse, opened his mouth over the creamy skin of her throat. He nipped and sucked, wanting her to see that mark, as well. The evidence he had touched and kissed her, that she had liked it. He scraped her sensitive skin with his teeth.

She purred like a cat.

Damn, but that sound nearly undid him. He wanted to hear her make it again and again. He wanted her to cry out his name as he thrust into her. He wanted…

"Ahem."

The loud, pointed clearing of a feminine throat dashed his thoughts of what he wanted. His blood roared in his ears, his heart thundering, lust coursing through him like a flooded river.

But there was an intruder, and he had gone too far.

Sin lifted his head and stepped away from Lady Calliope, whose eyes were dazed and so dark they were almost obsidian. Her lips were swollen from his kisses, her hair a tangle of brunette curls around her face, and the creamy flesh of her throat was pink from the abrasion of his whiskers. The roaring in his ears continued. He liked the way she looked, thoroughly ravished and utterly his.

Turning away from her required summoning all the control he had. But they had an audience, and even a man with a reputation as depraved as his knew he could not make love to his betrothed against a wall whilst someone else looked on.

Well, he could…

Grinding his jaw against the wicked thought, Sin turned, taking care to block Lady Calliope from view with his larger body. The aunt stood there, her eyes wide.

"Mademoiselle Beaulieu," he greeted, just barely keeping himself from calling her Aunt Feather-wit.

He offered her as courtly a bow as he could manage whilst sporting a determined cockstand.

"Lord Sinclair," she returned, dipping into an abbreviated curtsy. "Forgive me for the interruption. However, it would appear it was rather timely, *n'est-ce pas?*"

He raised a brow, attempting to look shame-faced. In truth, he was well-pleased by those kisses. "I am sorry. There is no excuse for my behavior. My sole defense is that I cannot wait to make my betrothed my countess. Pardon me for my lapse in judgment, I beg you."

"I understand young hearts all too well," said the aunt. "I had one, once, long ago now."

He took a moment to study her, truly. She had the same

dark hair and eyes as Lady Calliope, but that was where the similarities ended. Still, she was a handsome enough woman.

Lady Calliope emerged from hiding then, frowning as her fingers fumbled to restore her coiffure to its previous state, to no avail. "Forgive us, *Tante* Fanchette. It was remiss of me to meet Lord Sinclair alone."

"Just a few more days, and then the two of you will have the rest of your lives together," said the aunt, her tone cautioning. "I have already been remiss in my duties. Westmorland will never forgive me if there are any further lapses in propriety, and nor will I forgive myself."

"Lord Sinclair was just about to take his leave, *Tante* Fanchette," Lady Calliope said, casting him a furtive glance of warning.

Actually, it was more glare than warning. The virago was angry with him. Likely, she was probably angry with herself as well for having responded to him in the manner she had. Such glorious fire. He could scarcely wait to bed her.

"Do not be silly," said her aunt, waving a dismissive hand in the air. "Tea is ready, and of course his lordship must join us. I insist. We are to be family soon, after all. I must have time to better acquaint myself with him before my darling niece becomes his bride."

"He cannot stay," Lady Calliope said.

Sin grinned. "It would be my honor to join you both for tea."

If looks could kill, his betrothed would have slit his throat. "I distinctly recall you saying you had other engagements for the afternoon."

Did she truly think she could be rid of him that easily, particularly if his remaining would nettle her as much as he supposed? Foolish Lady Ruthless. He was made of sterner stuff than that.

"Nothing could be more important than spending time

with my beloved betrothed and her aunt," he returned with false gallantry.

"It is settled," said the aunt decisively. "Do come with me, the two of you. No more nonsense!"

Lady Calliope's lips pinched. Sin's grin deepened.

Oh, yes. The wedding night was going to be one delicious clash indeed.

CHAPTER 11

If you feel pity for the Countess of Sin, dear reader, pray try to banish it. She is not worthy of your concern. She earned her death by daring to desecrate our marriage vows with the Duke of W. I would kill them both again if I could.
~*from* **Confessions of a Sinful Earl**

"*Y*ou look as if you are being sent to the gallows," observed the Earl of Sinclair.

Callie kept her gaze upon the hands in her lap, which clenched the silken skirts of her wedding gown. There was a thin, golden band upon her finger that felt more like a prisoner's irons than a lifelong promise to love and obey. Her white gloves hid the ring. But she felt it there, burning her as if it were a brand.

She was too numb to speak, to even offer a response.

Earlier that morning, she had spoken her vows in the drawing room at Westmorland House. The occasion had been presided over by Aunt Fanchette, Lady Jo, and a small handful of other friends from the Lady's Suffrage Society, followed by a small wedding breakfast. There had not been time to arrange for a church, and it had seemed fitting to Callie to marry in the only place she had ever felt truly at home. Fitting, too, to begin her new life in a place of familiar comfort.

She had the sinking feeling that comfort would be the last she would know for some time.

"It is going to be an awkward marriage indeed if you do not deign to speak to me," Lord Sinclair added, his tone wry.

She rolled her lips inward and held her tongue, saying nothing. What *could* she say? The days had blurred together, passing by too quickly, until she had collided, headlong, with her unwanted fate.

She was married to the man seated opposite her in the Westmorland carriage. Her new husband had not possessed the funds to provide an adequate conveyance. He had nothing more than the dilapidated barouche and one mount. Ironically, it was Lewis, the coachman he had left with the splitting headache back in an alleyway near her former publisher's office, who was driving them to Sinclair's townhouse.

Her new home.

Not that it would feel like home.

Lord Sinclair gave an irritated sigh to accompany the sound of him strumming his long fingers upon his thigh. "Have you nothing to say, wife?"

Wife.

Yes, she was that. To him. To a man she still did not dare trust. A man who had once been her nemesis. A man she did not know, beyond the span of a week and a few, turbulent kisses. To say nothing of a forced carriage ride and an overnight abduction…

She stifled a shudder. She would be damned before she would show him a single weakness.

"Damn you, speak to me," he growled.

She met his gaze at last, startled by the intensity she saw reflected in his countenance. His jaw was rigid, his dark eyes sparkling. "What would you have me say, my lord? You have gotten what you wanted. You will have my fortune, such as it is. I must bear your touch until I present you with an heir. There seems hardly anything worth speaking about."

His expression shifted. "You must *bear* my touch?"

Suggesting she was unaffected by him was a lie, and she knew it. But she did it to spite him. "Yes. Just as I said."

"Come here," he told her in a voice of silken menace.

Molten heat pooled between her thighs. She pressed them together, doing her utmost to banish the unworthy sensation. She could not afford to want the Earl of Sinclair. Not when she could not be sure she could trust him.

"No," she denied, fixing him with a challenging stare.

She was not his to order about.

His nostrils flared, the sole indication of his irritation. For a few moments, the carriage swayed over the congested London street, the only sound between them the jangling of tack and the noises of the city beyond the enclosure of their conveyance.

And then, he struck. Fast as lightning, his hands clamped upon her waist. He hauled her across the carriage. The voluminous skirts of the gown Aunt Fanchette had chosen for her and the petticoats beneath tangled as she landed in his lap.

His hand curled around her neck, holding her still. "Your defiance is futile, darling."

Her hands settled upon his broad shoulders as the carriage hit a rut and swayed, nearly sending her sprawling. "I am not your darling. Release me."

"Kiss me first."

His order stole the breath from her. She stared down into

the harsh planes of his handsome face, certain she had misheard him. "I beg your pardon?"

"No." He gave her a grim smile. "I beg yours. You said you must bear my touch. Prove how detestable you find me. Kiss me now and show me you feel nothing at all."

The sensation between her thighs flared into something bigger, bolder, brighter, hotter. She was pulsing. Aching. All from his nearness, his body beneath hers, the mere suggestion of a kiss. His scent hit her—citrus, musk, man.

Sin.

No. She refused to think of him as that.

He was the Earl of Sinclair to her. Enemy. Captor.

Husband.

The last word shook her more than she would ever admit, even to herself. Enough of his foolish games. She had married him, but she was not his chattel. He could not order her to do his bidding.

"I do not want to kiss you," she told him stiffly, pushing at his chest in an effort to slide from his lap and return to her side of the carriage.

Where it was safe.

"Liar," he accused softly.

His lips quirked into a knowing smile. She could not seem to keep her stare from them. From that perfectly sculpted mouth, that broad jaw. *Merciful heavens*, even the delineation of his philtrum was perfection.

She wetted her own lips. "You are acting the boor."

"Perhaps I *am* a boor." He cocked his head, watching her with a heavy-lidded gaze that did strange things to her insides. "Or perhaps you are afraid to kiss me, Calliope. Mayhap you are afraid you will like it."

Of course she would like it.

She had every time thus far.

Not that she would admit it to him. She hated even

admitting it to herself, for it still felt like a betrayal to Alfred. To everything she had spent the last year believing.

"I am not afraid of you, Lord Sinclair," she denied.

And yet, she remained oh-so-very aware of his muscled frame beneath her. The haste of his movements had meant that she was seated in most unladylike fashion, her bottom wedged against the thick ridge of his manhood.

She squirmed, trying to get away. The action was instinctive, and yet it only served to grind her down upon him.

"Keep moving," he gritted, "and see what happens."

Her cheeks went hot. Indeed, she was reasonably certain that every part of her had been spontaneously engulfed in carnal flame. What was the matter with her? She had no right to feel an ache deep in her core. Her breasts were heavy, her nipples sensitive and hard against the stiffness of her corset. And his breath fanned over her lips. His eyes threatened to devour her whole.

She went still. "Lord Sinclair, you must release me."

"Sin," he said in that deep, wicked baritone of his.

It was gruff and yet smooth as velvet, all at once.

She felt it like a caress. Her tongue flitted over her suddenly dry lower lip, and his gaze followed the movement.

"What about sin?" she asked, breathless, even though she knew what he was asking of her.

She had merely blindly seized upon an excuse to delay the inevitable. Or to invent a distraction. A means by which she could escape.

You do not want to escape, taunted a wicked voice inside her.

Oh, how she hated the voice. Because it was right.

"That is my name," he said. "I would hear it on your lips. There is no need for formality now that we are husband and wife. Indeed, I dare say there was never a need for formality between us."

There was every need. Formality made it easier for her to cling to her defenses. The Earl of Sinclair was the man she had believed guilty for so long, the man she had loathed, the man against whom she had plotted her revenge. But Sin? Well, Sin was a different man entirely. The word itself was tempting. Wrong. Wicked.

She forced herself to recall that his former mistress, the beautiful duchess, had called him Sin.

"No," she countered, "that is not your name. No one is named Sin."

"It has been mine for as long as I can recall. Say it, princess."

"Justin," she said. For she knew his Christian name now. She had watched him sign it in his slanted, distinctive scrawl.

He tensed beneath her. "No one calls me that."

"Justin or Lord Sinclair," she said stubbornly, somehow feeling as if the distinction mattered, even if she did not know why. "Which would you prefer?"

"Sin," he repeated.

"Sin," she spat. "There, are you satisfied? Now let me go."

"Not until you kiss me."

The carriage rocked to a halt.

"We have arrived at our destination," she argued, pushing at his chest again. "This is unseemly. Let me go."

"Too afraid?" he asked calmly, lifting a hand from her waist to stroke her cheek.

Curse him. She could not bear to allow him to believe he scared her, or that she did not possess enough control to kiss him and feel nothing. Even if both were, in part, true.

"Never," she vowed.

He ran the backs of his fingers over her skin. Although he wore gloves, there was something about the caress that stole her breath. Gave her pause. There was a surprising tenderness in that touch. In his expression. She did not know what to do with it.

But he had left her with little choice. With a deep inhalation, she lowered her head and sealed her lips to his.

* * *

Her defiance.

Her mouth.

Fuck, the weight of her in his lap.

Those dark, flashing eyes, that cloud of mahogany hair.

Everything about her was driving him to the brink. Sin had never wanted a woman more than he wanted Lady Calliope Manning. Strike that—Calliope, Countess of Sinclair.

His *wife*.

How surreal it seemed. Today was a day of victory. The culmination of the battle he had waged with her. He had won. But she was not about to surrender. He knew that much. Strangely, he found the notion of her fighting him erotic as hell.

Mayhap that was why lust was crashing over him like waves on a storm-tossed sea. That, and her lips. They moved over his, soft and hard at once. He could almost taste her rebellion. He remained still, allowing her to kiss him, waiting for her to retreat.

But she did not.

Instead, she kissed him harder. Deeper. She was the one in control. The hands on his chest slid around his neck. She knew how to kiss, his new wife. And well. The thought had occurred to him before, at Helston Hall, but it returned to him now, along with a sharp stab of something akin to jealousy. Someone had taught her.

And that someone had not been Sin.

Perhaps she was not even a virgin.

The possibility had occurred to him before. There were all the rumors about her and the artist in Paris, to say nothing of her former betrothed. He would worry about that later, when he came to her chamber.

For now, he simply allowed her to kiss him, careful to keep his lips still. Careful not to respond. The fight to win her as his bride was over, but a greater war was about to begin. And Sin had every intention of winning this one as well.

Her tongue traced the seam of his lips, seeking entrance.

With a kittenish sound of frustration, she broke the kiss, staring down at him. "You are not kissing me back."

"Make me," he challenged her.

Her eyes widened. "What manner of game is this, my lord?"

"Sin," he reminded her. "No game. If you want me to kiss you back, you will have to do better than the tepid effort you have put forth thus far."

How he loved taunting her. In truth, there was nothing tepid about her perfect mouth on his. Nothing tepid about *her*. She set him on fire.

The driver gave a discreet knock on the door.

"Not yet," Sin called, keeping his gaze locked upon Calliope's.

For a moment, she remained as she was, frozen in his lap, and he thought she would retreat. Suddenly, she caught his face in her gloved hands and slanted her lips over his. This kiss was as skilled as the others that had come before, but it was aggressive. Almost forceful. She bit his lower lip.

His cock twitched.

This time, she did not draw blood as she had done at Helston Hall when she bit him. Rather, she exercised sensual precision. He opened, and her tongue swept inside his mouth. His restraint fled, as did his ability to resist her.

Sin kissed her back with all the burgeoning need inside him, the need that had begun as a spark in this very carriage and had grown into a raging inferno. Her tongue glided against his. He sucked on it, drawing it deeper into his mouth.

His hands were in her hair, cupping the base of her skull. He was no longer keeping her imprisoned in his lap. Instead, he was angling her so he could devour her back with every bit as much ferocity. He poured all his fury and his pent-up desire into this meeting of mouths.

A groan tore from him when she writhed on his lap. Her bottom, separated from him by her underpinnings and gown, was still a delicious temptation against his raging cockstand. She kissed him harder, knocking his hat off his head and sinking her gloved fingers into his hair.

He wanted nothing more than to lift her skirts and ram his cock deep inside her.

But he could not do that.

With great reluctance, he broke the kiss, gratified at Calliope's ragged breaths and the dazed expression on her lovely face. Her lips were swollen from kissing him, her cheeks flushed, her pupils huge in her gold-flecked eyes.

"I suppose that shall do," he drawled. "For now."

His gibe stole the sensual stupor from her countenance. "You are an arrogant oaf."

Yes, he was. And he was going to enjoy having her beneath him later.

"You had better get off me, darling," he said. "Unless you want me to consummate our union right here in this carriage for the first time? I do hate to keep the servants waiting, however."

The scarlet flush on her cheeks deepened, and it blossomed down her creamy throat. He would have liked to open her bodice and see if it reached her pretty breasts. But that, too, would have to wait until this evening.

"Scoundrel," she hissed, sliding from his lap and attempting to straighten her skirts into some semblance of order.

He wanted to haul her back into his lap and kiss her senseless. Her discomfiture was bloody adorable.

The thought left him bemused. Since when did he find anything to do with the woman who had done her damnedest to ruin him *adorable*? Since when had he been this desperate to sink his cock inside a woman?

Never, taunted a voice within.

A voice he stifled as he leaned forward and rapped on the carriage door. "We are ready to disembark."

Feeling grim, he slammed his hat back atop his head. He would have to steel himself against this rampaging desire he felt for her. He must not lose sight of the reason for their marriage—her ruthless act of vengeance against him for sins he had never committed. He could not trust her. Did not dare want her too much.

She was a means to an end.

He would have her dowry and her body. That was all he required.

The door to the carriage opened to reveal that the ominous-looking clouds which had been hanging overhead since dawn had decided to open up and vent their fury at last. There was a raging downpour flooding the streets. Somehow, he had been too caught up in Calliope to even take note.

"Your new home awaits you, Lady Sinclair," he told her mockingly.

It was fitting, he thought, to be greeted by a deluge.

"I can hardly wait," she said, her voice as grim as her countenance.

CHAPTER 12

Of all the vices I have enjoyed, the sins of the flesh are my favorite,
dear reader.

~*from* **Confessions of a Sinful Earl**

allie found herself in the countess's apartments, soaking in warm water up to her chin. She had grown accustomed to the bathrooms at Westmorland House —the height of modern convenience. Warm water at the tap whenever she wished. A chamber specifically designed for the bath, with a water closet. Her new home had no such amenities. The footman and the coachman had hauled the tub into the center of her room and filled it to the brim with buckets of water heated in the kitchens below.

At least her lady's maid, Whitmore, had brought her oils, soaps, and perfumes. And after the exhausting day she had experienced, she was pleased to finally have some time alone. Upon their arrival in the midst of the storm, she had been introduced to the small number of domestics in Lord Sinclair's employ. She had been permitted some time with her lady's maid in her new quarters to settle herself.

And then, Callie had been given a tour of the townhome by the kindly housekeeper, Mrs. Lufton. An abridged tour, she thought with a frown as she rested her arms on the lip of the tub and closed her eyes. There was a chamber she had not been shown. When Callie had questioned the reason, Mrs. Lufton had politely informed her that his lordship did not wish for the tour to include that chamber.

With *his lordship* nowhere to be found, Callie had been forced to accept the odd explanation. Inwardly, she had vowed to find out what was hiding on the other side of the chamber door as soon as possible. Or at the very least to confront her new husband about it.

Following her introduction to the skeletal staff he had retained, Lord Sinclair had disappeared. She had been irked at his abandonment of her. She still could not entirely say why. It ought to have suited her to be free of his unwanted presence.

But by the time he had joined her at dinner, she had been quite cross with him. He had treated her with cool politeness as the servants waited upon them. Dinner had hardly been an impressive affair. His cook was not nearly as talented as Rochelieu, the chef her brother employed at Westmorland House.

Sinclair had accused Callie of being spoiled once. She had not believed herself spoiled in the least. But a few hours into her new life as the Countess of Sinclair, she was beginning to realize just how right the earl had been. His townhome, like the crumbling ancestral pile to which he had spirited her, was in desperate need of repair.

It seemed to have been robbed of everything of value. The missing pictures—evidenced by the squares and rectangles where the wall coverings were new and brilliant rather than faded—were not limited to the main hall. Here in the countess's chamber, the walls were utterly bereft of ornamentation. There was no silver in sight. The carpets were threadbare. There were not enough servants for a house of this size.

Callie sighed. Her work as the mistress of this dilapidated townhome seemed insurmountable. She would need to hire a chef and countless other domestics, replace the carpets and wall coverings...the entire, once-proud edifice was in desperate need of a thorough cleaning, from below stairs to the attics.

To say nothing of the expectations the Earl of Sinclair would have.

She was expected to share his bed.

The night loomed before her, uncertain, distressing.

Tempting.

Her bath water had grown cool. Reluctantly, Callie rose and stepped from the tub. She could not hide within it forever. Reaching for a towel, she thought again of those kisses in the carriage. Callie did not know what had happened to her. His challenge had sent her over the edge, and she had forgotten herself. For those few, wild moments, she had been driven only by desire, by the undeniable attraction she felt for him.

Following dinner, the earl had informed her he had called for a bath in her chamber.

I will give you some time to prepare yourself for the evening, he had said.

The warning in his voice settled between her thighs now as a new pulse of yearning. She was turning into a wanton, and she could scarcely understand why or how. She still considered the Earl of Sinclair her enemy. Her body, however, did not.

Callie wrapped herself in the dressing gown her lady's maid had waiting for her. Simon would have been ashamed of her, if he could see her now. If he could see what she had become.

As she thought of the man who would forever own her heart, tears pricked at her eyes. She swore to herself that she would not allow them to fall. But she was weak, and one slid from her lashes, rolling down her cheek. For the first time since becoming the Countess of Sinclair that morning, she allowed herself to mourn what she had lost.

Her wedding day would have been two years prior. She would have been married before everyone she loved. Alfred would have been there. She would have had a society wedding, filled with laughter and happiness. Perhaps she would have even been a mother by now, had the future she had planned for herself not been so viciously stolen away with Simon's death. Instead, he had gone to Italy to ease his constitution, and he had returned in a coffin.

"Contemplating the rest of your life as my wife, princess?"

The grim drawl at her back took her by complete surprise. Callie spun around, a startled shriek escaping her.

"What are you doing in here?" she demanded, shocked at the sight of him standing before her, clad in nothing more than a dark-blue dressing gown that was belted loosely at his waist.

A mesmerizing sliver of his chest was visible. Strong, muscled, and covered in a smattering of dark hair. She did her best to ignore the pulse of yearning he brought to life within her once more. The arresting sight of his masculine beauty meant nothing to her, she told herself. He was so unfairly handsome, but other men were handsome, too. Simon had been, with his tousled, golden curls and his deep-blue eyes.

The man who should have been her husband and the man she had married could not be more different. The contrast had never been so vivid. The Earl of Sinclair's dark beauty made her heart pound and her breath hitch in her chest.

"I knocked." His searing gaze traveled over her. "You did not answer. I was worried."

She had heard no knock on the door adjoining their chambers. But it was possible that she had been too lost in her tumultuous emotions and musings to hear.

Still, his heated stare reminded her she was naked beneath her dressing gown. She folded her arms protectively over her breasts. Belatedly, the last of his words dawned upon her.

"You were worried," she repeated, disbelief lacing her voice.

"Yes." He sauntered nearer, not stopping until he stood before her.

She did not want his admission of concern to mean anything. It was not as if he cared about her. He had married her for her dowry and to gain revenge against her for *Confessions of a Sinful Earl*.

Callie raised a brow, clinging to all the calm she possessed. "Did you fear I had attempted to flee through the window again?"

"The notion did cross my mind, I confess." He startled her even more then by reaching out and catching one of her forgotten teardrops upon his thumb. "Why are you weeping, Lady Sinclair?"

"Do not call me that," she bit out. The name felt wrong. As if it belonged to someone else. She did not want it.

He brought the pad of his thumb to his mouth and sucked. "It is your name now. You must reconcile yourself to the choices you made, princess. You, alone, are the reason you are my wife."

Somehow, the sight of his sinful mouth sucking up her sorrow made her core tingle. There was something so very sensual about the Earl of Sinclair. His every move, every stare, word, and touch seemed alive with carnal intent.

"I am hardly alone in the reason," she reminded him pointedly. "If you had not held me captive and blackmailed me into marrying you, I would not be here now."

He inclined his head, watching her with that fathomless midnight gaze. "If you had not told the world I am a murderer and decimated my ability to secure a bride before I lost everything, I would not have had to marry you. No matter how you try to deflect, the paths all lead back to you, darling."

The way he called her darling was so cutting. Part of her knew she ought to fear him. He was a dangerous man. At least, she had spent the last year believing he was. Certainly, his actions thus far—abducting her, threatening her, forcing her into this unwanted union—suggested she had not been wrong.

And yet, he had never been cruel. He had never done her violence. Even when she had attacked him with the porcelain that night in the countryside, he had retaliated by kissing her. What a contradiction he was.

She did not like it. Nor did she like the way she responded to him. Especially when she remained so uncertain as to whether or not she could trust him.

"You are as guilty as I am," she insisted for the sake of her pride, and because she refused to shoulder all the blame for this marriage of inconvenience in which they now found themselves hopelessly mired. "I have yet to complete my preparations for this evening, my lord. Will you not leave so I may call for my lady's maid and finish in peace?"

"No."

She could scarcely believe him. "No?"

He was close enough that she could smell the sweet scent

of port on his breath. At this proximity, he stole all the breath from her lungs. "Just as I said. No."

She forced herself to inhale. To speak.

"Do you intend to play lady's maid for me?" she demanded, the idea causing her equal amounts of outrage and titillation.

The consummation of their union loomed. She had never been entirely nude in the presence of a man before. Surely her fear of what was to come was the reason why her heart beat so madly now. Why her mouth had gone dry.

"I intend for you to tell me why you were crying when I entered," he said easily. "And then yes, I intend to assist you myself."

She had not anticipated such a response. So personal, so intimate, both of those answers.

"It is none of your affair," she snapped. "And I do not require your assistance. My lady's maid is more than capable of aiding me."

"Everything about you is my affair," he told her calmly, his stare never wavering. "You are my wife."

She could not look away from him, no matter how much she wanted to. He commanded all her attention. "You married me for my dowry. Why should you care?"

"Tell me."

His demand shook her. As did his presence. There was something about the Earl of Sinclair that was so different from every man she had ever known before him. Something strangely magnetic. Alluring. Her reaction to him outraged her. She needed to put some distance between them. She needed him to return to his chamber and leave her alone until she was ready to face him. He had caught her at her most vulnerable, and she did not like it. Callie would have to chase him the only way she knew how.

"I was thinking of Simon," she told him defiantly. "There.

Are you satisfied? I was thinking of the wedding day I should have had. Of the husband I would have loved."

The earl's jaw tensed, but he did not go or fly into a rage as she had hoped he would. Instead, he remained where he was. "Love and marriage have nothing to do with each other, princess. Trust me. I have more than adequate experience in the matter. You shall be better off despising me from the start than had you married your beau. He would have only disappointed you or betrayed you, had he lived."

What a desolate view of marriage he had. "He loved me, and I loved him."

Sinclair's lip curled. "Love is a poison."

"Like the poison your wife swallowed to escape you?" she snapped.

The instant the question fled her lips, she regretted it. She was not a cruel woman; at least, she had not believed she was until this very moment. She had wanted to hurt him. Had wanted to cut him deep, because he had brought her to this point. He had forced her into this unwanted union. He made her want him when she should not. He made her weak. She had precious few defenses against him.

But his sudden pallor made her sick instead of filling her with triumph.

"Forgive me," she hastened to say. "That was unfeeling of me. I did not mean it."

Still, he did not go. "You meant it, Calliope. If you are going to be bold enough to strike, then do not pretend it was an accident."

His low voice shook her. Of the two of them, he was being calm and considerate, and she was the one being the ruthless beast. This was not the way it was supposed to happen.

"Very well." She held his gaze, unflinching. "I meant it. I do not trust you, my lord. I am not certain I ever will."

"Sin," he said. "Give me your comb."

His request took her by surprise. "I beg your pardon?"

"Your comb," he repeated. "Give it to me."

"I am perfectly capable of combing my own hair myself, my lord."

"It is Sin." He stalked past her then, and retrieved her comb himself.

She held herself stiffly as he returned, eying him warily.

"Justin," she said, hating the way the name Sin felt upon her lips, the way it made her tingle all over. Here was a victory she refused to give him. "Return to your chamber, if you please. You may visit me for your husbandly duties when I am ready."

"Is that how you imagined our union would be?" he asked, sounding amused as he stood behind her and began gently running the comb through her wet locks. "That you would snap your pretty fingers, and I would do whatever you wished of me?"

Of course that was not how she imagined their union would be. Nothing about the Earl of Sinclair suggested he was a man who would do her bidding. She maintained her silence as he worked, trying to ignore the unsettled way his commanding presence felt at her back.

When he finished his task, he brushed her hair over her left shoulder, and then his hands settled upon her. His fingers found her muscles, massaging. *Good heavens*, it was as if he knew inherently how to find all the places where her tension dwelled.

"You never answered my question, princess." Knowingly, he kneaded the tautness from her flesh. "Is it?"

She had forgotten what he had asked.

"Go away," she said without heat. In truth, his ministrations felt delicious. She was conflicted and confused and so very aware of him. Of his masculinity, his intensity, his sensuality.

This was all new. So very, *very* new.

"I am not going anywhere, darling," he warned, but there was no threat in his voice now. Only pure, wicked seduction. "You seem to be confused, so allow me to enlighten you. You are mine now. You are no longer Lady Calliope Manning. You are Calliope, the Countess of Sinclair. If I want to play lady's maid for you, I will. If I want you to call me Sin, you shall. From this day forward, your life changes, wife."

It already had. From the moment he had first stolen into her carriage, her life had changed. It would never be the same. Nor, she suspected, would she. He expected her surrender, utterly and completely. She was going to fight him. She *had* to fight him. But she also had to fight herself.

"I am not so easily commanded," she warned him on a gasp as his fingers found a particularly sensitive place near her neck.

"We will see about that," he promised. "Bow your head."

She obeyed, because she did not want to forego his hands upon her. Because she was weak. Her head tipped forward. He continued working the muscles of her neck in slow, steady motions. His long fingers upon her felt good. So good.

Too good.

"Stop fretting," he crooned. "Give yourself over to me, princess."

"How can I?" she shot back, even as she allowed him free reign of her body.

What was the point of denying him? His touch was not at all unwanted, much to her everlasting shame. He worked his way over her shoulders once more with skilled caresses. She found herself exhaling, some of the tension leaving her body. For a long time, there was no sound save her own, relaxed breaths mingling with his. No sensation but his touch.

"You see?" His mouth was devastatingly near to her ear. His lips grazed her as he spoke. "It is easy to give yourself to me. I have no wish to hurt you. Contrary to what you think about me, I am not a beast."

He kissed her ear, and then there was the hot, wet glide of his tongue over her. Dipping behind her ear, to a place she had not even known could appreciate touch. The mellow glow of pleasant sensation hovering over her vanished. Instead, a white-hot rush of longing shot to her core. The place between her thighs ached with unanswered longing. Her breaths emerged in heavy pants.

"I do not trust you," she said.

"Does it feel like I will hurt you, Calliope?" he asked.

She did not dare answer him, lest he stop. Lest she reveal too much. If she had been conflicted before, she was even more hopelessly confused now.

His hands traveled down her upper arms, and then, abruptly, his touch left her momentarily before returning somewhere else. Somewhere far more intimate. He cupped her breasts in both hands. His fingers found her nipples, rolling and plucking through the thin fabric of her dressing gown.

Pleasure washed over her.

"You are going too far," she forced herself to warn.

But she made no move to halt him. Her eyes slid closed once more. She surrendered to feeling. To his masterful touch. He pulled on her nipples and nuzzled her neck. Instinctively, she tilted her head to the side, giving him better access. He required no prodding. In an instant, his mouth was upon the tender cords of her throat, feasting. Kissing, sucking, nibbling.

"Shall I stop?" he asked, his voice husky and laden with the same desire she felt coursing through her veins.

Never, said that traitorous voice within.

"If you wish," she forced out, her pride taking the reins.

"Do you truly want me to stop?" He sucked on her flesh.

She stifled a moan. His hands had stilled on her breasts. Her nipples ached with the need to be touched. Every part of her was alive in a way it had never before been. His presence at her back, his mouth on her throat, his touch upon her body—it was nothing short of glorious. Nothing could have prepared her for this carnal onslaught.

He removed his hands then, his lips, too.

"Answer me," he demanded at her back.

His tone brooked no argument. He was giving no quarter.

"No," she whispered.

"No what, princess? You will have to be more specific. I want to be certain I understand you."

"No, I do not want you to stop," she gritted.

The admission was torn from her.

Her reward arrived in the form of his long fingers expertly opening her robe, leaving it gaping, and his hands, returning to cup her breasts. Bare skin upon bare skin this time. His fingers toyed with her aching nipples. She exhaled the breath she had not realized she had been holding. She *liked* his hands upon her.

Heaven help her.

"I have been waiting all day to do this," he murmured in her ear, catching the lobe between his teeth.

Simultaneously, his right hand slid down her belly, gliding over her in the whisper of a caress. He paused for a moment, so very near to her center and all the frustrated longing building within her.

And then, his hand settled over her.

The shock of his touch there was electric. She nearly jolted away from him. Her instinctive reaction was to press her thighs together, but all that accomplished was trapping his hand.

"Relax," he coaxed.

How could she do so when he was touching her there? In her most intimate place? When her entire body felt as if it were doused in flame?

"What are you doing?" she asked, breathless. Frozen. Unable to move. His hand remained wedged between her legs.

She should shove him away. Release her grip on him. Flee. But she could not.

"Touching my wife," he whispered in her ear.

His finger moved, gliding through her folds, sending sensation skittering through her. His thumb found an incredibly sensitive place and pressed.

She moaned.

The sound was foreign. Embarrassing.

She wished she could call it back, but the earl—Sin—was doing wicked things to her. Things she had never known she would want.

"I told you, I am not ready," she managed to say.

His other hand remained on her breast, caressing, toying with the hardened peak. His thumb moved again. He licked behind her ear. "Relax your legs for me, sweet. I want to touch you properly."

She swallowed. There was more? She could not even fathom it. Her heart was racing. The ache in her core grew by the second.

"Leave me to prepare myself," she pleaded, even though it was not what she wanted.

He had started a fever within her.

"Relax," he insisted, kissing her neck. His thumb grazed over that delicious place again.

She could not resist. Her body took control of her mind completely. She unclenched her thighs.

He made a low growl of approval, and then he shifted. His

fingers found the place where his thumb had been, and he swirled them over her. "Good wife."

His praise should have irritated her. She knew she ought to be putting up more of a fight rather than surrendering with such wanton ease. But the things he was doing to her, the pleasure radiating from the place where he touched her, astounded Callie.

Instead of protesting, she pressed her back to his lean form, resting her head against his chest. She was every bit as much his captive now as she had been the day he had taken her from London.

"Tell me now," he murmured against her throat, "how does it feel? Does it feel like I will hurt you? Does it feel like I am a monster?"

No. It felt…

She searched for a word that could aptly describe the sensations building inside her.

Wicked. Good. Delicious. Sinful.

Somehow, the only word it ought to be—*wrong*—occurred to her last.

His fingers stilled, remaining on her, but ceasing their magical feats. "I cannot hear you, princess. How does it feel when I touch you here, when I pet your cunny? Do you like it?"

She wanted to tell him she did not like it, but she could not form the words. He resumed playing with her, rubbing harder and faster, and the raw pleasure inside her continued to build. Her breaths were ragged. She felt as if she were seeking something, but she did not know what it was.

He sucked on her skin. "Say the words or I shall stop again. Tell me you like it, and I will make you come."

Callie knew what those vulgar words he had just uttered meant. Or, at least, she thought she did. The fast company she had kept in Paris had left her with knowledge no gently bred lady ought to possess. But there were words, and then there were actions. Nothing could have prepared her for ecstasy. Mere words could not possibly do it justice.

"Justin," was all she could manage.

"Say my name." He kissed her ear, her jaw. "Ask me to make you come."

He was depraved.

But she was desperate. She scarcely even recognized herself. She needed whatever he would give her. Needed *more*.

"Please, Sin," she forced out. "Make me come."

He resumed where he had left off, but this time, he increased his pace and pressure on her sex. "You are learning, wife. Now kiss me like you did earlier in the carriage."

She turned her head, and there was his handsome, wicked face. There were his beautiful lips. His gaze glittered in the low light. She was going to give him what he wanted. Because she wanted it, too.

Callie slammed her lips on his, kissing him hard. He groaned, the hand that had been on her breast moving to tangle in her hair and hold her still. His fingers tightened, angling her head to where he wanted her, and he deepened the kiss, sliding his tongue into her mouth. He was torturing her, the hand between her legs pleasuring her with insistent, carnal demand.

Everything inside her tightened. She felt as if she was going to burst.

And then she did. The most astounding sensation hit her. Pure, delicious bliss, so fierce it was almost painful. Something inside her clenched. She cried out into their kiss, and he answered her with a groan. The fusion of their mouths became furious.

She wrapped her arm around his neck, holding him to her. She did not care that she was surrendering to his seduction. Did not care about anything other than the exquisite pleasure throbbing between her thighs and the connection of their lips.

Slowly, the desire ebbed. As the last ripples of her pinnacle undulated through her, he gentled the kiss, his pace on her sex slowing. Until at last, he tore his mouth from hers. They stared at each other, their breathing equally ragged.

She wondered what he saw reflected in her countenance. What she saw in his was a man caught in the throes of desire. It made her feel powerful. It made her want more.

"The time has come," he rasped.

CHAPTER 13

I treated her to the most exquisite pleasure, and though I had ravished and ruined her, she returned to the ball without anyone aware of what had happened between us. Yet another secret, dear reader, I share only with you, that you might protect your wives and daughters and sisters from wicked men like me...
~*from* **Confessions of a Sinful Earl**

Sin reminded himself he needed to proceed slowly for what seemed at least the hundredth time since he had walked into his new wife's chamber to find her in delicious dishabille. If he had been a gentleman, he would have walked away and allowed her the additional time she requested. But, as his actions had just proved, he was anything but.

Head tipped back, she stared at him now with wide, dazed eyes, her lips swollen from the kisses they had just traded and slack from the aftereffects of the orgasm he had given her.

"Now?" she asked, sounding hesitant for the first time.

Ordinarily, she was bold and brash. She fought him at every step.

What a pleasant surprise—in the aftermath of her crisis, she was docile as a kitten.

Perhaps he would have to keep her tied to his bed after all.

Fucking hell. Wrong time to entertain that thought. The image of her naked, her glorious, ripe breasts on display, her slender wrists secured to his bed, sent another bolt of lust straight to his straining cockstand.

"Now," he ground out. "But not here. I want you in my chamber."

He had to pace himself, he knew. He could not merely have at her like a ravening beast. After all, there remained the possibility that she was a virgin. He must not forget.

"Await me in your chamber, and I will join you in a few minutes." The prim tone in her voice, after she had just made such throaty, wicked requests of him, was an unexpected delight.

If he did not take care, he would enjoy himself too much with his bride. He must endeavor not to do so. She was a means to an end, not a mistress to savor. Not even a woman he liked.

Or was she?

Blast.

"No," he denied, still holding her against him. He could not shake the notion she would flee if he allowed her. "Come with me now."

"At least allow me to fasten my dressing gown," she protested, her fingers already flying over the buttons he had undone.

"I am going to see you naked when I bed you anyway," he told her, amused in spite of himself. "What is the difference if I see you now?"

She nibbled at her lip, and he fought the urge to groan and feast upon her mouth again himself. "There will be no gaslights then."

"Of course there will be lights," he countered. "I want to see you. All of you."

In truth, he could see rather a lot of her now, thanks to his height and the manner in which the twain ends of her dressing gown had fallen apart. But he did not bother to point that out. He may have married her for her dowry, but she was his wife now, and he was enjoying his vantage point immensely.

"Aunt Fanchette said there would be no light," she protested.

Gone was his docile kitten. As the pleasure ebbed from her, the stubbornness returned. Very well. Challenge accepted. He would just have to make her spend as often as possible.

"What does Mademoiselle Beaulieu know of the marriage bed when she has never occupied it?" he demanded calmly, as if his prick were not harder than a block of marble, grinding against his wife's delectable rump.

"Please, my lord. I must insist you give me a few moments to compose and prepare myself."

She was not being unreasonable, he supposed. Except that he could see through her ploy. She was attempting to resurrect the walls he had just so summarily torn down when he had pleasured her.

"You do not require composure for what I have in mind," he told her, meaning it. "And the only preparation you need is the sort I have already done for you. But that is merely the beginning. There is more, much more."

His fingers still burned with the remembered feeling of her lush folds and the deliciously responsive bud of her sex.

Of her tongue lashing his. *Damnation.* This was not helping matters.

"More?" Her fingers were still frantically working over those bloody buttons, stealing his view from him.

"More," he repeated.

At long last, she sighed, and then accepted it. "Very well. We may as well get the bedding over with. I am tired."

He stepped away from her at last, keeping himself from responding through sheer force of will. She would be even more tired when he was through with her, but he did not say so aloud. Instead, he admired her as she turned to face him once more.

She was beautiful, this spitfire he had married. And he wanted her so much, he could scarcely breathe.

"Come," Sin told her, tangling their fingers together.

Sensation skittered up his arm—a spark, a heightened sense of awareness. Each time he touched her, it was the same. There was something about holding a woman's hand that was personal and intimate. It occurred to him that he had not done so since Tilly. Taking Calliope's hand in his had seemed natural. Instinctive.

Bloody hell. No more delaying. He had to consummate their marriage before he lost his damned mind.

He tugged her through the door joining their chambers. He did not stop until they reached his bed. He had never taken another woman here. When he had been married to Celeste, he had always visited her in the countess's apartments. But this was a new marriage. A new beginning, mayhap.

With a woman who had tried to destroy him.

He must not forget that.

He released her hand as if it were made of flame.

"On the bed," he told her, rougher than he had intended.

She moved toward it, still wearing the dressing gown.

He caught a fistful of the silk, staying her. "Not this. Remove it."

She hesitated before opening the buttons and shrugging it from her shoulders. It pooled on the floor in a whisper of sound. Her hair cascaded down her back, dry enough that it had already begun to curl. He could not take his eyes off her.

His bed was high, and Calliope was petite. She paused at the edge of it, which was above her waist, and cast him a look over her shoulder. "Do you have a step?"

"No step." He did not need one. Shaking himself from the trance that had come over him the moment she had removed the robe once more, he stalked toward her. "Allow me."

He grasped her waist in his hands and lifted her effortlessly onto the edge of the bed, spinning her to face him as he did so. Before she could retreat, he stepped to the bed, settling between her thighs. When she would have scooted away, his hands dropped to her smooth thighs, pinning her to the spot. He had a mouthwatering glimpse of the pink, beckoning flesh of her cunny. The urge to taste her there would not be denied.

And he would.

But first, he wanted her mouth again.

"My lord," she murmured.

"Sin," he reminded her, nettled by her return to formality. "We are about to be as close as two people can be. I will be damned if you are *my lording* me when I am inside you."

She chewed on her lip again, something he was coming to realize she did when she was anxious. "Why do you care what I call you?"

Keeping one hand firmly on her thigh, he lifted the other to cup her cheek. "You are my wife. Should I not care?"

"You hate me," she said.

He had persuaded himself he hated her. But that had been

before. And now? Now, he was no longer certain he did. He did not trust her, to be sure.

"I will not be able to fulfill my husbandly duty if you do not call me by my name," he lied.

In truth, nothing—not even an army—could stop him from bedding her tonight. He was ready. Now. He did not recall a time when he had ever been this desperate to fuck a woman. He had not even felt this all-consuming passion with Tilly.

She chewed on her lip some more, watching him from beneath lowered lashes, silent. On a groan, he lowered his head and took her lips. He sucked her abused lip into his mouth, flicking over it with his tongue. And then he bit it too, before deepening the kiss. He slanted his lips over hers. She tasted so sweet. Her kiss was like an elixir and a poison all at once. He wanted to feast on her mouth forever, but he also knew she was no better for him than his last countess had been.

One had pretended to love him and dealt him the cruelest of betrayals.

The other had ruined him and then married him.

He was going to make his new wife say his name again. Hell, he was going to make her moan it. Sin dragged his lips from hers, kissing down her neck. Her collarbone entranced him. He kissed a line over the delicate protrusion, then found the rounded slope of her shoulder. Her skin was so soft, floral scented, decadent.

He kissed down her breast, gratified at the way she inhaled sharply when his mouth traveled over the sensual curve. He dropped his touch to her breast, caressing it as he sucked her nipple. Her legs tightened on his hips and she cried out.

He bit her gently, catching her in his teeth and tugging. Her hands flitted to his hair. Instead of pushing him away, she held him there, arching her back, offering herself to him. Sin did not know if she did it with carnal intent or if she was merely acting instinctively. Either way, it sent white-hot lust roaring through him like a locomotive.

He liked pleasing her.

She was dangerous, his little wife.

Far more dangerous than he could have predicted.

He sucked her pebbled nipple, lashed it with his tongue, and then blew on it softly.

"My name," he somehow found the wherewithal to prod.

But she was stubborn, too. She said nothing, maintaining her silence, aside from her uneven breaths.

He nipped harder, then sucked, teasing her other nipple between his thumb and forefinger and simultaneously sliding his hand between her legs once more. Drenched, delicious heat greeted him. He ran his fingers up and down her seam, parting her, finding her pearl.

"Sin," she gasped, jerking against his hand.

"Better," he praised, holding her gaze as he swirled his tongue in slow, languid circles around the peak of her breast.

Her breasts were gorgeous, just enough to fill his hands. He loved the way she responded to his mouth on her.

"Oh," she said when he rubbed her pearl again.

It was deliciously swollen and slick. Each rotation made her hips buck. She did not want to desire him any more than he wanted to desire her. And yet, she was as helpless to the magnetism they shared as he was. His cock was rigid and demanding.

But he ignored it and sank to his knees for her.

He vowed not to make a habit of this. He could not afford to allow her to think she had any power over him. He needed control. His disastrous marriage with Celeste had taught him that painful lesson. He would wield every weapon in his armory against his second wife. He would break her with desire. He would ruin her the way she had sought to destroy him.

Vengeance of the most delicious sort.

He smoothed his hands over her inner thighs, spreading her wide, exposing her fully. The dark thatch of curls on her mound gave up its secret. She was pink and feminine and glistening. The sweet perfume of her excitement—spicy and feminine—hit him.

"What are you doing?" she demanded. "Surely that is not…you cannot mean to…it is indecent."

"Hush." He kissed each thigh. Slid his hands to the treasure he sought. Using his thumbs, he parted her. Sin had never seen a more carnal, beautiful sight than Calliope, utterly at his mercy. Her hair was a wild cloud around her face and shoulders. Her lips were parted. Her throat bore the marks of his lovemaking. She wore his every kiss, suck, and bite like the finest Worth gown.

Pretty, fallen princess.

He lowered his head, flicked his tongue over her hooded pearl. Once. Twice. The taste of her blossomed on his tongue. God, she tasted good. Finer than any dessert. More decadent than chocolate. Sweeter than honey. He licked her in firm, steady pulses.

"Sin," she said again, writhing as if she wanted to get away.

But she did not seek to escape him. Instead, she scooted nearer, burying his face deeper in her cunny. She was all he tasted, felt, breathed. They were one, joined in pleasure and darkness and rage. But anger had never felt so delicious. He sucked her clitoris, taking his time, savoring her.

She whimpered. Her fingers were in his hair again, tightening, tugging. Pleasure and pain. Such a delicious commingling. Gently, he used his teeth on her. Not a bite—not yet—

but just a tender abrasion. An introduction to the world of pleasure to which he could introduce her.

Her cry echoed in the chamber.

She was close—so close—to spending once more.

She was exactly where he wanted her.

Sin gave her another slow, thorough lick. And then he rose to his full height, towering over her. She was breathless and naked on his bed, her eyes wide, glittering pools of golden brown. The need to be inside her would not be denied.

His fingers fumbled with the knot on his own dressing gown. In his haste, he tightened it. Frustration bit at him as he attempted to loosen the bloody thing.

"Fucking hell," he muttered. This was not part of the plan.

"Here, let me help," she said softly, taking him by surprise when she shooed him away and her small, nimble fingers made short work of the knot.

His robe parted and his aching cock sprang free. He was obscenely hard, and he knew it. Sin felt like a satyr. His wife's gaze was focused upon him, her countenance frozen with a combination of shock and curiosity.

He knew a moment of uncertainty—quite rare in his long and storied experience with the fairer sex. He wanted Calliope to want him. He wanted her to like what she saw. He longed for her to embrace their union. To let herself be free.

"Move into the center of the bed," he told her, chasing away the doubt.

The sooner he made her his, the better. It had to be done. But while his mind told him this was his duty, his body told the opposite story. It was pleasure. Anything but duty.

She did not even protest, shocking him. Instead, she did as he asked, the effort making her delicious breasts move in maddening fashion. He dropped his dressing gown to the floor, not caring where it fell, and joined her on the bed, settling himself between her thighs.

The tension he had felt in her body earlier was present once more. He saw it in her clenched jaw, her expression, felt it in the stiffness of her body beneath his. Although everything in him screamed with the need to sink himself inside her and make her his, to lose himself, he knew he could not. He had to go slowly. Temper his need.

He kissed her. Gently this time. It was a tender exploration of her lips and tongue. She kissed him back after a moment of resistance, and then her hands settled on his shoulders. Her nails sank into his flesh, and he liked the sting.

"Sin," she said, turning her head to the side and breaking the kiss.

His cock was burrowing into her belly. He was doing his best not to frighten her, but he could not last much longer. "What is the matter now?"

"My family calls me Callie," she said.

Her family?

For a moment, Sin was completely befuddled.

What the devil was she saying?

"I will call you Sin if you will agree to call me Callie," she added, her eyes meeting his in the light of the gas lamps.

Her defiance was still there, burning in the amber and mahogany depths of her eyes. But there was something else there as well. Acceptance? Desire? He could not say. And there was an answering *something else* within him. An unexpected surge of warmth at her asking him to call her what her *family* called her.

"Callie," he tried.

The abbreviated version of her name suited her. It felt right on his tongue. Just as she felt right beneath him. The taste of her felt right in his mouth.

"Yes," she whispered, her gaze searching his.

He did not know what she was looking for. Or if she found what she sought. He was desperate to be inside her now.

"I am going to make you mine, Callie," he told her, and damn him if those simple words did not make his ballocks tighten.

She frowned and bit her lip. "It will never work."

"Of course it will," he countered, uncertain if she was referring to their lovemaking or their marriage.

"How can it?" she asked. "It is far too large."

Sin stifled a startled laugh. "It shall fit, darling, I promise you."

Her befuddled expression touched him in a place he had not believed existed. "How?"

Curious woman.

Delicious creature. How could he resist her?

"Let me show you," he said, and then he kissed her lips once more.

He grasped his shaft and glided the head of his cock up and down her wet slit, making certain to coat himself with her essence to ease the breach. He was thick and hard, more than ready. But he was also cognizant that she was likely a neophyte, judging from her skittishness. He could not simply ram into her, no matter how much his body cried out with need.

She emitted a breathy little sigh into his kiss when he dragged himself over her pearl. Her eyes were glazed, her lashes low. Beneath him, her body was soft and supple and pliant. The tension had slowly ebbed from her. Her lips clung to his.

He had not expected to enjoy himself this much. To be so ensnared, so enamored. It was as if she had cast a sensual spell upon him. But Sin was beyond the point of caring. He would worry about his powerful hunger for his new wife later.

He released himself and ran his fingers over her silken flesh, parting her. When he found her entrance, he swirled his fingers over her, testing her readiness. She jerked against his hand, her hips lifting off the mattress, seeking. She was so wet.

He could not wait.

He guided himself to her cunny and slid into her with a tentative thrust. She tensed and cried out into his kiss. Sin paused, white-hot desire searing him. Being inside her felt so bloody good. Her slick sheath constricted on him, bathing his cock in blissful heat.

Her channel was excruciatingly tight. She was a virgin after all, in spite of all the rumors from her time in Paris and her dead betrothed. The knowledge should not have mattered, and yet, he could not stay the rush of primitive lust it sent arrowing through him. Remaining still was killing him. But he held tight to his control, simply breathing, allowing her body to adjust.

He broke the kiss and lowered his head to her nipple, sucking on it, then blowing on the stiff peak. "How does it feel?" he asked against the soft curve of her breast.

"Strange," she whispered. "Is it over, then?"

Hell.

He did not know whether to laugh, cry, or slide his cock all the rest of the way inside her. He nipped, reaching between them to where their bodies were joined to tease her pearl once more.

"Does it feel as if it is over, princess?" he returned when she moved her hips in response to his caress.

She dragged him deeper inside her, her cunny clenching on him. And he was lost. He moved again, another shallow thrust. Then another and another.

Callie was panting, moving with him, her nails scoring his back again. "Oh, Sin."

His name in a husky moan from her lips was the most erotic sound he had ever heard. The last of his restraint fell away. He swiveled his hips and seated himself all the way. She trembled beneath him, her cunny pulsing, making him wild.

He took her mouth again, kissing her hard. And then he began to thrust in earnest. Her arms were wrapped around his neck, her breasts flattening against his chest. He was a large man, and she was small and delicate and feminine. He felt like a rutting beast pinning her to the bed, but he was losing the battle. Slow and gentle was no longer possible.

Desire pounded in his loins. She was his. Every stroke of his cock inside her said so. Every scrape of her nails down his back said so. Even the connection of their bodies, the way they fit together, felt so damned right. So damned good.

He increased the pressure on the bud of her sex, sliding in and out of her, kissing her with all the raw hunger burning through him. His tongue sank into her mouth, and she sucked on it. She came undone on a ragged cry that he swallowed without breaking their kiss. She constricted all around him, milking him, bringing him to the brink.

Sin bit her lip and hooked her leg over his hip, readjusting so he could penetrate her even deeper. Finally ending the kiss, he braced himself on his forearms over her, watching her as he fucked her. She was gorgeous, her breasts bouncing with the force of his thrusts, her eyes closed.

"Look at me Callie," he ordered her. "Eyes open."

He reached for her hair—those glorious, dark strands spread over his pillow, and grasped a handful, gently forcing her head back to expose her throat. He wanted her to know who she had married. To look into the eyes of the man who was inside her.

God, she was beautiful. Her swollen lips were parted, her eyes dark. In that moment, he thought he could stay inside her forever.

But nothing lasted forever.

And neither did he.

His ballocks tightened. He buried his face in her neck and spilled inside her, filling her with his seed. Marking her as his.

As he collapsed against his new wife, he could not shake the notion that she had just marked him as hers every bit as much.

CHAPTER 14

Have I convinced you of my depravity yet, dear, gentle reader? If not, do read on. There is more...

~from **Confessions of a Sinful Earl**

*C*allie woke up in the Earl of Sinclair's bed, her body aching in strange places, naked, and alone. The bedclothes were twisted around her body. They smelled of him, and to her shame, that scent made a pulse of yearning pound to life between her thighs, where her soreness reminded her the earl was no longer a stranger.

He had been inside her.

And this tall, magnificent high tester—one of the few pieces of furniture in his townhome bearing any value—was her husband's bed. And that equally tall, magnificent stranger was her husband.

Husband.

What a strange word. An even stranger notion. In the span of one day, her life had been forever altered. She could not go back to being Lady Calliope Manning. She was the Countess of Sinclair now.

Once, that fact would have filled her with dread and fear.

Last night, however, had altered her perception of the earl. Her cheeks went hot, and a swirl of embarrassment joined the longing churning within her as she remembered in vivid detail what had passed between them the night before. Aunt Fanchette had told her not to expect a grand passion, for that was rare even amongst love matches.

She had been quite specific during their talk.

No lights. It would be quite quick. There would be pain.

How wrong Aunt Fanchette had been. Instead, there had been nowhere to hide. The earl had seen, touched—even *tasted*—her everywhere. He had been demanding yet attentive, making certain to give her pleasure, worshiping her body in a way she had not even imagined possible.

The consummation of her marriage had been nothing at all like what Aunt Fanchette had warned. And what had come afterward had been equally surprising. He had tended to her with a basin and cloth, and then he had kissed her long and slow.

Sleep here, sweet, he had ordered her.

And she had been too sleepy and sated to defy him.

She had fallen into her first deep, dreamless slumber since he had abducted her from London. Callie ran her hand over the dent in the pillow from where his head had rested. It was cool to the touch, which meant he had been gone for some time.

She sat up with a frown, noting the light pouring in through the window dressings. Just how long had she slept? And where had he gone? Most importantly of all, how would she face him after all they had shared?

There was a subtle rap on the door adjoining his chamber to hers.

Her lady's maid, Whitmore, she realized.

Callie was sure her flush extended to her ears as she

clutched the bedclothes to her chin, covering her nudity. What, precisely, was the etiquette for waking up the day after the consummation of one's marriage, in one's husband's bed, without a stitch of undergarments?

She adored her lady's maid. They had been together for years—indeed, Whitmore had seen her at her lowest, after Simon's death. And yet, Callie hesitated now.

"My lady?" Whitmore called.

Callie winced. "Yes, Whitmore, do come in."

Whitmore entered the chamber, bustling inside with her signature mien of practiced calm. She was tall and flame-haired, but her temperament was not nearly as fiery as her appearance would suggest. "Good morning, Lady Sinclair. His lordship rang for me, supposing you would want some assistance this morning."

"That was thoughtful of his lordship," she said, managing a polite smile. In truth, she did not know what it was.

Managing? His way of telling her she ought to be out of bed by now? Or perhaps he regretted allowing her to stay instead of sending her to the countess's apartments?

Callie had to admit, she did not relish the thought of sleeping in the adjoining room. Although she had found sleeping in Sin's bed foreign and strange, she thought she would far prefer to be mired in his territory rather than to be stuck in the chamber his former wife had once inhabited.

There were traces of her that lingered still—the wallcovering was a feminine shade of pink, adorned with roses. What little of the furniture that remained was also diminutive and elegant, clearly chosen by a woman. Seeing the chamber redecorated—along with the rest of the shabby townhome—would be one of her first acts as Lady Sinclair.

Lady Sinclair.

"Would you care for breakfast in your chamber, or will you be dining below?" Whitmore asked.

"I will join his lordship for breakfast," she decided on a whim.

After all, they were married, were they not? She could not avoid him forever. Best to face him, pretend as if what had happened had not changed a thing.

"His lordship has broken his fast and called for a carriage," her lady's maid informed her, holding up the dressing gown for Callie to don.

Callie swallowed down a rush of disappointment at Whitmore's announcement. He was going somewhere? Already? Where? Why?

Then she reminded herself she did not care where he went. At least if he was gone, she would not have to worry about the manner in which she conducted herself.

"Very well," she said, still clutching the bedclothes to her chest as she sidled to the end of the mattress. "I suppose I will take breakfast below."

She could hardly consider the countess's apartments hers. And she was not about to break her fast in a faded chamber haunted by the ghosts of her husband's past.

Somehow, she had forgotten just how high Sin's bed was. But she remembered now, as she dangled her legs over the edge. She felt like a child, her bare feet swinging through the air, nowhere near touching the threadbare carpets below.

How humiliating.

"Would you care for a hand, my lady?" Whitmore asked calmly.

"What I would like is a stool," she grumbled, "or a stair. This bed is insufferably high."

"Yes, my lady. Of course." Whitmore's expression did not change. "I will see about finding one for you."

"Blast," Callie grumbled before throwing herself off the bed. She landed with a dull thud on her two feet and stuffed her arms into the dressing gown, hauling it around herself as if it were a protective shield. "Thank you, Whitmore. You are a gem, as always. Does breakfast promise to be as wretched an affair as dinner was last night?"

Whitmore rolled her lips inward. "I fear so, my lady."

Callie sighed. "Is the situation below stairs as dire as I suspect?"

Her lady's maid did not answer. She did not need to—her expression said it all.

"Very well, Whitmore," she said. "I suppose we are not at Westmorland House any longer, are we?"

"No, my lady. We are not indeed," agreed her lady's maid, her tone stoic.

The day loomed before her, endless as the rest of her life.

How in Hades was she going to navigate these treacherous waters?

* * *

"You look like you need a whisky."

Sin threw himself into a chair and glared at his old friend. "Go to hell, Decker. It is not even yet noon."

"And the morning after your wedding," Decker agreed, placing a crystal glass filled with amber liquid on the low Louis Quinze table at his side. "What the devil are you doing paying me a call? Should you not be ballocks deep in quim at the moment?"

Mr. Elijah Decker was not the sort of man who minced words.

Sin scowled. "You are speaking of my lady wife."

Decker seated himself in the chair alongside Sin's in his extravagant library. "A lady who did her best to ruin you. You could have avoided all this if you had accepted my offer."

Sin exhaled. He had confided in Decker about all his woes. His friend had, of course, suggested he loan Sin enough funds to settle his debts, but Sin had refused. He could not bear to accept Decker's charity, knowing there was a chance he could never repay him.

Sin considered Decker the brother he had never had. Neither of them truly belonged in their worlds. Decker was the bastard son of the Earl of Graham, and Graham had bequeathed him everything he could aside from his title. He had wealth but not respectability and had used that wealth to amass a business empire. Sin, meanwhile, had a title without wealth. And now, he did not even possess respectability.

There was always the hope, however, that his marriage to Lady Calliope could alter that, in time. If he even gave a damn about such a thing, and he was sure he did not. All he wanted was enough funds to keep his mother comfortably ensconced.

He took the whisky and sipped it slowly. Like everything else Decker collected, it was very fine. The library, laden with curiosities—most of them lewd in nature—was a testament to his wealth, travels, and taste for the subversive.

"Your silence is telling, old friend," Decker observed, his tone pointed. Knowing.

Too knowing, blast him.

"You know I cannot accept a farthing from you and maintain even a modicum of my self-respect." He cast a glance in his friend's direction. "And why should I want to bed a woman who is my nemesis?"

"Why indeed?" Decker raised a brow.

Fuck. Sin was torn this morning. Last night had been…

It had been *splendor*.

There was no other way to describe what he had shared with his new wife. He had never experienced anything like it, and he had bedded any number of women in his life. Some of them, he had cared for—Celeste, once upon a time, and Tilly. Others had been beautiful and skilled, women who knew how to use their bodies and their mouths to bring a man to his knees.

Not one of them had ever made him feel even a modicum of what Calliope Manning had.

Sin took another lengthy draught of his whisky, savoring the burn. He deserved to be punished. Inflicting pain upon himself seemed the only solution for what ailed him. That, and burying his cock in his wife's sweet cunny.

"Hang me, Sin," his friend said into the silence. "Do not tell me you are getting soft for the evil little chit?"

He stiffened. "I am not getting soft. I am merely a man torn."

"Fucking hell," Decker muttered, taking a sip of his own whisky. "Need I remind you of what happened with your former countess? What happened with the Duchess of Longleigh?"

Sin drained the remnants of his glass. "Curse you, Decker. That was different. I was young and stupid when I married Celeste. I was thinking with my prick, and I had no notion of how mad she was."

"And the Duchess of Longleigh?" Decker prodded.

"She was a respite from Celeste," he admitted, realizing it was true.

He had not been in love with Tilly, and he understood that now, having seen her again. They would forever be friends, but they were not meant to be lovers. They had been two lonely, lost souls, seeking shelter from the ugly storms of their lives. He could only hope she was happy now.

As for Sin? He knew not if he could ever find happiness. He suspected it would forever elude him, and he had made his peace with that. As long as his mother could live out the rest of her life in comfort, he wanted for nothing more.

"And what of Lady Sinclair?" Decker asked.

It took Sin a moment to realize his friend was speaking of Lady Calliope—*Callie*. Their union was still so new, so fresh.

"What of her?" he asked, feeling defensive.

And confused.

And randy as hell whenever he thought of her.

She had been glorious last night. Her body, her response, her abandon. The way she tasted, the throaty sounds she made, the way she obeyed his commands in the bedchamber when she was so defiant in every other way…

Bloody hell, he had to stop all such thoughts.

It was deuced *de trop* to get a cockstand whilst enjoying a whisky with his old friend. Just how depraved was he?

"You like her," Decker observed.

Did he?

He did not *want* to like her, that much was certain.

"She is…" He hesitated, struggling to find the words.

A few, unwelcome adjectives came to mind. Beautiful, smart, seductive, sensual, alluring as hell.

"A conniving jade?" Decker supplied, tearing him from his ruminations.

"Yes," he agreed, uncertain why he felt protective toward her, as if he wanted to argue with his friend. *Good God*, he had every reason to trust Eli. He had no reason to trust his wife.

"The woman who went to every effort to destroy your reputation and send you into penury," Decker added.

Sin drummed his fingers on his empty glass. "That as well."

But she was also more than that.

So damn much *more*.

How could he explain it to his friend when he could not even make sense of it himself?

"The author of vicious lies about you," his friend continued, quite unnecessarily.

After all, he was not saying anything Sin had not already thought. Nor was he revealing information that was new. And yet, Sin found himself wanting to believe better of her. He found himself strangely attuned to her. It was true that they had not known each other for very long. But he had been as intimate with her last night as a man and woman could be.

"She believed everything she wrote about me," he said. Speaking the words removed a weight from his chest. "She thought it was true, that I had killed her brother and then somehow Celeste as well."

"Because she is mad," Decker snapped. "Good God, Sin. You cannot possibly be defending the wench, can you? She was ruthless in her determination to strip you of everything. You must treat her in the same fashion. Use her dowry. Restore your good name. Have your vengeance upon her."

"Vengeance is hollow, Decker," he said bitterly.

There was the crux of the matter. After suffering a union with Celeste, a woman who had been undeniably mad, he had been quick to believe the same of Callie. But he could see the differences between the two women already.

Celeste's moods had vacillated wildly, even from the beginning. She had gone from delirious happiness to deep, endless bouts of despair. And when she had despaired, she had done the most damage. One day, she would have professed her undying devotion to him, and the next, he caught her sucking a footman's cock. Then, she locked herself in her chamber for a week. Sometimes, he still woke in the middle of the night, drenched in sweat, having been trapped in nightmares of listening to the sound of her sobs.

But Callie was not the same woman. She was brazen and bold and daring. She fought him every step of the way. But she was not possessed by the same demons which had claimed Celeste. She fought him face-to-face. There was no pretense about her. She had owned her authorship of those vile books about him.

Sin blinked and realized his friend had somehow risen, gone to the sideboard, and retrieved the decanter of whisky without his notice. Decker hovered over him now, his expression grim as he splashed some more spirits into Sin's glass.

"Vengeance does not taste nearly as good as whisky," Decker quipped. "Drink up. I dare say you need it, old boy."

"I do not *need* your whisky," he growled at his friend, but he brought the glass to his lips just the same.

"Fine, then. You *want* it. Drink, my friend." Decker threw himself back into the overstuffed chair at Sin's side. "If you keep carrying on as you are, I will have no choice but to suspect you are falling in love with your sworn enemy. What the hell has gotten into you? Is her cunny made of gold?"

Sin choked on his whisky. He inhaled, and it burned a path of fire down his throat and nose all at once. "Bloody hell," he said on a cough. "I am not in love with her. And do not speak of her so rudely ever again, or I will blacken your eye."

Decker raised his glass. "There you have it! You are in love. You have never before objected to me speaking frankly of your conquests."

"Callie is not a conquest," he found himself saying. "She is my wife."

"*Callie*, is it?" Decker cast a knowing look in his direction.

"Go to the devil," he bit out. "I do not believe in love, and even if I did, I would not find it with a she-devil who has ruined my life."

"Hmm." Decker took another sip of his own whisky.

"Promise me something, Sin? That you will not forget what she has done to you? This cannot be another Celeste."

Sin bowed his head, staring at the glass he held in his lap. The amber liquid taunted him. Tempted him. He wanted to drown himself, to numb his thoughts, his feelings. Most of all, his emotions.

"There can never be another Celeste," he agreed. Because he would not survive it.

Wisely, he kept that bit to himself.

"Christ no," Decker agreed. "But enough of all that. Do you want to see my newest acquisition? It is a piece of true distinction, of Japanese origin and very cleverly done. You will not even know what you are looking at unless you know what you are looking for."

And was that not the way of it in life, not just in Decker's collection of erotic art?

He tossed back the rest of his whisky. "Show me."

Decker rose and stalked across the library, returning with a small, unframed canvas depicting a man standing alongside a woman. At first glance, it looked as if the two were not even touching. But upon a closer look, the woman's dress was not a dress at all, and the man's hand was claiming her in full, carnal, primitive possession.

"What do you think?" Decker asked.

It made him think of his wife. His conniving jade of a wife. The one he could not stop thinking about or wanting.

Fuck.

"I think I need more whisky," Sin said, raising his empty glass.

That was the most honesty he could manage at the moment.

* * *

Callie told herself she ought to be overjoyed that her husband had not returned.

She had eaten her bland supper in silence.

And now, she was lying in the darkness in her new chamber, staring into the murky shadows, telling herself she would not be bothered if he continued staying away. Forever.

But that was a lie, and she knew it.

Well, Callie? What did you expect? That he would fall madly in love with you and fawn over you like a lovelorn suitor after one day of marriage?

On a sigh, she rolled over. How foolish she was. She had allowed the earl's lovemaking to rot her mind. Theirs was not a happy marriage. It was a marriage of convenience.

Sinclair had what he wanted now—her dowry, her silence, and the consummation of their union. Having secured that, he had gone off to do whatever he wished, not even bothering to inform her where he had gone or when he might deign to return.

Where had he gone? To his illicit club?

Did he have a mistress? He had claimed he did not, but Callie was not certain he was to be believed. His sobriquet *was* Sin, after all. After last night, she could attest to the reason for it.

At the memory of his wicked caresses and kisses, her traitorous body heated up and a new awareness burned between her thighs. She promptly squelched the sensations with the reminder that her husband could, for all she knew, currently be visiting those same kisses and caresses upon another woman.

Or, worse, other *women*.

Feeling ill, she rolled again, onto her stomach.

And that was when she heard a thud from the chamber next door.

Apparently, her errant husband had returned.

Another thump echoed through the silence of the night.

Callie sat up in bed, scowling in the direction of the earl's apartments. How dare he return in the midst of the night and then proceed to make so much noise? Had he no respect for her?

Sadly, she suspected she already knew the answer to that question.

Callie's dudgeon would no longer be ignored. She slid from her bed, not even bothering to find her dressing gown. Her nightdress—long and high-necked and modest—would suffice. She made her way through the shadows, narrowly avoiding crashing into a chair, until she reached the door joining their chambers.

Light shone beneath it like a beacon.

Without bothering to knock, Callie swept the door open.

Her husband was seated on the edge of his bed, fully clothed save his boots, which she gathered were the source of the noise. They lay on their sides, half a dozen feet from him, as if he had launched them there. His neck cloth was loose, and his dark eyes devoured her as she hovered on the threshold. Somehow, the sight of him—dissolute yet handsome as ever—filled her with trepidation.

"You look like a bloody governess in that night rail," he said, breaking the silence.

How insufferably rude.

"Where have you been all day and evening, my lord?" she demanded, although she had promised herself she would not ask.

Would not act as if she cared.

She did not care.

Who are you trying to fool? whispered an insidious voice inside her. Stupid voice.

"I was visiting a friend," he said.

A *friend.*

Instantly, the beautiful Duchess of Longleigh rose to her mind.

"All day and night?" she pressed.

Curse you, Callie. What are you doing? Return to your chamber.

But she lingered, there at the threshold, awaiting his answer. The caring lover of the night before was gone. He seemed different this evening, but she could not quite define how or why.

"Did you miss me, wife?" he mocked, that sensual mouth of his quirking into a taunting smile.

Yes.

"No. There were merely some matters which arose I wished to discuss with you," she said, careful to keep her voice as even as possible.

"Matters?" Holding her gaze, he shrugged out of his coat and began unbuttoning his waistcoat.

She ran her tongue over her lips, thinking she ought to flee for certain now. "Household matters. What manner of friend were you visiting?"

His grin deepened, damn him. "Not a female friend, if that is what you are asking, princess."

The relief sweeping over her nettled.

She tamped it down. "Your affairs are none of my concern. Forgive me the interruption. I will speak with you tomorrow. Good evening, my lord."

"Wait."

She paused when she would have spun about and returned to the safety of her chamber, as was wise.

He crooked a finger at her. "Come here, little wife."

Little wife.

She did not know why the phrase, uttered in his silken voice, sent a rush of heat to her core. She also did not know why her feet were moving. Padding across the threadbare rug. Obeying him.

What was wrong with her?

Callie stopped just beyond his reach. "What do you want of me, my lord?"

"My name on your lips for a start," he drawled, his gaze dipping to her mouth.

She was sure she ought to deny him. "You would have heard your name on my lips quite a bit had you not been absent all day and night."

Her tone was tart. Drat him. He was getting the best of her. She did not want him to see a weakness.

"You are angry with me," he observed.

"Not any angrier with you than I was before," she lied, not sure why it mattered so much.

Her pride, she supposed.

"Since you are still awake, you may as well play valet for me." His brooding gaze was still upon her lips. "Help me with my shirt, will you?"

She swallowed. "You seem more than capable of disrobing yourself."

"Perhaps." His dark stare flicked back to hers, searing. "Or perhaps I merely want your hands on me."

Her heart pounded. "I do not want to play games with you. The hour is late."

"Who said anything about games?" His eyes lowered, settling upon her breasts. "Why the devil are you buttoned to the neck?"

She fidgeted with her night rail, acutely aware of his nearness and knowing gaze. "Why should you care, my lord?"

"Sin."

He was only saying his name, and she knew it, but she could not seem to quell the effect that wicked word, spoken in his deep voice, had upon her. "I prefer *my lord*."

"You even sound like a bloody governess," he said, pushing away from the bed and sauntering toward her.

She stifled the instinctive urge to move backward and maintain the distance between them. "What is wrong with governesses?"

"Not a cursed thing." His hands settled on her waist, and he yanked her into his tall, hard body. "Except when you frown at me and you get all proper and stubborn and you are wearing that virginal white nightdress, it makes me want to do wicked things to you."

Wicked things.

Her hands settled on his chest, but she could not, for the life of her, make herself push him away. What if she *wanted* him to do those wicked things to her? His warmth and sculpted muscle were deliciously tempting with only the thin layer of his shirt to keep her from touching his bare flesh. His scent invaded her senses: citrus, musk, and the faintest hint of spirits.

"What wicked things?" she dared to ask, though she knew it was a dangerous question to pose at this time of night when she was alone with her new husband and he was watching her as she imagined a predator did his prey.

The grin he gave her did strange things to her insides. "Help me with my shirt like a good little wife, and mayhap I will show you."

"I am not your valet," she protested weakly.

But something—some part of her that was entirely foreign and previously unknown—made her want to pull each button from its mooring. Made her want to divest him of his shirt.

Made her want to kiss him.

Oh dear.

"But you *are* my wife now." The hands on her waist caressed, then slid to her bottom.

Filling his hands with her, he pulled her more firmly against him. She could feel the thick ridge of his manhood against her belly. An answering surge of molten heat pooled in her core.

"What are you doing?" she asked, irritated with herself for the breathlessness in her own voice and the way she could not seem to control her reaction to him.

"Persuading you to undress me," he said, and then his mouth was upon hers.

CHAPTER 15

I am a wicked, sinful man, dear reader. A man you should never,
ever trust.

~from **Confessions of a Sinful Earl**

*H*er lips were so soft and giving and warm beneath
his. Her rump was two delicious handfuls. Her
curves melted into him.

Kissing her should not feel so good.

Sin had been determined to avoid his new wife for the
entirety of the day. Decker's taunts had kept him from
returning. Instead, he had spent his time dining, drinking,
and playing billiards with his old friend. Keeping himself
from returning to his wife's side like a well-trained mongrel.

He *was* a mongrel.

But he was not trained, *by God*.

Except, the moment he had seen Callie standing on the
threshold in her simple white nightdress, looking deliciously
innocent, all his good intentions had fled. She had wondered
where he had been. Had she been jealous? Had she cared?
Worried after him?

Why should he give a damn?

He did not know, other than that he did. He gave a damn about her. He liked her. He wanted her. He had been hungering for her all day. Even as he had distracted himself with drink and good company and Decker's collection of erotic art, she had never been far from his mind.

He feasted upon her lips now as if he could devour them. And the darkness within him wanted to. He wanted to tear her virginal night rail off her luscious body, carry her to his bed, and fuck her all night long.

But she was likely sore, and he could not treat her as if she were no better than a common strumpet. Instead, he would have to settle for kissing her. And for making her come. He wanted her in his bed again tonight, and Decker could go to the devil. Nothing was going to stop him from taking what he wanted.

Taking what was *his*.

Her lips moved, kissing him back. Her tongue glided against his.

Her head drew back, ending the kiss before it had properly begun, a frown marring her forehead. "You taste of whisky."

"How do you know what whisky tastes like?" he demanded, though he knew he should not be surprised.

His new wife was no ordinary English rose. She wore trousers and had been painted in dishabille by Moreau.

"In the ordinary way," she returned. "By drinking it."

"I had some whisky after dinner," he admitted.

And before dinner, as well, but she need not know that. He was not a souse, and he did not often over-imbibe. Indeed, the last time he had done so had been in the wake of Celeste's death over a year ago.

"You had dinner and whisky with your *friend*," Callie said, emphasizing the word. "Whilst I remained here alone, uncertain whether or not you would return?"

"Jealous, love?" he asked, unable to refrain from taunting her. In truth, he had supposed she would be relieved to be rid of him.

After all, she hated him, even if her body responded to his quite well.

She bit her lower lip. "No. Of course not. Why would I be?"

He groaned. "Stop torturing your lips, woman."

Her frown deepened. "I am not yours to order about."

"You are mine now, and if you do not cease nibbling at your lips, I will have to give them quarter the only way I know how."

His cock was ridiculously hard. He ought to have drowned himself in whisky. Perhaps then he would not be so desperate to be inside her again.

Before she could say anything, he kissed her. Why was she so irresistible? Why could he not keep his distance? Exercise some restraint?

She had spent the previous night in his bed. He would be lying if he said he had not known a stab of disappointment when he had entered his chamber this evening and found she was not waiting for him. His reaction to her did not make sense, and he knew it. He had shared a bed with lovers before her. There was nothing special about the act, about the woman.

And yet, he had found her presence oddly comforting. Pleasant.

He kissed her with bruising force, wanting to punish her for the way she made him feel. But all he succeeded in doing was heightening his own desire for her. She kissed him back with equal abandon, her tongue gliding foraying into his mouth. *Good God*, he was not sure which of them was teaching the other a lesson.

The need to pleasure her rose within him, surpassing all else. Consuming him.

He released his grip on her tempting derriere and scooped her into his arms, intending to get her into his bed before she could attempt to escape him. Her mouth jerked from his, ending the kiss.

"What are you doing?" she demanded. "Put me down at once."

He made it to his bed in three strides. "As you wish, princess."

Sin tossed her lightly. Manhandling her was pathetically easy—she was so damned small compared to his hulking frame. She landed in the center of the bed with a feminine squeak.

"I am not...giving you husbandly rights this evening," she protested, scrambling to her knees.

She intended to put up a fight. He was not surprised. Anticipation jolted through him. The hem of her night rail was trapped around her thighs, baring her knees. She was creamy perfection. Not helping his cockstand to abate at all, that sight. Her hair was a wild, dark halo of riotous curls around her face, streaming down her shoulders and back.

He remembered how it had felt in his fingers, silken and cool. How it had felt wrapped around his fingers, too.

"Calm yourself, Callie," he told her with a composure that belied the fire coursing through his veins. He began slipping the buttons on his shirt free, one by one. "I have no intention of bedding you tonight. You are likely sore, are you not? Do you think me an unfeeling cad?"

Her cheeks darkened to a pretty shade of pink. "My lord!"

He grinned. Her embarrassment was strangely endearing.

"Sin," he reminded her as he shed his shirt.

Stripping it off was likely unfair, he knew. He had not failed to note the manner in which her brown-gold gaze had lingered previously upon his chest. He could not deny he found her interest pleasing.

"Sin, I must insist you not speak of such personal matters aloud," she said, her prim governess voice returning.

The dichotomy of proper Callie with the flushed cheeks and the wild woman who kissed him with such skilled ferocity intrigued him. He had supposed their union would be bloodless and cold and marked with their mutual hatred.

But their hatred had sparked flames of a different sort.

And this was one particular inferno he did not mind being scorched by.

He unbuttoned the fall of his trousers next. "There is my prudish governess once more. Will you not undo a few buttons, love? I fear your night rail will choke you in your sleep, that endless line all the way up your throat."

"There is nothing wrong with my nightdress," she argued, fingering the lacey frills at her throat. "Aunt Fanchette said husbands prefer their wives to be clothed modestly when they sleep. She chose this herself."

He could not stifle his laugh. "How the devil does Aunt Feather-wit know what husbands prefer from their wives when she has never had a husband herself?"

Her little white teeth emerged yet again, nibbling at her lip. "You must not call her that dreadful name. It is disrespectful. Aunt Fanchette is the only female relative I have to guide me, with my brother and his wife still on their honeymoon."

True. But he would be damned if he would allow himself to entertain even a drop of remorse for denying her the chance to receive wifely guidance from her new sister-in-law. Had they tarried, Westmorland would have done something to interfere with the wedding. Of that, Sin had no doubt.

He removed his trousers in one swift move, and then bent to pull off his stockings as well. "Do me a favor, wife? Cease relying upon the advice of Aunt Featherbrains, will you?"

"Aunt Fanchette," she snapped, her gaze traveling down his chest to his torso.

When it dipped lower still, his cock twitched. His erection was tenting his bloody smalls, and he knew it. If he were a gentleman, he would turn away or adjust himself. Do something to ease her discomfit. Think about kittens and puppies and elderly dowagers to kill his cockstand.

Instead, he whipped his smalls away as well, standing before her nude, his prick at attention. He ached to stroke himself. To take himself in hand while she watched. To do everything wicked with her. But this was only their second night as husband and wife. No need to debauch her entirely just yet.

They had time.

The rest of their lives.

"Do you truly want to talk about Aunt Fanchette at the moment?" he asked politely as he turned down the gas lamps.

"What are you doing?" she sputtered.

So full of objection and shocked outrage this evening, his little wife. Last night, she had been naked and wanton in his bed, wet and sweet beneath his tongue.

Bathed in darkness, he settled into the bed.

"Going to sleep," he told her. "The hour is late."

"Oh."

Did he detect a note of disappointment in her voice?

He pulled the bedclothes over himself. "Are you going to sit there all night, princess, or are you going to get beneath the covers?"

"I will return to my chamber," she said stiffly.

The bed shifted.

Did she truly think she could flee him that easily?

"You will not," he clipped, reaching for her through the shadows.

Happily, his left hand met with her linen-covered breast. Her nipple was hard, prodding his palm.

She inhaled sharply. "You said you would not enforce your husbandly rights."

But she remained where she was. Her protestations did not fool him. She was a passionate woman, and her body responded to his each time he touched her.

"And so I shall not." He rubbed his thumb over her nipple. "But I must insist you remain here this evening."

"Aunt Fanchette said husbands and wives do not share the same bed."

Her persistence was maddening. Also, somehow, adorable.

Adorable again?

What the hell was she doing to him?

He rolled her beaded nipple between his thumb and forefinger. "Callie?"

"Yes?" Her voice was hesitant.

"If you do not get under the bedclothes where you belong in the next five seconds, I am going to lift your virginal governess nightgown and spank your rump. Is that what you want?"

"You would not dare," she breathed.

Oh yes he would, and he would enjoy it too. One spank, then a kiss to dull the sting. And then he would flip her to her back and sink inside her. Or, better yet, he would put a pillow beneath her and slide into her from behind.

Bloody hell.

There went his cock again.

"Tempt me," he muttered.

"If you ever try such a thing, I will plant you a facer," she warned.

It was his turn to bite his own lip now, to stifle an unexpected burst of laughter. He had no doubt she would try. And though she was a small scrap of silk, he was willing to wager she would manage to land a decent enough blow.

"Hmm," he said on a yawn. The whisky he had consumed was beginning to take its toll upon him. Though he was itching to take her again, he was also exhausted, and his honor was not allowing him to indulge this evening.

His honor and his concern for her. What the devil ailed him?

"Attempt it and you shall see," she warned.

But the bedclothes lifted, and then a rustling filled the silence, punctuating her pronouncement. She was settling in, his little wife. Sin realized a smile was curving his lips. Not one of victory, either. But contentment.

He *liked* having her here with him.

Not that he would ever tell her as much.

Decker was right. He needed to be wary where she was concerned, especially after all the trouble she had caused him. But that was a worry for another day.

"I see you are not willing to test your theory this evening, darling," he could not resist adding.

"You are insufferable, my lord," she accused.

But there was no heat in her voice. In truth, she sounded wearier than he was. Still, he could not let her *my lord* go unanswered.

"Sin," he prompted.

For an indeterminate span of time, she said nothing. There was no noise between them save for the slow, even sound of her breathing.

Stubborn wench.

Just when he was about to slide into slumber, her dulcet voice interrupted the night.

"Sleep well, Sin."

He smiled. "And you, Callie."

He fell asleep to the soft sound of her breathing alongside him, and her presence did not feel wrong at all. Rather, it felt far, far too right.

* * *

Callie woke with a foot pressed against hers. And a hand on her hip. And something thick and long nestled against her bottom.

Her eyes fluttered open to early morning sun.

For a moment, she was disoriented, forgetting where she was and why.

Slowly, reality returned to her. It was her second morning as the Countess of Sinclair. And she was in the earl's bed. In her *husband's* bed.

But this time, unlike the morning before, he was here as well.

And that was his foot large and warm and yet also somehow comforting against hers. That large hand splayed possessively on her hip was his as well. And as for the thick and long object prodding her...

Dear heavens.

She knew precisely what *that* was.

His hand moved then, traveling from her hip in a slow, seductive path to her breast.

Was he awake? His breaths were even and rhythmic, suggestive of slumber. Surely she ought not to disturb him? She should lie still lest she wake the sleeping beast. Yes, that was the only reason she remained as she was whilst his hand cupped her breast. Whilst his thumb moved slowly over her nipple.

Heat pooled between her thighs.

His nail grazed over the taut bud.

She arched into his touch instinctively. It felt so good. Too good. His long fingers tightened on her breast. She swallowed and tried to recall all the reasons why she should not indulge in the wicked sensations he brought to life within her. All the reasons why she should disengage and quietly slip from the bed.

But his presence, hot and warm at her back, kept her here. She liked his foot against hers. She liked his hand on her breast, his slow and even breaths stirring her hair. She liked his nearness, his scent, his bed.

Something was wrong with her, surely. This was the man who had spirited her away from London and coerced her into marrying him. The man she had once believed capable of murder. The man she had vowed to destroy.

She had changed, however. Her feelings had changed. Despite everything, she was attracted to him, and she could not deny that magnetism. But it was more than the physicality of their union. There was good in him; she felt certain of it, even as she feared what it meant.

As his thumb continued to lazily stroke her nipple, she thought back over the curious events of the day before. His disappearance. His return. His claim he had been with a friend. A *male* friend. His insistence she sleep in his bed. Did she dare allow herself tender feelings toward him? Dare believe him? Dare suppose he would be a faithful husband?

More remembrance washed over her.

The sight of him, naked.

Another pulse of need came to life at the apex of her thighs. All the forbidden flesh he had so thoroughly pleasured throbbed with remembrance. His invasion of her body had been unfamiliar and painful. But it had also been...

Blissful.

Delicious.

His foot moved, traveling slowly up her bare calf. The hem of her night rail had twisted around her thighs while she slept. His warmth seeped into her. Never had she thought the stroke of a masculine foot over her skin could be erotic.

Until now.

His hand left her breast, and she almost made a sound of frustration at the loss. Her nipples were painfully sensitive. She never wanted him to stop touching her there. But then, his hand drifted. Over her belly. Back to her hip. Down her thigh. Slowly, he dragged the hem of her nightdress higher. His caress chased every patch of skin he exposed beneath the bedclothes.

She shivered, but not because she was cold. Because the want was suddenly a vibrant, pulsating need quivering to life. His fingers dipped between her legs. She shifted, rolling toward him incrementally, holding her breath as she opened her thighs.

He parted her folds, his touch unerringly finding that bundle of sensation that demanded attention. In that moment, it was the center of her being. Need throbbed. He moved slowly. Softly. Petting her, tantalizing her.

She was impatient. Callie wanted more. Her body felt as if it were inhabited by a stranger. She scarcely recognized herself. She was aching. Needy and wanton and desperate. She undulated against his hand, seeking increased pressure.

Lips feathered over her ear in a soft kiss. "Are you awake, sweet?"

Sweet.

She liked when he called her that, too. Callie thought about feigning slumber. Pretending she was asleep so he could not see the effect he had upon her. But what would be the point in that? They were husband and wife. Every time he touched her, all her good intentions turned to ash and scattered in the wind.

"Yes," she admitted.

His fingers slid lower. One dipped inside her, stretching her. "Good."

In and out, his finger went, sliding with ease. She was slick, and the friction felt wonderful and frustrating all at once. He nuzzled her throat, kissing and sucking and nibbling a sensitive place. She stared at the wall, the dark squares where all the pictures gracing the faded damask had once hung.

"Did you sell them?" she asked suddenly, bothered anew at the thought of how near penury he had been.

There was pockets to let and then there was desperation.

His finger stilled, lodged inside her. "Pardon?"

"The pictures," she clarified. "They are almost all gone, and—Oh!"

She ended on an exclamation, because he curled his finger and sank it deeper, finding a new, deliciously sensitive place inside.

"Oh is right." He bit her ear. Not hard enough to even sting, but with just enough possessive pressure to make a surge of need pound through her. "Never mind that, Callie. I want inside you. Here."

His finger retreated and then sank into her again, joined by a second.

"Yes." It was all she could manage to say.

"How do you feel?" he asked against her ear, still tormenting her with his long, knowing fingers.

Words? He wanted speech from her? She could scarcely even think any longer. He had turned her mind to rubble.

Her body was awash with need. His thumb found the bud of her sex, swirling over it.

He nibbled on her throat. "Are you sore, sweet?"

"Yes," she gasped, her hips pumping against his wicked ministrations.

He stilled.

"No," she corrected herself. "Sin, please. Do not stop."

He growled against her neck. "You are so wet for me. So tight. Tell me what you want."

She did not know what to say. Instinct told her what she wanted. He moved his fingers in and out in a tantalizing rhythm. She wanted him to replace his fingers with his manhood. To fill her the way he had on their wedding night.

"Callie," he whispered, his breath hot against her skin, his teeth nipping again. "Say it. Tell me what you want."

"I want you to make love to me," she managed.

He withdrew his fingers and rolled her onto her back. In an instant, the bedclothes were gone, and he had settled himself between her thighs. His rod was thick and stiff and huge. She reached for him, wanting to touch him. Just one pass of her fingertips over the rigid length. He was warm, his heat searing her. Surprisingly smooth, soft as velvet.

A groan sounded from deep in his chest, and she released him, wondering if she had done something wrong in her neophyte enthusiasm. "Forgive me," she hastened to say. "Did I hurt you?"

"Hell no," he reassured her, taking her hand in his and bringing it back to his length. "I love your hand on my cock. Touch me again, sweet. Touch me all you like."

He wrapped her fingers around him, showing her how to stroke and bring him pleasure. Touching him like this sent a pang of pure, unadulterated need to her core. She loved the sense of power she felt—knowing he enjoyed what she was doing. Watching the way his dark gaze traveled over her, devouring her.

She realized then that she was still wearing her night rail, bunched up around her waist, whilst he was completely nude. The sight of him between her bare, parted thighs, his body naked and so blatantly masculine and ready to claim her, made her heart pound. She ran her thumb over the head of him, catching a bead of moisture leaking from the tip.

The urge to taste him as he had done to her—wild, wicked, shocking—could not be contained. Holding his gaze, she brought her thumb to her lips and sucked. He tasted salty and earthy.

"Damn it, Callie," he growled, grabbing his stiff cock once more before guiding himself to her entrance.

They were perfectly aligned. She ran her tongue over the pad of her thumb, making sure she got every drop of him. He hooked her legs around his waist and plunged forward, sheathing himself inside her in one powerful thrust.

This time, there was no pain. There was only the glorious sensation of being filled. Her body had never felt more alive. All the breath fled her lungs. She reached for him, pulling him down upon her, wanting to be as close to him as she could possibly get. Wanting to merge with him, to become a part of him.

His mouth slammed down on hers. She held him tight, banishing every other thought, fear, worry, concern—everything—from her mind except him. Her husband.

Sin.

He moved then, withdrawing almost completely from her body before sliding back inside, deep, so deep. She kissed him back with all the fury of the pent-up emotion and desire rioting within her. His tongue was in her mouth. Her hands found the hard planes of his shoulders, her nails scoring over his heated flesh. He surrounded her, filled her, consumed her.

And she wanted it. Wanted everything he had to give her, all the decadent sensation, the awakening of her body. Everything was Sin—his scent, his taste, the heavy weight of him atop her, his cock gliding inside her passage, his dark gaze boring into hers as he claimed her. She could not look away. Could not blink.

Again and again, he sank inside her. The feeling of him was exquisite. She clenched on him, dragging him deep. Her body bowed from the bed. She could not get enough.

Sin's lips tore from hers as he broke the kiss, his breathing harsh and ragged. Bracing himself on one arm, he stilled in his claiming long enough to grasp the neck of her night rail and tear it in two. Buttons popped off. The sound of the fabric rending echoed in the early morning silence, blending with their desperate breaths and her wildly beating heart.

"My night rail," she managed to protest.

"It was in the bloody way," he said, his glittering eyes boring into hers.

And then he lowered his head, kissing the peak of her breast. He sucked a nipple into his mouth, moving at a faster pace. The combination of his hot mouth drawing on her breast and his cock ramming in and out of her body was electric. Too much. Her hands sank into his hair, grasping handfuls. His hair was thick and luxurious. Her every sense was heightened to the point of painful pleasure.

Her nightdress lay in shredded halves, but she forgot to care. His fingers found the bud of her sex again, toying with her. It was all she needed. Pure bliss rocketed through her. He bit her nipple, then sucked harder as a potent rush infused her, bathing her core in wetness. Her eyes fluttered closed at last, her head falling back upon the pillow as wave after wave of intense pleasure pounded down. Bright bursts of light, sparkling like stars, lived behind her eyelids.

She clasped him to her, unable to muffle her cry.

His name.

"Sin!"

"Yes, sweet." He raked his teeth over the swell of her breast, then moved to her other nipple as he continued pumping into her. "Come for me. Come on me."

She did. His words, his mouth on her breast, his cock plunging into her, his possession, all mingled. She was mindless, helpless to do anything other than move with him, to let him feast upon her and give him her complete surrender. The second explosion of desire took her by surprise. He thrust into her and took her lips in another kiss.

Suddenly, his body stiffened, and the warm rush of his release filled her. Another set of tremors rocked through her body. She cupped his face and held him there, kissing him as he collapsed against her, pinning her to the mattress with his big body. They kissed long and slow, their tongues tangling, their ragged breaths uniting.

They were one.

He ended the kiss first, raising his head to stare down at her. "I am probably crushing you."

"No," she said, shaking her head as her eyes searched his. She did not know what she was seeking. "I like the way you feel."

Far, far too much.

He caressed her cheek with his thumb, his expression almost boyish. "And I like the way you feel."

The more time she spent with him, the more impossible it became for her to believe he was the man she had once thought him. She caught her lower lip between her teeth, worrying it, feeling emotions she did not want to feel.

"Stop torturing your beautiful mouth," he said, kissing her swiftly before withdrawing from her and rolling away.

He thought her mouth was beautiful? She lay there, pressing a tentative touch to her lips, wondering just what manner of man her husband truly was.

CHAPTER 16

I cannot wait to marry my next victim, dear reader. Poor, naïve,
innocent Miss V. I will take great enjoyment in debauching her...
~from **Confessions of a Sinful Earl**

He was a ruthless savage.

He had torn Callie's night rail to shreds and slammed into her, riding her without thought and care. Because she had felt so bloody good, all tight, slick heat. Because she had touched his cock and then licked his seed from her thumb.

Because she was an erotic siren sent from the fiery depths of hell to torment him.

And because he possessed no restraint, no control at all when it came to her. Decker was right. He needed to exercise greater caution when it came to her. But how the devil was he to do that when he could not think straight in her presence?

Sin ran a hand over his jaw and tried to stop fantasizing about throwing his wife over his shoulder and hauling her from his study. There were a great deal of tasks awaiting him. His wife had plans to hire new servants, refurbish his pathetic excuse for a townhome, and Lord knew what else.

The only new hire he planned to concern himself with was a replacement nursemaid for his mother. A better nursemaid. One who did not get into the laudanum with alarming frequency. But that was his affair and not a worry with which he would encumber his wife. His mother's condition was too delicate to burden her with the addition of a new face. She still thought Celeste was alive, when she had moments of lucidity.

Mama would never understand that he had a new wife now.

A new wife who was currently seated opposite him, clutching a book and pen in her dainty hands, making notes in her flowery script. At least he knew what she had been doing yesterday in his absence. The perplexing woman had made a list.

"What is left?" he asked her now. "You hardly need my approval for household changes. Hire as many domestics as you like. Hang all the pictures you wish. Tear down the wall coverings. Replace the Axminster."

"The piano needs to be tuned," she said without looking up.

Hell. She had been in the music room?

"Have it tuned, then." He paused. "Do you play?"

She glanced up, her expression startled. "Of course."

"I would like to hear you play, after the old monstrosity is in proper working order again," he said.

A smile curved her lush lips. "I would like that."

If she kept looking at him that way, he was going to ravish her right here on his study desk.

"Excellent." He cleared his throat, feeling foolish and overwhelmed with lust all at once. He needed to put some distance between them. With haste. "Was that all you wished to discuss, then? I do have some other matters requiring my attention today."

Her expression fell, and he felt like an arse.

"Oh, of course. Forgive me, my lord." She turned her attention back to her list. "There is just one more thing. Your butler, Langdon."

Ah. Good old Langdon.

"What of him?" he asked.

"He is quite deaf, as you know," she said calmly.

"He is hard of hearing," Sin corrected. "What of it?"

"He also appears to be near-sighted," she added.

Sin sighed. Of course she would have taken note, a mere few days into their marriage. She was a dreadfully observant female. And a beautiful, maddening, vexing one.

"His eyesight has been growing worse of late," he allowed.

"Have you kept him on because you could not pay another butler?" she queried, her tone crisp.

He was not accustomed to discussing household matters with his wife—this was rather a novel situation. Celeste had not bothered to run the household at all. She had deferred all the details to the housekeeper. That Callie was already taking an interest in their home and servants was…pleasing. It was a sign that she meant to take their union seriously.

A strange sensation slid down his spine.

How was it possible that the woman he had coerced into marriage—the woman he had not wanted to wed at all—was already a better wife than Celeste? He tried to think upon the first days of his marriage to her, and all he could remember was a vast sea of disappointment and shopping.

Celeste had adored shopping.

And gambling.

And other men's cocks.

"Sin?" Callie prodded, bringing him back from the angry

maw of the past. "You did not answer my question about Langdon."

Sin sighed. The devil of a headache was descending upon him. He pinched the bridge of his nose. "I will speak with him. If you deem it necessary to hire a replacement, we shall. But he has been an excellent and trusted retainer, all these years. I would like to see him situated in the country, with a pleasant cottage. Eloise would enjoy that as well, I think."

"Mrs. Langdon?" Callie asked, frowning. "I had not realized he was married."

"He is not. Eloise is his Skye terrier," Sin explained. "If you have not yet met her, you shall. She usually accompanies him, keeping near so he does not trip over her. It is the oddest thing, but I vow that little dog knows Langdon has difficulty with his sight."

Realizing his wife was watching him with a new, curious expression on her lovely countenance, Sin decided to stop speaking.

"You allow your butler to keep a pet, and you know the dog's name," Callie said, eying him as if she had never seen him before.

"Of course." Sin frowned at her. "I can hardly part Langdon from his beloved companion. She keeps him out of trouble."

"Hmm," his wife said, before lowering her head to peruse her list once more.

He did not particularly care for her noncommittal hum of a response. "What do you mean by that?"

"You are unexpected," she said simply. "I am beginning to think you are not at all the man I thought you were."

Odd. He was beginning to suspect the same about her. What a pair they were.

Decker's words of warning returned to him, reminding him he dared not indulge in such fantasies. He must think with his mind and not his prick. But the trouble was, they seemed to be one and the same.

"While I am grateful you no longer think me a raving lunatic, do not underestimate me, my dear. You will find I am a more-than-worthy opponent when tried," he cautioned.

After all, it would not do for her to think him vulnerable or weak. Or, worse, for her to somehow develop some maudlin notion of him.

"I have already found that," she said softly. Sadly.

He was the cause of that sadness, and he knew a sharp stab of pain at the reminder.

Preposterous, that. Why should he care? Why should her upset bother him at all? She had done her damnedest to make a mockery of him before all society and make certain he had no hopes of saving himself from ruin.

He cleared his throat. They were venturing into dangerous territory. "Will that be all, wife? As I said, I do have other matters requiring my attention."

"Of course. That will be all for now." She rose and dipped into a formal curtsy as if he had not just shagged her silly hours before and torn her nightdress into shreds. "Will I see you at dinner?"

No, he wanted to say, for it would be far safer to keep his distance.

He stood and offered her a cursory bow in return. "Yes."

* * *

Sin opened the door to the large, private apartments where his mother lived and stepped over the threshold, closing the door hastily at his back. There was a large sitting room, where she almost never sat any longer, and an adjoining bed chamber overlooking the small gardens where she had once tended roses. These days, she was often in her bed.

A quiet, withered shell of her former self.

The nursemaid was seated in his mother's favorite chair, working on a piece of needlework. She stood at his entrance.

"My lord," said Miss Wright, dropping into a passable curtsy. "I was not expecting you to visit today, so soon after your nuptials."

"I wish to see my mother," he said coolly.

His dislike for Miss Wright was palpable, crawling up his throat, clenching his gut. Already, he had begun undertaking the task of finding a more suitable replacement. She was tall and broad, but spare of form, rather like a wizened oak. And although she was calm and composed in his presence, he had seen bruising in the shape of fingerprints on his mother's wrists not long ago that had sent him into a fury. He had warned her.

Miss Wright had claimed she knew nothing of the bruising, that perhaps his mother had gotten them during one of her nighttime wanderings. She had suggested he install a lock on the inside of his mother's apartments so that she could not leave without the key. But he had balked at locking his mother inside her apartments like an animal in a menagerie.

"Of course, my lord," Miss Wright said. "She was just napping now. I gave her a touch of laudanum to calm her about an hour or so ago. She was in another one of her fits."

He searched the nursemaid's eyes, wondering if she had tippled from the laudanum herself as well. He had no proof that she was consuming his mother's laudanum aside from the rapidity with which it disappeared, according to his ledgers, and the alacrity with which Mama found her way out of the apartments in the evenings.

"I will not wake her if she is asleep," he said. "Thank you."

Miss Wright inclined her head and dipped into another curtsy, this one more abbreviated than the last. He stalked past her, for the first time in a year or more noting the disparity between his mother's apartments and the rest of his home. Toward the end, he had forbidden Celeste from visiting Mama for more than one reason. Her blatant thievery had been chief amongst them. His mother's apartments were cheerful and decorated with the pastoral landscapes she preferred, along with many pictures of the Shropshire countryside, the place she had spent much of her girlhood.

Everything that would comfort her.

Nothing that would further upset her.

Anything for his mother.

He opened the door to her chamber and found her sitting up in bed, propped against pillows, her snow-white hair unbound and wild around her face. Her sky-blue eyes seemed far away at first as she took him in. But then she held out her hands.

"Ferdy, my love, is that you?" she asked, sounding confused.

His heart broke as he stepped forward and took his mother's hands, seating himself in the chair alongside her bed. He had learned long ago not to correct her unless it was an absolute necessity. She grew confused and disconsolate when anyone tried to separate the past from the present. Sin no longer existed to his mother on most days, and it was something he had been forced to accept.

"How are you, my dear?" he asked instead of answering her question.

Pretending to be the German archduke who had most likely sired him gave Sin no pleasure at all. But for Mama, he would do it if he must.

"I am well, Ferdy," she said, sounding like a breathless girl in spite of her advanced years and the toll her illness had taken upon her. "I do so miss dancing with you. What was it we danced that night?"

"The mazurka?" he guessed, for it was a dance she had oft mentioned.

"Oh yes." Her gnarled fingers tightened upon his, and a beautiful smile lit her face. "The mazurka! How could I forget? I dare say my feet scarcely even touched the floor. I have never felt as at home as I have felt in your arms, Ferdy."

Sin swallowed against a rush of pain that his mother more often than not no longer recognized him, not even on her good days. Instead, she mistook him for a former paramour.

"How is Miss Wright treating you?" he asked, changing the subject.

"Not well," his mother pronounced grimly. "I hope her cunny falls off."

Sin battled his shock. His mother had always been a quiet and polite woman. One of the first signs of her ailment had arrived in her inability to control her tongue. Suddenly, she had been cursing and muttering oaths at dowagers and spouting all manner of vulgarities, without qualms.

"What has she done?" he pressed. "Has she hurt you in any way? Has she handled you in a rough manner?"

"I asked for cocoa tarts," Mama said, raising a brow, "and the bitch gave me pudding."

"Scandalous," he managed. "Have you been walking in the evening again? Rearranging the busts?"

"I don't like their eyes," his mother said. "Sightless eyes. Not looking anywhere. Preposterous little villains, always watching me. What are they looking for? Miserable, gloomy arses, the lot of them."

He could not argue about the busts as he did not care for

them either. "You know you are not to be lifting them," he chided gently. "You could do yourself injury."

"I am always doing everything wrong, am I not?" Her eyes welled with tears.

And for the second time that day, he felt like a complete arse. "I am merely concerned with your welfare, dear heart. Do not fret over it. The busts have all been restored to proper order. It is you I worry about."

"Oh, my darling lad. Do not worry over me." Mama smiled, then released his hands. "I have never felt finer. When will my grandchild be born? Celeste told me, you know. Where is that girl?"

Her abrupt change—going from mistaking him for her Ferdy to realizing he was her son—was also commonplace. But nevertheless, navigating it remained difficult. He did not know precisely when his mother had become frail-minded. Years ago, perhaps. It had begun slowly, with simple things.

She had forgotten words. Names. Places. Later, it had grown worse. She forgot him. She became paranoid. One day, she had become utterly convinced that Langdon was planting spiders in her chamber. Another, she had cursed her best friend, and then announced she was not wearing her drawers at a garden party.

But it had been some time since she had mentioned his dead wife. And her grandchild, which had been stillborn. Sin's daughter. At least, he had believed Opal had been his. Another wave of sadness hit him at the memory of the little angel brought into the world too soon. Years had passed, but he would never forget.

"Mama, do you remember me?" he asked softly, focusing upon his mother's seeming lucidity instead.

She had sudden, beautiful flashes when she seemed to return to herself, like a sky after a brutal rainstorm. But always, inevitably, the clouds returned. Eventually, he knew, they would forever remain.

"Justin," she said. "Of course I know you, my wonderful son. Why do you not visit me more often?"

"I visit you almost every day," he reminded her. "If you ever have need of me, I am here. Ask Miss Wright or any of the staff."

"Oh Ferdy," she said, smiling again. "What would I do without you?"

And just like that, she was gone.

Again.

"Would you take some tea with me?" he asked her.

"Oh, yes Ferdy. I will *always* take tea with you," Mama said.

He could not keep himself from wishing that once, just once, his mother would take tea with *him* again. But he also knew that was not likely. Her glimmers of lucidity grew fainter by the day.

Soon, there would come a time when she would not know him at all any longer.

He had never dreaded another day more, aside from the day his daughter had been commended to the earth.

"I will ring for the tea," he said, rising.

"Have the girl ring for it, Ferdy," Mama called. "What is her name, again? The trollop ought to earn her bloody keep. And you will tell her I want tarts, won't you? Not the pudding. I have never been able to abide by pudding. I would sooner eat a fucking shoe."

"Of course," he agreed, wondering where the devil his mother had gotten her colorful vocabulary.

Then again, perhaps it was best he never knew. Some secrets were best kept.

CHAPTER 17

Do you know how delicious it is, dear reader, to fool everyone around you? To know that you have murdered two innocents and you will never be imprisoned for your crimes? It is a wondrous secret, and yet, confiding in you is equally thrilling. Sooner or later, the truth must be told...

~from **Confessions of a Sinful Earl**

*H*er husband was keeping a secret from her, and Callie did not like it.

Not.

One.

Bit.

He had been attentive that morning in the bedchamber. Even in his study, he had been patient. He had listened to her concerns and given her carte blanche to correct the deficiencies in domestics and the running of the household. He had given her leave to replace the faded, thin carpets. To have new wall coverings installed. To acquire art to adorn the walls.

Already, she had a painting of Monsieur Moreau's in mind, along with some of her favorite artists.

And then, Sin had disappeared once more.

Oh, he had claimed he had pressing matters requiring his attention. But Callie had not trusted him. Wisely, as it turned out. She had not forgotten that when she had been given her tour of her new home, one room had not been included. Callie had been so overwhelmed by the newness of her situation and surroundings, the mysterious apartments had slipped from her mind. Until she had witnessed her husband disappearing into them earlier that afternoon.

And yet, when she had inquired, at dinner, as to what he had been about all afternoon, he had smiled a bland, false charmer's grin and told her he had spent the day in his study.

He was a liar after all.

She had known that—suspected it. But the confirmation gave her no joy. Especially not after the closeness she had felt with him just that very morning.

The dessert course was removed. Unlike the rest of the dinner, the raspberry fool had been appealing. And yet, Callie had not been tempted to eat it. The bland fare prepared by her husband's cook had grown increasingly unpalatable with each course.

She attempted a gracious smile she scarcely felt. This was her first night at dinner as a wife, and she was furious with her husband. She scarcely knew the proper etiquette for such a moment.

"If you will excuse me, my lord?" Callie asked, averting her gaze.

She could not bear to look at him just now. Not when she had given him every opportunity to tell her the truth. She had asked several leading questions.

And he had failed to volunteer the pertinent information.

"Where are you going?" he shot back. "You need not run

off so quickly. And you scarcely touched your dinner this evening. What is amiss, princess?"

Princess again.

Not *Callie* as she had been that morning in his bed. Nor *sweet*.

She hated herself for taking note of the distinction.

"I am tired," she said, and that was not entirely a falsehood. "I will leave you to your evening entertainments."

He stood when she did. "If you are retiring early, perhaps I will join you. I find myself rather exhausted also."

Callie hesitated, reluctant to say too much before the lone footman who was attending them. Her husband took note of the direction of her gaze and promptly dismissed the servant, leaving them alone in the dining room, standing at opposite ends of the table. Their positioning was rather symbolic, she thought.

"What is it you wished to say to me?" he demanded the moment the footman had gone. "Your face is very expressive, wife. It gives you away."

She hated that he read her so well.

"I saw you," she blurted.

He raised a dark brow, looking regal and sinful all at once. "You saw me when? Where? During dinner? I expect so as we were seated across from each other."

She did not smile at his gentle teasing. "Going into the mystery apartments this afternoon when you said you were in your study."

"Ah." His expression hardened. "And you are suspicious of me, are you not?"

His tone of voice and demeanor suggested she ought not to be. He sounded hurt. As if he had expected better of her. Which was ludicrous, because he was the one keeping secrets. She was the one who had every right to doubt him.

"I have made no secret of my distrust," she said calmly, holding his gaze.

His jaw hardened. "Do you still think me guilty of murder?"

Did she? Once, the answer would have been easy—a resounding yes.

Now, she did not know for certain. And there remained the matter of his reputation. Of whether or not she could truly trust him. There was so much she needed to learn about him.

"You have not given me reason to fear you," she hedged.

"How gratifying," he snapped, stalking around the edge of the table.

He was angry. She told herself she would not retreat, even as he crowded her with his large, powerful body.

Callie tipped up her chin, all too aware of his greater height. "What do you want from me, my lord?"

"Honesty."

"I want the same of you." She searched his shuttered gaze, seeking answers. "Why are you keeping me from that chamber? And why did you hide yourself within it this afternoon and then lie to me?"

He caught her chin in a grip that was tender but firm. "Tell me something, princess. How is it that you can give yourself to me so thoroughly, that you can lie beneath me crying out with your pleasure, and all the while believe me a depraved murderer?"

His thumb traced a path of pure fire over her bottom lip as he awaited her answer.

His touch was clouding her mind. Sending unwanted pulses of warmth between her thighs. Making her come to life for him. Drat him and the way he made her feel. Curse him and the weakness he inflicted upon her.

She swallowed. "Why are you keeping secrets from me?"

"Why are you watching me?" he returned. "Hmm? Am I a prisoner in my own bloody household?"

"I was your prisoner once," she reminded him bitterly. "It is the reason we are now trapped in this hopeless marriage."

"Hopeless, is it?" His voice went cold. "Need I bring forth the true reason for our marriage, princess? Your little vendetta and all the lies you were intent upon spreading about me are what landed you in this hopeless marriage. Nothing else. I would have happily married Miss Vandenberg had she not cried off."

Callie was certain he would have terrified the quiet, shy heiress. She and Miss Vandenberg had only met once, but Callie did not think her impression had been mistaken. Miss Vandenberg was meek as a mouse. The very notion of Sin kissing her and making love to her as he had done to Callie was…

Untenable.

Infuriating.

"I would wager my dowry compares quite nicely to hers, and I would also wager that you would have terrified the poor woman. *Confessions of a Sinful Earl* did her a favor."

"Oh?" His hand moved, tracing her throat, grasping her gently, his thumb pressing to the hollow where she knew her pulse was pounding. "Is that how you justify your misdeeds, madam? Perhaps I was in love with Miss Vandenberg. Did you ever think of that?"

His query and his anger, coupled with his hand on her neck, gave her pause.

Of course she had not contemplated that. She had supposed he was marrying Miss Vandenberg for her fortune because he was desperately in need of one. It shamed her to realize she had been so focused upon her own need for vengeance that she had not stopped to think of who she might be hurting in the process. Or of the possibility that Sin was innocent.

"What is the matter, wife?" he asked silkily, his fingers tightening incrementally. "Nothing to say for yourself? Tell me how it feels to be such a temple of perfection. I truly want to know."

"*Were* you in love with her?" she asked, hating herself for asking the question.

Hating the possibility his answer would be *yes* even more.

He lowered his head, until his lips were nearly grazing hers. His breath was hot. His mouth was a temptation she knew from experience she could not resist.

"It is a bit late to ask that question," he growled, his lip curling into a sneer. "Do you not think, princess?"

He was attempting to intimidate her, she realized, and it was likely because he was trying to deflect her attention from the secret chamber. "That is not an answer, my lord. Were you in love with Miss Vandenberg?"

His thumb rubbed slowly over her throat in a predatory caress that should not make her breathless and yet somehow did. "No."

What was wrong with her that she liked being his prey?

The urge to touch him back could no longer be contained. She found her daring and caught his face in her hands. The fine prickle of his whiskers against her palms was welcome and yet uncomfortable all at once.

Fitting.

Pleasure and pain.

"What are you hiding in that chamber?" she demanded.

"Answer me first." His gaze slid to her lips, but his hold remained upon her throat, part threat, part caress. "Do you think me a murderer?"

She stared into his eyes, unable to look away, searching herself for her response. He was a confusing and complex man, the Earl of Sinclair. But even when he had abducted her, he had been concerned about her eating, about her sleeping on the floor. She had smashed a figurine over his head, and he had kissed her…

He confused her.

Left her flustered and aching and hopelessly muddled in the head and heart.

"No." Her answer left her suddenly. The moment the word fled her lips, she had to admit it was true. She did not believe he had hurt Alfred any longer. And nor did she believe he had killed his former countess. Callie had been alone with her husband enough to know she did not need to fear him. But not enough to know she could trust him. "That does not mean I accept you keeping secrets from me, however."

His expression shifted. The anger seemed to drain from him. In its place was, unless she was mistaken, sadness. "You do not know what you are asking of me."

She searched his gaze, trying to find answers that continued to elude her. "Honesty, Sin, as I said. That is all I am asking."

His lips thinned. He was still near enough to kiss. A tip of her head, a push forward onto her toes, and his mouth would be upon hers. She told herself she should not want that kiss. She ought not to desire his mouth upon hers. And yet, she was helpless when it came to him.

"You want to know what I was doing in that chamber today?" he asked abruptly.

"Yes." Her answer was instant. "Of course I do. If this marriage of ours has a hope at all, we must be as honest with each other as possible, Justin."

His nostrils flared, and she knew it was at the use of his Christian name. "What makes you think I give a proper goddamn if this marriage has any hope or not, princess?"

His response filled her with disappointment. "If that is how you feel, then this dialogue is a moot point."

But when she attempted to free herself from his hold, he held fast, his grip on her throat tightening just enough to keep her frozen in place. To remind her which of them was the more powerful when it came to strength. "Calm yourself, little wife. This is not easy for me."

His frank admission caught her by surprise.

She could not be sure if he was talking about their marriage or about her request for his honesty. "What is not easy for you?"

His sensual lips compressed. "Having a wife again."

She wished his answer had been different. "I did not want to marry you. This marriage was forced upon me."

"It was forced upon us both." His tone was cool, his expression unreadable. "Need I remind you of that? Of all the reasons why?"

Her patience snapped. "What are you so afraid of me discovering? Why will you not simply tell me what you are hiding from me and why?"

"Because there is nothing simple about it and you are once more being a brat, madam," he bit out.

She was still cupping his face in her hands, the heat of him searing her. Part of her wanted to rage at him. Part of her wanted to slap him. Or kiss him.

No, not that.

"What a pair we make," she said then, shaking herself from her thoughts and trying to tamp down the effect he had upon her. "For you are being an arse to my brat."

His jaw clenched beneath her touch. "Fine. You want to know what lies within that chamber, I will show you. But first, I will have your promise that you do not speak while we are in the chamber unless I ask you to do so."

What the devil was in those apartments?

"You have my promise," she said without hesitation, releasing her hold on him at last when she realized how desperately they clung to each other.

He nodded, then removed his grasp as well. "Come."

With a small jolt of unease, she settled her hand in the crook of his arm and allowed him to lead her from the dining room. Whatever it was, she was about to find out.

* * *

Sin paused at the door to his mother's apartments, turning to his wife. "Remember, no speaking. I will speak for you."

Her full lips took on a mulish moue, but she surprised him with her acquiescence. "I understand."

Undoubtedly, she did not like the notion of holding her tongue. But he could not afford to take the chance that she would upset or confuse Mama. Hell, he was not even sure he could trust Callie with the information that his mother was frail-minded. If she were to unleash her poison pen yet again, she would have the world believing he would soon descend into madness as well.

He had been biding his time, wanting to wait until he was more assured of his standing with his new wife, to make the revelation. But she had forced his hand, and he knew her well enough to suspect she would sneak into his mother's chambers alone to investigate if he continued to evade her questions and bar her from entering the apartments.

Once more, she had left him without a choice.

He opened the door and gestured for her to proceed him into Mama's sitting room. Miss Wright was within, seated with her needlework as she had been earlier in the day. This time, however, she bore the appearance of someone who had dozed off. She blinked slowly and rose as if doing so required an elaborate effort.

She curtseyed, and Sin could not help but to note the glazed quality of her gaze, the dilated pupils. "My lord, my lady."

"Miss Wright, I would like to introduce you to my wife, the Countess of Sinclair," he said. "My lady, this is Miss Wright, my mother's companion and nursemaid."

His wife's shocked inhalation was the only indication of her surprise.

She smiled warmly, however, her countenance elegant and composed. "I am pleased to meet you, Miss Wright."

"It is my honor, my lady," said Miss Wright.

Her speech sounded lucid enough, though he remained suspicious of her.

"Is my mother awake?" he asked. "Lady Sinclair would like to meet her as well."

"She would not take her dinner this evening," Miss Wright said, frowning. "I saw to it that she swallowed some broth and a bit of tea, but she may be sleeping now."

"There has not been much change since my earlier visit, then?" He already knew the answer, but this question was for his wife's benefit rather than his.

"I am afraid not, my lord."

He inclined his head. "If she is sleeping, we will not disturb her. Thank you, Miss Wright."

Sin did not often visit his mother after dinner. Nights were typically worse for her, he had discovered. It was as if the happy veil that enshrouded her mind was replaced. She became angry and sometimes closed herself off. He preferred the happy Mama who thought he was Ferdy and relived the magic of her youth.

But he was not making this visit for himself.

He was making it for the woman at his side, so that she could be reassured. So that she could understand the magnitude of the secret he had been keeping from her. Because— God help him—he cared what she thought. He cared about the tentative, fragile truce they had formed since becoming husband and wife.

Fool that he was.

He led Callie to his mother's chamber, cursing himself for his weakness where this woman was concerned. Telling himself he had already had the devil's own marriage and a wife who had made an art of causing him misery. He had no reassurance he could trust the woman at his side.

And he was about to introduce her to the most beloved person in his life.

The door clicked open to reveal Mama was not in her bed but rather standing at the window in her night rail. Her white hair was a knotted, matted mess, revealing what he had not seen during his earlier visit. A sharp arrow of anger found its home in his gut. Miss Wright ought to have been brushing her bloody hair instead of napping into her needlework.

As if sensing his anger, Callie slid her hand from his elbow and tangled her fingers in his. Her touch was gentle, reassuring. And Sin was suddenly grateful, so damned grateful, for the woman he had married in desperation and fury. There was far more to her than he had supposed. She was a complicated woman, but he was beginning to see that she was not the vicious, heartless shrew he had once been eager to believe her.

He cleared his throat, chasing the unwanted knot of emotion from it. "Good evening," he said to Mama, who was still trapped in her vigil at the window.

She turned at last, her gaze going first to Sin and then to Callie. "Ferdy! Why the devil have you brought the duchess with you? You promised to see me alone when you came to call. You know I cannot abide that bitch."

She was agitated this evening. Her voice was cutting, lacking the whimsy that so often infiltrated it these days. The curses peppering her speech told him she was in one of her more fragile moods.

"Calm yourself, Mama," he cajoled, pulling Callie with him as he approached his mother. "It is Justin."

"Justin?" Her brow furrowed, confusion clouding her countenance. "Who is Justin? Do not play tricks on me, Ferdy, it is not bloody well sporting of you. Why would you bring *her* here? Do you not know how much I love you?"

Although he knew Mama could not control the vagaries of her mind, he could not quell the disappointment flooding him. He had not expected her to remember or recognize him any more this evening than she had earlier in the day, or the day before that. His mother's mind was mostly trapped in a past where he did not exist.

Callie gave his fingers another squeeze and then released him, moving forward to put a soothing arm around his mother's back. "Ferdy brought me here to tend to your hair, my dear. I am hardly a duchess, as you can see. Come and have a seat. I shall fetch a brush."

Sin watched, amazed, as his wife swiftly guided Mama to a chair and saw her settled. He was not certain which surprised him more—Callie's swift understanding of the situation, or his mother's easy capitulation. Mama did not ordinarily do well with new faces, which would make replacing Miss Wright all the more challenging. Change upset her.

"I would love to have my hair brushed," Mama said, a note of cheer entering her tone. "My lady's maid has not been doing her duty, I fear."

Her time-worn hands went to her hair, investigating the tangles.

Callie discovered a silver-handled brush on a nearby table and cast him a shy smile as their gazes met. More gratitude hit him. *Thank you*, he mouthed to her. She nodded and turned to her task, gently running the brush through his mother's hair.

"Do come closer, Ferdy," Mama called to him then. "I can scarcely see you over there."

Sin obligingly crossed the chamber and seated himself in a chair opposite his mother while Callie continued her ministrations with slow, careful motions. Of all the reactions he had anticipated—and feared—she would have, compassion and tender understanding had not been one of them.

"Is this better?" he asked with an indulgent smile for his mother's sake.

"Much better, yes." Mama smiled. "You are such a handsome fellow. You look like someone I used to know. What is your name?"

"Justin," he told her.

"Justin," Mama repeated softly, as if she were testing the name. "A fine name. It means just and fair."

"I am not certain I have always lived up to my name," he said grimly, his gaze flitting to Callie.

Sin was far more apt.

"I knew a little lad named Justin once," Mama said softly. "He was the most beautiful boy, with big, dark, sparkling eyes."

Something in his chest constricted. It was at once a relief and a painful burden to know that some memories of him lingered in his mother's mind. He was not entirely gone. Though he feared the inevitability of a day when she did not even have these brief moments of recollection. They had been growing increasingly scarce in the last year.

"Would you tell me about him?" Callie asked before Sin could answer.

"He was mischievous," Mama said fondly. "He had his father's disposition, always ready to smile, and a bit of the devil in him. Once, he caught a bucket full of toads and let them run wild in the drawing room. You ought to have heard the maids and their bloody squealing."

Callie raised a brow, meeting his gaze over his mother's head. "He sounds like he must have been quite the little rogue."

"I had forgotten about that," he admitted with a wry grin.

He *had* been a devilish lad.

"The sweetest rogue, with an endless heart," Mama said, her smile abruptly dying. "Where the hell did he go? Have you seen him?"

Her agitation was rising again. She fussed with her night rail, rearranging it in her lap. Before he could offer a soothing word, Callie calmly patted her shoulder. "Shall I braid your hair?"

"Oh, yes," Mama said, the distraction appearing to calm her. "My lady's maid is a lazy whore. She never braids my hair any longer. Will you be my lady's maid now, dear?"

Sin winced at his mother's effortless vulgarity. The complexities of the mind were beyond his ken. Perhaps he ought to have warned Callie of his mother's singular new vocabulary beforehand.

"I would be more than happy to braid your hair for you, each day if you like," Callie told her, using the brush to separate his mother's hair into three equal sections.

"I would like that," Mama agreed, smiling. Her fingers went still in her lap. "When will you be having the babe, Celeste? I am excited to become a grandmama at last, you know."

Damnation. Of all the times for the not-so-distant past to return in his mother's mind, now was not it. Sin could feel his wife's gaze upon him, questioning. But he had revealed enough to her for one day. He could not bear to relive the death of his daughter as well.

"I am not certain," Callie said, her voice hesitant as she began weaving the strands of his mother's hair into a braid.

"Why do you look so bloody Friday-faced, Ferdy?" Mama asked him. "You know I cannot abide by sadness. Smile, if you please."

Sin did as his mother asked. For her, he would *always* find a smile.

CHAPTER 18

How wicked is the heart, dear reader, that it leads to such vile treachery?
~ *from* **Confessions of a Sinful Earl**

*C*allie stared at her reflection in the looking glass, wondering if Sin was going to come to her. Her hair was unbound, and she had already had her bath, partially in the hopes he would interrupt.

But he had not.

He had been quiet after their visit to his mother's chamber. Withdrawn and cooler than he ordinarily was. He had excused himself and told her that she ought to go to bed without waiting for him. She had sensed he had not been ready to discuss everything that had been revealed to her this evening.

Of all the secrets she had suspected him of keeping, she had never supposed that one would be a beautiful, white-haired woman who had lost her mind. Or that his former wife had been pregnant with his child, a child who had obviously not survived. The haunted expression on her husband's

236

face had revealed far more to her than his mother's confused jumble of memories ever could.

Her heart ached for him.

The love he felt for his mother had been apparent. And as the elder woman had wandered in and out of the past and present, mistaking him for another and then seeming to remember him for a moment, Callie's inner anguish for him had grown. As had her compassion. Although her relationship with her own parents had never been close prior to their deaths, she could not imagine how difficult it must be for him to know his mother no longer recognized him.

And yet, he had navigated the situation with effortless aplomb, answering to Ferdy, smiling for his mother when she had demanded it. His mother had been in good spirits when they had left her in the care of her nursemaid. And as for Callie…well, something had shifted for her tonight.

The more time she spent in his presence, the more apparent it became that there was much more to the Earl of Sinclair than she had previously supposed.

Deciding she had spent too much time awaiting him, Callie took a deep breath and straightened her dressing gown. Beneath it, she was nude. Not even a night rail. After the tattered remnants he had left her last gown in, she had deemed it best. Besides, there was something about her naked flesh against the softness of her robe that heightened her awareness.

If only her husband would come to bed. Or invite her into his.

She knocked on the door joining their chambers and received no answer. Suspecting he had yet to come to bed, she opened the door to find his apartments empty, just as she had thought. There was only one solution to her problem—if Sin would not come to her, she would go to him.

Callie made certain all the buttons on her dressing gown

were buttoned up and she was not showing any excess skin lest she cross paths with a servant, and then she left her chamber. It did not take long to find him, for there was a light glowing beneath his study door.

She knocked.

"What is it now, Langdon?" her husband asked, his tone irritated. "I thought I told you and Eloise to go to bed."

Callie opened the door and crossed the threshold, closing it at her back. Sin was standing near the fireplace, holding a glass of amber-colored liquid in his long fingers. His dark gaze settled upon her, seeming to devour her from where he was, halfway across the room.

Her nipples went hard beneath her dressing gown.

"It is not Langdon," she said quietly, feeling unaccountably nervous.

Perhaps he wanted to be alone. Mayhap he did not wish for her company. Surely there was a reason he had delayed in coming to bed. Why would he prefer to remain in his study, drinking, by himself?

"I would like to think myself capable of telling the difference between my wife and my butler and his dog," he said, passing a hand over his angular jaw.

"Have you spoken with him?" Callie asked. "About a cottage in the country?"

"I have." Sin raised his glass to her in a mock toast. "The stubborn old goat insists he must remain here, where he is needed."

She had wondered whether or not Langdon would truly wish to leave. And whether or not her husband would make him. It would seem she had her answer. Sin's mother had been right. Her beautiful son did have an endless heart.

"You will allow him to stay?" she queried.

Sin took a sip of his drink and raked his fingers through

his hair with his free hand. "If the curmudgeon will not go, what am I to do?"

"Perhaps we can persuade him to train a younger domestic in the art of being a butler," she suggested. "That will give him a sense of purpose and it also may make the notion of leaving here more palatable."

"You are a clever woman," he said. "Far more than I originally supposed."

She was not certain if he meant the words as a compliment or an insult. But suddenly, she did not like the distance between them and what it represented.

Standing where she was felt foolish.

But so did getting in closer proximity to her husband.

Oh, well. Her feet had a mind of their own, padding across the threadbare rugs that would soon be replaced. She stopped a foot from him, her gaze traveling over the handsome contours of his face.

"I am not sure whether I should thank you or chastise you for that," she said softly.

A wicked half grin kicked up the corner of his mouth. "It depends upon the manner in which you choose to chastise me, little wife."

Heat flooded her. She was a wanton for him. Always.

"What did you have in mind?" she dared to ask.

He took another sip of spirits, watching her with an intensity that was at once unnerving and exhilarating. "You could tie me to my bed and have your way with me."

His suggestion shocked and intrigued her. An image of him, gloriously naked, and bound to his bed, rose in her mind.

"I will admit, that would certainly even our scores," she told him boldly. "I have still not forgiven you for being tied to the bed when you abducted me, you know."

"Then I shall have to make it up to you." He placed his

drink on the mantel and closed the rest of the space keeping them apart.

One hand settled on her waist and the other took her wrist, raising it to his lips for a fervent kiss.

The soft feathering of his mouth upon her skin made an ache flare to life in her core. But she knew she must not forget her reason for seeking him out. Her tongue flitted over her lips, wetting them. His gaze tracked the movement with undisguised carnal intent.

"Thank you, Sin," she told him.

He kissed her wrist again. "What is your gratitude for, sweet?"

"Trusting me tonight."

He stilled, his expression unreadable. "You gave me little choice."

"How long has your mother been like this?" she asked, instead of arguing.

"The past six years." He kissed her wrist again, then nipped her skin with his teeth.

"Why did you not tell me before now?"

"Why so many questions, darling?" he returned, kissing each of her knuckles before releasing her wrist and clamping his other hand on her waist.

He hauled her into him. Her breath faltered.

They were pressed together, hip to hip, chest to chest. If she rose on her toes, she could take his mouth. She wanted his kiss, very much. The subtle scent of spirits tinged his breath, suggesting he had not been tippling long. His eyes were lucid and clear. She wondered why he had lingered here on his own when he could have come to her.

"Mayhap I am attempting to understand you," she told him, irritated with herself for the husky quality of her voice, the overwhelming manner in which his touch, his nearness, affected her.

All her good intentions fled.

Her heart was beating so hard, she would not be surprised if he could hear its frantic pounding.

"Sweet of you," he said, his brilliant gaze dropping to her lips. "Perhaps you ought to have done that before you destroyed my reputation."

His pointed barb hit its mark.

Regret washed over her, joining the desire.

"I am sorry." The words spilled from her lips before she could think better of them, before she could contain them.

She had wronged him so badly. Little wonder he had been furious enough to hold her captive until she agreed to marry him. His properties were in ruins. His funds were depleted. He scarcely had any servants, and he had a mother who required constant supervision.

"Why are you sorry?" His hand slid from her waist to her breast, cupping it, his thumb unerringly finding the stiff peak.

She inhaled and arched into his touch. "I am sorry I destroyed your reputation. Sorry I wrote *Confessions of a Sinful Earl*. Sorry I hurt you."

"You are not wearing a corset beneath this dressing gown, are you?" he growled.

Of course, he must feel she was not. He rolled her nipple, then plucked at it with devastating intent. Heat surged between her thighs. Need weighed her down. The very air surrounding them seemed to change, growing heavy and potent.

"I am not wearing anything beneath it," she told him.

He exhaled, and the warmth of his breath flitted over her lips in the ghost of a kiss.

Sin pinched her nipple, sending an exquisite blend of painful pleasure through her. "You are sorry, princess?"

She nodded, unbearably aware of him. Her every sense

was heightened to delicious acuity. "More sorry than I can say. It was wrong of me, making assumptions, leaping to the wrong conclusions, and then setting out to get my vengeance."

"Show me," he said, his voice a low, decadent rasp laden with sensual promise.

The ridiculous thought struck Callie that she would do anything he asked of her.

"How?" she whispered.

"I want you naked." He released her breast, his fingers traveling to the line of pearl buttons down the front of her dressing gown. "Take this off for me."

His words should have shocked her. Insulted her, perhaps. All Callie felt was a rush of desire so sudden and all-encompassing that it almost brought her to her knees. As quickly as he had yanked her into his tall, lean form, he released her and stepped away. He watched her with a hooded gaze, his countenance harsh and uncompromising.

She could not be certain if he intended to punish her or pleasure her. Strangely, she would accept either from him. She had wronged him. Grievously. And she could not deny the way he made her feel.

She trusted him. He would not hurt her.

With his gaze upon her, she brought her fingers to the buttons lining the front of her dressing gown. One by one, she slid the buttons from their moorings. He reached for his half-empty glass on the mantel, draining it in one gulp. As she reached her breasts, she fumbled a button, then hesitated, shyness overcoming her.

"Go on," he urged in that smooth, delicious baritone that sent a frisson down her spine. "I want to see you."

Finding her courage, she continued. The dressing gown gaped as she traveled farther down the line of buttons. Cool evening air bathed her naked skin, but her husband's hot stare chased away the chill. She reached the end of the buttons, just above the apex of her thighs. Holding his gaze, she shrugged the fine cotton and silk from her shoulders, then pulled it past her hips.

The ivory garment fell to the floor in a whoosh, pooling about her ankles. Fighting the urge to shield herself from his dark gaze, she stepped free of the material, standing before him in not one stitch.

Silence fell as his eyes scoured her. Though he had seen her—and had touched, kissed, and caressed all of her—before, she could not shake the bashfulness warring with the desire.

"There is no need for shyness, darling," he said, his voice thick with desire.

"I have done what you required of me," she managed to return with nary a betraying tremble in her words. "What more do you want?"

"I want to look at you and to know you are mine. You are so bloody beautiful, do you know that?" His words held a note of reluctance, as if he hated allowing her to know she affected him.

He thought her beautiful?

"The Duchess of Longleigh is beautiful," she said. "I am not."

"No." He shook his head slowly, moving toward her with steady, deliberate steps. "She is a faded comparison. The two of you are akin to fire and water. One could quench a thirst, and the other could burn a man alive."

"Water is deadly as well," she could not help but to remind him, even as she wondered which of the two elements he thought she was, compared to his ethereal former paramour. "Water can drown you."

"Water is safer than fire." He stopped before her. "You can

swim through it for a time, if you must. Fire will consume you in seconds."

"And which am I?" she dared to ask. "Fire or water?"

"Fire, Callie darling." He ran one long, wicked finger over her lips. "Always, *always* fire."

She parted her lips, and his finger dipped into her mouth. The invasion was strangely erotic. She instinctively sucked.

"Damn," he muttered. "You are a dream, Lady Sinclair. A dream that emerged from a nightmare."

He withdrew his finger, and she pressed a kiss to the fleshy pad, feeling as if she were a different woman entirely now. She had always been bold and eccentric—at least, in the wake of Simon's death, she had—but the way she felt with Sin was different. He made her feel powerful and reckless and strong and wanted.

He made her feel *desirable*.

"I thought you said I was fire," she whispered, locking gazes with him and commending herself to the moment, to the spirits of wickedness and truth mingling in the air all around them.

"You are a bloody inferno," he said, sounding as breathless as she was. "And I have never wanted to be consumed by flame more."

That sounded desperately familiar.

He traced his wet finger over her lips, then dragged it down her throat, following his progress with his intense stare. He watched her as if she were the most glorious sight he had ever beheld. As if she were riveting.

"I love the way you look at me," she said, then inwardly kicked herself for revealing so much to him.

Too much.

Too soon.

"Mmm?" His approving hum made her pulse between her

thighs as he continued his light, teasing touch. "And how do I look at you, little wife?"

His finger trailed over her clavicle, then over her shoulder, before proceeding in a languorous caress down her arm. She had never before realized her elbow could feel so alive aside from the times she had inadvertently thwacked it upon a hard surface. But this was new. His finger swirled around it, circling.

"You did not answer me," he reminded her, still working his torture upon that most unlikely part of her body.

How could she unravel by a mere touch on her elbow? She did not know. All she knew was that his finger was lightly swirling over her flesh, over her bone, making her ache there and everywhere else.

Especially between her thighs.

"You look at me as if you want to consume me," she whispered.

His finger left her elbow at last, gliding down her forearm in a barely there touch that made her wild. He took her hand in his and brought her palm to his mouth, kissing her there. Slowly. His tongue flicked against her skin, tracing the lines, tickling and teasing all at once.

Another kiss, and then he raised his head, his gaze frank. "That is exactly what I want to do to you. I want to lick you until you come. I want to taste you everywhere. And then I want to bury myself inside you and get lost in your flames. In your sweet, decadent heat. In your tight, delicious cunny that is all mine."

His revelations shocked her. Exhilarated her. For she felt the same way. He astounded her, made her feel a depth of emotion and passion she had not believed she would ever experience again. And if she were completely, brutally honest with herself, she would acknowledge that the love she had shared with Simon had never been this intense, this profound.

Her love with Simon had been sweet.

Effortless.

They had never shared more than kisses.

The way she felt for Sin was...different. Deeper, darker, more potent.

The realization stole her breath and sent an accompanying rush of guilt.

Guilt her husband stole when he lowered his head and sucked a nipple deep into his mouth. The wet heat and suction thieved her capacity for thought. He caught her in his teeth and tugged, always knowing what she wanted, what she needed, before she did. Her hands sank into his thick, luxurious hair. She felt giddy, as if she had consumed too much wine, as if her head were floating somewhere above her body.

His finger trailed down her belly next, circled her navel. Then traveled lower. Over her mound. Finding that hungry bundle of flesh with expert precision. She jerked into his touch, gasping, arching. Her knees threatened to give out. She did not care. Everything was alive. All her senses. Her lungs were filled with him. Her body was his to play with as he liked. And she was weak, so weak for him. So hungry for him. The salty taste of him was still in her mouth, and she wanted more.

She was a sinner tonight, willing and ready and his.

His finger teased her, working over her hungry flesh. And then he skimmed over her seam, finding her entrance and sliding inside. Deep. This time, her knees truly did buckle. He caught her against him, his finger still buried within her.

And then, his mouth was on hers. He kissed her hard. Punishing. Voraciously. Deliciously. His tongue slid inside to the rhythm of his strokes, in and out. She whimpered into that kiss, need pulsing to life. She was trembling. On the edge. Desperate for his claiming.

He withdrew his finger and moved them across the study without breaking the kiss. Suddenly, she found herself sprawling into a chair. Sin was right there with her. He kissed down her throat, over her breasts and belly, and then sank to his knees between her legs.

She had a moment to realize he was still fully clothed while she was naked before he dipped his head and flicked his tongue over her pearl. Pure sensation rocketed through her. Callie forgot to care about her nudity. He licked her slowly, leisurely. Lightly.

"You taste so sweet," he told her, his breath hot against her core.

His hands were on her inner thighs, caressing, spreading her wider. His tongue tortured her some more, until she moaned and shifted closer, seeking increased pressure. Still, he tormented her with soft flutters that made desire coil deep within her.

"Keep your eyes on me," he commanded, before sucking on the tender bud of her sex.

How could she look away?

The sight of this beautiful man on his knees before her, his mouth on her most sensitive, intimate flesh, was unbearably erotic. She held his gaze, watching him pleasure her.

The most astonishing realization hit her, walloping her with the profundity of it.

Dear God, she could love him.

There was every possibility she was already falling in love with Sin.

Heaven help her.

* * *

He was in love with his wife's cunny.

With the breathy little mewls she made when he licked her.

With the way she rocked against his face, practically begging him to fuck her with his tongue.

He had told himself that he was growing far too attached to her. That his fascination for her would wane. He had convinced himself to keep his distance this evening, needing some time to puzzle through what had happened between them earlier.

But all it had taken was the sight of her standing in his study, wearing that innocent-looking dressing gown with its endless line of buttons and frothy lace at her throat, her magnificent hair cascading down her back, and he had been helpless to resist her. She entranced him. Seduced him with a mere look.

And she was looking at him now. Watching him as he pleasured her. Her lips were swollen and parted, her breasts thrust forward like ripe offerings. She was pale and glorious and he had never wanted to bed a woman more in his life.

First, however, he would give her what she wanted. Sin ran his tongue down her folds, then licked into her. She jerked, quivering beneath him. She was already close. Good. He wanted her close. He wanted her mindless and wild and uncontrolled. He wanted her in a frenzy.

In and out, he slid, holding her dark gaze, delving into her hot wetness. Then, he returned to her pearl, sucking hard while he slid two fingers inside her channel. She was perfection, gripping his fingers, dragging him deep, so slick.

"I want you to come for me," he whispered against her core. "Fly for me, darling."

On a keening moan, she did as he asked, tightening on his fingers in a wave of spasms as he nibbled on her swollen clitoris. Her hands were in his hair, caressing. He waited until the last ripples of her pinnacle ended to slide his fingers from her and replace them with his tongue. Slowly, still holding her gaze, he lapped up all her cream. He inhaled her sweet, musky scent, savoring this connection.

Savoring her.

He could not get enough.

Still fucking her with his tongue, he switched positions, using his fingers to swirl over her pearl in hard, fast circles. He wanted her to come again. And again. And again. And just when neither of them could bear another second of waiting, he wanted to slam his cock inside her.

The thought made his ballocks tighten and his prick twitch, reminding him he was still fully clothed whilst she was beautifully nude. In his need to feast upon her, he had neglected to remove any of his own attire. That could be rectified soon enough. And hell, he was not even certain he cared. As long as he could get his cock inside her, that was all that mattered.

He moaned his satisfaction as her hips pumped against him, seeking. Her lips parted wider. Her breath was coming in sweet gasps as he pleasured her. Her wetness coated his tongue, his lips. He increased the pressure and firmed his tongue, sinking it as deep inside her as he could.

She came on a strangled cry, her body stiffening beneath his. Sin stayed with her as she shook against him, trembling with the power of her release. He waited until the last tremor rocked her, and then he stood.

Her ecstasy heightened his own need. Catching her around the waist, he pulled her gently to her feet, and then traded places with her, so that he was seated and she was standing, naked and sated, her face flushed with the aftereffects of her orgasm. There was no time to remove his bloody clothes. He had to have her.

Now.

He opened the fall of his trousers and freed his cock. "Turn around, princess."

She did as he asked, further proof that she was far less stubborn when sated, giving him a view of her luscious backside. Her arse was perfection, her dark hair hanging down her back. He caught her hips in his hands, positioning her the way he wanted. "Now sit on me."

"Sin," she protested at last, breathless, "how will this work?"

"Trust me, darling." Gently, he guided her down on him, gripping his cock with one hand and easing himself into her cunny. "Seat yourself."

She did, settling herself in his lap and taking him all the way into her tight, slippery sheath. Her gasp matched his. She clenched on him as he caressed her hips, her back. He dragged a handful of her thick, silken locks back and settled his mouth on the patch of skin where her neck and shoulder met.

"What do I do now?" she asked on a moan as he cupped her breast, finding her hard nipple and working it.

"You move on me," he told her. "Ride me. Take what you want."

"Oh," she said as she lifted herself, and then settled upon him once more.

The friction was pure bliss, as was the fit of her around him. He let his hand drop to between her legs, then strummed her pearl with his thumb. She began to move faster, with greater confidence, rising and then falling.

Sin's fragile grip on his own control snapped. He moved with her, their bodies working together, thrusting deep, then withdrawing, then deep again. Her scorching heat made his ballocks go tight. He bit her shoulder, rocking, thrusting, fucking her.

Loving her.

Loving her?

No, not loving her.

He banished the unwelcome thought. Where the devil had it emerged from? He was delirious with the need to spend himself inside her, that was all. Too much blood had rushed to his engorged cock.

He increased the pressure on her pearl, and she came, tightening on his cock with so much force, he could no longer keep from filling her with his seed. She ground herself on him as he spent with a hoarse cry, pumping into her.

Darkness edged his vision for a brief moment from the ferocity of his release. He collapsed against her back, holding her close, his breaths leaving him in ragged bursts. He kissed her neck, her ear, paying homage to her in every way he could.

Curse her, this obsession he had for his wife was not fading.

It was only growing stronger.

CHAPTER 19

There is beauty in cruelty, dear reader. There is madness in each of us, waiting for the right moment. Will I kill again? Only time shall tell...

~from **Confessions of a Sinful Earl**

"Tell me everything," Jo announced the moment they had settled in for tea.

Callie had been a married woman for almost a month. Finally, she had ventured out for the first time, realizing that she could not forever remain trapped in her new home, alternating her time between mooning over her husband and overseeing the new domestics and redecorating.

So, she had emerged into the world once more, paying her best friend a call. Her marriage had thus far been surprisingly, startlingly happy. She had spent each night in Sin's bed, learning his body in the same way he did hers. He had even selected a stool to keep at his bedside for her use. Of course, their lovemaking had not been limited to his chamber or the evening. He seemed to be on a mission to make love to her in each room of the townhome, at least once.

Her cheeks went hot. She could not very well tell Jo *everything*.

"What do you wish to know?" she evaded.

"You are flushing!" Jo observed. "You look ridiculously happy, dearest. The earl is not mistreating you, I take it?"

"Quite the opposite," she admitted.

"That is wonderful," her friend exclaimed, grinning.

"Perhaps too wonderful," Callie said on a rush.

All the emotions that had been building within her over the course of the last month were ready to be set free. All the longing, the fears, the desire, the need, the dread, the caring, heavens help her, the love…

Jo frowned at her. "What is the matter, Callie? I would think the earl treating you well would be a source of relief for you. Not long ago, he was your bitter enemy. Do you trust him now?"

"I do." Callie sighed, searching for the proper words to convey the confusing mix of feelings inhabiting her. "That is the problem. I trust him implicitly. I have realized I was desperately wrong to ever think him capable of hurting another. I have learned so much about him in the last month. He dotes over his hard-of-hearing, near-sighted butler. His mother's mind is frail, but instead of sending her away, he has been looking after her, seeing to her care even when he had to sell off nearly all the pictures and household possessions of value to pay his debts. Everything I have seen of him thus far is surprisingly noble and good."

Jo pressed a hand to her heart. "The butler is hard of hearing? And there is a mad mother-in-law? Please tell me she is not hiding in the attics."

Callie laughed weakly. Leave it to her friend to find some lightness in the moment. "She is ensconced in a regular chamber, and she is being looked after by a nursemaid. We have hired a replacement because Sin did not trust the previous woman in his employ, but she was all he had been able to afford. When I think of how I set out to ruin him, I feel sick."

"You were hurting, Callie. Your brother's death was unusual, and Lady Sinclair passing away on the same night was suspicious. I do not blame you for wondering and for wanting to do everything in your power to find the truth." Jo's voice was sympathetic.

Callie did not think she deserved her friend's sympathy or understanding.

"But was I trying to find the truth, or was I only seeing what I wanted to see and believing what I wanted to believe, regardless of who I hurt in the process?" Sadness cut through her. How wrong she had been.

How selfish.

How careless.

She had ruined a good man. A man who was far better than she had ever imagined. A man whose bed she slept in each night, who touched and kissed her with such tenderness that it made her ache just to think of it now, when he was nowhere in sight.

"You have a good heart, Callie," Jo said. "It looked damning. There is no denying that. And his reputation was blackened before you even wrote *Confessions of a Sinful Earl*."

He had indeed achieved a reputation for running with a fast set. For seducing legions of women. For being wicked. For doing whatever he wished and not giving a damn about the repercussions.

But it was increasingly difficult to reconcile the Sin she had heard about with the Sin she had come to know. The Duchess of Longleigh had told her Sin was a good man, and Callie had seen the evidence herself.

"I know all that, but he is nothing like what I expected

him to be." She sighed. "Oh, Jo. What if I am falling in love with him?"

There it was, her biggest fear. Because Sin himself had told her theirs was a marriage of convenience. He had told her he did not believe in love. His last wife had left scars upon his heart, that much was undeniable.

Jo's brows rose. "In love? You think you are falling *in love* with the Earl of Sinclair?"

Callie gave a miserable nod. "I never expected to like him, let alone care for him. But there is something about him that makes me feel emotions I never felt before. Not even with Simon."

The last admission came with a pang of accompanying guilt. She could not help but to feel she tarnished his memory by feeling such a depth of emotion for another man, and in such a short amount of time. A man who she had not long ago considered her enemy. A man she had been determined to destroy.

"Do you think he feels the same way?" Jo queried softly, giving voice to another of Callie's fears.

"I hardly know." Her voice trembled. "He has not been forthright with his emotions."

"But he is otherwise attentive?" her friend pressed.

Quite attentive.

Deliciously so.

Her cheeks went hot all over again. She could not meet Jo's inquisitive gaze. "Yes, I dare say he is."

"Your cheeks are red as an apple," Jo accused, chuckling. "Good heavens, I never thought to see the day Lady Calliope Manning was embarrassed over something."

"Lady Sinclair now," she reminded her friend.

And herself as well.

How strange it felt, rolling off her tongue. Stranger still, how right. A month ago, she never would have countenanced it. Now, she could not deny that marrying Sin had given her a sense of purpose for the first time since Simon and Alfred had died. Aside from her work for the Lady's Suffrage Society, she had been adrift. Her life in Paris with Aunt Fanchette had been nothing but a lavish swirl of parties. Her life in London had not been much altered, aside from her devotion to her cause.

"You are the happiest I have seen you in as long as I can recall," Jo said softly, cutting into Callie's turbulent musings. "I do believe marriage suits you, my dear friend."

"It does," she agreed, the admission nevertheless laced with worry.

Her happiness had always been cut short by a death, an unexpected end. She hated to bask too much in the moment, or to allow herself to grow too complacent. Surely this contentedness, too, would be dashed upon the rocks like a ship caught in a maelstrom before too long.

"You do not sound pleased with the realization, however."

Jo was ever observant and wise. Those were some of the traits that made her such a wonderful friend. That and her loyalty and sharp-as-a-blade wit.

"I am afraid," she confided. "He has made it more than clear to me that he expects me to give him an heir, and after that time, we shall go our separate ways and lead our own lives. Part of me is convinced he is still in love with his ex-mistress. And his last marriage has left him wary. Apparently, it was quite a bitter affair on both sides. I do believe he loved her at some point."

The notion of her husband's heart having been broken by other women before her left Callie feeling both melancholy and possessive, all at once.

"Oh dear." Jo's expression was commiserating as she took a sip of her tea and then made a face. "Good heavens, the tea has grown cold. Here I am chattering on, asking you all these insufferably rude questions. Just tell me to stifle it, do. I know I am too inquisitive for my own good."

That was one of the many curious facets of Lady Jo Danvers. By all appearances, she was a shy, quiet wallflower. It was only with those she knew and trusted that her true personality came to life. Meanwhile, Callie was the opposite. She was bold and boisterous and unapologetic. Mayhap that was why she and Jo had connected as friends on such a deep level. They were each what the other was not. Together, they understood each other and flourished.

"Never mind the tea," Callie said, feeling selfish for dominating the conversation with her own troubles and feelings. After all, she had meant to visit her friend, not to fret over the budding feelings bursting to life in her treacherous heart. Surely they could be tempered, no? "I came here to visit you, and that is all. I missed you, dear friend. Forgive me for being so serious and weighing down our visit with this nonsense. You must forget it all. I fear becoming a married woman has addled my wits. Let us speak of something else, anything else!"

"I missed you as well." Jo grinned then. "You must tell me what the marriage bed is like, Callie. No one will tell me anything. I swear I shall die a spinster wallflower without ever having even been kissed."

It astounded Callie to think her friend had never been swept into a darkened alcove by a handsome lord and kissed senseless. Jo was uniquely beautiful, sweet, smart, and wittier than anyone Callie knew. She could only suppose it was fear of Jo's brother, the Earl of Ravenscroft, which kept suitors at bay. That and Jo's own retiring nature whenever she found herself in large gatherings of people.

"You will not die a spinster wallflower, never having been kissed," Callie denied. "I promise you that, Jo."

Her friend sighed. "Sometimes, it feels as if I will. I have begun a list, you know, of all the things I want to experience in my life. I have grown quite tired of watching everyone I love go on with their lives while I remain here, the same as I ever was."

Callie felt a pang of guilt all over again. "I have not gone on with my life, dear heart. You will forever be my dearest friend, and you know it. Time, marriages, titles, nothing matters. You are the sister I never had."

"But you have a sister now," Jo pointed out, quite correctly.

"Yes, but she cannot replace you," Callie said soothingly, taking a sip of her own tea at last only to find that it was disgustingly tepid. "No one can replace you, Jo. I have Isabella, and I have you."

"And your wickedly handsome husband who makes you smile like a besotted fool," her friend added.

Jo's grumbling told Callie that perhaps her friend was, at last, ready to relinquish her role as wallflower and seize her life. "No one said you cannot find a handsome husband of your own who also makes *you* smile like a besotted fool."

Jo sighed. "I shall have to live vicariously through you, I am afraid. There is no such handsome gentleman forthcoming. All the lords I know are empty-headed and weak-hearted and dreadfully uninteresting. Not all of us can be carried off by an earl named Sin, you know."

Callie smiled at her friend's sally. "I should hope not. If he is off abducting others, I will box his ears."

Jo took another sip of her own tea, wrinkling her nose. "This is wretched, is it not? Forgive me, darling, I will ring for a fresh pot. One that does not leak."

The teapot had, indeed, leaked. It had rendered Jo's pouring quite humorous. The two of them had collapsed into a fit of giggles over it.

"Fresh tea would be wonderful," Callie agreed. "Now tell

me about this list of yours, if you please. I cannot wait to hear what is on it…"

* * *

His wife had been gone for—Sin checked his pocket watch—three hours.

Precisely.

He paced the length of his study, newly refurbished with fresh, plush Axminster. All the way to the door. He threw it open.

"Langdon!" he bellowed.

"My lord? How may I be of service?"

As if conjured, Dunlop, the younger domestic Langdon had been tasked with training in the role of butler, appeared. He was far too handsome for Sin's liking. Callie had chosen him, and Sin had eagerly foisted all the duties concerning the household off upon her. But now, he found himself regretting his decision. For Dunlop was too young as well. Sandy haired and blue eyed, with a mild manner and an easy disposition that made Sin instantly suspicious of him.

"I called for Langdon," he snapped at the butler-in-training. "Where is he?"

"He is having a nap with Eloise," Dunlop explained, his voice calm and tranquil, as if he were dealing with a recalcitrant child. "How may I help you, my lord?"

He did not want to ask this whelp for anything. Indeed, as Sin looked upon him now, he feared the blasted fellow was too pleasing of face and form. There was no paunch about the middle, no thinning hair.

All Celeste's indiscretions slammed into him in that moment. Her every betrayal. All the pain he had buried and done his damnedest to ignore. He looked at Dunlop, and he saw Callie kissing him. He saw Dunlop in Callie's bed.

Fuck.

Sin ran a hand from his jaw down his throat, feeling itchy in his own skin. Callie had never betrayed him. Nor had she given him any indication she would. But his mind was playing evil, wicked tricks upon him, returning him to the days when his wife had bedded half his staff with glee.

He told himself this was different, that Callie was nothing like his last wife. And yet, his mind would not cease. He could not stop his thoughts, tumbling over each other like the waves in a waterfall. Threatening to inundate him, to drown.

Celeste had taken great pleasure in hurting him.

So had Callie.

Curse it, was he doomed to continue repeating the same mistakes?

"My lord?" Dunlop prodded him, returning Sin to the present.

Reminding him that he was a jealous, foolish wreck. That he was a man who had been married for the span of a month, whose wife had hired a handsome young butler and then disappeared for hours.

"Has Lady Sinclair returned from paying calls?" he forced himself to ask like a normal, rational husband.

He told himself it was Celeste and her machinations that made him feel so uncertain.

That it was not Callie.

She had pledged to be true to him until she gave him an heir and spare, had she not?

"She has not yet returned, my lord," Dunlop told him. "Shall I report to you when her carriage arrives?"

"No," he snapped, feeling foolish, before thinking better of his response. What need had he to guard his pride? "On second thought, yes, Dunlop. Please do. I have a matter of urgent import to discuss with the countess."

That was a lie, of course, but the young, handsome, far-too-muscular butler did not bloody well need to know that.

"Of course, my lord," said the new domestic. "I will report to you as soon as her ladyship returns to the residence."

With a proper bow—which Sin found himself rather aggrieved he could not even offer improvement upon—Dunlop turned on his heel and disappeared. Grinding his molars, Sin watched the new servant stalking away. If the bastard even sent a lingering glance in Callie's direction…

No.

He could not forever allow himself to be entrapped by Celeste's actions. Could he? Celeste had been mad. Not like Mama, who was confused. Celeste's mind had been different. She had been wild, determined to destroy anything that was good. But Callie was…

Callie.

Different.

Unique.

Beautiful and bold and so very unlike every other female he had known. Not even Tilly had made him feel the way his new wife did. All the more reason for his concern, for his fear. Sin knew better than anyone that his past did not exactly mean that he was capable of following his heart.

His heart?

Fuck.

Sin slammed his study door and commenced pacing. There it was again, that unwanted, persistent feeling nettling him just as it had every day since he had made her his bride. Emotions were dangerous. Emotions could not be trusted. He had to cure himself of the lust fog inhabiting his brain. Surely that was all this was? Decker had been convinced of it.

One quarter of an hour later, a knock sounded.

His wife was finally home from paying all her calls. She crossed the threshold, wearing purple boots trimmed with rosettes and matching divided skirts. Her blonde-lace-adorned bodice emphasized her petite curves.

"Lady Sinclair has returned," Dunlop announced.

Sin cast the butler-in-training an irritated scowl. "As I can plainly see. That will be all, Dunlop."

Dunlop wisely made himself scarce, closing the door and leaving Sin and Callie alone. Silence reigned, broken only by the muffled sound of Callie's boots treading over the new carpets. She stood before him in half a minute, her dark gaze searching.

"Is something amiss, Sin?" she asked. "Dunlop said there was an urgent matter you needed to discuss with me."

How the hell was he supposed to concentrate when she was wearing those bloody boots? All he could think about was finding the hidden closures on her divided skirts and tearing them open.

"Sin?" she pressed.

He blinked, telling himself he could not act like a ravening beast because his wife had been gone from beneath their roof for a mere three and one quarter hours. And then he told himself he did have a reason for summoning her immediately upon her return.

But curse him if he could recall what it was.

"I do not like the replacement butler," he blurted.

There, that was true enough.

"Dunlop?" Her eyebrows rose. "But he has only been with us for two weeks. How can you find fault with him after such a short period of time?"

"He is too young." And far too handsome.

"He is older than the both of us," Callie argued, frowning. "I think we should give him more time to grow accustomed to our household before we make any decisions."

"I do not like him," he repeated, feeling childish.

But he also did not care for the manner in which his wife continued to champion the blighter.

Her brow furrowed. "Are you displeased with me?"

No, damn it all. He was displeased with himself.

He forced his whirling mind to calm. Callie was not Celeste. His rational mind understood that. But the old emotions remained. He was a wary, jaded beast. Every modicum of good sense he possessed told him his trust was not wisely placed in a woman who had done her best to destroy him.

"I am not displeased," he gritted, finding the words difficult to say. "I am merely hesitant. My last marriage did not precisely imbue me with a great deal of trust in others, particularly the fairer sex. You were gone for quite some time."

"I was visiting my friend, Lady Jo Danvers." She laid a soothing hand upon his forearm. "We had tea. We chatted for a few hours. The teapot leaked, and the tea grew cold, and we had to ring for another pot. Now I am home. I hardly think my short absence cause for concern."

Her touch seared him through his shirtsleeves. He was being an arse, and he knew it. He inhaled and then exhaled slowly, trying to calm the jumbled mess of his thoughts.

"Celeste would disappear for days." He ran his hand through his hair. "I am sorry, Callie. Forgive me. I know you are not her, but the circumstances of our marriage hardly lend themselves to trust. Not long ago, you were doing everything in your power to ruin me."

She flinched as if he had struck her, withdrawing her hand from his arm. "Do you think I was calling upon other men? Do you... Do you think I am enamored with Mr. Dunlop? Is that what you are telling me?"

Curse her. She was making him feel again. There was that

rush, uncontrollable, threatening to overwhelm his good sense. He wanted to drag her into his arms and kiss her senseless. To ravish her upon his desk. He wanted her naked on his lap, his cock buried in the welcome warmth of her tight cunny.

He turned away from her and stalked to the other end of the chamber, attempting to gain control over himself. Callie brought out the best in him and the worst in him, all at once. There was no denying that.

And of course, she was chasing him down in those delicious purple boots, determined to give him a piece of her mind. When he turned to find her close enough to kiss, he was not at all surprised.

"Answer me," she demanded. "Do you not trust me?"

"It is complicated," he bit out. "I do, and I also do not. I cannot explain it."

"What have I done to make you doubt me?" she asked, her voice softening.

Her honey-and-chocolate eyes glimmered with the traces of tears.

He was a bastard for making her cry. Once, he would have enjoyed her tears. He would have adored bringing her low, making her weak. But that had been before he knew her. Before he had slept with her in his bed each night. Before he had been inside her.

"Sin," she prodded, cupping his jaw as she searched his gaze. "What did she do to you?"

He wanted to tear himself away from her touch, and yet, simultaneously, he never wanted to move. He wanted her to caress his jaw and gaze upon him with such a tender need to understand him forever. No one had ever looked at him thus.

And this, from a woman who had believed him a murderer.

"Tell me," she whispered, stroking his cheek with her thumb.

"We were young when we married," he remembered. "In love, or so I thought. But after I inherited the earldom, she changed. She became consumed by the social whirl. After our daughter was stillborn, it grew worse. She hated me, blamed me. Celeste refused to allow me to touch her, to comfort her. She pushed me away, and she threw herself back into society with a vengeance. Before I knew it, she was gambling away everything she could, disappearing for days. Once, I caught her with two of the footmen."

Callie's soft gasp cut through him, settling deep, lodging somewhere perilously near to his heart. Her eyes were luminous. "Oh, my darling. I am so sorry."

My darling.

It was the first time she had used a term of endearment for him. The effect it had upon him was furious and wild. Suddenly, the last thing he wanted was her tenderness, her sympathy. The compassion in her gaze, in her dulcet voice, threatened to crush him. He could not bear it. He had no wish to relive the dark days of his marriage with Celeste.

Rather than continue unburdening himself, he lowered his head and took his wife's lips. Her kiss was laced with tea and sweetness. Her tongue slid against his. He kissed her as if he could devour her. Because that was what he wanted to do. He wanted her naked on his desk, wearing nothing but those purple boots of hers.

Hell, he was a monster. His wife had gone for tea with her friend, and she returned to a jealous fiend who all but accused her of planning to bed the bloody butler. There was no excuse for his reaction. His feelings for Callie had him desperately confused.

He did not want to feel.

Feeling made him vulnerable.

He wanted the physical. Lust roared through him, along with the frantic need to possess her. His heart pounded. He nipped Callie's lush lower lip, then kissed away the sting. Dragged his mouth down her throat. His hands found her rump. Delicious handfuls. He ground her against his aching cockstand, letting her feel what she did to him. How badly he wanted her.

"I am an arse," he whispered against her creamy throat. "Forgive me."

He sucked on her flesh. Her exotic, floral scent invaded his senses.

"Sin," she murmured.

Her small hands were on his shoulders, caressing, holding him close. He would do penance with desire. Make her come. This was what he knew best—sensuality. All he had to do was figure out how the hell to get her out of her divided skirts.

His heart was pounding harder. Louder.

Too loud.

"Sin?" she breathed, a question in her voice. "Dunlop is knocking."

Curse the blighter.

"My lord? My lady?"

"Go to the devil," he called.

"The Duke of Westmorland is requesting an audience, my lord," said the butler-in-training. "He says he will not leave until he has seen her ladyship."

Damn it all.

His wife stiffened and extracted herself from his embrace. "Benny! Oh dear heavens, he must be returned from his honeymoon. He will be furious with me, I expect. And you as well."

The desire coursing through him died.

"Send him in, Dunlop," he called grimly.

The timing was bloody poor, but he had always known that sooner or later, Westmorland would return, and Sin would have to face his reckoning. Perhaps it was just what he needed, a means of reminding himself of all the reasons why he would be better served to forget about his maddening infatuation with his countess.

CHAPTER 20

I am dangerous, dear reader. I am a bad, bad man. If you see me about Town, run.
~from Confessions of a Sinful Earl

*C*allie braced herself for her brother's wrath. Struggling for composure after her husband's painful revelations followed by his potent embrace, she smoothed her fingers over her hair. She probably looked as if she had been properly ravished. Then again, any time she was within close proximity to her husband, that seemed to be quite common.

Benny was going to be furious with her.

And hurt.

And confused.

"What are we going to tell him?" she asked Sin, making certain he had not dislodged any of the buttons on her bodice.

Her husband scrubbed his hand over his jaw. "The truth, I expect."

She bit her lip. "You intend to tell Benny about *Confessions of a Sinful Earl?*"

"No, wife." He raised a brow, his countenance uncompromising. "I expect you to tell him. You are, after all, the one responsible for the straits in which we now find ourselves."

She found herself frowning at his choice of words. Was he referring to their marriage, or to her brother's impending interrogation? She did not have the chance to seek clarification, because the study door opened and Dunlop announced their Graces, the Duke and Duchess of Westmorland.

Benny stalked into the chamber looking utterly enraged as expected. His new wife Isabella was at his side, looking fretful.

"What the devil is the meaning of this, Sinclair?" he demanded.

Callie winced, rushing forward to place herself between her husband and her brother, lest either of them come to blows. "Benny, please do not be angry," she begged.

Sin took his place at Callie's side, sliding a possessive arm around her waist. "Westmorland, Duchess. How lovely to see you both. Have you come to welcome me into the family?"

"I have come to beat you to a bloody pulp," Benny snarled.

Isabella placed a staying hand on his coat sleeve. "Darling, you promised you would be calm."

"Has he harmed you in any way?" her brother asked, his gaze searching hers. "How the devil did he coerce you into marriage? Aunt Fanchette swears the two of you are a sudden love match, but I would sooner eat my own shoe than believe such tripe."

"I have not harmed her," Sin said, exhibiting more of his signature sangfroid. "I did, however, abduct her from London and persuade her of the wisdom of saving herself from a ruined reputation by marrying me."

Isabella's eyes went wide. Benny stalked forward with a clenched fist.

"Benny, stop," Callie intervened, holding up a staying hand. "Please, listen to what I have to say before you do something you will regret."

"I will not regret planting this bastard a facer," her brother growled.

"My love, you are turning into a snarling bear," Isabella protested.

"He forced my sister into marrying him whilst I was out of London on my honeymoon," Benny accused, turning a glare upon Sin. "Do not think I have not immediately consulted my solicitor. If you coerced her…"

"He did not coerce me," Callie denied. "At least, not in the way you think."

"Perhaps we should sit down," said her husband coolly. "Ring for tea."

"Not unless you want it pitched in your face," Benny threatened.

"Only if you would care for a broken nose in return," Sin bit out.

Callie lost her patience. "Stop it, both of you! Benny, I am the author of *Confessions of a Sinful Earl*. Sin discovered I was behind the serials, and that I was responsible for the complete ruin of his reputation and his betrothed crying off."

"Callie." Her brother shook his head. "What the hell were you thinking?"

"I was wrong." She made the admission with utmost conviction now. "I was blinded by the pain of losing our brother and I was consumed with grief. I…I was not thinking clearly. So you see? I married Lord Sinclair to keep my secret safe, and to atone for the wrongs I visited upon him."

Some of the fight seemed to seep from her brother. "To keep your secret safe? Did you threaten her, Sinclair?"

Sin held her brother's gaze. "I did. Desperate times, desperate measures, etcetera."

"By God, I am going to trounce you, you despicable bounder!" Benny hollered, surging forward once more.

Sin was certainly not aiding their cause. She could not help but to wonder why. While she knew he was correct in being honest with her brother and sister-in-law, there were far more tactful ways of going about it. Part of her wondered if he *wanted* Benny to attack him.

"Benny, it is not what you think," she attempted to reassure him. "I chose to marry Lord Sinclair."

"He just said he threatened you so that you would marry him." Her brother was incredulous.

Well, that much was true. But how could she explain to her brother the incipient happiness she had found with her husband without revealing too much and embarrassing herself?

"I did," Sin said amiably.

She frowned at her husband. "You are making this worse."

He flashed her a rakish half grin. "Ah, but how can this little tragedy of ours be made to seem better than what it is? We are being honest with your brother and sister-in-law. We were both forced into marrying each other, if you must know." He turned to Benny. "Your sister left me without options. I left her without any in turn."

"You are a callous son of a bitch," Benny accused.

"Are you happy, Callie?" Isabella asked then, her worried tone stealing Callie's attention. "That is what matters the most. Your brother and I want to be assured you are content and being treated well."

"I am," she confessed.

For she *was* happy with Sin. Too happy, almost. What had just passed between them—the revelations of his distrust and his disastrous marriage to his first wife—lent a troubling undercurrent to that knowledge. She wondered if he would ever trust her, especially after the manner in which their union had first begun.

What cruel irony.

Her brother shook his head again. "I do not believe this, any of it. You could have waited until I returned from my honeymoon. Instead, you rushed into a marriage in secret without waiting for my blessing. You have been reckless in the past, Callie, but this, marrying a man you scarcely know —being blackmailed into marrying him—and now claiming you are happy…"

"Sin was doing his best to protect his mother," Callie said softly. "She is ill and in need of a caretaker. He is a good man, Benny. I was wrong about him, and I know that now."

"I would not say I am good, sweet," Sin said, giving her a look packed with so much intensity, it stole her breath.

But he *was* good. He was so much more than the sum of his reputation. So much more than she ever could have comprehended. And he was her husband, and she wasn't just falling in love with him.

She *was* in love with him.

Heaven help her.

The realization left her feeling giddy and lightheaded all at once, as if she would faint. How could she have fallen in love with him so quickly? So effortlessly?

And more importantly, what would she do about it now? Sin was hardly ready to accept her love or to trust her. The scars of his past had not yet healed, and she did not know if they ever would. What if he would never love her in return? What if their marriage was doomed to be one of convenience, and after he had his heir and spare, he would carry on with his life of excess and wickedness, without her in it?

"Bloody hell," grumbled Benny, "none of this makes sense. Not one whit. The least you can do is allow my duchess and I a moment alone with Callie, Sinclair. I would like to speak with her in private."

Callie expected her husband to object, but Sin inclined his head. "As you wish. Join us for dinner tonight as well, if you like. There will be no harm in two more place settings."

Benny's mouth was set in a harsh, unforgiving line. "Thank you for the invitation, Sinclair. However, only having just returned from our travels, we are tired. Nor would we wish to overstay our welcome."

"The choice is yours, Westmorland." Sin shrugged indolently, as if he did not have a care in the world. "I will leave the three of you to your familial tête-à-tête."

With a perfunctory bow, he turned and sauntered from the study.

The moment the door closed at his back, Benny descended upon her.

"What the devil were you thinking, marrying a man like the Earl of Sinclair?" her brother asked, his voice vibrating with his fury.

"My love." Isabella once more laid a staying hand on Benny's arm. "You must not be so angry with Callie. She has done nothing wrong."

"My wonderful wife is your champion, of course, because she has the patience of a saint," Benny said, still frowning ferociously at Callie.

"Of course she does," Callie could not resist teasing him. "She is married to you, after all, dearest brother."

"And now you are married as well." Benny pinched the bridge of his nose, as if he were attempting to stave off a dreadful case of the megrims. "Forgive me, Callie. I do not mean to shout, but surely you can appreciate my shock at returning after being gone a mere month to find you married. And not just to anyone, but to the Earl of Sinclair.

My God, do you have any idea what sort of reputation the man has?"

Grim uncertainty stole over her, making her stomach churn. "Of course I know about his reputation. I helped to create it, if you will recall from my earlier admission."

"I knew I should have been firmer with you." Benny raked a hand through his golden hair. "You have been through so much, losing Lord Simon, then Alfred. I never should have allowed you to go to Paris with Aunt Fanchette. And I never should have left before she had arrived. By God, I hold her partially responsible for this farce."

Callie bristled at her brother's assertion that he ought to have been firmer with her. "Benny, I am my own woman. If you had been firmer with me, I would have thrown more surprise balls."

Her joke was weak, a reference to his frustration with the many entertainments she had planned without his knowledge in the last year.

Benny did not find humor in it, but her sister-in-law smiled.

"I admire your daring, Callie. I always have." Isabella's smile turned sad. "Are you truly certain you are happy, dearest?"

"Despite the unconventional beginning to our marriage, yes," she answered. Though the doubt and questions remained, swirling through her, infecting her thoughts. Dogging her with unfair persistence.

"You have only been married for a month," scoffed Benny. "You scarcely even know him. He is a member of a depraved club that is renowned for its wickedness. He is the last sort of man I would ever wish to see married to my beloved sister."

The reminder of his club hit Callie like a pail of ice water.

She had known, of course. She had mined all the scandals and rumors surrounding her husband to write *Confessions of a Sinful Earl*. But it was difficult indeed to reconcile what she had known about him with the man she had come to know.

"I know about the club," she said.

"He has dared to take you there?" Benny asked, outraged anew.

"Of course not," she hastened to say. "He has not spoken of it to me."

The moment the confession left her, doubt blossomed. So, too, fear. Sin had never once mentioned the club. And he had been gone for so long the day after their nuptials. He had claimed to be visiting his friend. What if he had been lying?

"I wonder what else your new husband is keeping from you," Benny said grimly, giving voice to her fears.

"Nothing, we hope," Isabella said, swatting her new husband's arm. "You promised on the carriage ride here that you would remain calm. That you would not berate her or attempt to ruin her spirits."

Benny frowned at his duchess. "I wanted her to have a love match, as we have. Callie is worth far more than some arrogant, penniless earl who has the ballocks to abduct her, force her into marrying him—"

"I chose to marry him," Callie interrupted.

"Because he threatened to reveal you as the true author of those scandalous memoirs all of London is agog over," her brother countered. "By his own admission! My God, Calliope, I thought you were more intelligent than this. I never thought I would see the day that you would fall prey to a heartless rakehell out to destroy you."

The virulence of Benny's words sank deep into Callie's heart. They found her fears and mingled with them, until her stomach was an endless, churning sea. What if her brother was right? What if she had allowed the glimpses into Sin's softer side to blind her to the truth of the man that he was? They had only been married for a month.

She must not allow herself to forget the manner in which their marriage had begun. He had abducted her from London, bound her wrists, and even gagged her. And then, he had blackmailed her.

"Callie?" Isabella's worried voice cut through her madly spinning thoughts. "Are you well? You look dreadfully pale all of a sudden."

No, she was not well. She felt...dizzy. Sick. Overheated. Her skin was hot. The room seemed to spin. Her eyes could not find a safe place to fall. It was as if she stood still whilst everything and everyone else was whirling around.

The edges of her vision went dark. Benny and Isabella seemed suddenly too far away. Their voices were hushed and strange. And then Callie was falling, falling, falling.

Backward, into the abyss.

Darkness claimed her.

* * *

Sin paced the hall outside his wife's apartments, trying to tamp down his rage and his worry. Callie had swooned. His strong, fierce, fiery wife had bloody well *fainted*. It still seemed impossible to believe. He had abducted her, bound her, dragged her through the countryside, done his best to frighten her, and she had remained stalwart.

Ten minutes in the presence of her brother and sister-in-law, and she was requiring smelling salts. By the time word had reached him, she had already been awake, propped with half a dozen pillows which had been fetched from God knew where, in a chair in his study. Her pallor and the sheen of perspiration on her forehead had convinced him she was ill.

Dreadfully so.

She had told him she had a terrible megrim.

Sin had summoned a physician.

A physician who had been attending her, along with the Duchess of Westmorland, for…

He plucked his pocket watch from his waistcoat.

One whole fucking hour.

"Have you done something to her?"

The question, more snarling growl than respectable query, emerged from his wife's brother. The Duke of Westmorland had taken news of Sin's marriage to his sister worse than he had supposed. He had taken Callie's sudden fainting spell even harder.

But no harder than Sin. He had broken into a run when the news reached him, so desperate had he been to reach her.

"You believe I have somehow done my wife ill?" he asked, doing his best to quell his inner fury and failing. "What is it you think I have done to her? Have I poisoned her? Pushed her down the stairs? Good Christ, man. I was not even near her when she grew ill. If anyone should be asking questions, it should be me. I left her alone with you for scarcely any time at all, and suddenly I need to summon the physician."

Westmorland was pale. He stalked toward Sin, and Sin held his ground, remaining where he was, refusing to back down. The duke's eyes were wild, his upper lip curved into an unforgiving sneer. "Do not think I will not kill you because you are a peer, Sinclair. Or because you have somehow ingratiated yourself to my sister, and cast your spell over her. She is too kindhearted to know what manner of snake she has married."

He had never had any quarrels with the duke before now.

"What manner of snake am I, hmm?" he asked. "You seemed happy enough to receive me on prior occasions when I visited you at Westmorland House."

That was true enough, but he had known quite well that

the duke was merely tolerating him, not that he liked him. Sin had been so caught up in his desire to gain proof against Callie that he had not given a damn. His call had not been a social one. Rather, it had been the means by which he had sealed Callie's fate.

And his own.

How long ago that seemed, almost a lifetime. So much had altered between then and now.

"That was before you blackmailed my sister into becoming your wife, you bastard," Westmorland growled. "You are a rakehell and a scoundrel. Do you deny being a member of the Black Souls?"

Sin refused to flinch or retreat. "No. Of course not. I have never made false claims about myself. Not to your sister, and not to anyone. I am a member of the Black Souls club. I have been for years. It hardly signifies."

The Black Souls was a private club. Their reputation for depravity and licentiousness had been well-earned by some members, it was true. But the club was not solely a bastion of sin and wicked excess as all the rumors suggested. Rather, it was also a safe haven for lords with dark souls to convene. There was no judgment within the walls of that club.

And Sin had been grateful for that. He had done some things of which he was not proud, none of which had anything to do with the Black Souls. They had rescued him from his lowest depths. He could not lay the blame for his sins upon the Black Souls. Some of his best and oldest friends were members. Men he would trust with his very life. Decker, among them, who owned the club itself.

"Everyone knows the members of the Black Souls are depraved," Westmorland insisted, his nostrils flaring as if he scented something unsavory. "If you have harmed my sister in any way, I will not hesitate to end you."

Westmorland was lethal. He had killed two Fenians. Sin

did not discount the danger his new brother-in-law presented. He had no doubt that the duke meant every word he said. His devotion to Callie had been apparent, and surprisingly comforting to Sin. His loathing of Sin—that was another matter entirely.

However, he could not entirely blame Westmorland. Had their situations been reversed, Sin had to admit that he would likely feel the same.

He met his brother-in-law's gaze unflinchingly. "If I ever harm your sister in any fashion, I will end myself first. I have no intention of hurting Callie. Ever. She is my wife, and I will do everything in my power to keep her happy and well."

The duke's eyes narrowed into icy slits of disbelief. "I do not trust you, Sinclair. Not one whit."

Sin almost chuckled. Instead, he raised a brow. "I never asked you to trust me."

"Why did you marry my sister?" Westmorland asked.

"Because she owed me," he answered honestly. "She ruined me, quite intentionally. I had no recourse. I am being utterly honest with you, Westmorland. If you think I have anything to hide, you are wrong."

"Your first wife," the duke said slowly, "what happened to her?"

"Bloody hell," he muttered, disgusted. "If I had wanted to murder Celeste, I would have done so years before she took her life by her own hand. She was mad, Westmorland. I know you and Callie want to believe your sainted brother could not have been duped by her, but I am living proof, standing before you, to tell you that woman was a poison. To herself, to everyone she knew. But I would never have harmed her. And likewise, I would never harm your sister. She is my wife, my countess, the mother of my future children."

"You married her for her share of the Manning fortune," his brother-in-law accused.

He looked Westmorland in the eye. "You are damned right I did, and she married me because she had to."

Before the duke could counter his bold statement, the door to Callie's apartments opened at last. Dr. Gilmore emerged.

"Well?" Sin demanded, stalking toward the physician, his heart pounding in his chest as he forgot all about the need to defend himself against his irate brother-in-law.

"What is the matter with her, Doctor?" Westmorland asked in unison, striding forward also.

The physician looked from Sin to the duke, then back to Sin, clearly wondering which of them he ought to direct his words toward. Sin scowled at Westmorland. Damn it, he was beyond his bounds. Callie was Sin's wife now, and that bloody well took precedent over the relationship between siblings.

"How is Lady Sinclair?" Sin pressed curtly.

Westmorland pinned him with a glare.

Sin ignored him.

"Her ladyship is well and resting now," Dr. Gilmore said calmly. "You may see her if you wish."

"Resting," Sin repeated, loathing the word. He had never known Callie to rest. Or to faint.

"But what is the matter with her, Dr. Gilmore?" he snapped, out of patience. "Why would she swoon for no good reason?"

Dr. Gilmore gave him a small smile. "I do believe there was a good reason. A reason which will make itself decidedly known over the course of the next few months."

Was something dreadfully wrong with Callie? Was she ill? The thought stole the saliva from his mouth, the breath from his lungs. She was so vibrant and bold and alive. The notion of losing her, of watching her wither away, was hideous. Eviscerating.

Confusion swarmed him, mingling with the fear.

"What the devil does that mean?" he bit out, longing to shake the physician. "Cease speaking in riddles, man. Is she ill?"

"Oh dear, pray forgive me, Lord Sinclair," said the physician. "It was not my intention to worry you. Judging from my examination, she is in the finest of health. However, this is a delicate matter, and one generally best left to a discussion between a husband and wife. Why do you not go and see Lady Sinclair now? She will explain everything she and I discussed."

The answers were no clearer to Sin now than they had been before. Perhaps if he throttled the man? Planted him a facer?

"Bloody hell," Westmorland breathed, looking suddenly pale and dazed. "I am to be an uncle?"

An uncle?

His brother-in-law's words reached him as if from afar, from the opposite end of a tunnel. A babe.

Callie was already carrying his child?

It seemed impossibly soon, and yet, they had been married for nearly a month. She had not had her courses in all that time. It had scarcely concerned him, so besotted had he been with his wife. Sleeping with her in his bed each night, making love to her until they were both limp and sated, had become commonplace. He had not stopped to contemplate the possibility she could be with child so soon.

"As I said," Dr. Gilmore spoke again, piercing the haze that seemed to have settled upon Sin's mind, "it is early. But all indications suggest that you will indeed be an uncle, Your Grace. And you, Lord Sinclair, will be a father."

A.

Father.

Those two simple words nearly knocked him to his arse. The notion of an heir had been distant and removed. Indistinct. Unlikely, even. He swallowed against a knot rising in his throat. Terror and elation struck him at once, rendering him immobile and speechless. He could say nothing. Could not move. He stood there like a fool, until at last his reluctant brother-in-law broke the spell.

"You ought to go to her, Sinclair," the duke muttered. "You are her husband, after all."

Sin did not miss the bitterness lacing Westmorland's words, particularly *husband*. Part of Sin was pleased Callie's brother seemed to be every bit as protective of her as she was of him. The bond between brother and sister was undeniable. Ultimately, it had been what had driven Callie into Sin's arms, into his bed, had made her his wife.

He nodded, feeling as if the heavens had fallen upon his head. "Go to her. Yes. I shall."

Sin moved toward his wife's chamber, but paused, his fears still rising like the ocean's tides. "You are certain she is otherwise healthy, yes?"

"Yes," Dr. Gilmore affirmed with a nod. "Her ladyship is in excellent health."

Relief pummeled him like a fist. There was a rushing in his ears he had not experienced since the day he had seen Celeste's lifeless body, enshrouded in her coverlets, in that selfsame room. It was little wonder he wanted Callie to spend each night in his own chamber. There remained so many ghosts haunting this home, haunting *him*.

But there was also hope, astonishing and brilliant and equally petrifying.

He barely found the presence of mind to thank the doctor —Westmorland's personal physician, of course—before entering his wife's chambers. He found Callie seated on the chaise longue she had so recently selected. She smiled when she saw him, but the smile did not reach her eyes.

The Duchess of Westmorland rose upon his entrance, giving Callie a brief, though warm, embrace. "I shall leave you to visit with your husband. Send for us if you need anything, and visit when you are feeling well. *Tante* Fanchette is returning to Paris soon. You must not forget to call. She is missing you."

"I shan't," Callie reassured her sister-in-law with a grateful smile. "Thank you for sitting with me, Isabella. You are the sister I have always wanted, and I am so happy to see you and Benny together at last."

"You are the sister I have always wanted as well." The Duchess of Westmorland smiled wistfully before turning a frank stare upon Sin. "Lord Sinclair, you are, of course, most welcome to join Lady Sinclair in her visit. In fact, I insist you do."

The fierce, golden-haired duchess was not what he had expected. She was formidable. A beauty in her own right, but in spite of that, undeniably…unique. He would wager she kept Westmorland on his toes. Sin liked her. He liked that she cared for Callie. And he liked that she appeared more willing than her forbidding husband to give him a chance.

He bowed. "It would be my honor, Your Grace."

The duchess smiled. "Please, we are family now. You must call me Isabella."

Oh, yes. Far more willing to give him a chance. *Thank God.* "Isabella, then."

She cast a quick, questioning glance from Callie to Sin, then back to Callie. "I shall leave the two of you alone to discuss what Dr. Gilmore discovered then, shall I? Westmorland and I will see the both of you soon."

Sin waited until his new sister-in-law had excused herself from the chamber and the door had closed behind her to go to his wife. She was still pale, and she looked very much unlike herself.

He hated that.

He seated himself on the edge of her chaise longue. "How are you feeling, sweet?"

"Shaken," she admitted with a wan smile. "I had not thought enough time had passed since we wed, but Dr. Gilmore assured me that it had. You have heard the news?"

He swallowed. Nodded. "I have."

She bit her lower lip, worrying its lush fullness. Her right hand fretted with the fall of her skirts. "You are pleased, then?"

Pleased. Shocked. Panicked. Terrified. Elated.

Any of those would do.

He was going to be a father again. The notion seemed impossible and yet, he was startled by how much he wanted it. And with Callie.

"Of course, sweet." He covered the hand that had been plucking at her gown, staying her motions. "You know I am in need of an heir. I had not expected it to happen this quickly, but I am pleased. And I am relieved you are well. Are you still dizzy?"

Sin tried to resurrect memories of Celeste, when she had been carrying their daughter, and he could not. It was as if his mind had obliterated all painful recollections. He did not know what to expect. He did not recall Celeste being dizzy or swooning. But every woman was different. He could only suppose a pregnancy was different for each woman as well.

"Somewhat, yes, and tired." Her voice was subdued.

It was as if the spirit had been stolen from her.

This faded, weary, quiet version of the woman he had wed weighed down upon his chest as heavily as a stone. "Do you need to rest? A nap, perhaps?"

"Yes." She nodded, then closed her eyes. "Mayhap a nap

would be best. I may have overexerted myself today in my delicate condition, without realizing it. Paying a call to Jo, facing my brother's outrage."

Callie seemed…distant. Unlike herself. He did not like it. Earlier, before Westmorland had arrived, before she had swooned and the doctor had been summoned, everything between them had been so different. Now, he could not shake the feeling that something had been severed.

"I am sorry about the scene with your brother. Had I realized you were *enceinte*, I would not have countenanced leaving you to an interrogation." Sin frowned. "What can I do now? Shall I ring for your lady's maid?"

"Please." Callie sighed. "Whitmore will know just what to do. She always does."

The ease with which she would dismiss him rankled. Part of him had been hoping she would ask for him to remain instead. But Sin stood, then stalked to the bell pull.

For the first time in his life, he was jealous of a bloody lady's maid.

He could not help but to wonder how Whitmore would know what to do when he had not one fucking inkling.

He was going to be a father again.

Bloody hell.

CHAPTER 21

Be warned, dear reader. I ruin everything I touch. Sooner or later, I will ruin you, if you let me.
~from **Confessions of a Sinful Earl**

Sin was sotted.

So sotted, the walls of the Black Souls club were swirling around him. Churning, dancing, taunting him. The ceiling was a whirling blur. His ears rang with the sounds of his fellow club members laughing and talking. Occasionally, the dulcet giggle of a woman, a smooth voice, joined the din.

He blinked and struggled to focus his gaze upon Decker, who was dressed all in black this evening, from his shirt to his neck cloth, waistcoat, and coat. He looked like he had been torn from the bowels of Hades.

Ironic, that. Sin felt as if *he* had been torn from the bowels of Hades as well.

He struggled to recall why he was here, within four walls he had not inhabited in months. And then it all came rushing back to him in one befuddled mess. His argument with Callie, facing an irate Westmorland, her sudden swoon and the fear it incited, the doctor's unexpected announcement, Callie pushing him away… Always, always, back to *her*.

And the babe growing within her womb.

His child.

God, he was elated and terrified and weak in the knees, even though he was sitting down. He was sitting down, was he not? Sin glanced down to confirm, lest he fall on his arse.

"I am going to be a father," he announced, slamming his glass on the table before him.

Closing one eye, he peered into the empty vessel. He supposed he had drained it. Again.

Blast.

"So you have said, and so I have offered my felicitations," Decker said. "No less than five times now. Would you care for another whisky? Or perhaps you would prefer another form of distraction?"

Even as soused as he was, Sin bloody well knew what *another form of distraction* was at the Black Souls. He had not forgotten. A woman, for his pleasure. Warm, soft lips on his cock. Or something more. Bindings. Birches. Once upon a time, he had experienced all the depravities this club had to offer.

Why the devil was he here now?

Ah, yes. He had been looking for Decker in the wake of the realization his wife was going to have his child. He had been in need of support. Commiseration. *Hell*, anything. But Decker had not been at home. Instead, he had been at the club—one of the many businesses Decker owned.

And so, Sin had come here. Because he had been lost in a vast sea. Because he had not known where else to go. Because discovering his wife was carrying his child rocked him, shaken him. Dinner had been a bleak affair as she had still been feeling unwell. She had gone to sleep in her own bed for the first time since their marriage had begun.

Alone.

At her request.

And no matter how much he told himself he should not mind, that his objective had been achieved, that he could now carry on his life as he once had, he could not deny the truth: he did not want to.

"Sin?" Decker prodded, breaking up his whirling thoughts. "Another whisky? Some quim?"

"Do I look like I need more whisky?" he asked his friend. "Or anything else, for that matter?"

"You look like shite," Decker told him, unrepentant. "But you have been a boring, married chap, shagging your wife silly every night. If you are here at the Black Souls, especially after receiving such happy news, I can only assume you have come to your senses and you are once more ready to throw yourself into my den of iniquity."

"No petticoats," Sin grumbled, for the notion did nothing for him. Not even a twitch of his cock. Rather, it made his stomach churn and bile rise in his throat. "And do not speak of my wife, lest I be forced to plant you a facer."

There was only one woman for him now.

What if she *no longer wants* you?

He told the insidious voice to go to the devil and banished it.

"I ought to call for the books and memorialize this occasion, the Earl of Sinclair turning down a tumble," Decker said, grinning.

"Go to the devil," he returned. But, if he were honest, he would admit the nettling brought to life his old demons, mingling with the new.

Even in his inebriated state, Sin knew his friend's mockery was well-intentioned. It was a joke, a lark, not at all biting. Not meant to cut him to the marrow. And yet, it did. He had read every word of *Confessions of a Sinful Earl*. And each one of them returned to him now. All the ugly accusations, the hideous representation of himself. What if that was what his wife still believed of him? His reputation had been wicked before she had started her serials, and there was no denying it. Not without reason.

An endless onslaught of questions rained down upon him.

What if, now that she was possibly carrying his heir, she intended to put up a wall between them? What if tonight was just the beginning? What if their child was stillborn? What if Callie died in childbirth?

The thought of a life without his fiery, beautiful, dark-haired wife with the honey-and-chocolate eyes was impossible. Unacceptable. He could not bear to lose her, now that he had her. Over the course of the last month, everything he had never believed possible of changing...had.

And so had Sin, along with it.

"Why are you here, old chap?" Decker asked, his tone softening, marked with concern.

Decker rarely showed emotion. But he was the closest Sin had to a brother. Their friendship was old and deep. It spanned years. They were both pariahs in their own way. Always had been. Perhaps, even, always would be.

Sin sighed and blurted the words that had been doing their damnedest to escape him all night. The whisky he had consumed finally made it easier. "I think I am in love with her."

Decker whistled. "Good God, I was right. You *have* read the serials, have you not?"

He rubbed his jaw. "Of course I have."

"And you *do* know she is a wrongheaded, vindictive bitch? One who believed you capable of committing murder and made certain the rest of the world did as well?"

Sin winced. "She was wrong about me, but I cannot

entirely blame her. I hardly have the reputation of an angel. Be fair warned, however. If you ever dare to refer to her thus again, I will beat you to a fucking pulp, Decker."

"Not in your current state," his friend pointed out.

True.

Sin was not entirely certain he could stand. But he could still throw a punch. Could he not? Yes, he decided, he damn well could.

"Shall we test it?" he asked, raising a brow.

"I would prefer not to have an altercation with my oldest, best friend." Decker's voice was stinging. "Especially not over a woman who did her utmost to destroy you."

"She is not what you think," Sin found himself defending Callie as his whisky glass was miraculously refilled. "She loved her brother. Her devotion to him is…"

Something he envied.

As was her devotion to her dead former betrothed.

Because Sin wanted it for himself, curse her.

"Her devotion to him is enough to make her mad?" Decker guessed. "Because from where I stand, madness is the only excuse for what she did to you, Sin. She almost decimated you. How can you love such a treacherous—"

"Enough," Sin bit out, scowling at his friend, who was becoming more blurry by the moment. It was a distinct possibility there were two Deckers. At least, according to his eyesight. "I will not hear another ill word about her, and that is final."

"Fair enough." Decker inclined his head, his gaze searching. "But answer me this, Sin. If she is such a bloody angel, why are you here tonight? Why are you not at home, reveling in the marriage bed, reciting poetry to each other, that sort of tripe?"

Salient questions. Sin could not deny that, even if he hated them.

"She does not want me there," he admitted. "She was ill tonight, and she wanted her bloody lady's maid to attend her."

Instead of him.

That still hurt.

Fucking hell, how was his glass empty once more?

"Another whisky?" Decker asked him.

Sin ought to say no.

"Yes," he said instead. He was not ready to return home.

Home to his wife who had been…strangely withdrawn in the wake of the news she was carrying his child. Home to his wife who had been pale and quiet. Home to the realization that everything between them was about to change. Home to the fears that had not ceased to torment him ever since bloody Dr. Gilmore had made his announcement that Callie was carrying his child.

Thoughts of his daughter, stillborn, returned.

The realization he could lose another child, and that he could lose Callie too, slammed into him with the force of a fist.

His glass was full once more. He took a long, steady draught. The burn down to his gut was not enough to make him forget. But it was enough to distract.

For now.

She was going to be a mother.

How impossible it seemed.

Alone in the sitting room of her apartments, Callie rested her hand upon her belly. The chamber was eastward facing, which meant that whenever it was in abundance, rich sunlight spilled into the room, bathing it in warmth. On ordinary days, she adored this cheerful room. She spent time in here reading. Once, Sin had surprised her and made love to her on the divan. Another occasion, upon the newly replaced carpets.

But the joy she ordinarily found in this chamber was nowhere to be found today, and those memories of love-making haunted her like bitter ghosts.

It was still so much to comprehend, Dr. Gilmore's shocking proclamation the day before, that she was pregnant. Initially, she had been stunned. Utterly flabbergasted. For all that she and Sin had been making love at every opportunity, she had somehow foolishly believed that growing a child in her womb would take time. That it would not happen immediately.

However, fate had proven her wrong.

When Sin had come to her, she had been in shock. She had been dizzied, tired, and terrified. She still was tired. Still terrified. But now, she was also plagued by another painful truth: her husband had not returned home last night. He had left her as she had asked, and he had never come back.

The hour was nearing two o'clock in the afternoon.

Each tick of the arms on the ormolu mocked her. Like everything else in this newly decorated room, she had chosen the ornate bronze clock with a warrior as its focal point. The pictures on the walls, including one of Moreau's, filled her with bitter sadness. In the last month, she had made changes upon this home. It had begun, gradually, to feel like a place where she belonged.

As had Sin.

Where was he? And why? Had he decided that, having secured the possibility of an heir, he no longer needed to share her bed? Had he gone to his club? To another lover? To the ethereally beautiful Duchess of Longleigh?

At long last, she detected a flurry of motion in the hall. Footsteps. Voices. A door opening and closing. Callie knew what those sounds meant. Sin was back.

She rose to her feet and made her way through the door adjoining their apartments with all haste. When she saw him, she wished she had not, for the evidence of what he had spent the night doing was all over his handsome, dissolute form.

He was wearing yesterday's clothes. His hair was disheveled, his eyes bloodshot. His neck tie was missing, and his trousers were rumpled.

"Callie," he said, scrubbing a hand over his jaw.

She did not have the capacity to exchange greetings. A rush of raw fury made her tremble. "Where were you?"

"At my club," he said, moving toward her. "And after that, I bedded down at my friend's house."

She flinched away from his touch when he reached for her. "A *friend's* house?"

"Yes." His jaw hardened as his gaze searched hers. "A friend. Forgive me for not sending word. Yesterday's news left me surprised. I am afraid I did not handle it well."

"Were you with a paramour?" she asked, hating herself for the need to ask.

Fearing the answer and what it would mean even more.

"No." He shook his head. "Christ, no, Callie. I drank too much bloody whisky. My friend Decker took me to his townhome to sleep it off. That is all."

Fear had already sunk its talons into her heart. So, too, had doubt. Yesterday, he had been the one with doubts. Today, it was her turn.

She wanted to believe him. But part of her said she would be a fool if she did.

"Yesterday, I took tea with my friend, and when I

returned, you all but accused me of plotting an affair with Dunlop," she reminded him.

"Forgive me, Callie." He raked his long, elegant fingers—those fingers that knew every inch of her skin so well—through his hair. "There is no excuse for my behavior, save that I am hopelessly flawed. I am trying to be better, for you."

Another swift rush of outrage surged over her.

She gestured toward him, encompassing his disheveled state. "This does not look like trying, Sin. This looks like surrendering."

"I should have come home to you last night," he said on a sigh. "Forgive me, please."

She was not ready to forgive him with such ease. "Why did you go? Why get yourself so thoroughly inebriated that you could not return home until the next afternoon? Imagine how you would feel, had I been gone all night without word."

"I am an arse." He reached for her again, capturing her hand and tangling their fingers together. "And I am sorry."

How easy it would be to fall into his arms, into his bed. But that was what she had been doing for the last month, and look where it had landed her: she had fallen in love with a man she scarcely knew. She was carrying his child in her womb. And on the day she made the discovery, he had run off to drown himself in drink.

Benny's words of warning returned to her, then, and the doubts she had been entertaining yesterday, all last night, and every minute of his absence, blossomed.

You scarcely even know him.

He is the last sort of man I would ever wish to see married to my beloved sister.

I wonder what else your new husband is keeping from you.

She withdrew her hand from Sin's grasp. "I am going to pay a call to my brother and sister-in-law at Westmorland

House. I do not like the manner in which we left things yesterday."

"Of course." He clenched his jaw, studying her. "Allow me to dress, and I will accompany you."

"No." She could not give in to him. Not now. She needed time to sort out her feelings. To make sense of this wretched muddle. "I will go alone."

"Alone?" he asked, his voice grim.

"Yes. Alone."

He inclined his head. "As you wish, Callie."

It was not what she wished, but Callie did not bother to say it. Instead, she walked away.

* * *

"Her Grace, the Duchess of Longleigh," Dunlop announced.

Sin scowled at the butler-in-training. From bad to worse, it would seem. His head was still aching, his mouth felt as if it had been stuffed with cotton, and no amount of tea he had consumed since his ignominious return a few hours ago could cure what ailed him.

Mostly, he was filled with self-loathing.

And now, Tilly was here.

Tempting though it was, he knew he could not send her away. If she had sought him out, there was every possibility she was in need of aid. Moreover, she had been gracious to him, agreeing to meet with Callie, when the risk to her had not been worth the reward.

"See her in," he relented even as he knew Tilly paying him a call was the last complication he needed to add to this carriage wreck of a day.

He stood when Tilly entered, offering her a bow.

She was beautiful as ever, the drapery of her gown cleverly constructed to hide her pregnancy. Her mien was grave. She smiled, but it did not reach her eyes.

"Thank you for seeing me, Sin," she said softly.

"Of course," he told her easily. "For you, I always have time. What is the matter, my dear? Is it Longleigh?"

Her smile fled. "Is it not always Longleigh?"

Sin cursed. "You never should have married that bastard."

But he did not follow the statement he had oft made to her over the years with the additional accompanying sentence. *You should have married me.*

Because he no longer felt that way. When he had been consumed by misery with Celeste, marriage to Tilly had certainly seemed the better option. Her husband was a detestable, heartless bastard and Sin's wife had been a faithless, vindictive wretch. Now, however, Sin had found something deeper and far more meaningful with Callie. They were not just friends. She completed him in a way no other woman ever had or could.

If you did not bollix everything up with your stupid bloody trip to visit Decker last night, his conscience reminded him.

"But I did marry him, did I not?" Tilly shook her head. "I, alone, am to blame for the desperate straits in which I find myself. I had believed it would be different between us, if he finally had what he wanted. But I was wrong."

"Has Longleigh hurt you?" Sin pressed.

It was not his business, he knew, but the worries which had first surfaced upon his visit to Haddon House with Callie returned, and they would not be silenced.

"He has not raised his hand against me, if that is what you are asking. He would not dare to cause harm to the babe," she said. "Afterward...I cannot say. But I have not imposed upon you today to fret over what might happen. I am here seeking your help because of what has happened."

"Come," he said, gesturing for her to have a seat on the divan Callie had selected for his study as part of her campaign to refurbish his townhome. "Have a seat."

"Thank you, Sin," she whispered, her voice tremulous. "You are a great friend to me. I have missed you."

He had a feeling this conversation was going to be long and her feet would need the rest. Sin settled himself in a chair opposite. "Tell me everything, Tilly."

* * *

Callie emerged from her visit to Benny and Isabella feeling calmer. It had been good to spend a few, unhurried hours visiting with them. The distraction had been welcome. And it had granted her some time to realize she had been hard on Sin earlier that afternoon. After all, he had shown her he was trustworthy, had he not? The wounds left behind by his first marriage were deep, and she could not forget that.

"Where is his lordship?" she asked Dunlop upon her return, determined that she would see Sin and do her utmost to resume where they had left off earlier.

"Lord Sinclair is with the Duchess of Longleigh, in his study, my lady," the butler-in-training announced helpfully.

The Duchess of Longleigh?

Callie's stomach dropped.

"Thank you, Dunlop." The words had scarcely left her lips when Callie's feet were moving.

Feeling as if she were in a dream—a nightmare—she reached the study door. It stood slightly ajar. Through the crack, she saw the duchess in her husband's arms. Saw Sin's hands tenderly stroking up and down her back.

Heard her husband's beautiful, deep voice.

It was a lover's embrace. The intimacy and familiarity were undeniable.

"I will always care for you, Tilly," he was saying. "Whatever you need..."

Callie could not bear to hear the remainder of the words. The tentative understanding and hope she had spun, delicate as a spider's web, was obliterated. Everything gone. In a moment. In the sight of the duchess in Sin's arms, watching the way she clutched him, as if she would never let him go.

Dear God, it was just as she had always suspected. There were still feelings between the two of them.

Perhaps even love.

Callie fled, the sting of tears in her eyes, and ordered the carriage brought around once more. She was going back to Westmorland House.

She was going home.

CHAPTER 22

*I will never forget the expression on her face when realization
dawned upon her, like the sun illuminating the morning sky,
chasing away the shadows and darkness of night. It was in that
moment, dear reader, when she realized she had never known me
at all.*

~from **Confessions of a Sinful Earl**

"She does not want to see you, Sinclair."

The cold pronouncement of the Duke of Westmorland cut through the silence of the salon where Sin had been awaiting his wife. For the second day in a row, he had returned to Westmorland House, determined to gain an audience with Callie.

This time, he had not been turned away at the door by the disapproving butler. Mayhap because Sin had finally threatened to plant him a facer if he did not at least allow him inside the sprawling castle where his wife had chosen to hide herself. Regardless, this was not the interview he had been hoping to achieve after suffering through the longest night of his life.

Two nights in a row without her in his bed.

It had been fucking torture, and he was at fault for both.

"She is my wife," he told his forbidding brother-in-law. "I have every right to see her and to speak with her."

"You do not deserve an audience with her," Westmorland snarled. "After what you have done, you are damned fortunate I do not shoot you where you stand."

Sin returned the duke's glare with one of his own. "As far as I am aware, murder is still a crime, Westmorland."

"So is what you have put my sister through." Westmorland stalked toward him, menace in his step. "First, you blackmailed her into marrying you whilst I was on my honeymoon because you are lacking even a modicum of honor. Then, she discovered she was carrying your child, and you spent all night getting soused at a depraved club. After which you promptly made love to your mistress in your study, in plain view of the servants."

Sin's ears went hot, but he refused to retreat. "I will own that I blackmailed her into this marriage, and that I drowned myself in whisky that night, but the Duchess of Longleigh is not my mistress, and nor was I making love to her in my study."

When he had belatedly learned, after Tilly's departure, that Callie had returned from her call to her brother, only to suddenly leave once more, he had instantly known what she must have seen and the conclusions she had reached. Once again, his own actions looked damning. The fault for that was his, and he would own it. But he had hastened to Westmorland House only to be denied entrance. That Callie would hide from him for an entire night and not even allow him the chance to explain felt like a betrayal.

"Why should anyone believe what you say, Sinclair?" the duke bit out. "You are a known and admitted liar."

"All I want is the opportunity to speak with my wife," he returned, undaunted.

"Callie does not want to speak with you," his brother-in-law snapped. "You have done enough damage. When she is ready to see you, she will let you know."

Sin was tired of waiting.

He wanted his wife back.

He wanted the woman he loved. It had taken her leaving him to force the realization that he was not just *falling* in love with Callie. He had fallen a long bloody time ago. Perhaps even the moment she had smashed that worthless piece of pottery over his head back at Helston Hall. When she had demonstrated all her stubborn fire and fearlessness. He could not choose the exact second the balance had shifted. Nor how it had happened. All he did know was that he loved her. And like the sun rising each morning, that love was constant and true.

"I am not leaving until I see her," he countered evenly.

Westmorland raised a brow. "Then I suggest you enjoy bedding down on the carpets like the mongrel you are."

His brother-in-law did not like him. Whilst Sin was pleased Callie's brother was so loyal and protective, he would have preferred a bit less unadulterated hatred being directed toward him. He could admit it was not entirely undeserved.

"All I want is to see her, speak with her, and to give her some things that belong to her," he said simply, unwavering.

"I will see him, Benny."

Callie's voice cut through the thick mutual enmity inhabiting the salon. Sin turned to find her standing on the threshold. A jolt of awareness went through him when their stares met and held. He wanted to run to her, to take her in his arms, to beg her never to leave him alone for another night again.

But he remained where he was, tempering himself. The

manuscript in his hands rendered such an action impossible anyway.

Instead, he bowed. "Callie."

My love. My beautiful, stubborn, delicious woman.

"You do not have to see him," Westmorland addressed his sister. "If you are not comfortable with this, Callie, I will send him on his way."

"No." She shook her head, her gaze still lingering upon Sin. "Thank you, Benny, but I want to speak with my husband. Alone."

"I am not sure that is wise," the duke countered, his voice stern.

"What do you think I am going to do to her, Westmorland?" he demanded, nettled.

"Please, Benny," Callie said, her voice gentling. "I promise you, I will be fine."

Westmorland sent Sin a vicious glare. "If you hurt her in any fashion, I will break off both your arms and beat you with them. And then I will cut off your ballocks and stuff them down your throat."

"Gruesome bastard, aren't you?" Sin muttered.

His brother-in-law merely raised a brow. "Try me, Sinclair."

"Benny," Callie said pointedly.

Thankfully, the duke at long last took his leave, but not before sending one more threatening glance in Sin's direction. When he was gone, Sin and Callie stood alone, facing each other.

"How are you feeling today?" he asked on a rush. "Any dizziness? You have not swooned again, have you? Perhaps we ought to sit. Are you too warm? Too cool? Have you eaten enough?"

As the last question fled him, he understood how foolish he sounded. But it could not be helped.

"I am as well as can be expected," she answered, her voice taut. *Controlled.* Distinctly unlike his fiery countess. "And I do not need to sit. I am perfectly capable of standing. I am not so fragile."

He nodded, drinking in the sight of her. She was bloody ravishing. Her dark eyes were doing the same to him, he realized. But her expression remained guarded. They were eying each other like two prize-fighters attempting to determine which of them would land the first blow.

"You look well," he observed, deciding it would be him. "Indeed, you look better than well. You are so damned beautiful, it hurts to look at you."

Her cheeks went pink. She caught her berry-red lower lip in her teeth. "Thank you. I could say the same of you."

He did not believe that for a moment. He looked like a man who had scarcely slept the night before. Who had paced the freshly replaced Axminster in his chamber, searching his mind for ways he could make amends with the woman he loved.

He itched to touch her, but there was still the matter of the manuscript in his hands. He thrust it toward her. "This is for you."

She took it from him, their fingers brushing in the exchange, and Sin felt the shock of that touch—so simple—so innocent—in an electric pulse that shot up his elbow and landed in an ache in his ballocks.

Callie glanced down at the manuscript. "This is the last installment of *Confessions of a Sinful Earl*," she noted, sounding surprised.

He nodded. "It is. Your former publisher returned it to me, at my request. But I want you to have it."

Her brow furrowed. "Why?"

"Because it is yours."

She gazed back up at him. "But why now?"

"It was wrong of me to keep it from you, just as it was wrong of me to get sotted at my club and spend the night at Decker's townhome." He paused, struggling for his words. Everything he had rehearsed on the carriage ride here dissipated in the wake of her glorious presence. "It was also wrong of me to abduct you. Wrong of me to blackmail you into becoming my wife. Hell, Callie, I have committed a great deal of wrongs in my life. But one I swear I have not committed against you—and never would, for that matter— is adultery. Whatever you think you saw between myself and the Duchess of Longleigh was purely friendship. Nothing more."

"You were embracing her," Callie said. "Holding her in your arms as if she were made of finest porcelain. Telling her you would always care for her and be there in whatever she needs. And this, after you were so protective of her. After you revealed to me that she had once been your *mistress*, and lest we forget, you had just spent the night carousing. Tell me, Sin, what was I to think?"

"You were to think that I spoke vows and intend to uphold them," he countered.

"For how long?" she asked bitterly. "You were more than clear with your expectations. You told me you would bed me until I provided you with an heir, and then we could live our lives separately, however we wished. As soon as I was pregnant, you were gone all night long, and then I caught you in the arms of the duchess, making promises to her."

Tilly's story was complicated. He had promised her his utter discretion, but he could not keep the truth from Callie. Not when doing so could cost him his wife.

"Longleigh is a despicably cruel man," he said, struggling to give voice to the ugliness Tilly had revealed to him yesterday. "He is unable to perform his husbandly duties, but he requires an heir. There was a time when he allowed Tilly to live as she wished, to discreetly take lovers. However, he decided he was no longer willing to take the chance that she would, as he phrased it, birth him a bastard that was not of his stock. He forced her into bed with one of his nephews."

Callie gasped. "Are you saying he allowed his nephew to rape his own wife?"

"That is what it was to have been, yes," Sin said grimly. "However, at some point before their affair began, it became something more for the two of them, and they fell in love. Now, the nephew is suddenly, inexplicably missing, and Tilly is convinced Longleigh had something to do with it. She asked me for assistance in finding him. That is what you saw. She is worried over her lover, the father of her child. Terrified what Longleigh has done to him, and worse, what he may do to her. I was doing my best to reassure her, and to promise her that I will aid her in whatever fashion I can."

"That is despicable," Callie said, her voice hushed with shock, her countenance reflecting the same disgust swirling in his own gut. "I feel so badly for her. You are going to help her however you can, are you not, Sin? We can also speak with Benny about it—given all his connections at Scotland Yard, no one would be more capable of looking into the disappearance of Longleigh's nephew."

"It is indeed despicable," he agreed. "I have promised to do what I can in that regard. I am, however, quite certain your brother does not hold me in the highest esteem at the moment."

That was rather an understatement, he thought wryly. Westmorland had been eying him like an executioner ready to start sharpening his blade.

"Benny is exceedingly protective, but when I explain everything to him, he will see reason. Believe me." Callie paused, then worried her lip again. "I feel so foolish now. I was terrified that you had chosen her. That you would no longer want me now that I am pregnant."

Her confession slayed him. It required every modicum of restraint Sin possessed not to groan and cover that much-abused lip with his. There was far too much at stake to lose himself in kisses just yet. Later, there would be time for that. He *hoped*.

"Never, sweet. I will always, only choose you." He flashed her his best attempt at a smile. "Forever. And I want you now more than I ever have."

"I had thought for certain you were still in love with her."

He held his wife's stare, willing her to read the sincerity in his. He had never meant anything more than what he was about to say. "I promise you there is only one woman I love."

Callie stilled, her gaze searching his. "Sin?"

He moved forward, closing the remaining distance keeping them apart. Her scent filled his senses, her wide eyes all he saw. That sooty fringe of impossibly long lashes. The flecks of honey in the dark-brown depths.

"You, Callie," he said softly. "You are the only woman I love."

"You...love me?" Her eyes glistened. The manuscript fell from her fingers, fluttering all over the floor around their feet.

She did not remove her gaze from his.

He took her hand in his and held it over his madly thudding heart so she could feel how she affected him. "I did not just bring the manuscript back to you. This belongs to you also. My heart."

Her fingers curled in the fabric of his coat. "Sin..."

"I never wanted to fall in love with you," he continued, praying she would not reject him. That she would believe him. That she would trust him. "From the start, I was determined to hate you. I told myself I was using you, that you were a means to an end. That I was only marrying you to solve my problems. But from the moment I first kissed you, I knew that was a bloody lie. I thought I was marrying a treacherous witch, that this marriage would be no different than my last, and similarly doomed to misery. It did not take me long to realize how wrong I was and how right *we* are, together."

"Oh, darling." Tears clung to her lashes, slid down her cheeks.

"I love you, Callie," he continued, his own eyes stinging. "I love your stubbornness, your loyalty, your compassion. I love your passion and your caring. I love the kindness you showed my mother, the way you tirelessly pursue what is right. I love going to sleep each night with you in my bed and waking up each morning with your face the first thing I see. I love the way you taste, the way you smell, and I bloody well love the way you kiss. I love everything about you."

He would have said more, but he stopped, afraid he had revealed too much. Afraid he had not revealed enough.

She cupped his face. "I love you, too."

He lost the ability to think. Or speak.

Instead, he could only act. Sin hauled Callie into his arms and took her lips with his. No kiss had ever been sweeter. She surrendered to him with a breathy sigh, her arms going around his neck as she rose on tiptoes to return his kiss with all the ferocity he had come to expect from her.

Their mouths sealed in perfect union, and never in his life had any kiss felt better. It was a kiss of reunion, of relief, of love. So much love. They kissed and kissed and kissed, until they were breathless. Until his next thought was that he was going to drag her to the bloody carpet and take her on a bed of the scattered pages of her unpublished manuscript.

Before he could do something so foolhardy, he tore his lips from hers.

For a moment, they stared at each other, two lost souls inexplicably found. And then she traced her finger down his cheek, trailing wetness he had not realized had been there before over his skin. Tears. His.

Fucking hell.

This woman had him in tatters.

This woman made him whole. She picked up the jagged shards of the man he had once been and sewed him back together into a new man. One who not only loved her, but one who was worthy of her love in return.

"I love you so much it hurts," she told him, a sentiment he knew all too well. "Do you forgive me for doubting you, for letting my fears get the best of me?"

"I forgive you anything," he vowed. "Come home with me, sweet. Come home where you and our babe belong."

Her smile hit him in the heart. "There is nowhere I would rather be."

* * *

Fate had an odd way of taking the worst of life—the heartbreaks, the losses, the ugliness—and fashioning them into something unbearably good, Callie had discovered. Sometimes, the road to redemption was long, winding, and perilous.

Sometimes, fate stole into your carriage and made you his captive. Sometimes, fate was named Sin, and he was wickedly handsome, and his kisses turned your knees to pudding, and he made you fall in love with him and all his battle scars.

Sometimes, you had to suffer to appreciate that goodness when it finally arrived.

Callie snuggled against her beloved husband's chest. She could not help but to feel, this night, a new sense of rightness. A sense that she was exactly where she was meant to be, where she had *always* been meant to be.

In her husband's big, tall bed. The one where he had first made love to her.

The one where he had made love to her again, with exquisite tenderness, not long ago. His heart was a reassuring hammer beneath her ear, the musky, citrus scent of him invading her senses. The smattering of crisp, dark hair on his chest was soft against her cheek.

She kissed his bare skin, inhaling deeply. His fingers stroked through her unbound hair. Callie hated to halt the sweet simplicity of the moment, but she had a question for him, one which had been troubling her ever since he had thrust the pages of her work into her hands earlier that day at Westmorland House.

"Why did you truly give me back the unpublished installment of *Confessions of a Sinful Earl*?" She tilted her head back to see his face as she posed her question.

From this angle, she was treated to the sight of his strong jaw and proud chin, shaded in whiskers. His full, sensual mouth, those wickedly sculpted lips that brought her so much pleasure, were swollen from their kisses and glistening in the lamplight. He was still and silent for so long she wondered if he had heard her.

But then, at last, the deep rumble of his baritone emerged.

"Because they are your words. You are an incredibly talented writer, sweet." He paused, swallowing, and she greedily tracked the subtle dip of his Adam's apple. "I had been keeping it since your publisher returned it to me. But the story is yours. If you want to complete it, publish the final volume of the serial, I will not object. Lord knows all London is awaiting it."

Her husband was willing to allow her to further trample his reputation into the mud, and for no reason other than that he loved her. She absorbed that knowledge. And if she did not fall in love with him even more in that instant, the stars did not shine in the night sky, and nor did the sun rise in the east each morning.

How wrong she had been about him. She had believed him a heartless, dangerous villain. A man capable of anything. Instead, she had discovered a man who was sweet and compassionate, who would sacrifice anything for those he loved.

Even himself.

"I do not want to publish it, Sin." Her fingers trailed over the hard plane of his abdomen. "I never want to hurt you again."

He lifted a hank of her hair, allowing the strands to fall onto her bare back, ever so slowly. "Then never leave me. I need you here with me, princess. At my side, in my bed, in my arms."

"I am here to stay." She kissed his chest once more.

"Promise?" His hand swept beneath her hair, following the line of her spine in a gentle caress.

"Promise." She flicked her tongue over his flat nipple, feeling wicked. "I love you." She nipped him lightly. "Do you promise *you* will never leave *me*?"

"Hell yes," he growled. "You are quite stuck with me forever, love."

"Good." She kissed down his chest, taking her time to marvel at him. "There is no one else I would rather be stuck with, darling."

Her lips traveled lower. Her hands, too. He was so beautiful, masculine strength at her mercy. She wanted to worship his body the way he did hers. His skin was warm, his muscles rippling beneath her touch. He inhaled sharply when she kissed down his ribs, over his abdomen.

His hand fisted in her hair. "Callie, what are you doing?"

"Loving you." She settled herself between his legs, where his cock was already hard again, standing stiff and proud. "Tell me what to do, Sin."

He was watching her with a heavy-lidded gaze. "Damnation, woman." But even as he bit out the words, he gripped his thick length, holding it out to her like an offering. "Take me in your mouth."

Callie did not hesitate. She sucked the tip of him, reveling in the way he tasted—salty, musky, like both of them mingled together. She swirled her tongue around him, gratified at his low groan of approval. Callie glanced up his body, meeting his intense, dark stare.

"More?" she asked.

He swallowed. "More. Take me in your throat, princess."

Sin removed his hand, giving her free reign over him. She lowered her head, taking as much of him as she could, and gripping the base of his shaft with her hand. His fingers tangled in her hair, guiding her, showing her what he wanted.

Up and down, in and out. He surged into the back of her throat, huge and demanding.

"Yes," he rasped. "Let me fuck your mouth."

Oh.

His vulgar demand made her pearl pulse and an aching wetness blossom between her thighs. She understood what he wanted, and she wanted it, too. Wanted him. Was ravenous for him. Callie moved her lips up and down his shaft, alternating between bringing him deep into her throat —so deep she almost gagged—and then retreating to lavish attention upon his cockhead.

A drop of his seed leaked from the slit at the tip, and she licked it up, savoring every drop of him she could get. Then she lowered her head again. The thick slide of his manhood over her tongue, down her throat, was intoxicating. His hips were pumping beneath her, and each moan she wrung from his perfect lips felt like a victory. His cock was so beautiful, as beautiful as the rest of him. She could not get enough of him. She wanted his seed in her mouth, wanted to swallow it down.

Wanted to make him lose control.

But her husband had other ideas.

Sin tugged on her hair, pulling her head back until he slid from her lips.

"I was not finished yet," she protested.

"If you do not finish, I will be finished," he growled, hauling her up his body and rolling them as one so she was pinned beneath him, legs spread. "And the first time was far too fast. I want to go slowly this time. To enjoy you properly."

Her aching cunny was perfectly aligned with his big, wet cock. She writhed beneath him, wanting to get him inside her.

"Enjoy me, then," she urged, desperate.

"I will." The grin he gave her was full of wicked promise.

The bud of her sex pulsed. Sucking him had left her desperately hungry for him. She was drenched. But he was not doing what she wanted. Instead, he was reaching for something…

His discarded neck cloth, she realized.

"Give me your wrists, sweet."

She would give him anything.

Callie did as he asked, and he tied a knot around both wrists, then secured them over her head. She was tied to his bed, as she had been on the day he had taken her from

London, but this time, everything between them was different.

So very, wonderfully different.

He grinned down at her. "I like having you at my mercy, little wife."

"I like being at your mercy," she confessed on a gasp when he dipped his head to suck her nipple into his mouth.

The hot, silken suction was exquisite. He palmed her other breast, working his thumb over the pebbled peak. When he rasped his teeth over her, Callie's core clenched.

"What will I do with you?" he asked.

"Anything you want," she said, breathless.

His tongue licked a tormenting circle around her nipple, then flicked over it. She bucked from the bed, trying to bring him nearer, wanting his cock to fill her, stretch her. But he retreated, the only part of him touching her his mouth and his knowing fingers. He lapped at her breasts, long leisurely strokes over first one nipple, then another. When she swore she could bear no more of his torture, he sucked.

His fingers traced over her belly, lingering there, where their child grew.

"I love you," Sin said against her skin.

"And I love you." The words, now that she had spoken them once, were easy to say. Easy to embrace.

Just as Sin was easy to love.

He dragged his light touch lower. To where she was on fire for him. Long fingers stroked her slit, then parted her. He circled her aching bud with slow, light strokes. Not enough pressure. Callie thrust into his hand. He gave her what she wanted, sucking her nipples and stimulating her at the same time.

And then he kissed down her body, spread her thighs wider, and settled his mouth on her. He sucked her pearl, the wet sound echoing through the chamber, along with her ragged breathing.

She moaned. There was something delectably erotic about being tied to his bed. About not being able to touch him. About being completely his. About the sight of him pleasuring her, his handsome face buried in her mound.

He groaned as he suckled her, then ran his tongue over her in firm, wet strokes that had her on the edge. After their first round of lovemaking, all her senses were heightened. The needy ache in her sex turned into a crescendo of pure bliss. She cried out, jerking against his lashing tongue, against the bonds on her wrist. Warmth blossomed from her core as she spent. She quivered beneath his masterful tongue as he stayed where he was, prolonging the pleasure with steady pulses and the abrasion of his teeth.

Sated, limp, mindless, she struggled to catch her breath as her husband kissed her inner thigh and met her gaze. His lips glistened with the evidence of her desire. She wondered if she would taste herself on his lips, or if she would taste the both of them, mingling, blending, becoming one.

He kissed his way back up her body, and she had her answer when he claimed her mouth. Deep, soul-baring kisses. His tongue in her mouth. She sucked. Both of them, that was what she tasted—the blended saltiness and musk of their union. The hope and the joy and the love.

Us.

Yes, that was it. *Us.* They were one, now and forever.

He rubbed his cock up and down her folds, coating himself in her wetness, then found the nub he had just so thoroughly pleasured and toyed with her some more. She mewled into his kiss, writhed against him. Her hard nipples grazed his chest.

The weight of him atop her was delicious.

He raised his head, his dark gaze glittering with intensity.

"Tell me what you want, sweet. Make those pretty lips say dirty things."

"I want your cock inside me, filling me, stretching me." She licked her lips, finding her courage. "I want you deep in me, Sin. I want you fast and hard and wild."

"Good little wife," he praised, notching his cock to her slick core. "I have no choice but to give you what you want, do I?"

"No you don't," she agreed, lifting her head to seal their mouths in another slow, carnal kiss before letting her head drop back onto the pillow. "Make me come. Fuck me, Sin."

The naughty words fled her lips. She did not even know where they emerged from, only that he had taught them to her. He had shown her what they meant, had brought her to shattering heights of pleasure. And now, he was going to give her even more.

On a guttural groan, he thrust into her, gliding through her wetness and planting himself as far as he could. She was gloriously filled. He moved, withdrawing from her, only to slam his cock back into her again.

He took her lips in another drugging kiss, biting her lower lip as his rhythm turned frantic. In and out he drove, hips pumping, bed shaking. She wrapped her legs around him, meeting him thrust for thrust. And though she longed to touch him, to run her fingers over his back, to sift through his hair, the inability somehow heightened the potency of her desire. She loved being tied to his bed.

Loved him inside her.

Atop her.

Taking her to the edge of that dangerous cliff of desire.

In and out. Faster. Harder. More.

He caught her bottom in his hands and angled her so he could plunge even deeper into her. Callie lost all control. The knot of desire grew tighter. Her heart was pounding, the slide of him in her cunny making her feel as if sparks were raining down on her.

"Come for me, sweet," he murmured against her lips.

One more frantic slam of his hips into hers, and she did.

She clenched on him, her entire body seizing as a burst of pleasure exploded, radiating outward. Tremors rocked her. She gasped his name. In the next breath, he stiffened, the warm rush of his seed making her tremble.

He collapsed against her, breathing heavy, his heart pounding against her breast, his face buried in her hair. She came down from her cloud slowly, gasping for breaths, reveling in the intensity of their lovemaking.

After a few moments, he stirred, then untied the knots on her wrists.

She wasted no time in wrapping her arms around him. He gathered her in his embrace, drawing her against his chest once more. They clung to each other as if they were each other's only chance of surviving the raging waters of a flood. And that was what it felt like, this bond between them.

They were each other's. Simple as that.

He pressed a kiss to the crown of her head.

Callie smiled. "Sin?"

"Yes, sweet?" His baritone was lazy. Sated. Happy.

Her smile deepened. "That was a vast improvement upon the last time you tied me to a bed."

Her husband chuckled, then stroked her hair. "If you thought that was good, my love, wait until the next time."

Callie was feeling saucy. "Is that a threat or a promise, darling?"

"For you, Callie mine, *everything* is a promise."

EPILOGUE

*I have a confession to make, dear reader, and it is not a confession
of which I am particularly proud. Nevertheless, it must be done.
You see, I am the true author of* Confessions of a Sinful Earl. *I
wanted to believe the worst of my Sinful Earl, dear reader, and I
deliberately sought to destroy him, one word at a time.
But he showed me the best of him. And in the end, I fell in love.
How could I not?
Dear reader, I married him. I do not deserve him. Nor do I deserve
you.
This memoir is my attempt to make amends. In it, you will discover
the truth of what happened to the Duke of W. and Lady S. You will
also find the real truth about Lord S. I hope you will forgive me for
the damage I have done...*

~from **Confessions of a Sinful Countess**

*C*allie held the small, bound volume in her hands,
studying the fine leather stamped with gilt letters.

"What do you think of it?" Sin asked her, sounding
anxious.

"I think it is beautiful and frightening, all at once." She ran a finger over the embellished words. "At last, everyone will know what truly happened."

The memoir she had written over the last few months of their marriage was not just a gift to her husband—Callie's way of atoning for the ruthless manner in which she had destroyed his reputation—it was also her means of putting a painful chapter in both their pasts behind them forever.

"You are certain you wish for the copies to be sold?" Sin searched her gaze. "Decker has reassured me that he will have them destroyed if you or Westmorland change your minds."

"No." She shook her head. "This is what is right, Sin."

As it turned out, fate had one more surprise in store for Callie and Sin. Not long after their reconciliation, Callie had made a stunning discovery tucked in a hidden compartment in the countess's chambers: Celeste's journal. The final entry had been a grim declaration of guilt.

Confessions of a Sinful Countess would finally resolve the questions surrounding the deaths of Alfred and Celeste. The truth had been on the page, written in shaky scrawl. Alfred had told her he wanted to end their affair that night following Sin's angry confrontation. Celeste had fought with him and pushed him in a fit of rage. He tumbled down the stairs, his neck broken. She had fled and had ended with the conclusion that there was no means of escape save her own end.

"There may be ramifications for both of us," Sin reminded her, his countenance serious. "Scandal. Rumors. This may undo all the good we have done over the last few months. There will be little question as to who is the author."

Sin had been the first person to read her manuscript. With his blessing, they had given the memoirs to Sin's friend Decker, who was using the publisher he owned to print not only the memoirs, but also all future publications for the

Lady's Suffrage Society. Decker was a cunning businessman, and he understood the demand for the memoirs would likely be an excellent opportunity for his company. Scandal and salaciousness sold in abundance.

Callie was no fool. She knew how unconventional it was to admit she had written *Confessions of a Sinful Earl*. She also knew the risk she took in revealing the truth of Alfred's and Celeste's deaths.

"This is the only means of removing all traces of doubt concerning you," Callie told him, resolute. "It is the right thing to do, for everyone."

"I do not give a damn if the whole world thinks me guilty." Sin's hands closed over hers atop the book. As always, his touch awoke her need, unending when it came to him. "You know the truth. If I have your faith, trust, and love, I have everything I need. All I could ever want."

"I care," she told him softly. "I am responsible for all England believing you a murderer. It is time to rectify that, and this is the only way."

"I told you, everyone else can go hang, save you," he insisted stubbornly.

He was so keen to protect her. How did she deserve him?

"If they must go hang, I will make certain they know you are an innocent man first," she countered softly. "I love you too much to keep this a secret any longer."

"Ah," he drawled, plucking the book from her hands and depositing it on a nearby table before pulling her into a loose embrace, "but I am hardly innocent, little wife. You ought to know that by now."

As always, he knew what she needed, and when. Their discussion was at an end. The book would be sold. Everyone would read it. Tongues would wag. Callie's mind was made up.

The undercurrent of desire in Sin's voice sent an

answering surge of yearning through her. Her belly was between them, burgeoning and immense, keeping her from the closeness she longed for from his big, powerful body. Callie's arms wound around her husband's neck.

"I do know you are a very wicked man," she said, her stare dipping to his sensual mouth. "In only the best way possible, of course."

He lowered his head and kissed her, long and slow. Their tongues glided together. He tasted of tea and sugar. Of sweet temptation. Of promise and hope and redemption. Of love. He took his time, worshiping her mouth. His hands cupped her face, holding her still for his ravishing.

He did not need to worry she would move; there was no other place she would rather be than here, with him. Always. She told him with her kiss, with her lips and tongue.

When he pulled back, straightening to his full, impressive height, his expression took her breath. "I want you."

She felt positively bovine in her current state. She was large, ungainly. In Callie's estimation, and according to her mirror, her petite frame looked utterly ridiculous carrying a child. But Sin's desire for her had never waned. If anything, it had increased as her belly swelled with their babe. She did not mind, for she was every bit as ravenous for him in her current state, if not more so.

Still, she had to remind herself it was the midst of the day and they were in the music room, where she had been playing a tune upon the piano before he had arrived. The door was still ajar. Langdon, who had yet to retire to his country cottage because he was not ready to entrust the household to Dunlop—Langdon's words—could wander in at any moment. Or Sin's mother, whose spirits had lifted in the care of her new nurse. Or even Eloise.

"The door is open, Sin," she protested weakly.

She wanted him so badly, her drawers were soaked, and

her sex was pulsing. All from his nearness and those kisses. Her body wanted his the way her heart did. The wickedest part of her was not sure she cared about the door or the possibility of interruption.

"That is a problem easily solved," he said, releasing her and stalking across the chamber.

Callie would be lying if she said she was not admiring the sight of her husband's long legs and his delightful arse as he went. He was in shirtsleeves and waistcoat. Who could blame her?

He closed the door and spun around in one deft move. The intensity of his stare turned Callie's insides to liquid as he made his way back to her. His hands settled on her waist, such as it was these days. He pressed his forehead to hers.

"Better?"

Everything was better when he was touching her.

"Yes," she whispered.

"Good." He gave her one of his rare, beautiful grins—the sort that crinkled the corners of his eyes and made him somehow even more deliciously handsome. "I need to taste you."

"Oh." It was the only word she could manage.

"Yes, *oh.*" His grin deepened. Carnal intent emanated from him.

Wicked, wonderful man.

He guided her backward, to the piano bench. Before she knew it, she was seated upon the bench, facing him, legs parted, skirts and petticoats clutched in her hands as he sank to his knees on the Axminster before her.

"You are lucky I am not wearing divided skirts," she teased.

"No." His hands were on her knees, on her thighs, caressing through her drawers. The thin, delicate barrier between her skin and his made her wilder, more desperate.

"*You* are lucky, darling. I am going to lick your pretty cunny until you come all over my tongue. And then, I am going to fuck you hard. So bloody hard. Until you come again on my cock."

If she had not already been seated, she would have melted into a puddle on the floor.

"Yes," was all she could manage. And then, as an afterthought, "please."

"Mmm," he hummed as his head settled between her thighs.

The first stroke of his tongue over her engorged pearl was electric. He sucked. Licked down her seam. Sank his tongue inside her.

"Oh, Sin," she moaned. He felt so good. His tongue was hot and warm and firm.

"Delicious," he whispered against her folds, his breath stirring more delirious want.

She leaned against the piano, limp and helpless and mindless. The discordant sound of a half-dozen keys rang through the air. The ivory cut into her back. And still, she did not care. All she wanted was more Sin. More of his tongue. More pleasure. More everything.

Because she knew how he liked when she spoke wickedly, and because she was greedy, she found her voice again. "Make me come. Fuck me with your tongue."

He did. Oh, how he did. He groaned into her core. His tongue was long and knowing, thrusting into her again and again. She planted her left hand on the piano bench to keep herself from tumbling down, and her right hand went to his head. Her fingers slid through the thick, silky strands of his hair. She grabbed a fistful, and then she pressed him deeper into her cunny, showing him what she wanted.

He licked into her until she came, her channel convulsing with such force, she cried out and shuddered and lost all control. She would have slid to the floor had Sin not caught her. But even as the throes of her release tremored through her, he was not finished. Gently, he drew her to her feet, and then moved them as one to the side of the piano.

"You are a goddess," he said, planting her hands on the sleek, polished wood. He kissed her ear, then tongued the hollow behind it. "I want inside you."

"Yes." The word left her, a needy susurrus.

Her skirts lifted again. Sin's mouth found her neck, and he lavished kisses upon her greedy flesh. His fingers dipped inside her, testing her readiness. She moaned. He did not need to test. She was more than ready. Heavens, she was desperate.

"Now," she ordered him, unable to stand any more of his torment.

"Demanding little wife," he breathed, nibbling on a particularly sensitive part of her throat. "I like when you order me about."

"I want you," she told him, thrusting into his hand, his fingers.

He withdrew from her, and she knew a moment of agonizing waiting until he brought his cock to her entrance. "I want you more."

If it was a contest, Callie was sure she would win.

If she could manage a coherent word, that was.

Which she most decidedly could not.

It did not matter, anyway, because in the next breath, her husband impaled her with his thick, rigid cock. Sensation burst. Over her. In her. Everywhere. She was delirious with need, with bliss. He was buried deep, so deep. And it felt good, so good.

He started moving, thrusting slowly, building the momentum, the need. With each stroke, she cried out. The only sound in the room was their ragged breathing and the wetness of her cunny as he pumped into her with gradually increasing speed. She slid her hands to the edge of the piano to keep from collapsing atop it. The ridge gave her purchase as she began moving against him, seeking more. Deeper, harder, faster.

He gave her everything she wanted, just as he always did.

His fingers found her pearl, stroking with expert precision.

It did not take long for her to reach the heights of passion again. She spent once more, clenching on his cock, rearing against him to drive him deep, and he lost himself in almost the same moment, spilling inside her. She milked every last drop from him, reveling in the warm torrent of his release until at last, sated and drained, she collapsed against the piano.

He kissed her nape. Whispered his love for her in her ear.

And she whispered hers for him right back.

* * *

Sin paced the length of his study for the hundredth time. Or the thousandth.

Mayhap millionth?

Millionth. Was that even a word?

He ran his hand over his jaw and then over his whole bloody face, closing his eyes. "Fuck!"

"Whisky?"

Decker's calm, wry voice shook Sin from his inner torment. He opened his eyes again to find his friend standing before him, a half-full glass extended between them like an offering to the gods.

Sin plucked the glass from Decker's fingers. "Hell yes."

He lifted the fine crystal to his lips and poured the whisky down his throat before offering it back to his friend. "More."

Decker raised a lone, dark brow. "Certain? I thought you were no longer touching the stuff after the time you were too obliterated to go home and Lady Sinclair nearly cut off your ballocks."

It was true. After that horrible night, Sin had not touched another drop of whisky. Nor had he gone to the Black Souls club. He had been doing his utmost to be a husband worthy of Callie. To show her she could always trust him. To banish the demons of his past forever. And he had done so.

But today was a different sort of day.

It had begun in ordinary fashion, waking to Callie in his bed. They had made love slowly and deliciously. Then, breakfast. Followed by all hell breaking loose.

And now, he was awaiting the birth of his daughter or son. Callie had been upstairs with Dr. Gilmore, her sister-in-law, and her best friend Lady Jo for hours. Suffering. Laboring. Sin could only pray that both his wife and their child would survive. It was harrowing. Terrifying. He had faith, but he was petrified, nevertheless.

"What time have you?" he asked Decker, instead of answering his friend's question.

It had been deuced rude, anyway.

"Half past eight." Decker tipped a decanter, splashing more whisky into Sin's empty glass. "Bloody hell, man. Is this what I have to look forward to?"

Sin took a frantic gulp of liquor, feeling it burn all the way to his gut. He probably ought to offer his friend an encouraging word. But fuck the blighter. Sin was not his keeper.

"Absolutely," he said, without a hint of conscience.

Decker poured himself a glass. "Fuck."

Sin toasted him mockingly. "My sentiments precisely."

And then he promptly drained the rest of his glass.

But the whisky was not helping him. It did nothing to assuage his worries. He slammed his glass down upon his desk and resumed pacing.

"It has been far too long," he worried aloud. "Westmorland went to check on the progress ages ago."

"This sort of thing takes time, does it not?" Decker asked.

"Yes," Sin bit out, turning back to his friend and stalking back down the length of the study. "Too much time. Too many risks. Too much danger. My God, Decker, if I lose her…"

He could not finish the sentence. Could not bear to do so.

"Lady Sinclair will be well," Decker promised him. "And you shall soon have a squalling, red-faced girl or boy child who hopefully takes after your wife when it comes to appearances…"

"Ha," he bit out, momentarily distracted by his friend's antics. "I shall tell you the same bloody thing when it is your turn."

Decker glared at him. "Go to hell, Sin."

It was Sin's turn to raise a brow at his friend. "Already there, old fellow. Currently."

Suddenly, a knock sounded at the study door.

"Enter!" Sin bellowed, desperate for word of Callie and their babe.

The door opened, revealing the Duchess of Westmorland, who was herself heavy with child. Westmorland was at her side.

Sin rushed forward. "How is she? How is the babe?"

The duchess smiled. "They are both well."

Relief hit him.

Thank God.

"You have a son," Westmorland added. "Congratulations, Sinclair."

His relationship with Callie's brother had improved over the last few months. Sin appreciated Westmorland's protectiveness over Callie. Westmorland appreciated that Sin would do everything in his power to keep Callie happy.

The words echoed now.

A son.

He was a father.

He scarcely heard Decker congratulating him. Blood was roaring in his ears, and for a moment, he feared he would swoon like a milksop. But Sin gathered himself and focused on the duchess, who had been in the birthing room.

"May I see them now?" he rasped.

"Of course." The duchess smiled. "Go."

Sin did not need to be told twice. He was up the stairs in a blur. Jogging down the hall. Crossing over the threshold.

Drinking in the most beautiful sight in the world.

Callie looked tired but glorious, her dark hair tamed into a neat braid, a swaddled bundle nestled in her arms. He scarcely took note of Lady Jo, quietly excusing herself from the chamber. The doctor was already gone.

"Come, my love," Callie said softly, "meet your son."

He did not require further invitation. Sin's strides ate up the distance between them, until he was at her side, gazing down at the perfect, pink face of their son. Awe and love hit him with so much force, his knees buckled. He sat on the bed at Callie's side, reaching out with a trembling hand to gently touch the fine, dark hairs on the babe's head.

"He is perfect," he murmured, turning his attention back to his wife. "Just like his mama."

"He is handsome," Callie said. "Just like his papa."

Sin stroked her cheek, filled with wonder. "How are you, sweet?"

"Happy." She turned her head and pressed a kiss to his palm. "Happy beyond words."

Sin could not resist covering her lips with his. "Thank you for loving me and for giving me a son, my darling wife. I could not be more content."

Then, he kissed their son's smooth little brow.

Callie caressed Sin's cheek, love shining in her eyes. "Nor could I."

Who would have thought this fiery, daring minx—a woman he had once considered his nemesis—would be the one to conquer his heart and make him whole again?

Not him.

But Sin was bloody well glad she had.

* * *

THANK you for reading Sin and Callie's story! I hope you enjoyed this first book in my Notorious Ladies of London series, all about daring ladies who know what they want and aren't afraid to get it.

You can read *Lady Wallflower*, Book Two in the Notorious Ladies of London series right now, featuring Callie's friend Lady Jo Danvers, handsome businessman Elijah Decker, and a *very* naughty list. One-click!

P.S. If you're looking for the Duke and Duchess of Westmorland's love story, you can find it in *Fearless Duke*. Tilly's story is available in Book Five, *Lady Lawless*.

Please consider leaving an honest review of *Lady Ruthless.* Reviews are greatly appreciated! If you'd like to keep up to date with my latest releases and series news, sign up for my newsletter here or follow me on Amazon or BookBub. Join my reader's group on Facebook for bonus content, early excerpts, giveaways, and more.

Keep reading for an excerpt of *Lady Wallflower*…

* * *

Chapter One

London, 1885

Decker stared at the list on the desk before him.

He had read the flowery script at least half a dozen times since finding it tucked between the pages of a pamphlet he had been tasked with printing for the Lady's Suffrage Society.

The words taunted him.

Tempted him.

Reading them made his cock hard, partly because he had never been meant to see them. Partly because of the woman who had written them. Quiet, shy Lady Jo Danvers, who loved to frown at him. Who looked at him as if he were a footpad about to filch her reticule. Who had delivered her pamphlet to his offices buttoned to the throat, not a hair out of place, looking very much like a governess he longed to defile.

Damn it, he had to stop thinking about her. Had to stop perusing the list. And he would, Decker promised himself. Soon. But first, he was going to read it again.

Ways to be Wicked
1. *Kiss a man until you are breathless.*
2. *Arrange for an assignation. Perhaps with Lord Q?*
3. *Get caught in the rain with a gentleman. (This will necessitate the removal of wet garments. Choose said gentleman wisely.)*
4. *Sneak into a gentleman's bedchamber in the midst of the night.*
5. *Go to a gentleman's private apartments.*
6. *Spend a night in a gentleman's bed.*
7. *Make love in the outdoors.*

8. *Ask*

Bloody hell. The items on her list were delicious enough to incite his lust and his interest in equal, ballocks-tightening measure. But that incomplete number eight—only just begun, as if she had stopped in *medias res*, as if she had *more* wonderfully sinful items to add to her list—made his prick twitch every time. He had tortured himself with it. So many possibilities.

What did she want to ask? And who did she want to pose the question to? Was there a number nine? What else would she add to her list?

Most importantly, who the devil was Lord Q?

That question bothered him more than it ought to. Decker told himself it hardly mattered. Lady Jo was not the sort of woman with whom he dallied. First, she was a lady. Second, she was an innocent.

Or *was* she?

The list before him mocked.

It hardly seemed the composition of a virginal miss. But then, how the devil would Decker know what a virginal miss would write? He had not been a virgin in years, and he had never been a damned miss. Moreover, he had not bedded an innocent in...well, *ever.* His predilections tended to be far more depraved than a virginal miss could satisfy.

But oh, how delightful it would be to debauch Lady Jo.

Curse it, his trousers were too tight, drawing against his erection each time he shifted in his chair to ease his discomfort. The spell of yearning Lady Jo's list cast upon him was heavy and thick, unbreakable. He was going to have to take himself in hand if he was going to get anything accomplished today.

There was only one answer to his current predicament.

He had to rid himself of the list.

Remove the temptation.

Return it to its rightful owner, and then forget he had ever seen it.

Right. That last part was never bloody well happening, was it?

On a sigh, he composed a terse note to Lady Jo Danvers.

* * *

I believe I have something of yours.

THE NOTE WAS in Jo's reticule as she waited for the hulking Scotsman who served as Mr. Elijah Decker's *aide-de-camp* to announce her. Seven words. Signed with his initial. She had instantly known who had sent her the message. And she had also known what he had in his possession. What she had inadvertently given him.

Her cheeks were hot.

Misery churned in her stomach.

Her list had been missing for three days. She had searched for it everywhere. Initially, she had believed she had somehow misplaced it, shuffling it with some of her correspondence. But when a thorough investigation had failed to produce the list, she feared her older brother Julian, the Earl of Ravenscroft, had taken it. However, after his protective, brotherly wrath had not been unleashed upon her, she had reached another, far more troubling conclusion.

She had unintentionally mixed her list into the pages of her pamphlet for the Lady's Suffrage Society. And she had given it to the odious, sinfully handsome, utterly self-absorbed rake who owned the publisher that was now printing all the society's pamphlets.

Those seven words written in his arrogant hand, burning a veritable hole of shame through her reticule, confirmed it.

Of all the people to whom she could have unintentionally given her list, why, oh why did it have to be *him*?

She detested him and men of his ilk.

Mr. Elijah Decker was rather like a whore. A *gentleman* whore.

Only, he was no gentleman.

"What is it, Macfie?" growled Mr. Decker from somewhere within his office, sounding irritated. "I thought I told you not to interrupt me for the next hour."

"Forgive me, sir, but ye have a visitor," Mr. Macfie offered. "Lady Josephine Danvers."

Jo clutched her reticule so tightly her knuckles ached. Less than a minute to attempt to compose herself before she had to face him. She inhaled. Told herself she would be firm. That she would not show him a modicum of embarrassment. She would demand he return the list. She would require his silence.

Mr. Macfie turned to her. "He is ready for ye now, milady."

She thanked him and reluctantly moved into Mr. Decker's lair. Mr. Macfie snapped the door closed with more force than necessary, making Jo jump.

Mr. Decker rose to his full, imposing height, his impossibly blue stare upon her. "Forgive Macfie. He does not know his own strength."

She stared at Mr. Decker, trying to make sense of what he had just said. She blinked. No words were forthcoming. Her heart was pounding so loudly, she was certain Mr. Decker could hear it.

"The slamming of the door, my lady," Mr. Decker elaborated, raising a knowing brow.

Her ears felt as if they were on fire. "Of course. Mr. Macfie is forgiven. You, however, are not. Where is my list?"

Clasping his hands behind his back, Mr. Decker sauntered toward her. "I do not recall asking for your forgiveness, my dear."

She stiffened. "I am not your dear, and you failed to answer my question. Where is my list?"

He stopped before her, insufferably handsome. "Which list are you referring to, Lady Jo?"

The blighter.

He was toying with her. She would wager her dowry upon it.

"You know very well," she charged.

"Hmm." He tapped the fullness of his lower lip with his forefinger, as if he were thinking. "I believe you may have to give me a hint. What did it say, this list of yours?"

Her cheeks were scalding. "You know what it says."

"Do I?" He grinned, like the devil he was.

She had no doubt he had read every word she had written. Every shocking thing she had drafted thus far after seizing upon her plan to live her life and experience true passion the way everyone else around her was. Her sister was blissfully married. Her dearest friend was happily wed and wildly in love.

And yet, Jo had never been kissed.

"Yes," she hissed. "You do."

"I am afraid my memory is dreadfully faulty. Remind me, my lady." His voice was low. Teasing. Taunting.

Daring.

He did not think she had the audacity to say it, she realized.

Jo kept her gaze trained unwaveringly upon him. "Ways…"

She faltered.

"Ways," he prompted, his stare dipping to her lips.

"Ways to be wicked," she blurted.

"Oh, yes. *That* list. Now I recall." The grin he gave her was sin in its purest, most tempting form.

Curse him.

And curse the curious flutter that started in her belly and slid lower, pooling between her thighs.

Jo was doomed.

Want more? Get *Lady Wallflower* here!

DON'T MISS SCARLETT'S OTHER
ROMANCES!

Complete Book List
HISTORICAL ROMANCE

Heart's Temptation
A Mad Passion (Book One)
Rebel Love (Book Two)
Reckless Need (Book Three)
Sweet Scandal (Book Four)
Restless Rake (Book Five)
Darling Duke (Book Six)
The Night Before Scandal (Book Seven)

Wicked Husbands
Her Errant Earl (Book One)
Her Lovestruck Lord (Book Two)
Her Reformed Rake (Book Three)
Her Deceptive Duke (Book Four)
Her Missing Marquess (Book Five)
Her Virtuous Viscount (Book Six)

League of Dukes
Nobody's Duke (Book One)
Heartless Duke (Book Two)
Dangerous Duke (Book Three)
Shameless Duke (Book Four)
Scandalous Duke (Book Five)
Fearless Duke (Book Six)

Notorious Ladies of London
Lady Ruthless (Book One)
Lady Wallflower (Book Two)
Lady Reckless (Book Three)
Lady Wicked (Book Four)
Lady Lawless (Book Five)
Lady Brazen (Book 6)

The Wicked Winters
Wicked in Winter (Book One)
Wedded in Winter (Book Two)
Wanton in Winter (Book Three)
Wishes in Winter (Book 3.5)
Willful in Winter (Book Four)
Wagered in Winter (Book Five)
Wild in Winter (Book Six)
Wooed in Winter (Book Seven)
Winter's Wallflower (Book Eight)
Winter's Woman (Book Nine)
Winter's Whispers (Book Ten)
Winter's Waltz (Book Eleven)
Winter's Widow (Book Twelve)
Winter's Warrior (Book Thirteen)

The Sinful Suttons
Sutton's Spinster (Book One)

Second Chance Manor
The Matchmaker and the Marquess
The Angel and the Aristocrat
The Scholar and the Scot

Stand-alone Novella
Lord of Pirates

CONTEMPORARY ROMANCE
Love's Second Chance
Reprieve (Book One)
Perfect Persuasion (Book Two)
Win My Love (Book Three)

Coastal Heat
Loved Up (Book One)

ABOUT THE AUTHOR

USA Today and Amazon bestselling author Scarlett Scott writes steamy Victorian and Regency romance with strong, intelligent heroines and sexy alpha heroes. She lives in Pennsylvania and Maryland with her Canadian husband, adorable identical twins, and one TV-loving dog.

A self-professed literary junkie and nerd, she loves reading anything, but especially romance novels, poetry, and Middle English verse. Catch up with her on her website http://www. scarlettscottauthor.com/. Hearing from readers never fails to make her day.

Scarlett's complete book list and information about upcoming releases can be found at http://www. scarlettscottauthor.com/.

Connect with Scarlett! You can find her here:
    Join Scarlett Scott's reader group on Facebook for early excerpts, giveaways, and a whole lot of fun!
    Sign up for her newsletter here.
    Follow Scarlett on Amazon
    Follow Scarlett on BookBub
    www.instagram.com/scarlettscottauthor/
    www.twitter.com/scarscoromance
    www.pinterest.com/scarlettscott
    www.facebook.com/AuthorScarlettScott

Printed in Great Britain
by Amazon